Dedicated to Wilma,
Thank you for your service
I'm just glad my stories were there to keep you entertained!

Riley Parra

Season Two

Geonn Cannon

Supposed Crimes LLC • Falls Church, Virginia

Published in the United States.
Supposed Crimes LLC
Virginia

Second Edition

ISBN: 978-0-9828989-6-3

www.supposedcrimes.com

This book is typeset in Goudy Old Style,
licensed by Ascender Corporation.

Table of Contents

The Heavenly Host

The church was smaller than Riley expected; the stone tower was just barely as tall as a two story house. A waist high wooden fence blocked off the golf course green lawn, and the gray stone, steep roof and tall, thin windows gave the building an air of piety, but Riley couldn't shake the image of a friendly mountain cottage as she approached. The open gate was crossed by a thin stripe of crime scene tape and a small stone sign identified it as the St. Isidore of Seville Catholic Church.

Riley parked at the curb behind the black medical examiner's van. When she unfastened her seatbelt, she saw Priest was looking at her. "What?"

"First case back from... vacation," she said. "Are you sure you're okay?"

Riley sighed and leaned back in her seat. The tower of the church had wide openings on all four sides to expose an empty space once occupied by a bell. Riley stared at the spot, wondering where the bell had gone while she formulated her answer. Finally, she said, "I'm back. The city is still a shit hole, but it's my shit hole. You guys put me through hell so I could protect it. That's what I'm doing. And I'll do it better without you acting as if I'm going to fall apart every five seconds. Can we go in now?"

Priest said, "I just feel responsible."

"Just because you set me up and abandoned me when I needed you most?" Priest looked stricken, but Riley shook her head. "I'm kidding, Priest. You were just following orders. Come on. Let's go see what horrible thing happened here."

A cop in a damp rain slicker lifted the tape so Riley and Priest could duck underneath. "Detectives," he said as he let the tape fall back into place. Riley saw him looking at the wounds on her neck. They had faded in the two months since her trial, but they were still visible. She resisted the urge to turn up her collar, and pretended to examine the exterior of the church as she waited for the inevitable comment. "Those druggies really did a number on you, huh?"

"Yeah," Riley said. The official story was that Riley had been held hostage and tortured by a meth cook. It was easier than trying to explain that a group of archangels held her hostage and left her at the mercy of a vengeful fallen angel just so they could feel comfortable with her as the city's protector. She fabricated the fake story with Priest's help: she stumbled over a meth lab while she was on her own and was taken hostage by the main cook. He and his buddies held her prisoner for a few hours until Riley managed to escape, accidentally setting off an explosion that destroyed the lab and killed her captors. It was messy, but it did the trick.

Riley cleared her throat and gestured at the building. "Body is in the main sanctuary?"

"Yes, ma'am," the cop said. "Can't miss it. The medical examiner is already inside."

Riley kept her face expressionless at this news; she merely nodded and continued walking toward the doors.

Despite the damp weather, the doors were standing open to the elements. Riley and Priest stepped into a dark foyer, which had three chairs flanking the two doors that led into the main worship hall. Riley looked at the floor and saw scorch marks on the carpet. Priest stepped up to the font of holy water, dipped two fingers in, and crossed herself. She turned to Riley, thought better of suggesting she do the same, and followed Riley into the crime scene.

Rows of pews ran down the walls on either side, split by a wide aisle down the middle to the altar. Stained glass Bible stories colored the wall behind the pulpit, the meager sunlight barely lifting the room's mood above gloomy. Almost directly in the center of the aisle was the body, currently swarmed over by a group in navy blue windbreakers and white rubber gloves. Riley was focused on the lithe redhead kneeling next to the body, neck craned to examine the victim's head.

"Well, how about that?" Riley said. "Crime scenes are fun again."

Gillian looked up, smirked, and said, "It's pretty easy to be the life of this party."

Riley stood well outside of the crime scene unit's work area and examined the scene. The body was laid on its back, arms outstretched and palm up. Blood stained the shoulders of the man's polo shirt and spread away from him in a pool that narrowed as it moved out. His eyes were closed, his lips parted slightly. Riley said, "Alright, Gillian. Remind me why we let you back in."

Gillian said, "We've got a seventy-three year old man, Bernard Wright. Been dead for about three or four hours. Single, lived in the building behind the church. He worked the grounds, made sure the place wasn't vandalized too often. The priest's assistant said they leave the church doors open all night, so he made the rounds to keep kids from acting up. First blush, I'd say he was walking through the sanctuary when someone surprised him, they struggled, and Mr. Wright got overpowered."

"Cause of death?"

"I'm guessing a candlestick in the conservatory," Gillian said, holding up a plastic bag. A candlestick had been lain length-wise inside, one end smeared with blood. "Or close enough. We think the killer got him down onto his knees, then whapped him on the back of the head."

Riley frowned and looked at the blood pool again. "All of this came from a head wound?"

"No, you asked for cause. The head wound didn't bleed. You know what they say; the first hit is always a freebie." She reached down and turned the body so Riley could see his back. The material of the shirt underneath the collar was torn and soaked with blood. "After he was down, the doer pulled out a knife and sliced open his back. Then he smeared the blood out onto the floor."

Riley grimaced and looked at the blood again. Knowing it hadn't been spilled naturally made her realize the pattern. She stepped over the pool, moving next to Gillian so she could see the body right side up. The blood spread out on either side, wider near the body and narrowing near the pews. The ends tapered off into thin rivulets. Riley pressed her lips together and said, "What do you see?"

Gillian glanced at Priest and eyed the rest of her team before answering. "Completely objective? The killer gave his victim bloody angel wings."

Riley and Priest were directed to a narrow corridor at the back of the sanctuary. The hall was dark, the windows shaded with the early morning storm. The carpet smelled slightly of mildew, and the paneling on the wall needed to be repaired or replaced. Riley assumed that the majority of the tithe went to maintaining the exterior of the church and the sanctuary; places the worshippers rarely saw, like the reverend's office, were far down on the list of necessary repairs.

The door to the office was open, and Riley saw the priest seated at the desk with the phone to his ear. He had one slender hand on his forehead, pushing back a shock of orange-red hair as he listened to the person on the other end. He turned jade green eyes toward the door when Riley knocked, and held up one finger. Riley nodded and stepped back into the hallway with Priest.

Priest glanced toward the sanctuary and looked at Riley. "Angel wings."

"Could just be a coincidence. I mean, we are in the church. Maybe the guy just has a sick sense of humor."

"Do you truly believe that?"

Riley shrugged and leaned against the wall. Since she jump-started the war between angels and demons two months earlier, things had hardly gotten better. The local population was unaware of the supernatural warfare waging in the streets of their city, but they could see the aftereffects. People grew angry for no reason, started brawls in the streets, and domestic disturbance calls were up almost sixty percent. According to Priest, it was a side effect of the war. Being in the vicinity of warring seraphim was bad for a human's mental health.

Riley definitely saw the likely connection between her actions and the body currently being loaded into the back of Gillian's van. There was a chance that a side effect of the war she threw into high gear had caused Bernard Wright to die, but she pushed away the guilt. She wasn't going to blame herself for every casualty of someone else's war, even if she did shoot the opening volley. The war would have happened sooner or later; at least she was there to pick up the pieces.

The pastor appeared in the door and gave a weary sigh. He knew he had gotten over one hurdle only to be faced with another. "Detectives. Father Denis Lawrence. Please, come in." Lawrence led them back into his office, waiting until they were seated before he sat down himself. He braced his hands on the edge of his desk and gingerly lowered himself into his chair.

"Father Lawrence, I'm Detective Riley Parra, this is Detective Caitlin Priest. I know this is a bad time, but we'd like to ask you a few questions."

"A bad time, yes, but when would this conversation actually be easy?" He offered a wan smile and shook his head. "It's been a difficult morning. I've been on the phone with members of the parish who have already heard the news. Bernie was very well loved by everyone in the church."

"You were the one who found him?"

"Yes. I came in this morning at my usual time. Around five thirty. No rest for the wicked, so the righteous might as well be available." He smiled weakly and folded his hands together. "I thought it was some sort of prank at first. Some horrible... prop. I couldn't believe it was really him. I checked his pulse. I got... blood... on my hands..."

"The blood on the floor," Riley said. "Did you notice anything unusual about it?"

Lawrence frowned and shook his head. "I barely even noticed the blood. All I could see was... Bernie's face. Although now that you mention it, there seemed to be two pools. One on either side of the body. That's a bit unusual, isn't it?"

"A bit," Riley said. She kept her tone flat, unemotional. "So you can't think of anyone who would want to hurt Bernie?"

"Him personally? No. Unfortunately, the list of possible attackers is much larger when you consider Bernie may have just been in the wrong place at the wrong time. The church has a donation box, which we regularly transfer to a safe. The top has been pried off by crowbars more times than I care to remember. I think Bernie was just making his rounds and discovered someone trying to rob us. It's happened before, but never..." He sighed. "About a year ago, I was knocked down by a teenager I caught in my office in the middle of the night. It screwed up my hip. I should have realized it would only be a matter of time before..."

"It wasn't your fault," Priest said.

Lawrence sighed and nodded. He glanced at Priest and, as he started to turn away, flicked his eyes back to her face. There was something in his gaze, a sense of recognition. Priest didn't shift her weight or look away; she held Lawrence's gaze. Riley watched them both, waiting for Lawrence to figure out why Priest seemed just a little different than anyone else who had ever sat in that chair. He started to speak twice before he stopped himself. He furrowed his brow and shook his head before focusing on Riley.

"Bernie wasn't a saint. He had... a past when he came here, I knew that. But he was a good man. He didn't drink anymore, and he didn't gamble. He spent the majority of his time here at the church, tending the grounds. I can't imagine how he would get involved with the kind of person who could commit a murder. But—" The phone rang, and Lawrence closed his eyes for a moment to gather his strength. "You are welcome to examine his apartment. My assistant can show you where it is. Anything you require on the church grounds, you will have access to as well."

"Thank you, Father," Riley said as she stood up. "We'll let you take care of that call."

"Thank you, Detectives."

Lawrence stood and shook their hands. When he clasped Priest's hand, he frowned as if he felt a shock. He stared at her for another long moment, focusing on her eyes. Finally, he shook his head and released her. "My apologies."

"Don't worry about it," Priest said. "Thank you for your time."

Riley stopped outside Lawrence's office and waited for Priest to join her. "I've been wondering about that. If clergy could sniff you out."

"The very religious often sense something," Priest said. They began walking down the hall to find the pastor's assistant. "They rarely make the connection. It's like a whiff of perfume in a crowded room. You know you smell it, but it's impossible to pinpoint where it's coming from. Usually people don't even pay attention."

A woman in a black dress and white sweater stepped into the hall, looked toward them, and nervously approached. "Are... you the police detectives?"

"Yes, ma'am," Riley said. "Detectives Parra and Priest. Are you the pastor's assistant?"

She nodded, her golden earrings jangling under the smooth canopy of straight white hair. "Faye McElroy. You can call me Faye. Father Lawrence told me to show you to Bernie's apartment." Her eyes suddenly filled with tears and she pressed her lips together. "I just... can't believe..." She took a deep breath and let it out slowly. "Well. You wanted to see Bernard's home. This way." She turned and led them to a small office at the opposite end of the corridor.

Faye's office was cramped, overflowing with potted plants and flowers, with a window that looked out over the church's back garden. There was a door behind Faye's desk that led outside, and she picked up an umbrella before leading the detectives through the door and into the rain. A stone path led from the door to a small cottage at the back of the church's property.

"Did he go out much?"

Faye held the umbrella just high enough to clear her head, hunkering under it as she led them outside. "Oh, no. His time was occupied with the garden or taking care of the interior of the church. It was like his mission in life, to make sure this place was in tip-top shape. I don't have a clue what we'll do without him."

Riley looked back at the church and again noticed the missing bell. "What happened to the bell?"

Faye looked at Riley, followed her line of sight, and shook her head. "I... don't know. I think it was already gone when I started coming here."

Riley nodded and examined Bernie's home. The cottage was shaded by an oak tree, rain pouring out of the gutters and gathering in the small ditches dug along either side of the house. Faye stepped onto the porch and dug a keychain from her pocket, unlocked the door and pushed it open. She stepped back and gestured for them to enter.

"I'll be in my office if you need me. Unless you need me to stay here..."

"We'll be fine," Riley said. "Thank you, Ms. McElroy."

They waited until Faye was back in her office before they went inside. Priest said, "What was with the question about the bell?"

"Gave her something else to think about," Riley said. "Come on."

She expected a typical bachelor pad, with clothes and take-out containers on every horizontal surface. Instead, Bernard Wright seemed to have made an effort to make as little impact on the home as possible. The living room furniture was standard display room fare, with matching pillows on the couch and armchairs. A small TV stood on a cart next to the window, with a porcelain Jesus standing on top of the TV Guide.

"Must have made it hard to watch porn," Riley said, pulling on a pair of rubber gloves.

Priest looked at the statue, frowned, and moved deeper into the apartment. The kitchen was at the back of the house, separated from the living room by a counter and cupboards. Priest went down the hall to the bedroom, and Riley went to the dining room table. It was there that the most clutter had been accrued; newspapers, crossword puzzles, piles of junk mail. Riley picked up some of the envelopes and looked through them.

There was a beer stein in the center of the table, flanked by salt and pepper shakers, and Riley flipped open the top to look inside. Piles of chips shifted inside, and she saw four years, six months, and three months. "Seems Bernie was a member of Alcoholics Anonymous," Riley said, raising her voice to be heard at the other end of the house. "At least four years sober." She looked in the fridge and saw a box of soda cans, sandwich fixings, and a half-eaten sub sandwich from Subway. She let the fridge door close and turned around as Priest came out of the bedroom. "Anything interesting?"

"Nothing of note," Priest said. "The bedroom looked lived in, but clean."

"No personal letters in the mail," Riley said. "Credit card offers, bank statements." The kitchen counter was spotless, and the sink was empty save for a handful of dishes. "If he hadn't died, I would hire him to be my butler."

Priest picked up an address book from the end table and thumbed through it.

Riley put her hands on her hips and scanned the room, trying to get a feel for Bernie. "Okay. Bernie was found at about five thirty. Gillian said he was killed around two or three this morning. Seems to fit the vandal theory. Bernie just happened upon someone trying to steal from the church, and he got a candlestick to the head for his reward."

Priest said, "And the wings?"

Riley shook her head. "If a vandal hit him, they probably started running as soon as he went down. All they would have cared about is the fact he wasn't chasing them."

"Maybe the attack and the blood are unrelated."

"You mean Bernie was killed, and someone else came into the church and decided the crime scene was a little too bland? Did a little art project?"

Priest shook her head. "Perhaps it was meant as a message. A demon may have sensed what happened and decided to use the body for its own purposes."

"How could a demon even enter the church?"

"A man had just been murdered here, Riley. The seal was broken."

Riley said, "Oh. Can you—"

"I restored the seal when I came in. With the holy water."

"Oh. Well, that's good." She walked into the living room and looked at the television. "Seems like the only time he would have to leave the house was for AA meetings - if he was even still going to them. We'll let the crime scene unit go over this place for any hiding places with juicy secrets. Let's go see if the rain left us any evidence of a break-in."

Riley convinced Priest to go into the diner and pick up some breakfast to go, including something for Gillian. She got out to stretch her legs while she waited, leaning against the car with her hands in her pockets, and stared down the street. There was a corner grocery store not far from where they had parked, the windows boarded over. Crime scene tape attached to one side of the front entrance waved in the breeze like a scarf held out the window of a speeding car. Riley remembered reading something about a clerk being murdered over the thirty-two dollars in the cash register. He handed it over, and the robber pulled the trigger anyway.

She turned her attention to the yellow sky, filled with the dark storm clouds that had finally stopped raining on her. She could see flashes of lightning in the clouds, could hear vague clattering that might be mistaken for hail, but she knew the real source. She was hearing the sound of angels and demons battling each other, their war renewed when Riley crashed a car into the front of Marchosias' hotel. At that moment, angels and demons began converging on the city, reinforcements and ringers called in from both sides in an attempt to shift the tide of the war.

Regular folk went about their days without seeing, or allowing themselves to notice, the creatures in their midst. But everyone felt the change in the air, and the increase in violent crimes was a testament to that.

And Riley could only blame herself for it.

Priest came out of the diner with two bags of food. Riley pushed away from the car. "Hey. How come you're not..." She gestured at the sky. "I mean, it is your fight, isn't it?"

"No," Priest said. "My fight is yours." She gestured with one of the bags. "I asked them to put Gillian's breakfast in a separate bag so you could deliver it yourself."

Riley smirked and got back into the car. "You know me too well, Caitlin." She waited until Priest got into the car before she added, "Thanks. For having my back."

"Always," Priest said.

Riley paused outside the doors of the morgue and peeked through one of the narrow windows. The room looked the same as it always had, three tables and a row of coolers to the right, with a large stainless steel door at the opposite end of the green and white room. The lights were harsh and brilliantly white, reflecting off every smooth and polished surface.

For the last few months, Riley had hated this entire floor of the building. But there was one thing present that made all the difference, and she was standing at the foot of one occupied table, making notes on a clipboard. When Gillian looked up, she spotted Riley in the window and smiled. She waved Riley in before she finished whatever she had been writing.

Riley pushed the door open and stepped inside. "Hey."

"Hey yourself. Find anything at the crime scene?"

"Signed confession," Riley said. She crossed the room slowly. "How are you doing?"

Gillian rested the pen against the paper and looked around the morgue, as if just realizing where she was. She nodded. "I'm doing fine. I was a little anxious when I first got here this morning, but I scrubbed up and checked the overnights and..." She pressed her lips together and nodded. "I can do it. I can handle it."

Riley smiled. "Good." She put her hand on Gillian's arm just below the sleeve of her scrub top and squeezed. She had offered to be there for Gillian's first morning in the room since being tormented there by a tag team of demons, but Gillian insisted she had to do it alone. Riley held up a brown paper bag. "I got you some breakfast on the way from the crime scene. Where do you want it?"

"Office," Gillian said. "Thanks, babe."

Riley took the food into Gillian's office and left it on her desk. When she came back into the main room, she was in full cop mode. "Have you checked out Bernie?"

"Yes," Gillian said. "Just a rudimentary once over when we got him here. I told you the back wound was post mortem. That wasn't precisely true." She walked back to the table and Riley followed. "Bernard was incapacitated by the knock to the head. He suffered a subdural hematoma, which would have killed him within a few hours. But the stab wounds in his back were what killed him. The killer laid him down, sliced across his shoulders with the knife, and let Mr. Wright bleed out for his little art project."

Riley said, "Are you admitting your first guess was wrong?"

"Medical examiners are detectives, too. We adjust our theories according to the facts we're presented with."

"Sounds like a fancy way of saying you were wrong."

Gillian said, "Can we focus on the dead body, please, Detective Parra?"

Riley smirked. "Anything else interesting about him, Dr. Hunt?"

"He was in decent shape for a man starting his seventh decade. He got a lot of exercise taking care of the church, I guess. If he hadn't gotten hit over the head, he might have lived another twenty years."

"Shame we can't penalize murderers for stealing years from their victims, huh?" She touched Gillian's arm again, brushing her fingers over the smooth flesh. "I'll probably work through lunch. See you at home?"

Gillian nodded. "If you want to check in on me later, feel free."

Riley said, "I could probably work that into my schedule. Hopefully no one else will die today, and Bernard's killer will be overcome with guilt and come walking in."

"We can always hope," Gillian said. She rested her hands on the side of the table and turned to face Riley. "Do you have a minute?"

"For you, always," Riley said.

Gillian smiled. "I want to apologize. While we were away together, I kind of gave you the impression that everything would be fine when we got back up here. I haven't exactly lived up to my end of the bargain. Intimacy-wise."

Riley smiled. "What, because we haven't had sex since we got back? We sleep in the same bed, Jill. That's intimate enough for me, until you're ready." Since their return to the city, they had stayed relatively chaste. Sleeping together in pajamas, cuddling on the couch and kissing and stroking each other through clothes. Riley could sense Gillian's apprehension at being back in the place where she had been so horribly violated, and she was willing to take baby steps.

Gillian reached out and touched Riley's hand. "Thank you. I thought I would be okay. And for the most part I am. I can stand being in our apartment, and being here in this room. But touching... even when I know it's you, it feels like *her* touching me. I just need a little time."

Riley kissed Gillian's temple and said, "You have it."

Gillian wrapped her arms around Riley and held her for a long moment, breathing in her scent. Finally, Gillian pushed Riley away and said, "Good. Now, get out of here. I need to work my magic."

Riley smiled. "I'll see you tonight."

Gillian nodded. "I love you."

Riley pushed the door open with her shoulder and blew Gillian a kiss as she left the room.

The bullpen had been rearranged during Riley's recuperation, and she was still getting used to the changes. Her desk and Priest's had been moved to the back of the room, nearer the stairs and also within earshot of Lieutenant Briggs' office. She tried not to think too much about what the new placement meant.

Riley hung her coat on the back of her chair and looked at the pegboard Priest had set up next to their desks. A street map of the city was hung in the middle, with small red flags taped in areas of increased violence. The majority of marks were in No Man's Land, naturally, but the incidents were beginning to bleed over into the center of the city. It almost looked as if Marchosias' stronghold was growing.

"Riley," Priest said, pausing by the corner of Riley's desk until she turned to look at her. "I called Father Lawrence and he gave me the address of Bernard's AA meetings."

"All right," Riley said. "I'm not sure it'll tell us anything we need to know." She took a piece of the red tape Priest had been using, found the church, and added the mark.

Priest said, "You think this is just an extension of the rising violence?"

"For all accounts, Bernie Wright was a regular man. Quiet, kept to himself. I think someone tried to rob the church and Bernie got in the way."

Priest nodded. "And the bloody wings?"

Riley chewed her bottom lip and took a seat. Priest walked back to her desk and sat down, turning her chair to face Riley. Riley finally said, "Okay, here's a hypothetical. Let's say a guy was walking in the park. He went under a bridge, and a piece of masonry broke off and happened to hit him on the head. He falls down and dies. A little while later, another man comes along. Maybe he's not a bad guy; he just needs some cash for food. He sees the dead man and decides 'hey, he doesn't need money anymore.' So he takes the wallet and walks off. Body is discovered, and the cops see the missing wallet and assume he was killed in a robbery."

"You think the wings were a crime of opportunity?"

"The timing is hinky," Riley said. "Bernie was hit on the head, and he was knocked out. We're not sure how long he would have been out, but probably not very long. So the artist would have had to come along fairly quickly or else Bernie would have woken up and stumbled off to die somewhere else."

Priest nodded. "So what is our next step?"

"We need to call Father Lawrence and see if they had problems with anyone specific. If someone was using the church as their own personal ATM, maybe we'll get lucky."

"And if we don't?"

"We canvas the neighborhood," Riley said. She sighed and picked up the phone. "Let's hope we get lucky."

Riley spent the morning on the phone with Father Lawrence and Faye McElroy, but neither of them knew of any specific repeat offenders. Lawrence suggested a few members of the congregation who might know, so Riley started through the list. Some people were available, but had no information. Others didn't answer and Riley decided to call them back at a decent hour.

She filled out an initial report of the crime, taking time to decide whether or not to include the bloody wings. She occupied herself with busywork, emptying out the paperwork that had taken over her inbox.

When she finally looked at the clock, it was closer to noon. She dialed a few more people on the list, hoping to catch them at lunch. Her third attempt, Thomas Bailey, answered on the first ring. "Mr. Bailey," she said. "This is Detective Riley Parra. I was wondering if you had a few minutes to speak with me about Bernard Wright."

Bailey sighed. "Father Lawrence told me to expect your call." He groaned, and Riley assumed he was taking a seat. "I've only got a few minutes, but I'll tell you what I can. Bernie was a good man. A *good* man. I was just starting to get sober, and he helped me out. He took me to a meeting. I have a one year chip because of him. I'm not sure what I'm going to do now."

"I'm sorry," Riley said. "Mr. Bailey, Father Lawrence mentioned that the church had issues with break-ins over the past few years. Do you know anything about that?"

"Hooligans," Bailey said. "Father Lawrence keeps the church open all night, just in case anyone needs the Lord outside of business hours. God knows the night can be really dark, especially here lately. But people take advantage. They take advantage. They can't be trusted." He sighed heavily. "I've seen them a couple of times, but only one I could name. Kevin Gibson. I grabbed the boy when all his friends ran off and I tried to talk some sense into his head. Told him if I ever heard of him doing this again, I'd take him to the police."

"Did you tell Father Lawrence?"

"No, no. Kevin's a good kid. He's just hanging around with a bad crowd. I was hoping he just needed to be talked to, given a warning. Get a good scare."

"Do you have an address for him?"

"Oh, you don't have to harass the boy..."

"Mr. Bailey, he might have information about who was stealing from the church. That could lead us to Bernie's murderer."

Bailey sighed again and gave her an address. "His parents are named Carol and Harlan."

Riley wrote it down and said, "Thank you, Mr. Bailey. We won't tell him where we got his name."

"It's not that. He's basically a good kid. He just... he's in with the wrong crowd," he said again. "I grew up on the same streets he's on, and I know a little bit about where he's coming from. I hope he didn't have anything to do with this."

"So do I, Mr. Bailey. Thanks for your help." She hung up and waved to get Priest's attention. "Feel like taking a little field trip?"

Kevin Gibson lived in a brownstone near the church, the building's three segments flanking a small courtyard of dying brown grass. A fleet of bicycles stood near the stone wall between the grass and the sidewalk, and Riley eyed them as she walked past. Half of them looked brand new, name brand bikes. She doubted the people who lived here could afford new clothes for their kids, let alone top of the line bikes. She followed the cracked pavement to the front door. The foyer was dark and damp, flooding from a leak somewhere upstairs. They could hear a steady trickle of water coming from somewhere unseen as they stepped inside.

A boulder-shaped bald man in a tank top looked up from his mopping. He squinted suspiciously at them and spoke in a thick Russian accent. "You plumb?"

"Police," Riley said, showing her badge. "We're looking for Harlan and Carol Gibson's apartment."

The super muttered, "*Dalbayob*," and jerked his thumb toward the stairs. "Third floor. Up there. Second door."

Priest followed Riley up the stairs, pausing to look down at the Russian man ankle-deep in foul water. She looked toward the ceiling, and the trickle of water suddenly stopped. The Russian man looked toward the back of the foyer, muttered something under his breath, and continued to push the water toward the door. Riley glanced at Priest. "Didn't know you could do that. I might need to invite you over to Gillian's for dinner sometime."

"I just asked for a little assist."

"God has time for things like that?"

Priest shrugged. "When other people are asking for world peace and cures for cancer, doing little things that have immediate results is kind of a fun distraction."

Riley knocked on the apartment door and said, "Ah. So God is easily distracted. That's comforting."

The door opened and a boy barely out of his teens leaned against it. He wore a pair of jeans that hung low enough to reveal his boxers, his sunken chest marked with what looked like cigarette burns. He scratched his cheek with the back of one hand and said, "You the girls I ordered?" He smirked, then chuckled, then coughed.

Riley held up her badge again. "Kevin Gibson?"

The guy grunted and slumped away from the door. "Asshole, what did you do?"

"Nothing," a kid shouted from the back of the apartment. There was a loud banging, and then heavy footsteps on the wooden hallway floor. "God, Bradley, every fucking thing that goes wrong, and you're—"

A kid in his early teens appeared, spotted Riley and Priest, and immediately turned and ran. Bradley grabbed for the kid's shirt, but his fingers slipped over the cotton and he almost fell on his face. "Hey, you fucker, get back here! These're the cops!"

Riley said, "Outside," to Priest and then ran into the apartment. Bradley stepped out of her way with his hands held out to show he wasn't fighting.

Riley reached the window in time to see Kevin jumping onto the next building. She growled at the delay and said, "We just want to talk to you, you little…"

Riley ran across the roof after him. She reached the edge and knew that she would never make the leap if she slowed down even a little. She launched herself off the barrier and stumbled when she hit the other roof, dropping just far enough to slap her hands against the hot tar before she rejoined the chase. Kevin was already across the roof, ready to take another leap. He glanced back to make sure she wasn't closing in.

The moment he was distracted, Priest rose into view with her wings spread out to either side. They retracted as her shoes touched the edge of the roof and stepped into Kevin's way. He slammed into her and fell back, and she grabbed him before he could recover. She looped her arms around his and pinned him as he struggled to break free.

"Stupid bitch! Let me the hell go!"

Riley caught up to them, trying hard not the show how out of breath she was. "Pace yourself, Kevin. We only let you have four insults before we start charging you."

"Shut up, pig. Think I'm scared of you?"

"That's three," Riley said. "You only have one more before we run you in and lock you up. Want to try your luck?"

Kevin pressed his lips together, twisted against Priest's grip, but stayed quiet.

"Smart man. We hear you're the guy to ask about things happening around Father Lawrence's church after dark. Sort of the inside man."

"I'm not telling you a damn thing."

"Yeah, you are, you little prick!" Riley turned and saw Bradley stalking toward them. He had taken the time to pull on a T-shirt before coming outside. "You're gonna tell 'em every damn thing they wanna know."

Priest relaxed her grip and stepped to one side, resting a hand on his shoulder. "Think about it, Kevin. If we give up on you, we go to the next name on our list. Maybe they'll be more talkative. Maybe they'll have some things to say about you."

Kevin hesitated, shook his head, and then said, "I di'nt do nothing. I wasn't even there last night. Sure, I gone in a couple of times. But not last night."

Riley turned to Bradley. "Mr. Gibson, where was your brother last night, say from one until three?"

"I got no idea," Bradley said.

Kevin lunged at his brother. "Liar! You're a damn liar! I was here. I was here all night."

Riley said, "Kevin. If you saw something, you better tell us now. You help us out, we'll be inclined to believe you if you tell us you were just a witness. Understand? The longer you keep quiet, the more we think you have to hide."

"I'm his legal guardian," Bradley said. "You wanna take him downtown, you got my permission. Maybe it'll do the little punk some good."

Riley shrugged and looked at Priest. "Maybe he'll prefer a few hours in a cell."

Kevin scuffed his feet into the gravel on the roof. "Wait, stop." His body sagged, but Priest didn't relax her grip on his arm. "I was hanging out at the church last night. They got a fence, so when pig—" He glanced at Riley and amended what he was going to say. "When people drive by, they can't see you. We go there sometimes."

"Last night?"

"Yeah," Kevin said. "We were there and we saw Bunny going in through the side door."

Priest said, "Who?"

"The maintenance guy," Kevin said, looking like a kid for the first time. "He... he slurred his words sometimes. It sounded like he said Bunny when we asked what his name was."

"Okay. Then what happened?"

Kevin shrugged and said, "I don't know. Nothing."

Bradley lunged forward and reached for his brother. "You little prick, if you don't…"

Riley grabbed Bradley by the arm and twisted, changing his angle of approach and forcing him to his knees. "Why don't you just stay by me," Riley said. "Kevin, we just want to know what you saw last night."

Kevin shifted his weight from one foot to the other. "There was someone else with me. He went inside, because he said that Bunny left the door open and that made it too easy to pass it up. So he went in, and then he came running out like a second later and he said we had to get the fuck out of there."

"What was this other guy's name?"

Bradley was the one to answer this time. "It had to be a kid called Hawk. Philip Hawkins. He was here last night, and they left together. I got his address inside."

"You fucking narc!" Kevin shouted. "Ratting out my friend?"

"To keep you out of jail, you ungrateful little fucker!" Bradley snapped. He looked at Riley and said, "Come on. I'll show you."

Riley started to follow Bradley, but Kevin called out to her. "Cop! Hey, cop!" She turned. "There was another person there."

"Inside the church or in the courtyard with you guys?"

"At the door. Hawk and I got out of there fast, and he was hauling ass. I didn't know what the hell was going on. I thought that old priest may have been coming after us. So I looked back. And I saw a guy standing by the door. He was standing there like he was about to go in, but he was making sure we were gone first."

Riley said, "What did he look like?"

Kevin shook his head and shuddered. "I don't even know, man. I mean, he was standing there with the moon and everything, but I couldn't tell you what he looked like. Just black, you know? Not black like a black guy, black black. Like there was nothing. Like he didn't even have a face."

Riley and Priest exchanged glances, and Riley nodded. "Thank you, Kevin. You've been a big help. Don't worry, we won't tell your friend where this information came from."

Kevin scoffed and pulled away from Priest. This time she let him go, and he trudged across the roof to his brother. Bradley swatted at Kevin's arm as he passed and said, "Go inna the house, you little fucker." He watched Kevin to make sure he went back home, and turned to Riley. "Sorry my brother wasn't any help. I mean, good luck finding a dude without a face, right?"

Priest said, "Actually, it might not be as hard as you think."

Riley waited until the apartment door was closed before she spoke. "Demon?"

"Or demon-possessed man," Priest said.

Riley grimaced. "Don't suppose you could call in any of your winged buddies to lend a hand?"

Priest shook her head. "You underwent the trial so the others could trust you to protect this city. You passed. That means they won't interfere. You're all on your own."

"Wonderful," Riley said. "Talk about the ultimate booby prize." She checked the addresses Bradley had given them; one was Hawk's apartment and the other was the diner where he sometimes washed dishes. She started toward the stairs. "Come on. Let's go see if we can catch this kid."

"Even if this Philip Hawkins hit Bernard Wright with the candlestick, the demon is the true murderer."

"Wright would have died from the head wound eventually. He would have maybe woken up and crawled somewhere else to die, but he would have been just as dead. The demon just happened to get there before the victim's heart stopped beating."

"So we're going to arrest a fifteen year old kid for murder?" Priest said.

"Maybe manslaughter," Riley said. "Trust me, I don't like it any more than you do."

When they reached the foyer, they saw that the Russian super had mostly cleared out the flooded floor. He glared at them as they came down the stairs. "You run all over my roofs? That was you?"

Riley tried to look contrite. "Yes, sir. Sorry. If it helps, he started it. Hey, at least the leak has stopped."

The man sneered and shook his head, pushing his mop with renewed vigor as he muttered in Russian.

Riley shook her head. Some people couldn't appreciate a miracle when they were handed one.

The diner filled the narrow space between a pawn shop and a building for lease, the window papered with hand-written specials. The small bell over the front door chimed as Riley came in, pausing to look around the cramped room. Next to the door were two arcade games that looked older than anything else in the place, the chimes and whistles from the machines echoing off the chipped tile floor. There were four tables, all vacant, covered with checkered tablecloths.

A slender man with a thick head of white hair stood behind the cash register. The sleeves of his white shirt were rolled up to the elbow, and Riley saw the faded blue ink of old tattoos on his forearms. Behind him, she could see a teenager standing at the sink with his back to the restaurant. Riley took the badge from her belt and held it by her hip, making sure the clerk could see it but the kid wouldn't if he turned around.

"Um, hello. What can I get for you?"

"I don't know," Riley said. "What would you recommend?"

The clerk stepped to the side and flipped up a section of the counter to allow Riley through. She stepped inside, nodding her thanks to him as she moved to the kitchen door. She kept her badge out, holding it up where he wouldn't miss it, and said, "Philip Hawkins?"

The kid turned around and, the instant he realized a stranger was standing nearby, started running in the other direction. He grabbed the back door, flung it open, and ran into Priest's waiting arms. She spun him around and gently guided him back into the kitchen.

Riley hooked her badge back on her belt. She nodded her thanks to Priest. "If this cop thing doesn't work out, you may have a career as a kid catcher."

Riley looked at the kid. He looked older than Kevin Gibson, but not by much. His dark hair was a mess, a shock of it standing straight up away from his forehead and twisting back to tangle with strands from the sides. There was a hint of peach fuzz on his upper lip. "Hi, Mr. Hawkins. We have a witness that says you and another boy were seen at St. Isidore's last night. Want to tell your side of the story?"

"The other kid's name is Kevin Gibson," Hawk said. "He did everything. If you want him I can find him for you. I can even tell you where the little fucker lives."

Riley looked at Priest. "Kevin Gibson. Write that down, Detective Priest. Come on, Hawk, get your things."

"Where'm I goin'?"

"You just fingered Kevin Gibson for the murder of Bernard Wright.

There's paperwork to do. We have to take your statement downtown." She looked at the clerk. "Sorry to leave you short a dishwasher. We'll try to get him back to you as soon as possible."

The clerk looked at Riley, Priest and Hawk. "I... okay. Whatever you have to do is fine."

"We need his parents' contact information, please."

"Yes, of course."

The clerk wrote down several numbers and held the slip of paper out to Riley. She snatched it as she led Hawk out of the kitchen. "Come on, Hawk. Let's give your parents a call and get them down here."

Hawk looked at Priest, decided he wouldn't be able to get past her, and trudged after Riley through the store.

Riley called Hawk's parents and his father gave them permission to drive Hawk down to the station. He planned to meet them there, but Riley and Priest arrived first. Riley led Hawk into the office and gestured at the first interrogation room. "Go on in there and take a seat. I'll be in there in a second." She closed the door behind him and motioned a uniformed officer over. "Get the kid a soda and then stand guard. He's already tried to run once. Act friendly. Talk with him."

The cop nodded and went to the break room to find a soda.

Priest said, "You're not going to talk to him?"

"Not without his parents or guardian present," Riley said. "Besides, it'll be a good tactic. He's going to sit in there by himself for a while and wonder what I'm doing. Coffee?"

"No, thank you."

Riley went to her desk and sat down, staring at the closed interrogation room door. When Priest sat down at her own desk, Riley rubbed her face and shook her head. "I really don't want to arrest a kid for murder. But I'm not going to let him slide."

"I understand. But Bernard Wright was murdered because young Mr. Hawkins was committing a crime. It was only a matter of time before he escalated to mugging, or armed robbery. Taking him off the streets now may be the thing he needs to put him back onto the right path."

"All we can do is hope," Riley said, as her phone began to ring.

"And pray," Priest amended.

Riley picked up the phone. "Detective Parra. Yeah, send him up." She turned to Priest. "Hawkins' father is downstairs. Let's go."

They saw Mr. Hawkins hurrying toward them. He spotted them and said, "Detective Parra?"

"Yes, and this is—"

"I don't care," he said. "I'll have your goddamn badges by the end of the day. I let you bring my son down here so my lawyer can see a boy, a *teenager*, dragged into an interrogation room and treated like a common criminal."

He opened the interrogation room door, obviously prepared to see a waterboarding in progress. Instead, he saw the uniformed cop Riley assigned to stand guard was sitting on the edge of the table looking at the trading cards Hawk had laid out on the table. Hawk was in the middle of taking a drink from his soda can when he saw his father.

"The kid will be traumatized," Riley said.

Lieutenant Briggs came out of her office, alerted by the shouting. She looked at Riley without surprise and then focused on Mr. Hawkins. "What's going on here?"

"Your detectives—"

"I was *asking* my detectives," Briggs said. She turned and looked at Riley. "What's going on?"

Riley nodded at the boy. "Philip Hawk was spotted at St. Isidore's last night. He was there when Bernard Wright was murdered, and he identified the boy he was with as the killer. We just want to get his statement and he'll be on his way if everything adds up for us."

"Sounds reasonable to me," Briggs said. She turned to Mr. Hawkins. "You can join your son in the room while Detective Parra speaks with him. But I will ask that you lower your voice and calm down. Am I clear?" Hawkins reluctantly nodded. Briggs nodded back, and then said, "Carry on, Detective."

"Thank you, Lieutenant."

"I'll be watching," Briggs said, her words carrying half a warning as she went to the video observation room.

Riley gestured for Mr. Hawkins to lead the way into the interrogation room. She entered behind him, closed the door, and walked to the seat across from the teenager. "Hi, Philip. Can I call you that, or do you prefer Hawk?" The kid shrugged. "Well, maybe we should stick to Hawk for now." She opened the file. "You said the boy with you, Kevin. He was the one who went into the church."

Hawk nodded. "Yeah. I didn't even want to be there. He's always asking me to tag along."

"Why do you go? You're older than him, right?" She smiled. "I mean, when I was a kid, I was always trying to tag along with the older kids. Younger kids, who had the time for 'em. They were brats."

Hawk shifted in his seat.

"Why did Kevin go into the church?"

"He knew they had some money in the safe. Or in the donations box. It's pretty easy to get into 'em, so he thought it would be quick."

Riley nodded. "Did he tell you what he saw in the church?"

"He said Bernie was there. Caught him trying to open the donation box."

"Mm-hmm."

Hawk shrugged. "So, like, Kevin hit him."

"Murdered him?"

"No," Hawk said. "He didn't... I mean. He just didn't want Bernie to follow us. Him. Wh-when he ran away." He glanced at his father and looked down at the table. "He just wanted to knock him down so we could get away. He didn't think he would kill him. You know?"

"Yeah," Riley said. She glanced at Mr. Hawkins and saw that he wasn't buying the story either. "Philip, I have to say I have some problems with this story. See, we've already spoken to Kevin. He told us that you were the one who went into the church."

Hawk said, "Well... well, yeah. I mean, he said that because he was scared, right? I mean... yeah. He didn't want to go to jail."

Riley said, "Philip, look at me." He reluctantly lifted his eyes. "I don't want to send you to jail for this. I just want to know what happened. I want to know exactly what happened in that church so I can figure out the best way to deal with this. A man died, and that's tragic. You were involved, and I can't ignore that. I can make it easier for you. But you've got to help me, right now, in this room."

Hawk swallowed hard and seemed to shrink. "I-I went into the church."

"Damn it, Phil..."

"Sir," Riley said, holding up a hand to silence him.

Hawk's lower lip trembled. "I saw a candlestick, and I knew this guy. He owns the pawnshop next door to the restaurant. I thought he'd, you know, want it. I could get money or something. I don't know. It looked expensive. So I picked it up. I didn't even get to the safe, 'cause I heard this noise behind me. And I turned around and..." He shuddered. "I'd seen

Bunny before. But this didn't look like him. Like not at all. I thought it was a fu— a-a freakin' monster or something. It was huge. I just, I swung the candlestick at it, and it went down, and then I got the fuck out of there. I-I mean the... I got the heck out."

Riley leaned back in her chair. The demon Kevin saw outside obviously played a bigger part than just coming in afterward to play with the blood. It needed Hawk to assault Bernard Wright to get access to the holy ground. It had taken his anxiety of getting caught and transformed Bernie into something out of a nightmare. Hawk had still swung the candlestick, and maybe he would have anyway, but he wasn't much more than a weapon.

"Thank you, Philip. That was very helpful. I'm going to speak with my lieutenant for a moment, let you have some time to yourselves. I'll be right back." She pushed her chair back and left the room, meeting Lieutenant Briggs in the hall.

"Kid saw a monster?" Briggs said.

"I believe him," Riley said, even though she couldn't explain the reasons why. "Anxiety, fear of being caught, his mind probably turned Bernard Wright into a monster. A lawyer could argue he was acting in self-defense."

"Imperfect self-defense," Briggs said. "It's still a crime."

"This kid is robbing donation boxes from church," Riley said. "But he's still a kid. Sending him to prison will turn him into a career criminal."

Briggs nodded. They had both seen it happen too many times for her to argue. "Suggestions?"

"There's a rehabilitation program upstate, Project Rescue. They take violent juvenile offenders and teach them to train rescue dogs for adoption. It could be the best thing for him, and his best chance to have a normal adult life. Or as normal as it gets."

"The charge is manslaughter," Briggs said. "Give him the option of ten to fifteen years in prison, or this rehabilitation program. Leave it up to the kid to decide. Could be his first step to being reformed."

"Right," Riley said.

"What about the bloody wings?" Briggs asked. "Priest filled me in."

A demon playing games with us, having a joke at our expense. She shook her head and decided Briggs wasn't ready to be brought in on the truth. "Crime of opportunity. Priest and I could canvas the neighborhood and see—"

Briggs stopped her with a shake of her head. "No, there are enough dangerous wackos out there for you to chase without adding this guy to your roster. Good work today, Riley."

Riley nodded and watched Briggs walk away before she went back into the interrogation room. Hawk's eyes were red, filled with tears he was refusing to cry. Riley put her file down on the table, sat down, and hoped against hope that Hawk would make the right choice.

Riley managed to wrap up her paperwork early and fulfilled her promise to Mr. Hawkins to get in touch with Project Rescue on Philip's behalf. They would send two administrators down to meet with his father and escort him to the camp themselves. The night was just beginning to darken the windows when she pushed away from her desk and shrugged into her jacket. Priest was still at her desk, typing something. Riley said, "Are you going to stick around for a bit?"

Priest blinked as if waking from a trance, but she didn't look away from her screen. "Um... yes. I think so, just in case anything comes up."

Riley smirked. "Heaven doesn't have broadband, does it?"

Priest looked sheepish. "It's so much information. From all over the world. The history of every religion at your fingertips."

"Whatever floats your boat, Caitlin," Riley said. "Hey, do they have a list of saints on there?"

"Yes."

"Who was St. Isidore? What was she the saint of?"

Priest said, "*He* was the patron saint of several things. Computer sciences, technology..."

Riley stopped her with a wave of her hand. "Whoa, hold on a second. There's a patron saint of *computers?*"

Priest smiled. "Yes." She looked back at the screen. "He is also the patron saint of schoolchildren."

Riley's smile faded. "Lot of good it did Kevin Gibson and Philip Hawkins."

"I think it worked out very well for Philip Hawkins."

"How do you figure?"

"He got you assigned to his case."

Riley didn't know how to respond to that, so she decided to let it drop. "Good night, Caitlin."

"Good night, Riley. Say hello to Gillian for me."

Riley saluted and headed downstairs. She made a detour to the morgue to see if Gillian was still there, and continued to the garage once she saw the night shift coroner was already on duty.

On the drive home, she thought about Hawk and Kevin Gibson. She had high hopes that Hawk would turn himself around, but Kevin was another story. All she could do was hope he realized how lucky he had gotten this time around. She drove a few blocks out of her way and drove along the border of No Man's Land. There were people out in the streets, in the alleys, dying and killing each other. She would get assigned one of them in the morning and she'd have to pick up the pieces. Everything would begin again.

She parked in her usual spot in the garage, trudged upstairs and let herself into the apartment she once again shared with Gillian. During Gillian's sabbatical, Riley had hated the place. It never felt like home when she was there alone, and she always felt like an intruder. Coming back to a lit, warm home after a long day was so welcome that she leaned against the closed door for a moment and let the feeling wash over her, smiling at how good it felt. Kevin wasn't the only one who had gotten lucky.

Riley took off her coat and dropped it on the arm of the couch. "Jill?"

"Kitchen."

Riley changed direction and went into the kitchen. Gillian was just closing the fridge door, holding a jar of mustard in her hand. She had changed into a white T-shirt and an old pair of scrub bottoms. "I was just going to make a sandwich. Did you want one?"

"No, I'm not hungry." Gillian put the mustard down and unscrewed the top. Riley watched her build the sandwich, her hands moving with quick, graceful movements. Everything she did was like a ballet; Riley could watch her read a newspaper just for the joy of seeing her flip from one page to the next. "How was your day?"

"Routine," Gillian said. She lifted the sandwich and inspected it before she started to eat. "Yours?"

"I caught the kid who killed Bernard Wright."

"That's great, sweetheart." She looked up from her sandwich, brow furrowed. "It was a kid?"

"Teenager. I set him up with Project Rescue. It'll do more for him than prison."

"Smart. Good for you," Gillian said. "Did he explain the blood?"

Riley shook her head. "That wasn't him. There was a demon in the area. Priest thinks he used the murder to get into the church and leave a little calling card for us."

"Why did it want into the church in the first place?"

"I don't know. I don't want to know. If it's not important right now, then I'm not going to worry about it. We'll burn that bridge when we get there. Come here please." Gillian abandoned her sandwich and walked across the room. She slipped her arms around Riley's waist and accepted her kiss. "Days should always ends like this," she said when they parted.

"Play your cards right, Detective..." Gillian smiled and kissed Riley again, her smile fading as she moved her hands down to Riley's hips.

Riley broke the kiss and pressed her cheek against Gillian's. "We should slow down."

"No," Gillian said. She moved her hand to the small of Riley's back. "I've been thinking about it all day. I want you. I'm ready."

Riley moaned as Gillian kissed her again, harder this time. Gillian turned Riley until she was pinned to the wall next to the fridge and broke the kiss to explore Riley's throat and the part of her chest exposed by the open collar of her shirt. Her hands slipped under Riley's shirt to tease the bare flesh with her fingers before she moved up, pressing through the material of Riley's shirt until she reached her breasts. Riley arched her back as Gillian pressed her palms against her, and they kissed again.

"I really have missed you," Gillian whispered when the kiss broke again.

"I've been right here."

Gillian pulled Riley away from the wall, her hands and lips still exploring as they moved toward the bedroom.

"I'm sorry it took me so long to find you again."

Riley took advantage of the pause in their kiss to pull Gillian's T-shirt over her head. It dropped to the floor and Riley followed the curve of Gillian's breast with light touches of her fingertips. She touched the black lace of Gillian's bra before leaning in for another kiss. "It was worth the wait," Riley said as she hooked her thumbs in the waistband of Gillian's pants and shoved them down.

Gillian put her hand on Riley's shoulder to brace herself as she stepped out of the pants. She turned and disappeared into the darkness of the bedroom and Riley followed her. Riley's shirt hung open, exposing her undershirt. She went immediately for the bedside lamp and snapped it on, turning to see Gillian standing at the foot of the bed. Gillian kept her eyes locked on Riley as she reached behind her and hooked her bra. She let it fall and pushed her underwear down, standing naked before her.

Riley's heart moved erratically against her ribs, skittering as she rounded the edge of the bed. She put her hands on Gillian's skin as they kissed. Riley slipped her hand around Gillian and touched her back, covering the crude tattoo Riley had given her with her entire palm. "You're safe now," Riley whispered, kissing and tasting the sweat on Gillian's neck.

"Yes," Gillian said.

Riley put her hands on the backs of Gillian's thighs and pulled. Gillian bounced slightly on the balls of her feet, hooking her legs around Riley. They twisted and fell onto the bed with Riley on top, kissing her way down Gillian's body. She sucked the nipples tenderly, swept her tongue over the moist flesh between her breasts, and swirled her tongue in Gillian's navel. Finally settling between Gillian's legs, Riley kissed the moist hair and curled her tongue along the familiar folds. She moved back, sliding off the bed and pulling Gillian to the edge of the mattress. Gillian put her legs on Riley's shoulders and crossed her feet at the ankles.

Riley bowed her head, and Gillian lay back on the mattress and closed her eyes. Riley explored with her lips and fingers, letting her lips part Gillian's sensitive folds as she teased the wet flesh. Gillian responded with gasps and sighs, whispering Riley's name as she reached down and found Riley's free hand, threading their fingers together and squeezing.

When she came, her shoulders lifted off the bed and she curled her body forward over Riley. She put her hand on top of Riley's head like a blessing, panting through her orgasm, eyes tightly closed and her teeth bared as she thrust her hips against Riley's mouth.

After a long moment, Gillian relaxed. She lay back on the bed and locked unfocused eyes on the ceiling. She looked down and saw Riley toss her blouse and undershirt aside, licking her lips as Riley unbuttoned her pants and pushed them down her legs. Her underwear was bright white against tanned flesh and was quickly tossed aside, and Riley covered Gillian's naked body with her own. She pressed herself against Gillian's hip, looked into her eyes, and began to thrust. She moved her lower body in slow, deliberate circles, and was soon matching Gillian's rough breathing.

Gillian touched Riley's face, letting her fingertips linger on her closed eyes, her lips and the pounding pulse in her throat. Riley lifted her head, said Gillian's name, and her body twitched in anticipation of her own climax.

Tears rolled down either side of Gillian's face, pooling in her hair. When Riley looked and saw the tracks, Gillian answered before Riley could ask. "I'm home."

Riley smiled. "Yeah." She bent down and kissed Gillian's lips, settling on top of her. Gillian ran her hands across Riley's naked body, feeling each and every curve, always moving, trying to make up for lost time and missed touches.

Riley stayed awake as long as she could, holding Gillian as she slept, but she eventually dozed off. When she woke, she slipped out of Gillian's grip and went into the kitchen for a combination of delayed dinner and a midnight snack. She put her blouse back on, buttoning it enough for modesty before she went into the kitchen.

Gillian's sandwich was still lying on the table, one bite taken out of it, and Riley sniffed it to see if it was still good. The mustard didn't smell too bad, so she took a bite and searched the fridge for something to wash it down. She had grabbed the milk carton when Gillian, coming into the room behind her, said, "That view alone is worth coming home for."

Riley straightened and turned to look at Gillian. She wore a tight baby blue T-shirt with a Roman helmet on the front, the hem just short enough to reveal the crotch of her underwear. Riley lifted the milk in a toast to Gillian's form and said, "Ditto."

Gillian smiled and said, "Is that my sandwich?"

"I'll make you a fresh one. Sit."

Gillian sat at the table and put her head down. Riley mimicked Gillian's preparations from earlier, making a sandwich that was just a bit sloppier than Gillian's but still edible. She put it on a plate, poured a glass of milk, and then kissed the top of Gillian's head to wake her. "Dinner is served."

"Mm."

Riley sat across from her and ate her own sandwich. Gillian peeled off the crust of hers, eating each strip slowly with her eyes half open. In the middle of the dinner, Gillian moved her hand to the middle of the table and Riley placed hers in it. She was about to suggest a return to the bedroom when she heard her cell phone ringing from the living room. "Damn it." She reluctantly released Gillian's hand and went to answer it.

She finally found her phone in the pocket of her coat and flipped it open. "This is Parra."

"Riley, it's me," Priest said. "Are you at home?"

Riley looked at Gillian. "Yeah."

"You need to get down to Third and Wilson."

"Why? Priest, it's the middle of the night."

"We have another one."

Riley resisted the urge to groan. She pinched the bridge of her nose and said, "We just closed one. Let another detective take care of it. Robeson or—"

"Riley," Priest interrupted. "We have another angel."

Riley opened her eyes and dropped her hand. "You mean like Bernard Wright?"

"Yes."

Riley looked at her watch. "I'll be there in twenty minutes." She hung up and hissed, "Goddamn it."

Gillian was standing in the kitchen doorway. "I'll keep the bed warm for you."

Riley sighed. "Thank you. I don't know if I'll be back tonight." She cupped Gillian's face and kissed her hard. "I love you. I'll see you tomorrow, if I can."

Gillian nodded and gestured at the bedroom. "Go get dressed. I'll clean up in here." Riley nodded and reluctantly pulled herself away from Gillian.

Riley pulled up outside a stretch of crime scene tape twelve minutes later, rather than the twenty she predicted and examined the scene as she got out of the car. Three police cars with lights flashing stood at the curb to detour any traffic away from the scene. The focus seemed to be on the sidewalk outside of a used book store. Riley spotted Priest and Briggs as she flashed her badge at one of the uniforms standing guard. He let her under the tape, and Priest met her halfway. "What the hell?" Riley asked.

"That's what we've been asking," Priest said. They walked back to Briggs together. "I was at the office when the call came in. I had to see it for myself. And I thought you—"

"You were right."

Briggs turned to face them. "You said the wings were a crime of opportunity."

"They were," Riley said. "I... thought they were."

Briggs said, "Come with me." Priest and Riley followed her to the spot the patrol cars were angled to protect.

A man lay in the middle of the street, arms outspread with the palms facing up. He was dressed in a sweatshirt and jeans, sneakers nice enough to be brand new still on his feet. His head was covered by a towel, a small dignity offered by one of the officers who had responded. Riley took all of this in, but it was the ground underneath him that she noticed.

Someone had spread the pool of blood out in wide arcs on either side of the man's body. The ends were curled, with narrow wedges like feathers running along the bottom. In the harsh light of a patrol car's spotlight, the blood looked like spilled oil.

Briggs stopped and faced the body as she spoke. "Owner of the bookstore saw it happen. He said the victim was crossing the street when someone came up behind him. He didn't think anything of it, until the second guy grabbed the victim and started stabbing him in the back. He saw four or five quick jabs, and then the killer lowered him to the ground. Owner called 911 while the killer drew the wings. Said he was afraid of going out and getting the same treatment. Guy finished drawing in the blood, got up, and ran away. Never even looked around to see if anyone was watching."

"Did the bookshop owner give a description?" Riley asked.

Priest said, "Black. As in completely without color. He said, and I quote, it was like the guy didn't even have a face."

Riley recalled Kevin Gibson's words and felt a chill.

"Maybe the first one was a crime of opportunity," Briggs said, "but this is a sign he enjoyed it too much. He's going to start killing people for his little art projects. It's bad luck, Riley, your first case back. But you started this one—"

"I want it," Riley said.

"Good to hear. It's yours." She looked down at the body on the ground and said, "Find this guy, Detective Parra."

"I intend to, Lieutenant."

Briggs nodded to Priest as she walked toward the group of uniformed officers on the sidewalk.

Riley looked at Priest and then turned to look up at the sky. It was hard to see anything, with the clouds blocking the moon. The darkness seemed to swallow everything up. But she knew they were nearby, the angels and demons warring with each other. Though she had started it, she never thought the war was her business. She had been doing the best she could to stay out of the war, as she knew that she wouldn't stand a chance against the combined armies of heaven and hell. She was content to focus on her priority of protecting the city. But now one of them, one of those damned demonic fighters, had dropped the gauntlet on her turf. Maybe the demons decided that if they couldn't bring her to the fight, they would bring the fight to her.

If it was a fight the demons were looking for, Riley was more than willing to give them one.

The Angel Maker

Riley went into the on-call room without turning on the light, finding the couch by memory and dropping onto the insufficient cushions. She draped an arm across her face and hoped for at least half an hour of uninterrupted dozing. What she really wanted, to be honest, was to be back at home in Gillian's bed, but she couldn't afford the time it would take to drive there. She would have to get up and leave as soon as she lay down. As soon as her eyes were closed, she saw images of the crime scene she had just spent an hour exploring.

She saw the shop owners of the all-night cigarette and liquor stores, their bloodshot eyes turned toward the street as they spoke to Riley and Priest about what they saw. The consensus was that no one saw anything but a dark form and a brief, violent confrontation in the middle of the street. There was no description of the attacker because "it was too dark," despite the working streetlights on either side of the block.

Riley saw Grace Stone, the tired-eyed woman with pillow creases on the side of her face. Riley first saw her on the opposite side of the crime scene tape, her hair a mess, holding her robe together with one hand as she looked around the area in confusion. Riley saw the uniformed policewoman sitting next to the woman on the curb as Riley explained why her husband never came back from getting his cigarettes. She heard the crack in Grace Stone's voice when she said, "But what do you *mean*, 'killed'?" She was relieved when she finally walked away and left the policewoman to comfort the new widow.

Grace Stone provided them with basic information about her husband. His name was Russell Stone, a part-time janitor with the firm Squeaky Clean. He left the apartment around three for a cigarette break. This apparently wasn't unusual; Russell could be an insomniac, especially when he hadn't gotten a job in a while, and he smoked outside on the fire escape. She fell asleep assuming he was outside chain smoking but worried when he wasn't home an hour later. She was too shocked to provide much else about why her husband may have been targeted.

When they finished at the crime scene, Riley and Priest returned to the station. Neither of them spoke during the drive. Riley put up a replaced the pegboard between their desks with a whiteboard, and filled it with the little information they had.

Their victims were Bernard Wright and Russell Stone. According to the official file, Bernie's death was unrelated to the angel wings. Philip Hawkins had confessed to involuntary manslaughter, and his trip to Project Rescue was already being set up. There was no reason to doubt his assertion that he had nothing to do with the angel wings, which meant that there was a second person at the scene. He was their artist. In her report, Riley would suggest that whoever their 'artist' was, he'd gotten such a thrill out of his little masterpiece that he moved on to actual murder to make another.

Only she and Priest knew the truth. Hawk was under the influence of a demon when he struck Bernie, shown a horrific vision that caused him to lash out with deadly force. The witnesses all agreed that the killer in the second murder was definitely the same person who drew the wings, which meant that the demon was now apparently doing the dirty work himself.

Riley didn't think she'd succeeded in sleeping until she felt a cool hand on her forehead. She recognized the touch and opened her eyes, smiling up at the silhouette of Gillian standing over her. The door to the on-call room was open, lighting her from behind. Riley smiled and said, "Morning."

"Hi. Priest told me you were napping. I brought you coffee and some clean clothes."

"Bless you," Riley said. Gillian took Riley's offered hand, pulling her up into a sitting position. Riley breathed deep, inhaling the aroma of the coffee Gillian brought for her. "Sorry about running out like that last night."

Gillian sat next to Riley on the couch. "Never apologize for that. It's your job. I just wanted to make sure you were okay before I started for the day."

"I'm much better now," Riley said. She took the coffee off the table and took a slow sip. "Oh, that's the good stuff."

"I figured it was my fault you didn't get much sleep before the call came in."

Riley smiled. "Some things are better than sleep." She rubbed Gillian's thigh and said, "Do you have the victim from last night on your table?"

"He's up first," Gillian said. "I'll let you know when I have something."

"Thanks." She kissed Gillian's lips and said, "I'll try to see you at lunch."

Gillian nodded and stood up. Riley watched her leave the room, nursed her coffee for another few seconds, and then picked up the folded clothes Gillian had left her on the couch. She had thrown on the most convenient thing when she left, and she was glad she wouldn't have to suffer for that for the rest of the day.

She changed in the locker room, splashing cold water on her face before she went out into the main bullpen.

Word had obviously spread during her nap; there was a serial killer in the city. Riley wanted to point out that three victims were necessary to make that designation, but doing so would only ensure a third victim would arise before the week ended. She could always hope the demon had, for one reason or another, wanted Bernard Wright and Russell Stone dead and he was now done.

Priest was sitting on the edge of the desk, staring at the whiteboard. She had filled out the information under Bernie's name, and added a few items to what they knew about Russell Stone. Both men also had pictures clipped above their names with magnets. Priest turned as Riley approached. "Good morning. I hope it was okay to send Gillian in."

"My favorite alarm clock," Riley said. She gestured at the board. "New information from the wife?"

"Yes, and I phoned Father Lawrence for anything else he could tell me about Bernard Wright. So far, there's nothing to tie the two men together."

Riley read the new information on Stone: he hadn't been called out on a job in almost two weeks, he was a chain smoker, and he was popular with the men at the bar down the street from where he lived.

"Bernie was in AA," Riley said. "Maybe he and Stone crossed paths there."

"Stone's wife said he never went to any of those meetings. Her exact words were that he drank a lot, but he didn't have a problem. They weren't patrons of the church where Bernie lived and worked. I called the janitorial service where Stone sometimes worked, to see if they ever did a job at the church, but the offices are closed for another twenty minutes."

"Bernie took care of custodial work for the church," Riley said. "That could be the connection. Both men are basically janitors."

Priest shrugged. "Janitors are invisible. They can get into places that are usually off-limits. But Stone hadn't had a job for two weeks. If he saw something incriminating, why wait so long to kill him?"

Riley glanced at Priest and chuckled. "Wow. We'll make a real cop out of you yet."

"Glad to hear it," Briggs said. Riley cleared her throat and straightened her posture as the lieutenant joined them. She looked fresh and showered, her dark hair pulled back in a braid. She looked at the board and said, "Anything new since this morning?"

"Filling in the blanks," Riley said. "We're trying to find the connection between the two victims. We're going to check out Squeaky Clean as soon as they open."

Briggs nodded. "Good. People are already calling this a serial case, even though there are only two victims. Close this up before they're proven right."

"I'll do my best."

Briggs shrugged and held her hands out. "That's all I can ask of you. Keep me apprised."

Riley stood up and took her gun and badge from the desk drawer. "All right. Let's go see if the Squeaky Clean guys are in yet."

Priest followed Riley downstairs to the garage. "I've been thinking about Bernie's murder. Maybe it wasn't exactly chance and opportunity."

"What do you mean?"

"The murder was inside of a church. And now we're pretty sure there's a demon involved. Bernie's death broke the seal on the church and allowed the demon inside. That's a pretty big deal, isn't it? I mean, breaking the threshold..."

Priest said, "You have a point. Perhaps we should investigate the church again. There may have been evidence we overlooked."

"Right," Riley said. She unlocked the door to her Nova and sighed. "Big day ahead of us. Serial killer, demons..."

"Do you regret coming back from vacation?"

Riley breathed deep and looked around the garage. "No. It's good to be back."

Squeaky Clean's corporate offices were located in a squat prefab building with white aluminum siding. The parking lot was filled with four identical green trucks and a fifth truck that had a white camper shell on the back. Riley parked in the street and walked up the sloped driveway. They were almost to the door when it opened and two men in white jumpsuits came out. The men barely glanced at Riley as they moved purposely toward their trucks.

"Excuse me," Riley said, moving into their way with her badge held up so they couldn't miss it. "I'm Detective Riley Parra. This is Detective Priest.

We'd like to ask you a few questions about one of your coworkers."

One of the men kept walking, but the other slowed a bit. "Which one?"

"Russell Stone."

The first man who was already at the truck turned to look at her. "Stone don't work here."

The second man said, "Yeah, he does. Sometimes."

"No, fool got fired."

"Yeah, you wish, Drew." The second man finally stopped walking and faced Riley with his arms crossed. "What did he do?"

Riley pointed at the man now leaning against his truck, impatiently watching her. "That's Drew, and you are...?"

"That's Drew Payne, I'm Travis Salda-a."

"I'm afraid that Mr. Stone was murdered last night."

Drew laughed hard before he could contain it, ducking his chin and wiping a hand over his mouth. Riley, Priest and Travis all looked at him, and he stayed silent as long as he could. "Sorry. But... just desserts, right? How'd she do it?"

"Sir?"

"His old lady. She get a gun or something?"

Riley said, "What makes you think his wife was involved?"

Drew looked at Travis and his smile slowly faded. "Oh, come on. Trav, you know what I mean, right? You hated working with that prick because he beat up on his wife all the time. We'd have to spend all day with him and hearing about how you gotta keep your bitches in line. I socked him myself once or twice. Just to keep 'im in line, understand." He snorted and turned his head to spit toward the street. "I'm just saying. Bad rubbish."

"Is that true?" Riley asked Travis.

He shrugged and looked down at his feet. "I don't like talking behind people's backs. And now that he's dead, shit..." He looked at Riley and saw she wouldn't be letting the issue drop. He rolled his eyes and said, "Yeah, okay, he talked about hitting his old lady. A lot of guys do. They get frustrated and they vent. But I never saw any bruises on the lady."

Riley had to admit she hadn't seen any bruises either. Of course she had only seen Mrs. Stone on a dark street when she had other things on her mind. She looked at Priest, who shrugged.

"Okay. We'll let you guys get back to work. Is your boss inside?"

"Supervisor is Mr. Bauer," Travis said. "He's inside."

Riley nodded. "Thanks for your time, gentlemen." She waited until they were in the truck before she started toward the building again. "Did you notice any bruises on Mrs. Stone?"

"None," Priest said. "But isn't it normal for the abuser to inflict injuries in places that are easily concealed?"

"Yeah, bastards are smart," Riley said. She went up the three wooden steps to the front door, knocking on the frame as she stepped inside.

The office was larger than it appeared from the outside, the interior space furnished with only a handful of desks and filing cabinets to maximize the open space. A man stood at the back of the room, jabbing the buttons on a fax machine. He spoke when he heard the door open. "Either of you idiots know how to run one of these things?"

Riley said, "Sorry. Not our area of expertise."

Bauer turned and glared at them until he saw their badges. "Oh, great. Whoever called you, tell them to stuff it. I don't know what happened to whatever file is missing or—"

"We're not here for anything like that," Riley said. "We'd just like to speak to you about Russell Stone."

"Stone doesn't work here anymore."

"So we heard. We were wondering why."

Bauer moved to his desk and sat heavily. "Why? You guys part of the wrongful termination unit or something? I fired him 'cause I found out he beats up on his wife. I don't much care for people like that. So I waited until I had a reason. He came in late one day, and I told him he could take off as long as he wanted. I had no use for him anymore."

"That was about two weeks ago?" Riley said.

"I don't know. That sounds about right. What's going on?"

Riley said, "Mr. Stone was murdered last night."

Bauer scoffed. "Is that so. Well, if his wife has a brother, I'll alibi him."

"That won't be necessary. Do you think any of his coworkers might have taken offense at some of his talk? Maybe they decided to take justice into their own hands."

"I doubt it. What time was the jerk killed?"

"Around two-thirty."

Bauer shook his head. "Couldn't have been any of my guys. They were all at work from eleven until five-thirty. The smallest one was a group of four."

Riley said, "And three of them wouldn't lie about where the fourth was?"

Bauer smiled. "Sure they would, if it involved that prick Stone. But I don't know why they would bother. He was out of sight and out of mind. I hadn't even thought about him since he walked out the door. Two weeks is a long time to hold a grudge."

Riley nodded. "Do you have a list of the businesses you sent Stone to clean?"

Bauer checked the files on his desktop and then tapped a few buttons on his computer. The printer next to the fax machine started to whir, and he handed them a sheet with twelve business names printed on the front. "Those were from his last month working here. I think it's a waste of your time, though. People have complaints, it comes to me. They don't know the specific people who work on their place."

"Unless the business owner happened to be there when the cleaning crew came in," Priest said. "Maybe Mr. Stone saw something he shouldn't have."

Bauer shrugged. "You're the detectives. I'm just telling you I wouldn't bother. Someone did that lady a favor takin' her husband out."

Riley forced a smile. "Well, we can't pick and choose what murders we investigate, Mr. Bauer. Thanks for your help."

He stood up to escort them to the door. "Sorry I couldn't be more help. Mrs. Stone was a really classy lady, the handful of times I got to meet her. Makes you wonder what she saw in a guy like Russ."

"Just shows there's someone out there for everyone," Riley said.

"Yeah. Some of 'em are victims." He scoffed and gestured at the badge on Riley's belt. "Look who I'm telling. Let me know if you need anything else from me or my guys. I'll make sure they help you out."

"Thank you, Mr. Bauer."

Priest followed Riley back to the car. "Are you going to talk to the other employees?"

"No point now," Riley said. "Bauer's probably already on the phone telling everyone to back each other up. There wasn't any love lost between these guys and Mr. Stone. No one seemed to care for him, and any number of them could have been pushed by a demon to take the last step."

"So the suspect list is the entire city?"

"No," Riley said. "We can probably eliminate the people who never met Stone."

Priest said, "Oh, good. For a second I was worried it would be impossible."

Riley smiled and said, "Get in the car. Maybe Gillian will give me more than coffee when we get back."

Gillian was in blue scrubs, masked and gloved, and her hair was hidden under a cap. She pulled off the latter as Riley and Priest came into the morgue. "Hey, guys. I was just about to give you a call. I finished the autopsy on Mr. Stone." She pulled down her mask so that it covered her chin instead of her mouth.

"Anything we didn't already know?"

"Cause of death was multiple stab wounds." She walked to the table and turned on the light so they could see. "The first was here, on the right side of the back. The wound is tapered, and approximately five inches deep. Two more wounds here, on other side of the spine. The second of these, the one on the left, was the fatal wound. The killer pressed, twisted, and pushed it up until he nicked the heart. There are a couple of other superficial wounds that bled a lot. The attack was not frenzied."

Priest said, "The killer wasn't angry."

Gillian shook her head. "I would be able to tell from the markings if he was angry. These wounds are relatively casual. There's enough force to pierce the clothing and muscle but nothing excessive. It would be like me or you cutting the tape off a package."

Riley said, "He didn't care about the murder. He just wanted the blood to make his wings."

Gillian nodded. "So... we're sure about what this is, right?"

"Not beyond a reasonable doubt," Riley said. "But it seems the most likely scenario. There's a demon out there that's using someone to murder people. The question is *why?*"

"For fun," Gillian said. She looked down at the body and said, "Looking at what connects the victims won't do any good. The victims are just a small piece of the equation for this. The demon doesn't even care about the murders, really. It's a mean to his end. He gets off on control. Forcing a human to do something outside of their comfort zone. Making someone kill." She blinked and looked up, locking onto Riley's eyes. "Sorry. I guess I had a little flashback."

"It's okay," Riley whispered. She touched Gillian's hand.

"I think Gillian has a point," Priest said. "I don't think we're going to find a connection between the victims. Or with their murderers. A demon would most likely use anyone in the vicinity, and then kill whoever was handy. Investigating this case officially won't do any good, because it won't be solved in the traditional manner."

Riley said, "We'll still have to go through the motions for Briggs' benefit. We'll keep digging into the victims' background and try to connect them while we're looking for the demon pulling the strings in the background." She sighed and pushed a hand through her hair. "And I thought a regular serial killer investigation would be hard."

"And you're screwed if Briggs assigns a task force," Gillian said.

"She won't do that until there are at least three victims. Hopefully that'll give us a little time." She looked at the body on the table and said, "This guy was killed at half past two."

"Yeah," Gillian said. "That was the time given by the eyewitness, and my exam confirmed it."

"Bernie was killed the night before. What was the time of death?"

Priest's eyes widened and Gillian said, "Oh, damn. Around two-thirty."

"Do you think there will be another victim tonight?" Priest asked.

"I don't know. God. I hope not. A new victim every morning would be just what this city needs. It's not like we can warn people to stay indoors between two and three tonight. Most people will be inside anyway. Those who are outside don't have much say in the matter. We need to look at the two scenes and see if there's any kind of pattern."

"I'll get the map ready," Priest said.

Riley watched her leave and then turned to Gillian. "Hey," she said softly. "Do you want me to stay down here for a while?"

"No," Gillian said. "Thank you. I just... have some... lingering issues to deal with. I'll be fine. Thank you."

"I'm a phone call away," Riley said. She kissed Gillian and whispered goodbye before she reluctantly pulled away and followed Priest upstairs.

Priest had already marked the location of the first two sites on their map. Riley looked at it as she approached, trying to let her brain fill in an obvious third location. She stopped in front of her desk and said, "None of the murders have occurred in No Man's Land yet. I guess that could be counted as a good thing."

"Unless it's another sign of No Man's Land growing," Priest said.

Riley sighed. "I try to see the glass as half full one time, and you shoot me down."

Priest smiled. "Sorry."

"Have you come up with any ideas about where we might find the next victim?"

Priest shook her head. "Without knowing if the first two are random or part of some kind of design, we can't do much. Even if we were sure it was a design, we don't know what it is just from these two points."

Riley dug in her top desk drawer until she found a roll of thread. She tied one end around a push pin, put it at the church site, and tied the other end around another pin on Russell Stone's murder. The thread ran down at a straight forty degree angle. "It could be the first leg of a pentagram," Riley said. "A small pentagram."

"Well, we can't tell much from a single line, but the angle isn't steep enough for any leg of a pentagram," Priest said. "Even if he was just trying to make a small pentagram, it would only cover about five blocks. If you're going to make the effort, why not cover the entire city?"

"Maybe there's something important in those five blocks. There's no need to cover the entire city if you can cover what you need." She looked at the map, trying to remember what was on the blocks that would be covered if they were right. Finally, she sighed and said, "We're theorizing about the size of something we're not even sure is being made. For right now let's just assume they were random killings. If there's going to be a third tonight, there's not going to be a way to predict where it will happen."

Priest said, "What's our next move?"

"We tell Briggs about our third victim theory, and then we go back to the scene where Stone was killed. If the killer wasn't waiting for Stone specifically, then he would have been waiting for someone, anyone, to show up. The victims weren't important, but the locations were." She chewed her lip and said, "Odds are that this street isn't very busy at two in the morning. Either way, he was waiting. Maybe he left us something."

The part of the street where Russell Stone died was still blocked off with crime scene tape. Traffic was slowed since it was reduced to a single lane, and Riley ignored the sour looks of people driving past as she ducked under the tape. The blood had unfortunately been washed away by the crime scene clean-up crew, but Riley had expected that. Priest stayed on the sidewalk and looked up and down the street.

"Did the bookstore owner say which direction the killer came from?"

Priest withdrew a notebook and checked the details. "He saw Russell Stone coming across the street toward the store, which is that direction." She pointed. "So he was almost all the way across the street before the killer appeared from behind him and to his right."

Riley took Stone's position, held her right hand behind her back, and looked over her shoulder. Each building on the street had a narrow alley separating it from the next building. The nearest alley was blocked off by a wrought-iron gate backed by a piece of plywood. The next one down the street was open and relatively empty save for a few trash cans. "What is that, about fifty yards? Our guy was waiting there."

They crossed to the alley and Riley said, "Did the crime scene guys check this out?"

"I'm sure they did," Priest said. "They were all over this area last night. Of course, searching with flashlights is hardly the same as looking in daytime."

Riley looked back at the crime scene. She couldn't go very far before it was out of sight. "Okay. Our boy was here. He didn't care who the victim was, but it had to happen here. Why?" She paced to the mouth of the alley and looked at the businesses she could see. "Bernie's murder, in the church. That makes sense. It broke the seal. I assume there was some kind of alarm that went off when the seal got broken."

"More like an aftershock from a powerful earthquake. But yes, it was felt."

"Feel anything last night?"

Priest shook her head. "Afraid not."

Riley said, "If the victims don't matter, then the locations have to be the key. But the middle of the street?" She looked up at the buildings she was standing between. Crime scene tape was still up, and a crime scene truck was blocking the opposite side street. "Maybe the killer needed traffic to be tied up here today. What are these buildings?"

Priest ticked off a list from her notebook. "A bookstore, a law office, a liquor store, a bar..."

"Okay, probably not blocking off the street. God knows we have enough liquor stores and bars in this town. Maybe the location is just near the killer's home. He didn't want to venture out too far." She sighed. "We're never going to get anywhere this way. Let's see if anyone remembers something they didn't mention last night."

They were halfway across the street when Riley spotted Russell Stone's wife. She was coming out of her apartment building, wrapped in a heavy coat despite the warmth of the day. Her hair was hidden by a baseball cap, and her hands shook as she closed the door behind her and stepped onto the sidewalk. "Mrs. Stone," Riley said. Grace's head turned quickly toward her. "Do you remember us from last night? Detectives Parra and Priest. Could we have a word?"

Grace's eyes widened slightly and she moved her lips in an attempt to speak.

"It'll just take a moment," Riley said.

Grace suddenly went limp and crumpled to the ground like a puppet with its strings cut.

Priest lunged to catch her and barely managed to keep her head from impacting the bottom step of her apartment building. Riley crouched next to the woman and checked to make sure she had only fainted, and then looked at Priest. "Nice catch."

"Thank you. Warn me the next time you're going to play hardball with a witness."

"Warn *you?*" Riley said.

When Grace came to, Riley and Priest helped her down the street to a diner. Riley found a booth and sat Grace down, keeping her company while Priest went to get something to drink. She came back a moment later with two cups of tea, for herself and Grace, and a cup of coffee for Riley. Grace accepted the cup with both hands, whispered a thank you, and took a slow sip. She swallowed and looked at Riley before she lowered her eyes to the cup in her hands.

"I apologize for my reaction, Detective. I've been feeling guilty all day. About Russ." She licked her lips and ran her thumb over the handle of her cup. "The truth is, I've been feeling relieved all day. The guilt is just a side effect. I took a nap, and I woke up knowing he wasn't there. And I was happy. I smiled. Isn't that horrible? When I saw you on the street, I just assumed... I don't know. I thought maybe you were coming to arrest me."

"We can't arrest people for not being appropriately sad when something like this happens," Riley said. "Otherwise the jails would fill up every time a politician died. We've spoken to some of Russell's coworkers. They told us that he wasn't exactly a good husband."

Grace smiled sadly. "He wasn't a bad man. He had a temper, but who doesn't? When he got depressed, he would take it out on me. If he hadn't worked for a while, he would have to prove he was the man of the house by whatever means he could." She shrugged. "Is your life perfect? It's the life I had. And I did love him. In a way."

"Mrs. Russell, we're fairly sure that your husband was simply in the wrong place at the wrong time. We think whoever stabbed him was looking for someone, anyone, to kill, and your husband was convenient."

Grace looked out the window and chewed her bottom lip. "I'm going to have something else for confession, I suppose. That's where I was heading when you stopped me. When you told me that he was a random death, I thought, 'well, at least they picked the right person.' You must think I'm a terrible person."

"No," Priest said. "You were pushed to those thoughts by years of abuse. Mentally and physically. Russell Stone will have to atone for what he has done to you. You're free now. You can have peace."

Grace stared at Priest for a long moment before she nodded. "Thank you."

"We won't keep you any longer. Thank you for your time, Mrs. Stone." They stood and Riley thought of a possible connection. "Your church. You don't happen to attend St. Isidore's, do you?"

"No. St. Rita's."

Priest smiled. "The patron saint of marital problems and abuse."

Grace blinked. "Is she?"

Priest stepped forward and wrapped her arms around Grace. She held her for a long moment, whispered something in her ear, and said, "I hope you find peace."

"Thank you," Grace said. She smiled nervously at Riley, adjusted her coat, and hurried from the diner.

"What did you say to her?" Riley said as they followed her outside.

"That's between me and her," Priest said. "I gave her a bit of comfort. I believe she'll get through this trial."

Riley said, "Well, at least that's one silver lining." She looked at the buildings nearest the crime scene. A liquor store and a law office. Odd to find those things right next to each other, but she had seen stranger things, especially this close to No Man's Land. She stepped off the curb and glanced down to where the bloody wings had been a few hours before. She looked at the sidewalk and did a double take. "Priest."

"What is it?"

The parking spot blocked by their crime scene tape was reserved. Black letters painted on a white background spelled out PARALEGAL. Riley pointed and said, "That."

"I know what a paralegal is," Priest said.

Riley knelt and pointed at the R. A smear of dark red ran down between it and the second A. "What does that look like to you?"

"Blood," Priest said.

"It looks like the letter R."

Priest squinted and said, "I suppose."

"That makes it Parra Legal."

"That seems like a leap, Riley."

Riley turned and scanned the street. "Stone was killed over there. How big were the bloody wings? A few feet? There's no way that blood was spilled all the way over here. This was put here deliberately."

Priest looked at where they had found Stone's body and seemed to visually measure the distance. "You may have a point."

Riley took her cell phone out and dialed. "Thank God the crime scene unit didn't wash this away." While the phone rang, she looked down at the smear of dried blood. She had thrown down the gauntlet when she realized there would be more murders, and she had vowed that she wouldn't back down from a war if it came to that.

This message, she was sure, was the other side accepting her challenge.

They waited for the lab guys to show up and watched as they took samples and photographs of the new blood smear. They didn't reveal the significance of the blood's placement; Riley wanted to wait until they knew it had a non-demonic explanation before they added it to the official report. When they were done, Riley suggested lunch and Priest let her choose where they would go. Riley found a restaurant a few blocks away with a large outdoor seating area and decided it would be good enough.

"What do they serve here?"

"Cheeseburgers, hamburgers, chili dogs... greasy and delicious."

Priest looked at the tables they passed dubiously. "Perhaps it would be best if you ordered for both of us."

"No problem. Two cheeseburgers with everything, fries, and cokes.

Their order was delivered quickly on identical red trays. Priest looked at her food with increasing trepidation. "Are you certain people eat this sort of thing a lot?"

"It's the main reason this country has an obesity problem, and a heart attack problem."

"And you're eating it because..."

Riley handed Priest the ketchup. "Because it's delicious. Dig in." She picked up two fries and chewed them as she looked out over the street.

Priest took a bite of her burger, chewed carefully, and then washed it down with a drink of her soda. "That's terrible."

"It gets better." Riley looked at the burger and said, "Oh. You don't have a thing about eating meat, do you? I mean, religiously."

"No," Priest said. "Why? Is there meat somewhere in this?"

Riley smirked. They ate quietly for a while. Priest discovered that the fries were fairly safe, so she focused on eating handfuls of them between bites of her burger. Finally, Riley said, "I've been thinking. Do you think this killer could be the guy?"

"What do you mean?"

"The other team's quarterback. Evil's champion. I mean, we know he's out there somewhere. Maybe these murders are his way of getting my attention."

"I suppose that's a possibility. I take it you haven't had any luck finding out who he is."

Riley shook her head. "I haven't exactly had much of an opportunity to look. I figure he's someone with power. Someone capable of influencing how things work in the city. But when you're looking at that level of government, it's hard to tell evil from flat-out incompetence." She looked at Priest's tray and saw she was slowly but surely making progress on the burger. "What do you think?"

"There's an awful lot of gristle."

"I mean about my theory on this murderer being the other guy."

"Oh. It's possible. I would question why he's taking the time to murder anonymous victims, but you're right. Maybe he is just doing this to get your attention."

"Of course, that would mean that the real fun hasn't even started yet."

Priest wrinkled her nose and dropped the remains of her burger onto the greasy wrapper. "I think I lost my appetite."

"Yeah," Riley said. She pushed her tray back. "Me too."

Riley found a note on her desk when she returned. *See me. Briggs.* She showed it to Priest and said, "These are never good news."

"Would you like me to say a prayer?"

Riley said, "If you've got one handy. You're coming with me. We can brief her together." Briggs' door was open, and Riley knocked on the frame. "You wanted to see us?"

"Yes. Come in." Briggs finished typing something and said, "CSU told me that you found another spot of blood at the scene."

"Yeah. On the sidewalk. We're not sure it means anything, but it's something."

Briggs picked up a newspaper and said, "Did you see this?"

Riley picked up the paper and groaned. "Police Seek the Angel Maker?"

"It's more a 'the cops can't protect you' story than actual facts about the case. Courtesy our old friend Gail Finney."

"You mean someone actually wrote this?" Riley said. "I thought newspapers just had a machine that spit this crap out."

"That's not important," Briggs said. "I'm concerned about this theory you have about the two-thirty deadline. How big of a threat do you think this is?"

Riley shrugged. "That depends. I think it will happen, but I don't think there's anything we could do to prevent it. We could put two cops at fourteen random locations and have them watch out for anything suspicious, but we don't have that kind of manpower. We're not even sure anything will happen tonight. The timing could have been a coincidence. It sucks, Lieutenant, but there's nothing we can do but wait for a call."

Briggs nodded slowly and said, "All right. Keep the deadline to yourselves. We don't need Gail Finney picking up on it and asking if we could have prevented other murders. That's all." They started to leave, but Briggs said, "Detective Parra. Stay a moment."

Priest stopped, but Riley motioned for her to go on. She shut the door and turned to face the desk.

Briggs said, "It's been brought to my attention that you're in a romantic relationship with Dr. Hunt. Is this correct?"

"Yes, ma'am."

Briggs folded her hands on the desk. "This is the sort of thing that you should have told me as soon as she came back. I have to ask if it's going to be an issue."

"No," Riley said. "The reason I didn't bring it up is because it has no bearing on my work. Jill... Dr. Hunt and I are both professionals."

"That's all I needed to hear," Briggs said. "That's all. Riley..."

Riley resisted the urge to roll her eyes. "Yes, ma'am."

"Get this son of a bitch before he kills anyone else."

Riley rested her chin in her hand, squinting at the map between her desk and Priest's.

Priest said, "Why do you have thread in your desk drawer?"

"I tore a seam on my blouse once while I was chasing some pickpocket. I keep thread in the desk drawer in case it happens again."

"You can sew?"

"Yeah."

Priest sighed. "Clothing is so cumbersome. It gets dirty, you have to clean it. And it's never clean for long."

"Must be better where you're from," Riley said. "You just wear the same thing every day. It can't get dirty. Can it? Is there dirt... there?"

"I don't know. But we don't wear the long flowing robes you see in paintings."

"What do you wear?"

"Nothing, usually." She frowned when Riley chuckled. "It's not sexual."

Riley nodded. "Sure it isn't."

Priest looked at the board. "Am I helping distract you? Has your subconscious locked on anything?"

"No," Riley said. She sighed and laced her fingers behind her neck to stretch. "Thanks anyway." She stood and stepped closer to the map. "The victims have no connection. The locations don't seem to be important. So why did the killer wait for Russell Stone? And if he wasn't waiting for Russell Stone, then why was it so important that someone be killed in that spot?"

"The paralegal sign," Priest said.

Riley shook her head. "There's a Riley Brothers Auto on Monroe. If he wanted to send me a message, that would be a better choice."

Priest said, "Well, maybe he had to stay where he was."

"Why?"

"I don't know why."

Riley walked slowly in front of the board. "Okay, Russell Stone was killed on Third and Wilson. Why would someone have to stay in that spot?"

Priest said, "Maybe he lives in one of the apartment buildings nearby."

Riley suddenly slapped the map. "Son of a bitch. Bus stop. There's a bus stop a block away." She ran her finger up the line and jabbed it at St. Isidore's. "Bus stop. The killer rides the fucking bus." She turned and grabbed her phone off the desk. "Get me the phone book. I'm going to find out what buses run there."

"We have the fourteen locations," Priest said. She looked at the map and corrected herself. "Actually, more like a hundred, but... we've narrowed it down considerably."

Riley paused and said, "I guess we do. Go tell Briggs, I'll— yes. Yes, this is Detective Riley Parra. I need to speak to one of your drivers." She turned to look at the map while she was on hold. She picked up a pen off her desk and began crossing off the icons that indicated a bus stop. If they stuck to downtown only, ignored No Man's Land, and stayed in the general vicinity of the two previous murders, they definitely had a workable number of places to check.

Briggs left her office as soon as Priest finished briefing her. Riley hung up with the transit authority. "We just narrowed down the number of locations. The St. Isidore and Wilson stops are on the same bus route." She picked up a pen and drew a line between them. "I talked to the supervisor. The bus driver is named Joanna Clark, and she's on her way in to the transit authority to talk to us. I wanted to check out the bus just in case our guy left us anything."

Briggs nodded. "Get me a list of the bus stops you think this guy will be using and I'll ask for increased patrols around them tonight. Maybe we'll get lucky. We'll put an officer on the bus to keep an eye on things."

"Actually, boss, that might scare the guy off," Riley said. "I suggest an unmarked car follow the bus at a reasonable distance. Just to keep an eye on things."

Briggs considered it and then said, "All right. Nice work, Detective." Briggs patted Priest on the shoulder as she went back to her office, and Riley gestured toward the stairs.

"Let's go talk to the bus driver."

Priest followed Riley out of the bullpen. "How many stops are on that particular bus route?"

"Twenty-one," Riley said. "Still a lot of places to check, but it's a drop in the bucket compared to what we could have been dealing with. After this,

I think I'm going to crash in the on-call room for a few hours."

"That's why you nixed Lieutenant Briggs' idea to have a cop on the bus. You want to be out there looking for him."

"It's my case," Riley said. "More than that, you and I both know what we're really dealing with. I'm not going to risk a uniformed cop who just thinks this is a run of the mill psycho."

Priest nodded. "I'll go with you. Maybe I'll be able to narrow it down even further."

Riley smirked. "Kind of like a disturbance in the Force?"

"I've seen that one, I think," Priest said.

"We'll head out around midnight. We have to assume the killer knows what we both look like but maybe we can think of a way around that."

Priest said, "What do you plan to do when we catch him?"

"Bring him in. Ask him some questions. It won't be easy if he has a demon riding shotgun, but I've got an angel in my corner."

"It could be bad," Priest said. "If this guy is who you think he is, if he really is evil's champion, he may be protected by a tattooed sigil like you used to be. There's a chance I won't be able to touch him."

"We'll burn that bridge when we get there." She gestured at the next landing and tossed the keys to Priest. "I'm going to stop in and see Gillian. Let her know that I won't be home tonight. It won't take long." Riley went through the door and down the corridor to the morgue entrance, pushing it open with her shoulder.

Gillian was at one of the examination tables with a body in front of her. She looked over her shoulder and turned off the microphone clipped to the collar of her scrub top. "Hey."

"Hey. I can come back if you're busy with a customer."

"No, it's fine. He's a lousy tipper." She pulled down her mask and said, "What's up?"

Riley said, "First of all, Briggs knows about us. She won't make it an issue if we keep it professional."

Gillian shrugged. "Sounds easy enough to me."

"That in mind, don't make a scene when I tell you I probably won't be home tonight."

"Did you get a break in the case?"

Riley said, "I'm not sure. We're going to talk to someone who might have seen him, but it's still very up in the air. If things go right, I'm going to be staking out tonight."

"Did you get any more sleep?"

"I will, after this interview. Promise."

"Okay. Be safe, and call if you can." She leaned forward, keeping her body away from Riley to prevent contamination. Riley pecked Gillian's lips. Gillian said, "Let me know if you have a few minutes for dinner later."

Riley realized that half a cheeseburger had left her particularly hungry. "That would be amazing, Jill. I'll let you know." She kissed Gillian again and gestured at the table. "I'll let you get back to work. Anything I should worry about?"

"Massive head trauma," Gillian said. "Four witnesses, totally accidental."

"All right. I'll leave you to him. See you tonight." Riley was at the door before Gillian said, "Be careful."

"You said that already."

"What, do I have a limit?"

Riley chuckled. "No. I'll be careful, promise." She blew a kiss to Gillian and let the door swing shut behind her.

The bus depot was crowded on three sides by tall buildings, its lot half-empty. Riley parked near the front of the main building where two women were waiting. The women were dressed identically in crisp blue blouses and dark blue sweater vests. They approached as Riley and Priest got out of the car. One woman said, "Are you the police detectives?"

"That's us," Riley said. She showed her badge. "Parra, this is Priest. Are you Joanna Clark?"

"No, that's her," she pointed at the other woman. "I'm Renee Long. I'm the supervisor."

Joanna Clark came forward and said, "Renee told me you were looking for someone on my bus. I don't know if I can help, but I can sure try."

"We think the man we're looking for boarded at Third and Wilson last night, and at St. Isidore's church the night before that. He might have been wearing dark clothes, maybe kept his hands in his pockets. He may have been out of breath, or..."

"I don't remember anyone like that on the bus," Joanna said. She scratched her cheek. "That time of night, I'm not really paying attention to the individual passengers."

Priest said, "This person is one you would notice. You would feel uncomfortable the entire time this person is on your bus. Anxious. You would feel like a crash was imminent. Your palms might sweat."

Joanna's eyes widened as Priest spoke. "Well... sometimes in the middle of the night like that, sure. I feel that way."

"But you don't associate that feeling with a specific person?"

"Why... why would I?" Joanna asked.

Riley and Priest exchanged a look and then Riley said, "We'd like your permission to be on the bus tonight. There will be an unmarked car following you and increased patrols around the stops, but we want to have all our bases covered."

Renee said, "Anything to help catch this guy. You really think this jerk is using our buses?"

"It's our best theory right now."

"Well, like I said, anything we can do to help. The bus leaves around nine for the late shift. You should get here around eight-thirty to be aboard."

Riley checked her watch. That gave her four hours to nap and have dinner with Gillian. "All right, I'll be here."

Joanna shuddered and said, "I hope you catch this guy. I'm not going to feel safe on my own bus now that I know he's walked right past me."

Riley said, "Don't worry. We'll do our best to make sure he doesn't ride your bus again after tonight."

The on-call room was basically a gathering spot for detectives who didn't want to take the time to go home and sleep during a hectic case. It had a TV and a small seating area with two donated couches and three chairs clustered around a low coffee table. There were two roll-away beds in the corner, but Riley preferred the couch. A doorway across from the couch led directly into the locker room, but the light never bothered her when she stretched out.

A few other detectives came in while she was napping, but she was only peripherally aware of their presence. She only woke when she smelled Gillian's perfume. She opened her eyes as Gillian quietly lowered herself into the armchair closest to Riley. She was carrying a brown paper bag, and the scent of what was inside finally prompted Riley to sit up. "Hey. Taquitos?"

"*Si*," Gillian said.

"*Te bendiga*," Riley said.

Gillian took the food from the bag and set it up on the coffee table.

She had been home already, her scrubs replaced by a red blouse and blue jeans. She used the paper bag as a plate and poured out a bit of salsa for dipping. She sat next to Riley on the couch, their thighs touching, and they began to eat. "Priest told me you were going to ride the bus tonight. Do you think you'll be able to spot the guy?"

"I'm hoping so. If not, I'll have Priest backing me up." She chewed her taquito slowly, hoping to fool her stomach into thinking it was a bigger meal than it was.

Gillian said, "I also have sopapilla if you're still hungry."

"You're brilliant," Riley said.

Gillian smiled. "I put a bag in your locker. Just some old clothes I had lying around that didn't fit me anymore. And my old glasses."

"You wear contacts?"

Gillian shook her head. "No. Laser surgery when I was a teenager. I kept the glasses because... well, I don't know. But promise you won't think less of me when you see them."

Riley smiled. "Why, are they big horn-rimmed nerd glasses?" Gillian pursed her lips and Riley laughed. "Oh, you have to put them on for me."

"Maybe if there's an incentive."

Riley leaned in and kissed Gillian's cheek. "Like maybe if you were a sexy teacher?"

Gillian grinned. "I like the way your mind works, Detective Parra. What time do you have to leave?"

"In about fifteen minutes. Enough time to finish dinner." She looked at the open door of the room and said, "Did Lieutenant Briggs see you come in here?"

"She was talking to another detective at her office door. I'm pretty sure she did."

Riley nodded. "Okay. I just don't want her to think we're sneaking around."

They ate quietly for a while. Riley finished her taquitos and moved on to the sopapillas. Gillian got a bit of salsa on her lip and Riley kissed it away with a sweep of her tongue. When they finished their meal, Riley cleaned up the debris and wiped her hands on a napkin Gillian provided. "I should probably go."

Gillian stood up and said, "I'll say it again..."

"I'll be careful."

"I'm not going to be one of those partners who says 'I love you' every time you leave my sight. That would remind me that every time you go out, you might die. But just because I don't say it, don't think—"

"I won't forget," Riley whispered. She cupped the back of Gillian's head and kissed her tenderly. "If nothing happens, I should be home around five or so."

"You can wake me."

Riley mouthed that she would and reluctantly stepped away. "Thank you for dinner."

"Hey, if it's the only time I get to spend with you..." She winked and said, "Be careful. I love you."

Riley chuckled. "I love you, too, Jill." She went into the locker room and found the bag Gillian had left for her. She opened it and pulled out the top layer of clothes. "Oh, you've got to be kidding me, Gillian."

Joanna Clark did a double take when Riley boarded the bus. Riley resisted the urge to take off the outfit and said, "Undercover. In case the guy saw me at a crime scene."

"Oh," Joanna said. "Right. Okay."

Priest followed Riley to the back of the bus. One bench seat ran along the entire back, giving them a view of every other seat. Riley sat down and caught a glimpse of herself in the mirror above Joanna's seat. She wore two of Gillian's bulky sweaters, a pageboy cap, and the thick glasses that she hadn't believed would be really that bad. She adjusted them so that she could look over the top of the frames, a necessity due to the strong prescription of the frames. She looked at Priest in time to see her stifle a grin.

"Hey, you're not going to win any beauty pageants either, Caitlin."

Priest wore a black wig they'd gotten from the evidence room and a pair of granny glasses. Her floral print dress was a bit too tight around the chest and shoulders, but that was hidden under a knit shawl. "Quiet," she said.

"You ladies comfortable back there?" Joanna called.

"Ready to go," Riley said.

Joanna fired up the bus and pulled out of the lot. Riley had the route printed out and folded in her pocket. There was a stop on every other block, snaking through the main section of town to the edge of No Man's Land. There it took a ninety degree turn and worked its way through a small segment of the wrong side of the tracks before trekking north and back into the "good" part of town. It made the rounds twice before going back to the depot in the morning.

"What do you think?" Riley said. "I'm assuming he gets picked up in No Man's Land and rides out."

Priest considered it. "It would make the most sense. Both St. Isidore's and the second murder are beyond that point."

Riley said, "Then it looks like we've got a long night ahead of us."

The bus slowly filled with other people, none of them paying much attention to the strange women at the back. Riley and Priest watched them all board, looking for any clues. People who boarded in pairs were less suspicious, and the surprising amount of the elderly who boarded were also discounted. Riley subtly pointed out a few likely candidates to Priest, but she eliminated them all with a simple shake of her head.

They had been in No Man's Land for only five minutes when Riley sensed Priest tensing. She looked casually toward the front of the bus as a man climbed up the stairs. He was average height, wide around the middle, and he had a hood pulled over a baseball cap that covered his down-turned face. He took one of the front seats and slid over near the window. Riley looked at Priest who nodded before Riley could ask the question.

Riley stood up and moved toward the front of the bus. She braced herself on each seat as she passed it, tucking her top lip under her bottom and wrinkling her nose. When she reached the man's seat, she glanced quickly toward him. His face was turned toward the window and she only got a blurry view of the reflection. She continued forward and leaned down by Joanna's shoulder.

"Excuse me, bus driver," she said, affecting a deep Southern accent. "Are we going all the way to the waterfront?"

"Not quite that far. You need to go back to your seat, ma'am."

Riley muttered and shuffled around to return to her seat. As she passed the man in black, she turned to look at him. He wasn't facing the window anymore, and Riley only got a flash of dark, angry eyes as he lunged at her. One of his hands slapped her face, covering her eyes and preventing her from seeing what he looked like. Riley shoved the man, and they both twisted and fell into an empty seat. The man was on top, and he pressed his weight on his hand, pinning Riley to the vinyl of the seat.

"Police, freeze!" Priest shouted.

"Stop the bus!" the man growled.

The driver had started pulling to the corner when the scuffle began, but the man's voice caused her to slam on the brakes. The bus lurched to a sudden stop, and Riley heard the thud as someone was thrown to the ground. She grabbed the man's belt and found a sheathed knife. She struggled to pull it free, but the man slammed his knee into her side. He lifted his weight and there was a deafening explosion that filled the tin can of the bus. The ringing in Riley's ears harmonized with the screams of other passengers, disorienting her as the man pushed off of her and ran to the door.

Riley sat up and rolled off the seat, one hand on her ear. She looked toward the back of the bus and saw Priest was the person who had fallen, and she was currently holding a woman who had been shocked by the gunshot. Her face was pale, holding her hands up on either side of her face. "Caitlin," Riley said.

"I'm fine, she'll be fine. Go."

Riley turned and stumbled toward the front of the bus. The driver was standing by her seat and pointed out the open doors. "I didn't know if I should try to stop him or..."

"You did the right thing," Riley said. "Stay here, keep these people calm."

She jumped the steps and landed hard on the pavement. She stumbled a bit, and Gillian's glasses fell off. She spotted the man in black ducking into an alley and she took off after him. The street was deserted, but she still fumbled to get her badge from the pocket of her coat just in case she needed it.

Riley pressed her shoulder against the wall next to the alley's mouth, dropped to a crouch, and checked to make sure the way was clear before she started running again. She could hear the rough breathing of her prey up ahead, his heavy footsteps echoing off the brick walls on either side of them.

Riley came out of the alley ten seconds behind the man in black, her eyes locked on his back as he ran blindly into the street. Riley was too busy worrying he would be hit by a random car to notice the other man until it was too late. He extended his arm and Riley ran into it, the air forced out of her as she fell to the ground. The man came down on top of her, holding her down. He straddled her, grabbing her collar with both hands. Riley brought her hands to his face, but he swept her arms out of the way and moved to place his knees on her upper arms. Riley fought against him, but he was too strong.

In the dim light, she could see his featureless face peering down at her. Even without a mouth, he seemed to be smirking. She knew he was the Angel Maker's demon associate.

"Well done," the demon said. His voice was a sibilant hiss. "We thought we would have to kill four or five before you figured out the pattern. Very impressive, Detective Parra. It would appear your legends do you justice after all. Allow me to save you and your friends some trouble. My associate will no longer kill every day."

Riley looked past her captor and saw the man she had been chasing disappear down a dark alley.

"After all, where is the fun in that? If you know when he'll hit, you'll stop him in no time. We merely wanted to give you a chance to know us. To understand what is at stake. Don't worry, Detective. We'll be back. You can take that to the bank."

She could tell the demon was smiling behind his mask as sirens began to fill the air.

"Looks like your partner has called in the cavalry. We'll be seeing each other again, Detective Parra. This is just the foreplay."

He pushed off of her and turned, running across the street before Riley could get back on her feet. A police car came around the corner with its lights flashing. Riley stepped into the street with her badge presented, and waved them in the direction the man in black and his 'associate' had gone. Riley watched the car speed past, knowing there was no way in hell they would actually find the man they were looking for.

"Riley!"

She turned and saw Priest running toward her. Riley rubbed her arm where the demon had sat on it and met Priest halfway.

"How are the passengers?"

"Fine. Stabilized. There's an ambulance on the way for one woman. The Angel Maker?"

"Got away. They both did."

Priest frowned. "Both?"

Riley sighed and shook her head. "I don't want to talk about it right now. Come on. Let's get out of here."

Two hours later, Riley quietly entered Gillian's apartment. She took off her shoes and socks before she went into the bedroom.

The lamp on Riley's side of the bed was on, casting a gentle glow on Gillian's back. The small gesture was almost too much, and Riley resisted the urge to cry at the sight. She took off her jeans and Gillian's sweaters, lay down on top of the blankets, and exhaled sharply as she sank into the soft mattress and blankets.

"Riley?" Gillian whispered. She rolled onto her back and touched Riley's stomach. "Hey. Did you catch him?"

"No," Riley said.

Gillian scooted closer and pressed herself against Riley's side. "I'm sorry," she whispered. "Do you want to talk about it?"

"No," Riley said. "Just hold me."

Gillian slipped her arm between the mattress and Riley's back, lacing her fingers together on Riley's other side. She kissed Riley's neck and rested her head on her shoulder. Within seconds, she was back to sleep.

Riley ran her hand down Gillian's back, stroked her hair, and stared at a spot of light on the ceiling as it slowly got brighter with the coming day.

The Sound of Drums (Part One)

Johnny Cash was singing from the jukebox in the corner, one of the few points of light in the barroom. The front windows were curtained at the bottom and the top half was darkened by rain. The bartender stood with her back to the bar, a paperback held in one hand while she stirred the ice in her drink with the other. Her brown hair fell down over one eye, covering the right half of her face. It was still early in the evening, and the bar had been quiet for most of the afternoon.

In the middle of *Solitary Man*, the door opened and brought a wave of conversation, laughter, and rain inside. The bartender closed the book and turned to take her station. She rested her hands on the countertop and forced a smile. She knew everyone in the group, and none of them inspired particularly friendly feelings in her. Rich Fitzpatrick and his girl Denise Carney, the two Dannys, and James O'Donnell, all with their various hangers-on. They took up four tables and a booth at the back of the room.

Alexander Kimaris was the last one inside. He paused to shake his umbrella on the mat outside before he closed the door and scanned the room. He wore a crimson shirt, open at the collar, under a charcoal black suit. His smile and eyes were reptilian, focusing on the bartender. His hair was a mess of black curls, neatly cut and forming a halo around his head. He slipped his long, slender hands into the pockets of his trousers and smiled.

"Hello, Brandi," he said, his voice dripping with seduction. "I would like a round for everyone, please, and a bottle of your finest wine."

"Whatever you say, Mr. Kimaris." She turned and went behind the bar to fill the glasses. She looked back and saw Kimaris taking his place at the center table. His captains flanked him on either side, with the combined entourage taking up the ends. The phrase *one of you shall betray me* flitted through her mind, but she pushed the thought aside as she carried the drinks over to the table on a tray.

"Thank you," Kimaris said. "Your service is appreciated, as always."

"I have to go into the back room to find the wine," she said.

Kimaris nodded. "Take your time. We have business to discuss."

Brandi glanced toward the door.

Kimaris waved her on. "You needn't worry. We'll keep an eye on the place for you."

"Sure," Brandi said. "All right. Come find me if you need anything."

Kimaris inclined his head slightly and she felt his eyes on her back as she left the room. The bar actually did have a wine rack in the back room, pitiful as it was, but she stepped around it to her small command center. She brushed the hair out of her face as she straddled the stool and eyed the monitor sitting on a milk crate. She picked up her ear bud off the table and adjusted the volume before she put it in. The image on the screen was a static image, focused on the seating area rather than the cash register or the door. Its purpose wasn't to prevent theft.

The security camera was the only way she could observe the bar without raising unnecessary questions. She hid the listening device in a lighting sconce, hoping the cone would help amplify the voices no matter where they were in the room. It wasn't the ideal way to spy, but it would do in a pinch. She made sure that she was recording as Kimaris spoke to his men.

"There will be no fewer than eight; I think that will be sufficient to get our point across. The city is already shaking from fear because of this Angel Maker nonsense. All they need is a little push in the right direction. We've been planning a long time for this, boys. I need to know I can count on you when the time comes."

There were murmurs of assent.

"Your loyalty means everything to me. But I'll need more than words this time. Something of this magnitude requires a bit of ceremony." On the monitor, she watched as Kimaris withdrew a knife from the pocket of his coat. It was wickedly long, sharp enough that it sent glints of light into the camera lens temporarily blinded it. When Kimaris lowered the knife, he handed it to the man next to him. "A ceremony of blood, drawn from the wrist. If anyone feels uncomfortable, they may leave now."

The bartender looked away from the monitor as the first man cut himself. She wasn't queasy; she had seen far worse. But something like this was more than she could handle on her own. She took out the ear bud and paced to the wall, turning on her heel as she debated what to do next. She knew it would be a big job when she started but the way Kimaris was talking... she needed help.

She looked back at the monitor and saw the men were still passing the knife around the table. Kimaris seemed to be gathering the blood in a cup, and she didn't want to see what happened next. She grabbed the coat off the hook, pulled it on, and flipped the hood over her head as she slipped out through the back door. The fire escape over her head caught the rain and propelled it down to the alley in an impressive waterfall, surrounding the door in a curtain of water. She hunched her back against the downpour and ran to the mouth of the alley.

There was a corner store nearby, lit like an oasis in the darkness, and she ran through the puddles and ducked inside. Canned music played through the ceiling speakers, a subliminal lullaby to shoppers. She smiled politely to the clerk as she hurried past. There were four payphones at the back of the store and she dug in her pockets for two quarters.

She dialed quickly and leaned against the partition as she listened to the buzz in her ear.

"Police."

"Yes, I need to speak with Detective Riley Parra. It's urgent."

"Detective Parra isn't available at the moment. Would you like to leave a message?"

"Yeah. Tell her..." She brushed the rain from her face with a sweep of her hand, brushing the twisted flesh caused by a roadside bomb. She didn't have enough time to explain everything, and she didn't want to even try doing so on a telephone message. "Tell her Kenzie Crowe needs her help."

In the two weeks since Russell Stone's murder, there were still no new developments in the Angel Maker case. Riley went back and interviewed all the witnesses again, going over the meager evidence they had acquired. Riley refused to admit defeat, and didn't pay attention to the media saying that the police had to "wait around for another body to drop so they could get more evidence."

Briggs gave Riley plenty of leeway on the case, but she eventually stopped by Riley's desk with a new file. People were still dying, and the department was overwhelmed as it was. The Angel Maker was reluctantly put onto the back burner. Briggs promised that the Angel Maker case would take priority as soon as any new information came to light.

Riley had to admit it was calming to follow a case from beginning to end. No dead ends, no confusion, just a simple explanation. Their first case was a shooting that was eventually ruled accidental, followed almost immediately by a man stabbed outside of his apartment building. They found the bloody knife in the communal trash can in a bag along with junk mail addressed to the victim's neighbor. The killer confessed as soon as he opened the door and saw their badges. Spare time, what little they had, was dedicated to decimating the stack of paperwork rising like monoliths on their desks. Through it all, the white board with everything associated with the Angel Maker stayed between their desks as a constant reminder of their true priority.

The rain that had been drowning the city all day finally tapered off as they returned to the station. They had spent their day at the courthouse giving testimony in past cases that were going to trial. Riley turned to Priest as they went inside. "So do you even have to put your hand on the Bible, if they ask you to testify in open court?"

Priest shrugged. "I would assume so. Why wouldn't they?"

"It seems kind of unnecessary."

"Only to you. You know that I'm really—"

Riley nodded. "Yeah. I'll just have to try to keep a straight face."

The desk sergeant called out to her as they crossed the lobby, and Riley reluctantly changed direction toward him. He was holding a memo, which meant that she couldn't close up shop and head home. She hadn't been sleeping very well, and all she wanted to do was go home and curl up with Gillian for a few hours. Last minute changes to her schedule made her grumpy. When she reached the desk, he handed her the note. "You got a call marked urgent."

"Is it about the Angel Maker case?"

"Dunno. Someone named Kenzie Crowe wants you to call her."

Riley immediately perked up and took the memo from him. "Kenzie. This is a local number." She turned to Priest and said, "Did you have any plans for tonight?"

"No," Priest said. "Do I have to go?"

"She called on an official line. I assume she wasn't just calling to chat. Why?"

Priest followed Riley to the stairs. "I don't particularly like Mackenzie Crowe. The last time she was here, she took you to the Underground at a very dangerous time. You could have been torn to pieces down there."

"She was my partner, Priest," Riley said. "She put her life on the line for me, more than once. We trust each other. If she needs help, I want to be the one she calls. But no, if you don't want to go, then you don't have to."

Priest nodded. "Just know that I will be there to back you up if what she wants is dangerous."

Riley patted Priest on the shoulder as they walked into the bullpen. "See? That's exactly what I'm talking about. You have my back, and I have hers, even if we're not partners anymore. When you do it right, it becomes a lifelong obligation." She sat down at her desk, dialed the number on the slip, and leaned back. "I have to call Gillian and let her know I'll probably be late." She checked her watch as she listened to the phone ringing. She was about to double check the number when the phone was answered.

"Stanton Investigations. Chelsea Stanton speaking."

Riley was unable to speak for a moment, and finally hung up the phone. "Oh, Jesus."

"What's wrong?" Priest said.

A detective passed by the desk, and Riley motioned for Priest to follow her. They crossed the room to the stairs. Only once they were out of the bullpen, Riley spoke in a low voice. "I'll call Kenzie and Jill from the road. Let me give you a ride home."

"Okay," Priest said. "What was all that about on the phone?"

"In the car," Riley said.

They remained silent the rest of the way to the car, but Priest could tell Riley was still reeling from the phone call. Riley waited until they were on the road before she spoke again. "Apparently the number Kenzie gave belongs to a private investigator named Chelsea Stanton. She was a detective here when Kenzie and I were still in uniform. We all idolized her. She was the first female detective in the station."

"The first?" Priest said.

"Glass ceiling," Riley said. "It wasn't that long ago women weren't allowed to be cops at all, forget about actually being detectives. She was like the superhero of the department for all of us in uniform. And then there was a case." Riley sighed and shook her head. "The death of a drug mule led Stanton to a crack house. Biggest bust of the year, a room full of cocaine ready to be distributed. Unfortunately some of the drugs, a pretty large amount, went missing between the crime scene and the evidence room. Stanton said it was a miscount, claimed some men in the department were trying to make her look bad. Her lieutenant tried to give her the benefit of the doubt, but things got... very tense. He opened an investigation of the men in the squad. It looked like Stanton stole the drugs but the men were being punished.

"Finally, someone had the bright idea to do drug testing. I mean, if someone stole the drugs why wouldn't they try it out? That's when Stanton gave it up."

Priest said, "She knew who set her up?"

"No. She did it."

Priest stared at Riley and said, "She what?"

"She skimmed some of the cocaine when she put it in the van. She kept it for herself. She'd gotten hooked by a confidential informant who wouldn't trust her unless she joined him in partaking. Before long she was using it recreationally. Buying off the street, blackmailed by more than one dealer who knew she was a cop. She admitted to doing all sorts of things to fund her habit. She whored herself out, looked the other way on busts..."

"How long was she in jail?"

"Three years. She made some deals, got some good behavior time, did a little dance for the prosecutors. Every cop in town was livid when her release was announced. She had not only lied, she tried to blame other cops for what she did. So when she got out of prison, someone was waiting for her. He shot her in the back of the head. He was too far away to do any serious damage, and a guard managed to grab his arm just as he fired. Stanton survived, but she lost most of her vision."

Priest shook her head as they rolled to a stop at a traffic light. "What happened to her?"

"She dropped out of sight for a while. A few years after the shooting, she showed up again with a private detective agency in No Man's Land. From what I've heard, she mostly does insurance investigations and cheating husband type of stuff. Keep in mind, I haven't heard much. Her name is pretty much banned around the station. She accused other cops to cover her own ass." She looked at the red light and drummed her fingers on the wheel. "What the hell is Kenzie doing with her?"

"Something dangerous," Priest said.

"Yeah," Riley admitted. "But with Kenzie, what else is new?"

Riley thought about Kenzie while she drove Priest home. She considered how often she and Kenzie had gone into a dangerous situation together. How often Riley had been in a dark corner, out of bullets, but she remained calm because she knew that Kenzie was somewhere out there. She owed Kenzie that same security. No matter how much time went by, no matter whether they were both wearing a badge or not, they could still count on each other for backup.

Riley pulled to the curb near Priest's building. The church underneath her apartment was in the middle of a service and Riley could hear the music even through the windows of the car. Riley said, "Got any plans tonight?"

Priest nodded toward the building. "The church is having a late mass. I plan to enjoy it."

Riley smiled. "Have fun."

"Riley, be careful. And if you can't... call me."

Riley held her hand out, and Priest took it. "Kenzie was my old partner. I still owe her after all these years. But you're my new partner. I owe you the same thing."

Priest said, "What if my idea of saving you is keeping you out of dangerous situations in the first place?"

"I'll take it under advisement."

Priest grinned. "I'll see you tomorrow. Hopefully not before, and hopefully in one piece."

"I make no promises," Riley said.

Priest got out of the car. Riley waited until she was inside the building before she pulled away from the curb. She was only sure of one thing; if Kenzie Crowe and Chelsea Stanton were involved, she was going to need Priest's help before it was all over. She took out her cell phone and dialed a familiar number, turning on the speaker and setting the phone on her thigh.

"Hey. I was just about to call you."

"You finally decided you can do so much better and you're going to break up with me?"

Gillian laughed. "Yeah. I got three people lined up waiting for my attentions. I'll be late to dinner tonight, I'm afraid."

"As long as your relationships with those three people are purely physical."

"Slicing and dicing," Gillian said. "Looking for the truth."

Riley smiled. "Turns out, I'll be late to dinner, too. I have... I have to check something out."

"That pause was interesting."

"I'll explain it when we get home," Riley said. "It's complicated. And controversial."

Gillian said, "I eagerly await your explanation. Be safe, love."

"You too," Riley said. She hung up and slipped the phone back into her pocket.

There was no physical border to No Man's Land, but the difference between the two sides of town was obvious. Driving through the neglected neighborhoods, Riley resisted the urge to touch the butt of her gun just to make sure it was still there. The streets were never really safe, and they had always gotten worse at night, but things had somehow managed to get worse after she slammed her car into Marchosias' building and jumpstarted the war between Heaven and Hell. The people on the street in No Man's Land after dark were not the kind of folks it would be good to meet unarmed.

Chelsea Stanton's office was the third storefront along the street, after a second-hand furniture store and a sports bar. Riley parked in front of the building and looked at the reflection of the sign in her side mirror. STAN-TON INVESTIGATIONS. She thought of all the horror stories over the years, all the whispered gossip. And how quickly she had gone from idolizing Chelsea Stanton to wanting to be nothing like her. "What are you doing here, Kenzie? Of all the places you could have ended up..."

Riley and Kenzie walked into the station, weary from their latest shift. Kenzie slipped her hand into the small of Riley's back, a silent invitation to come home with her once they changed into their street clothes. Riley accepted with a nod and a smile and let Kenzie lead the way up the stairs. Halfway to the first floor, Kenzie stopped and put her hand out, guiding Riley to the side of the stairs.

Detective Chelsea Stanton was coming down the stairs, straight down the middle as if they were her personal passage to the ground floor. She looked at Kenzie and Riley as she passed them. "Catch any bad guys tonight, ladies?" she asked.

Kenzie said, "We left a couple for you."

Stanton laughed without turning back to look at them. "Much obliged."

Kenzie stared after Stanton until Riley nudged her shoulder. "Hey. Should I just go back to my apartment alone and you can stay here and think about her ass?"

Kenzie grinned and said, "I have an appointment with a different ass tonight." She slapped Riley's rear end and continued to the locker room.

Riley sighed and shook her head to clear away the past before she got out of the car. The sky was still heavy with clouds, but a little sun was breaking through in the last moments before it set. Riley stepped over a puddle on the sidewalk and stared at the logo for Stanton Investigations. A sign on the office door revealed that it was still business hours, so Riley had no choice but to go inside.

The reception area was miniscule, consisting of just a currently vacant secretary's desk and three chairs lined up under the window. A wall with a built-in aquarium separated the front room from the back. Riley eyed the fish as she walked past the partition and looked into the main office. Two desks faced each other from opposite sides of the room. The back wall was mostly glass, looking out onto a greenhouse full of white flowers. Riley was about to announce her presence when the greenhouse door opened and Chelsea Stanton stepped into the office.

She still had the presence Riley remembered, the ability to own a room just by entering it. Age had only improved her looks, her high cheekbones and arched eyebrows. Her hair was still jet black, but now it was long enough to rest on her shoulders, and her eyes were hidden behind a pair of dark goggles. She wore a sleeveless white dress, her feet bare as she crossed the room to her desk.

Riley cleared her throat. Chelsea turned toward her, angling her head slightly before she smiled.

"Riley Parra. It's been a long time. I've been expecting you."

"That's a nice trick. Did Kenzie tell you she called me?"

Chelsea took a seat. "I'm not completely blind, you know. I can see things on this side." She waved to her right. "It's just the left side that's dark. Besides, we received a hang-up call from the police department a few minutes ago. I assume it was from someone who didn't expect to hear my name, so it was someone trying to reach Kenzie. You were the best choice for that."

"Is she here?" Riley said.

Chelsea's smile faded and she leaned forward to write something. "She's undercover at the moment." She held the paper out to Riley. "If she called you, I assume she wants you to come find her."

Riley moved into the room to take the address. Chelsea folded her hands in her lap and leaned back. "I've kept my ear to the ground, Riley. You've been making quite a name for yourself in the department."

"Yeah," Riley said. "Some of us know how to do that the right way."

Chelsea didn't react to the snap. "I know back in the day, you and Kenzie always looked up to me. I know my opinion doesn't mean anything to you, but you've definitely taken up my mantle in the best possible way."

"Thanks," Riley said. "I'll be in touch with Kenzie. Best of luck with your future endeavors."

She turned and left the office, eager for the fresh air to wash away the stain of being in Chelsea Stanton's presence. She knew that Stanton meant it as a compliment, but the last thing Riley wanted was comparison between the two of them. She walked the line between following the rules and playing by her own too often to think about the worst case scenario of what might happen to her if it came crashing down.

Riley found a parking space down the block from the address Stanton gave her. She dug a hoodie out of the backseat, pulled it on while she was still in the car, and flipped the hood up to conceal her face. She locked her badge in the glove compartment, but she kept her gun tucked in the front of her belt.

She scanned the dark street for signs that her car wouldn't be safe while she was inside, but seeing wasn't believing in No Man's Land. She had no doubt there would be a handful of kids snooping around it as soon as her back was turned. She unzipped her hoodie and made sure that her gun was visible from several vantage points before she untucked her shirt and covered the weapon. She hoped it would be enough of a deterrent to keep the vehicle in one piece.

Riley went into the bar and scanned the patrons. There were a few guys at the back, all three of them with bandaged wrists. They ignored her as she walked to the bar and took a stool.

Kenzie moved down the bar. She wore a sleeveless black T-shirt with the words Undisputed Truth written across the chest in faded letters. She smiled at Riley and said, "What will you have?"

Riley nodded at the shirt. "Any other night, I might ask for some truth." Kenzie's smile widened. "But tonight, I think just a beer. And maybe some of those pretzels."

"Coming up." Kenzie placed a bottle on the bar and opened it before she went to retrieve the bowl of pretzels. She knelt under the bar and, a moment later, came back with a full dish. "Here you go. Let me know if you need anything else."

Riley took a swig from the bottle and took a pretzel from the bowl. She saw the piece of paper at the bottom of the pile, but she ignored it until she could get a look without raising suspicions. She idly ate a few more pretzels and then looked down. *Pay and leave when you read this. Alley behind the building. You shouldn't have come here!* Riley took a long drink of her beer, ate a few more pretzels, and rapped the bar with two knuckles. "'Ey. How much I owe?"

"Two fifty."

Riley peeled three bills from her wallet and dropped them on the counter. "Keep the change."

"Gee, thanks."

Riley slipped off the stool and stumbled out into the night. She looked toward her car and saw a kid leaning against the wall next to it. He hooked his thumb at it and said, "Watch your car for ya. Twenty bucks."

Riley took her gun out and said, "Why don't you do it for free?"

The kid held his hands out in supplication and crossed his arms over his chest.

Riley walked to the corner and looked down into the alley. When the service door opened, Riley whistled, and Kenzie jogged down the alley. She wrapped her arms around Riley and hugged her tightly. "Riley Parra."

"Thought you were skipping town last time we spoke."

Kenzie broke the hug and said, "Are you kidding? This town is where all the excitement is. I can't walk away from that."

"Just how much excitement?" Riley asked, motioning for Kenzie to follow her out of the alley to her car.

"Enough that I wanted to talk it over with someone official. But at the department, where it's safe and well-lit. You shouldn't have come here."

"I can handle No Man's Land after dark. I've been doing it since I was ten."

"I don't mean that. But now that you mention it, No Man's Land is a lot different than when we were kids, Rye. The bad dudes who ran things back then are scared to come here in the daytime. I mean you shouldn't have come to the bar. Some bad people were still there, and there's a chance they could have recognized you."

Riley waved off the reluctant guard, and he scurried down an alley. When they got to the car, Kenzie said, "Your beautiful partner isn't with you?"

"She had to go to church," Riley said. "Besides, she's pretty new to being a cop. I didn't want to ruin her reputation. She could have been seen going into Chelsea fucking Stanton's building, and she would be done."

Kenzie laughed. "Wow. That didn't take as long as I thought it would."

"She put other cops on the chopping block to save her own ass," Riley said.

"She made a mistake. She admits she made a mistake. She's human, Riley. She paid her debt, and then she almost lost her eyesight as an added 'fuck you'."

Riley shook her head and dropped the subject. "Why did you call me?"

Kenzie sighed. "Something big is happening. Not just in No Man's Land, in this entire city. And I think you're involved."

"Me?"

"Last time we met up, there was definitely something you and Priest weren't telling me. I let you get away with it because at the time because I didn't think I was staying. But I'm here now. I'm invested in this town again. If something is happening here, I want to be part of the solution. I can't help if I don't know what the problem is."

Riley sighed. "Kenzie, if I told you..."

"If you told me, then I'd know, and you would have an extra hand. Two, if you let Chelsea help you out."

"Gee, that'll be great for my career. You can forgive her if you want, Kenzie. But the fact is Priest and I still have to carry badges in this town. Badges and Chelsea Stanton do not go together anymore."

Kenzie opened the car door. "Have a nice life, Riley."

Riley rolled her eyes. "Get back in the car, Mackenzie."

Kenzie turned and bent down to look into the car. "If you don't want to include Chelsea, then you don't want to include me. That's fine. Anything you can handle on your own, I can handle alone, too."

Riley got out of the car and followed Kenzie down the sidewalk. "That's not true this time, Kenzie. This is bigger than the two of us. It's bigger than you think. I don't have a choice. If you try to take it on by yourself, you'll die. Simple as that."

"You're the one tying my hands."

Riley groaned and looked down the street. Kenzie had to walk these streets every night. She was spending her evenings in No Man's Land. She had a right to know. She sighed and said, "It's a long story. We're going to have to go somewhere to talk. When do you get off?"

"Midnight," Kenzie said.

It would most likely put her in the doghouse with Gillian, but Riley nodded. "Where can we meet?"

"The waterfront," Kenzie said. "Where we used to stop. Say half past twelve to give me time to close up here and get across town."

Riley couldn't help but smile. "The waterfront, huh? Getting nostalgic in your old age?"

Kenzie shrugged. "Call me a romantic. I'll see you tonight."

Riley watched to make sure Kenzie got back into the bar without trouble before she went back to her car. She got behind the wheel, sighed, and dialed Gillian's number.

When Gillian answered, Riley heard the echo that told her she was on speakerphone. "Hey, sweetheart. I don't know how long you think an exam takes..."

"I didn't expect you to be home," Riley said. "I need to let you know I'll... be a little later than I thought. It'll probably be two before I get home."

Gillian sighed. "Do you remember what you promised me? What you said not twelve hours ago? 'Jill, I'll be in bed at ten tonight. I'll lie there, and I won't move until it's six in the morning and you have to wake me up when you go to work.' You haven't slept through a single night in, what, a month?"

Riley scratched her eyebrow with her thumbnail. She looked in the side mirror and saw three dark figures approaching her car from the alley.

She spoke into the phone as she reached for the glove compartment. "I swear if there was any way..."

"I know," Gillian said. "I'm just worried that the only sleep you get is on that damn couch in the on-call room. And then I feel guilty for distracting you when we do get to bed together."

Riley smiled with her eyes on the mirror. She saw the outline of a sideways baseball cap, and a baggy jacket on the leader of the kids.

"Never feel guilty about that. I have a few hours before my meeting. I want to spend them with you, if I can."

Gillian chuckled. "Sweet talker. Do you mind having dinner in the morgue?"

One of the kids moved toward the passenger side of the car, trying to flank her.

"No. I'll pick something up and be there in half an hour." She rolled down the window. "How do you feel about chicken?"

"Sounds great. With mashed potatoes."

"You got it. See you in about half an hour." She snapped the phone shut and held her badge out where the kids could see it. "Walk away right now and I'll forget all your faces."

The three wannabe gangbangers froze in their tracks. They were inches from the car, one of them fingering some weapon in the pocket of his baggy jeans.

"Limited time offer, Peace-Sign Earring," Riley said. She raised her gun and aimed it at the passenger window without looking. "Yo, Flat Nose. Want to risk it for a piece of crap Nova? Then back it up."

The kid in the lead started to back up. The other two, slaves to the hierarchy, went after him without comment.

Riley rolled up her window and shook her head as she pulled away from the curb. No Man's Land was dangerous enough as it was. With demons now officially on the warpath, things weren't going to get any safer. If Kenzie insisted on spending her evenings in No Man's Land for some crusade, the least Riley could do was make sure she was fully equipped with all the information she needed.

Riley didn't particularly like visiting the station after regular business hours if she could avoid it. The lights were all dimmed and the halls were haunted by a skeleton crew of workers and janitorial staff. Riley ignored them and went straight to the morgue with the bucket of chicken. Oddly, she had no problem with the morgue after hours. The lights there were bluer than they were in the rest of the building. It was soothing, and she liked the way her footsteps sounded echoing off the tile and metal. And, of course, the company couldn't be beat.

Gillian was at an exam table. Riley knocked, and Gillian looked up and waved her inside. There was a table with a mask and gloves, and Riley put them on before she ventured near the tables. "Hey. I'll take the food to your office."

"Okay. I won't be long."

Riley went through the room quickly. She didn't have a problem with the morgue, but having food there always made her think twice. She shut Gillian's office door and went to the cabinet to get the paper plates Gillian had started to keep there. She had just finished serving up both plates when Gillian came in. Her gloves, mask and cap were gone. "Hey. Seems like we're having all our dates here lately."

"I'll take you to a real restaurant one of these days," Riley promised. Gillian kissed her hello and took her plate. "You don't have a problem eating chicken after..." She gestured toward the exam room.

"No," Gillian said. "I killed my gag reflex when I was in med school."

Riley said, "All those boys you dated?"

Gillian slapped Riley's leg. "I never dated boys. I just slept with a couple before I figured things out." She sat down and draped a napkin over her thigh. "So what's this secret meeting you have tonight?"

Riley explained the call from Kenzie and their arrangement to meet after she got off work. She neglected to mention Chelsea Stanton's involvement in the case.

"Hm," Gillian said. "So you won't be going home with me because you have to meet your ex-girlfriend in the middle of the night at a place where you used to go parking."

"We didn't park there," Riley said. "I mean, we did, but..."

The day was starting to brighten. Riley watched the light as it seemed to float in on the water in front of them. She was fully dressed in her uniform again, but Kenzie's uniform blouse was still on the seat between them. She was wearing her white undershirt, and Riley looked at it and studied the swell of her breasts under the fabric. "It gets to me sometimes. That I'm from here."

"You're not from here," Kenzie said softly. She reached out and teased the hair at the nape of Riley's neck.

"No Man's Land, born and raised."

"Yeah, but you're not fro here. You just spent the first few years of your life living here. You're from somewhere else."

"Any idea where?"

"I'll get back to you on that one."

Riley reached over and put her hand on the back of Kenzie's neck. She massaged gently, and Kenzie rolled her head with the motion of the massage. Riley propped her foot up against the dashboard and watched the sun rise.

"Those mornings helped keep me sane. It was easy to lose hope working in No Man's Land every night. She made it tolerable. My feelings for Kenzie are entirely in the past. But if you want to come with me to chaperone, you're more than welcome."

"No thanks. I'll trust you. But I do want to meet Kenzie one of these days."

Riley said, "My first real partner and my last. Yeah, there's a combo I want to endorse."

Gillian paused with a chicken wing halfway to her lips. "What?"

Riley looked up from her plate. "What?"

Gillian leaned back. "Your last partner?"

"Yeah."

"I think you just meant I was the latest."

Riley leaned forward and kissed Gillian's lips. She let the kiss linger, tasting the grease from the chicken Gillian had already eaten. Gillian resisted touching Riley with greasy fingers, but she announced her pleasure with a quiet moan. When Riley pulled back, she said, "Nope. You're the last. I thought you knew."

Gillian smiled. "Well. I suspected. Hoped..."

Riley settled back in her seat and crossed her legs. "I don't know how long it'll take me with Kenzie. If it's very late, I'll just crash on the couch."

"No. Wake me. I want to check your collar for lipstick."

Riley smiled. "Do people really leave lipstick on collars?"

"Yeah. All the time. I'll show you one of these days."

"I'll look forward to that, Dr. Hunt."

Gillian winked and wiped her lips with a napkin. Her chicken was done, and all that remained were the mashed potatoes. "You're meeting her at midnight, right?"

"Twelve-thirty."

"Then go home. Lay down. I don't care if you sleep, just get in bed and rest your eyes a little. I know you think you're fooling me, but I know you're really only sleeping an hour or so every night."

Riley shrugged. "It's no big deal. I'll catch up on sleep once we catch the Angel Maker."

"People can't catch up on sleep," Gillian said. "You have three hours. I want you asleep for at least one of them. I'll be home before midnight and I'll wake you so you don't miss your meeting with Kenzie."

Riley put her empty plate on the desk and cupped the back of Gillian's head with her hands. She pulled her in and kissed her slowly. "Come home with me."

"No. I have work to do. And that would defeat the purpose of sending you to bed."

"You're more relaxing than sleep."

"Nevertheless."

Riley released Gillian and said, "Okay. For you, I'll try my best."

Gillian kissed Riley's eyelids and then stood up. She guided Riley's head to her stomach and stroked her hair. "Sweet dreams, Riley. You deserve them."

Riley wrapped her arms around Gillian's waist and pulled her closer. She buried her face in the smooth fabric of Gillian's scrub top and wondered if she needed sweet dreams when she already had Gillian in her waking hours.

Riley was more scared of Gillian than she was of Marchosias and all of his goons. She went home. She kept her clothes on, taking off only her jacket, shoes and socks before she climbed into bed. She stared at the ceiling, letting the room slowly take form around her. She crossed her ankles and laced her fingers together on her stomach. She remembered nights during Gillian's exile when it had been nearly torture to sleep in this bed. Nights when she'd dragged a blanket and pillow into the living room and curled up on the couch. Now that Gillian was back, it should have been easy to fall asleep.

Of course, it didn't help that the Angel Maker and his demon puppet master were still at large. Waiting to claim a third victim.

And the war between the demons and angels was growing more destructive with every day. That was all her fault.

It was a wonder she slept as much as she did.

An hour after she lay down, she heard Gillian's key in the lock. She moved onto her side, folded the pillow, and pulled her knees up to her chest. She kept her eyes closed, hoping her body would take the hint, but she was still awake when the bedroom door quietly opened and the hall light tinted the darkness yellow. She heard soft footsteps and she could feel Gillian standing over her.

"Nice try," Gillian said softly.

Riley rolled onto her back. "How can you always tell?"

"You snore," Gillian said. She touched Riley's ankle and sat on the foot of the bed to take off her shoes. Riley sat up and leaned against the headboard to watch Gillian get undressed.

"I don't snore."

Gillian chuckled, and Riley nudged her with her foot. "Are you going to shower?"

"Bath, actually. I want to soak tonight."

Gillian pulled off her scrub top, the T-shirt underneath riding up to reveal her back.

"May I watch?"

Gillian stood up, hooking her thumbs in the waistband of her pants as she walked to the bathroom. "If you sleep for more than an hour, I'll let you have a ringside seat." She pulled down the back of her pants to reveal her underwear just before she kicked the door shut.

Riley pulled the pillow out from under her head, covering her face with it and wondering if passing out counted as sleep.

"You know, *you* can sleep," Riley said. Gillian was curled up, her head on Riley's stomach. Riley alternated between stroking Gillian's hair and running her fingers down her back.

"That's okay. I'll wait until you go."

Gillian had changed into a slip and the expanses of bare flesh and lace were distracting. She focused on how Gillian's hair slipped through her fingers.

"Did you put this on to remind me of how hot you were before I went out to meet Kenzie?"

"Oh, was that tonight?"

Riley smiled.

"Riley, you could go out and meet all of your ex-girlfriends. I'm more worried about the fact you'll be in No Man's Land after hours."

"I'll be fine."

Gillian lifted her head and looked at Riley. "I took your protection. The tattoo..."

Riley shushed her. The tattoo that Riley's first lover gave her was her only protection from demonic possession and attack. Riley transferred part of that protection to Gillian, and she hadn't regretted it for a moment. "I gave it to you. I'd rather have you."

Gillian kissed Riley's lips. "It's almost midnight."

"I should probably go."

"Okay," Gillian whispered. She sat up and let Riley move out from underneath her. Riley put her hands on Gillian's shoulders and guided her back to the pillow. She pulled the blankets up and kissed Gillian softly. "I'll be home in a couple of hours. You can give me a massage and see if I loosen up enough to get some sleep."

"Mm," Gillian said, already half asleep herself. "That would be nice."

"Night, babe," Riley whispered. She kissed the corners of Gillian's mouth, smoothed the blankets around her, and tiptoed barefoot to the bedroom door. She looked back and, for a moment, envied the peace on Gillian's face. She closed the door and left the apartment to meet Kenzie by the waterfront.

In a city where decay seemed to be the only constant, Riley was surprised to find their spot was virtually untouched in the decade since she had last been there. The parking lot was a wide expanse of broken concrete and the weeds growing along the edge were tall enough to look like walls. Riley parked at the north end of the lot facing the water. She could see lights burning in No Man's Land and, when she rolled down her window, could hear sirens rising and falling in the distance.

She glanced in the rearview mirror when she heard the approaching car, moved her hand to the butt of her gun when the car pulled in behind her. The lights flashed three times, and Riley relaxed. Kenzie got out of her car and walked around to the passenger side of Riley's. She had changed out of her bar outfit to a plain white T-shirt and slacks. She smiled at Riley. "Glad you're here. I wasn't sure you would be."

"If you need help, I'll do what I can," Riley said.

Kenzie nodded. "How is this going to work? I'll show you mine, and so on?"

"Why don't you tell me what you need help with, and I'll fill in the blanks?"

Kenzie considered it and said, "I want the whole story eventually, Riley. I'm living in No Man's Land. If you can help me make sense of some of the shit that happens there, I have to know."

Riley said, "I'll tell you as much as I can without you thinking I'm insane."

"That'll do for now." She leaned back in the seat. "Chelsea was hired by an insurance company to see if a bar was padding its claims. It seems an inordinate amount of their bartenders got injured or killed or just plain disappeared, and the insurers were sick of paying out. So Chelsea sent me in undercover to see what was going on. What do you know about a guy named Alexander Kimaris?"

"I recognize the name. He's more of an organized crime division sort of guy."

Kenzie nodded. "I first saw him about three days after I started working there. Usually his boys are with him, but sometimes they come in alone. It didn't take long for me to figure out how things work. Kimaris is the boss, and the buddies are his employees. They do the heavy lifting and get their hands dirty while Kimaris just reaps the benefits. But he's not the top of the food chain. I did some digging. Kimaris makes frequent trips to report to his boss in No Man's Land. A guy named March."

Riley resisted the urge to groan. She looked out the window at the water.

"See, I thought you might recognize the name. It seems a few months ago, right around the time you were taken prisoner by that gang, someone drove a car through the front door of March's main base of operations. That was the start of escalations in No Man's Land. Murder, robbery, domestic violence, carjackings... it's like someone poked a stick into a hornet's nest. You know anything about that, Riley?" She looked at the dashboard. "Come to think of it, you've had some work done on this car since the last time I saw it, haven't you?"

"March's full name is Marchosias," Riley said. "He's the top of the pyramid. He has some lieutenants underneath him who run the real army. I guess Kimaris is one of them."

Kenzie said, "That's pretty much what I figured. Kimaris and his guys have been trying to get friendly with me. I figure the other bartenders who got hurt or killed were pulled into his ring and ended up casualties. I was going to wait until I had evidence before I took it to the cops. But then something else happened instead. Earlier tonight, I overheard him and his guys talking. They have something big planned. I'm not sure what, but it required a blood oath that none of them would turn on the others. I wrote down what they said." She passed Riley a notepad.

"No fewer than eight," Riley read. She noted the mention of the Angel Maker and said, "Could Kimaris and his people be involved with that?"

"I doubt it. His tone indicated he was speaking about an outside distraction. Like if you said 'we're going to be late because of the rain.' After that, they all cut their wrists to draw blood. Kimaris said that loyalty was required."

Riley remembered the three men in the bar with bandaged wrists. "His guys come into the bar a lot?"

"There's at least one of them there almost every night since I started. Two of them were still there when I closed. I had to usher them out."

"All right. So whatever it is, it's not going down tonight. I'll talk to Briggs and see if we can get some bodies to follow Kimaris and his men tomorrow. We'll see if they lead us anywhere interesting." Riley was thinking about Kimaris' words. She didn't know what "at least eight" meant, but with the Angel Maker terrorizing the streets already, they didn't need anyone else racking up points.

Kenzie said, "All right. You have my story. What the hell is happening to our town, Rye?"

Riley sighed. "Did you ever read the Bible?"

Kenzie said, "Nah, I never went in for that sort of broad comedy."

"All right, what do you know about angels and demons?"

Kenzie raised an eyebrow.

"When I was a teenager, I was involved with a cop. Christine Lee. I told you about her. She gave me a tattoo."

Kenzie said, "I remember it well."

"What I didn't know at the time was that the tattoo was... special. It granted protection from some of the No Man's Land powers that be. Christine Lee was chosen by angels to stand against the forces of darkness in... shit." Riley laughed and looked at Kenzie. "What the hell are you still doing in the car? This is insane."

"I've seen some strange stuff since I got back to town, Riley. Go on."

"Basically, there are demons installed in No Man's Land. I have no idea why they're here. I don't know what's so special about this town. But there are angels here as well. They do what they can to protect the innocent, but there's only so much they can do. So they appoint human champions to fight for their cause. A few years ago, I ran into Marchosias by chance. He killed me—"

"Time out."

Riley rested her hands on the steering wheel. "Marchosias threw me off a building. I was dying, but an angel made a deal to bring me back because I'd been marked by the previous champion. If I died, the city would have been left unprotected."

Kenzie whistled. "Why don't the demons just cut your head off and do what they want?"

"It's more fun for them to play with me, I think," Riley said. "They *can* physically injure me, and they can do a shitload of psychological torture, but they can't possess me because of the tattoo. So I guess they decided it would be more fun to break me before they finish the job."

"Does Priest know all of this?"

"Priest is an angel. My, uh... she's my guardian angel, actually."

"Shit."

Riley chuckled.

"So Caitlin Priest is an angel. March is a demon, and Kimaris is one of his lieutenants. That's a lot to take in."

"Yeah," Riley said. "Do you believe it?"

Kenzie considered the question and said, "If anyone else told me, no. Even with everything I've seen I wouldn't believe a word. But you? Yeah. I believe it." She looked at her watch and said, "I should go. I still haven't briefed Chelsea about tonight."

"All right. I'll call you tomorrow. If Briggs doesn't okay the manpower, you'll at least have me and Priest watching your back."

Kenzie got out of the car and said, "Thanks, Riley. I owe you one for this."

"You owe me about ten thousand, Kenzie. Luckily I don't keep score."

"Sure you don't," Kenzie said. She winked and shut the door, walking back to her own car. Riley waited until Kenzie pulled out of the parking lot before she followed. She thought she would feel relieved, sharing some of the burden of what was going on with Kenzie. Instead she just felt she had brought another person into a deathly dangerous fight. Someone else she would have to protect.

She got home just before two. Being in bed for so long earlier had screwed up her internal clock so that she felt like she'd passed an entire sleepless night and should be preparing for work. Instead, she took off her shoes and blouse before she went into the bathroom. She had resisted sleep aids in the past because she preferred to get her sleep naturally. But since that was looking less and less likely with every passing night, she poured two pills into her palm and swallowed them with a glass of water.

She wore her undershirt to bed, trading her slacks for a pair of pajama pants, and slid under the blankets next to Gillian. Gillian murmured and turned toward Riley. Riley shushed her, holding her until she was still again. She kissed Gillian's forehead, laced her fingers together in the small of Gillian's back, and waited for the 'may cause drowsiness' pills to do their work.

Gillian woke Riley the next morning in a way that was extremely popular with both of them. When she finished, Gillian kissed Riley's thighs and stomach and said, "You were sleeping so peacefully. I couldn't resist."

"Is that my reward for sleeping?"

Gillian grinned. "Don't expect it every morning I wake up before you."

"Not every time," Riley said. "Once a week would be fine." They showered together and drove to the Four-Ten Diner to meet Priest.

They ordered and Riley waited until the waitress left to begin filling them in on Kenzie's situation. When she finished, Priest leaned back and considered the information. "Kimaris is a lower level lieutenant. If Marchosias is planning something big, he wouldn't entrust it to Kimaris."

"So Kimaris is working alone," Riley said.

Priest shrugged. "Apparently. There are two possibilities. Either he's attempting to move up in the ranks by impressing Marchosias and earning his favor, or he's attempting a coup. I'm inclined to believe it's the second. Marchosias is distracted by the war. Now wouldn't be the time to curry favor with him. It is, however, the perfect time to strike. Marchosias is spread thin, and his attention is elsewhere. An attempt to overthrow him would have a chance of succeeding."

Gillian said, "Pardon me for being the dummy to ask this, but... would that be a bad thing? Maybe Kimaris would be a... more reasonable demon to have in charge. Sorry. I just heard how stupid that sounds."

"No," Riley said. "Marchosias is the devil we know, literally. We've come this far with him. Adding someone new would just change all the rules. He may decide he doesn't like the idea of having a champion and come after me directly. But stopping Kimaris feels an awful lot like helping Marchosias."

"Kimaris is planning something big," Priest said. "No matter what his intent, he'll throw the city into chaos to achieve it. You're fighting to prevent that. Any assistance that gives Marchosias is just an unfortunate, unforeseen side effect."

"That works for me," Riley said. "I'll talk to Briggs about the stakeouts. We need to follow Kimaris and his men and see where they go." She anticipated Gillian's comment and said, "I'll sneak in a nap in the afternoon if I'm going to be up all night."

Gillian smiled. She was about to say something when her pager began beeping. "Ah, duty calls." She checked the number and said, "People could at least wait until after breakfast to die."

"If they had any decency," Riley said. "I'll see you later."

"Yeah. Bye." She leaned in and kissed Riley's lips. "I'll see you, Caitlin."

Priest waved and watched Gillian leave. "Are you still not sleeping?"

"I slept last night," Riley said. "Almost four hours."

"Are you sure you're all right? You have the Angel Maker thing, the stress of Chelsea Stanton and Kenzie Crowe coming back into your life, and now the Kimaris situation. I worry you're spreading yourself too thin. Maybe you should let me deal with Kimaris, and you focus on the Angel Maker. And getting some sleep."

Riley said, "There are two problems with that. One, you can't deal with Kimaris because you hate Kenzie. Secondly, I'm fine. I don't need a night off. Even if I did agree to that, I'd just go home and lie awake worrying about what was happening. I'd be even worse off."

"Regardless, tonight is just a stakeout. Sitting and watching, right? So let me do it. I can tolerate Kenzie Crowe for a few hours if it means you can take a night off. Besides, you're a little too conspicuous to sit outside a demon bar all night."

Riley laughed. "And an angel would blend in better? They'll feel you a block away."

"No Man's Land is dripping with residual energy from the war. Anything they feel, they'll just attribute to combatants. I'll be fine."

Riley drummed her knuckles on the table and said, "If anything happens, or if you realize that something big is happening tonight..."

"I'll call you," Priest said. "On my honor, I won't leave you out of the loop. But you'll get rest, Gillian will be happy, and everything will work out fine."

"When you say things like that, I really start to worry."

Priest smiled.

Riley spent the morning with the Angel Maker murder book. She reread over every interview, stared at the white board, and mentally traced the bus route she assumed the killer took. He would get off the bus at a certain point. If there was a rhyme or reason for the places he chose, she couldn't find it. He would wait. He'd murder someone who was convenient, and then he would wait for the bus to come back around to take him home. He would most likely take the lag time between murder and the arrival of the bus to get rid of his bloody clothes. She assumed he wore a coat and gloves, something easily discarded. Uniforms had searched trash cans and sewers in a five block radius of the murders and hadn't found anything. Riley theorized that he removed the bloody clothes, but he took them with him. Maybe in a duffel bag.

After lunch, she ventured into Briggs' office to talk about Kenzie's story. She left out the supernatural elements and any mention of Chelsea Stanton. Kimaris was a well-known figure in the crime world. Riley assumed that even the slightest whisper that he was up to something would be enough for Briggs to assign a few people to the stakeout.

Briggs agreed and said, "I have a couple of detectives I could assign. I'll let you know by the end of the day. I assume you and Priest will be in charge of this?"

"Just Priest tonight," Riley said. "I've been running on little to no sleep because of this Angel Maker business. I'm letting Priest take over so I can take a mental health night."

"Probably a wise decision." Briggs leaned back in her chair. "When I took this job, I was told you'd be a handful. I was told you didn't play by the rules, lone wolf, all that crap. I don't know if I scared you straight when I came in, or if your new partner is just having a calming effect on you. Whichever it is, keep it up."

Riley said, "I'll do my best, boss."

She went back into the main bullpen where Priest was working. She tapped the edge of Priest's desk and said, "Briggs thinks you're a good influence on me."

"I'm a good influence on everybody," Priest said.

"Don't rub it in." Riley found the small black book in her desk drawer and flipped to the list of numbers at the back. Sleep wasn't the only thing Riley had been neglecting lately; she planned to make good on a promise she had made to Gillian.

Riley went downstairs a few minutes before Gillian went off-duty. Gillian was in her office, signing a report as Riley came inside. "There's a good sign," Riley said. "I assume it means you're going home on time."

"Yes, for a change," Gillian said. She filed the report and said, "I'm not even on-call, so I have the whole night free. How about you?"

"The same," Riley said.

Gillian smiled and leaned back in her chair. "What a momentous occasion. We should celebrate it properly."

Riley said, "I should take you to dinner. I promised you a real restaurant, after all. How about Melbourne's Grill?"

"Like we'd get in now."

"We would if someone made reservations."

Gillian smiled and stood up. "Riley Parra, are you being romantic?"

Riley put her hands on Gillian's hips. "I obsess over everything. The Angel Maker, Marchosias, this whole damn business. I obsess over everything except the one thing I should be focused on." She kissed Gillian tenderly and whispered, "I'm so glad you're back. I missed you so much last year. I'm so much more... sane when you're here. I love you. And I should have been taking the time to let you know that."

"You're going to make me cry, Detective Parra."

"C'mon. I'll help you carry your stuff to the car. We have enough time to get home, shower, and get changed before our reservation."

Gillian handed Riley her satchel and said, "The Riley Parra girlfriend experience. I'm not sure I'm ready for this."

"You're in for quite a ride," Riley said. "Come on. If we don't hurry we'll have to shower together like we did this morning."

Gillian followed Riley from the office, dragging her feet the entire way.

Priest was waiting outside for Kenzie to pick her up when Riley and Gillian left the building. She watched them walk to Riley's car and waved when they drove past. Spending an evening with Kenzie Crowe was a small price to pay in exchange for Riley getting a night to herself. It was well-earned.

Kenzie arrived not long after Riley left. Priest got into the passenger seat and Kenzie reached down to turn up the radio. A woman with a bluesy voice was singing *In My Time of Dying*. Priest said, "Funny."

"I thought so. It was either this or gospel music." She pulled away from the curb. "I always knew there was something different about you, Caitlin. I didn't question it too much because I knew you had Riley's back. Hell, anyone that would follow her into the Underground just to make sure she comes out in one piece is aces in my book. But angel? That was way down on my list."

"It's not exactly something we advertise. So if you could keep it to yourself."

Kenzie mimicked locking her lips. "I was gay in the police force, and then in the military. Trust me, I can keep secrets."

Priest nodded and looked out the window.

"Riley told me that you don't care for me too much, so I don't expect much conversation tonight."

"Good," Priest said. She was going to leave it at that, but she couldn't. "It's not that I dislike you. I don't like what your presence means. It's an indicator that Riley will be put into some dangerous situation or another."

"Sounds like she gets into her fair share of dangerous situations on her own."

They drove through the streets in uncomfortable silence. When they entered No Man's Land Priest broke the silence. "I'll stay outside in the car and keep an eye on the comings and goings. Is there a way for you to be in contact with me?"

"I can get you an ear bud," Kenzie said. "I'll let you know when anybody important is on their way out. I'll come out to check on you from time to time, when I can get away."

Priest nodded.

"So where's Riley tonight?"

Priest grinned and said, "She's taking care of something important that she has been neglecting."

Kenzie read between the lines and smiled. "Good for her."

Riley wore a black blazer over her nicest white shirt and a red tie. She had considered a dress, but Gillian saved her by saying, "I want to go out with Riley Parra, not some girly-girl look-alike." So Riley waited, sitting on the edge of the bed, drumming her fingers together between her knees as she waited for Gillian to get ready. She checked her watch and reconsidered wearing her hair up but decided to leave it alone. She looked toward the closed bathroom door and decided men had a point about waiting for women to get ready.

The door opened and Riley took back every bad thing she'd been thinking.

Gillian wore a black knee-length dress, and knee-high black boots. Her arms were bare, and her red hair was down. She did a spin and said, "Worth the wait?"

"Always," Riley said. She slipped her arm around Gillian's waist. "Shall we?"

Gillian gestured for Riley to lead the way, and she guided Gillian out of the bedroom. She had already called for a cab since they both intended to have wine with dinner. Her mind kept trying to bring up Kenzie and Priest, wondering if they were all right and wanting to check in with them. She turned her head and breathed the scent of Gillian's hair and the thoughts went away. For a few hours, on one night, she was going to focus on being in a relationship. That was bigger than anything Heaven and Hell could throw at her.

Kenzie stopped at a convenience store on the way to the bar, and refused to show Priest what she bought until they arrived. She parked at the end of the street, far enough from the bar so it wouldn't raise suspicion but still close enough that Priest could make out the faces of people coming and going in the dark. Kenzie pulled the brown paper bag out of the back seat and said, "Okay, this will be your first solo stakeout, so I thought I'd get you the basics."

Priest said, "I'm on the edge of my seat."

Kenzie tossed a bag of potato chips onto the dashboard. "Junk food and lots of it." She put a small bag of chocolate doughnuts on the seat next to Priest. "There's a shop down the corner where you can get some coffee that actually tastes like coffee if you swallow it quick. Call me if you need a bathroom break and I'll let you know if you have the time." She smiled. "And most of all have fun."

Priest picked up the bag of doughnuts. "I'm starting to regret suggesting Riley take the night off."

"It's just part of being a cop, seraphim. Get used to it. I'll check in on you later."

She got out of the car and Priest opened the bag of doughnuts. She sniffed it, wrinkled her nose, and dropped the bag on the driver's seat. She watched Kenzie walk down the street toward the bar and hoped Riley was enjoying her night.

After dinner, Riley and Gillian decided to walk to a nearby corner for a better chance of getting a cab. Gillian held her high heels in one hand, one arm wrapped around Riley's for support. Riley walked slow, trying to maximize the amount of time Gillian would be leaning so heavily against her. "Pretty nice night," she said.

Gillian chuckled. "Very nice night. It was wonderful." She kissed Riley's cheek. "You know, it was kind of unusual for us. We never got the whole romantic dating period. We just kind of jumped to the old married couple."

"Whoa. Old?"

"Okay, we're more like newlyweds. How's that?" She squeezed Riley's arm. "But we didn't have dates. We just kind of fell into a full relationship. What if we went on this date and decided we didn't really have that much in common?"

"I knew everything I needed to know about you before we kissed," Riley said.

"Really."

Riley nodded. "I knew you were a sweet, kind, funny woman. I knew you were smart. I knew that you could read me like a book. I knew that it made me happy every time I walked onto a crime scene and saw you. I didn't need a handful of dinners and some crappy movies to know that I belonged with you."

Gillian was quiet for a long time before she said, "Did you know that I knew you and Kenzie when you guys were still in uniform?"

"I assumed you did," Riley said. "You were the current medical examiner's assistant around that time."

"Yeah. I saw you for the first time at my first crime scene. You were the first cops on the scene. I showed up with Dr. Grant and I saw you when I crossed the park. You said something to me."

"I did?"

"'Deep breaths, doc.'" She chuckled. "It was just a passing comment. I was so afraid I would be sick, so worried that I wasn't cut out for the job after all. I guess I was green around the gills. You just walked past me and said, 'deep breaths, doc.' It wasn't mean or... condescending. You were kind. I remembered that the next time we met. And the next time."

Riley smiled and looked down the street for an available cab. "I can't believe I don't remember it."

"Maybe we crossed paths a lot of times and just didn't notice. Standing in line at the same check-out. Stuck in the same traffic jam."

"Everything else in my life has been fated," Riley said. "Why not you?"

Gillian turned to look at Riley. "I know you've been worried. And I should have put your mind at ease, because it might be contributing to your insomnia. But I'm not going anywhere, Riley. I know when things got hard last time, I ran. That was unfair to you. But I'm back, and I'm staying. For the long haul. I've been trying to let you know without saying it, but... it needs to be said. I'm here, with you. For good."

Riley squeezed Gillian's hand. "It's good to hear," Riley said. She was about to bend down to kiss Gillian when she saw a cab approaching. She brought her hand up and finished the kiss as the cab pulled to the curb for them. She opened the door and guided Gillian inside. She gave the address to the cabbie and let Gillian rest her head on her shoulder as they started to drive.

"If this was really our first date," Gillian said, "I don't think anything would have changed. I'd be just as crazy about you as I am now."

"Good. I've never been good at the romantic thing. I don't think I've ever really done the romantic thing. Dinners, yeah, but actual holding hands and just walking together after a meal is new to me."

Gillian started to say something, chuckled, and shook her head. She cleared her throat and lifted her head to whisper in Riley's ear.

"When you dropped your napkin at dinner, and bent down to pick it up, I thought you were going under the table."

Riley laughed and whispered to Gillian, "I considered it."

Gillian nipped Riley's earlobe. She moved her hand to Riley's thigh and gently massaged it. "I was scared to death you would disappear and then I'd feel you slipping between my legs. But at the same time, I was kind of turned on."

Riley kissed Gillian's neck.

"Will you, when we get home?"

"Will I...?" She knew Gillian was blushing, and glanced toward the front of the cab. Their driver was the picture of professionalism. There was no indication she could hear anything, but Riley knew that she at least suspected what was happening. "Will I what?"

Gillian chuckled nervously, and it was such a sexy sound that Riley shuddered. "Will you go down on me when we get home?"

"Why not here?" Riley whispered. She brushed her fingers along the bare skin between Gillian's dress and boots, and felt her shiver.

Gillian laughed and bowed her head, biting Riley's neck. Riley groaned as Gillian moved down her throat, teasing with her teeth and tongue until she reached the collar of Riley's shirt. She took the cloth between her lips and pressed down until she was sure her lipstick had been transferred. She moved back up Riley's neck and whispered, "Didn't I tell you I would give you some lipstick on your collar?"

Riley said, "I'd rather have it somewhere else." She pulled back just enough that she could find Gillian's lips, kissing her passionately as Gillian's hand moved teasingly over her thigh.

The driver cleared her throat. "We're here."

Riley reluctantly broke the kiss and pulled the money from her pocket. She tapped the driver on the shoulder, and she took it without turning around. "You ladies have a wonderful evening."

"Yeah," Riley said. "Planning on it." She took Gillian's hand and pulled her from the cab. She slipped her arm around Gillian's waist, but couldn't help looking toward No Man's Land. Kenzie and Priest were out there somewhere, without backup. She knew they could take care of themselves but that didn't make it any easier to stop thinking about them.

"Hey," Gillian whispered. "You with me?"

Riley turned her focus on Gillian. "Yeah. A hundred percent."

Doughnuts, as it turned out, weren't so bad. Dunked in coffee, they were almost acceptable as food. Priest didn't understand why she had started eating. She wasn't particularly hungry, but the food had been convenient and it gave her something to do with her hands. She wondered if that was why so many humans smoked themselves to death. Just to have something to do with their hands.

She had been watching the front of the bar for nearly an hour. Most of Kimaris' men were identifiable by the bandages around their wrists. She made notes of their arrival times. By her count, there were eight men inside by the time Kimaris finally arrived.

Priest felt him even before he turned the corner. He was dressed in a suit and tie, and he looked human to the naked eye. Priest saw him differently. To her, he was a stack of slides laid over each other to form a composite. The shadows seemed to cling to his suit, the air around him thick with unseen electricity. Priest focused on him as he glanced up and down the street. He was cocky, self-assured, and completely oblivious to the fact there might be danger around.

Kimaris went into the bar and Priest waited. Seconds later a shape emerged from the alley and hurried across the street. Priest took the remnants of her snack off the seat as Kenzie got into the car. "Hey. I guess you decided the doughnuts weren't so bad after all."

"Did they ask you to leave?"

"'Ask' is a bit too kind," Kenzie said. She held up an ear bud and said, "I figured you would want to know what they were saying."

Priest put it into her ear. She heard idle conversation and the clink of glasses, with a faint sound of music in the background. "How are things in there?"

"Tense. Whatever Kimaris wants to do, it's going to happen soon."

Kimaris spoke in their ears, and they both turned toward the bar.

"I hope everyone had time to make the appropriate arrangements. Once we begin, there will be no time for resting. Once we begin, we will not stop until the end. Is everyone ready?" There were murmured agreements. "Excellent. This is our time. We will not be silenced. By dawn, this city will know the name of its true leader."

"Shit," Kenzie said. "Riley picked a great night to take off."

The door to the bar opened and the men started to exit. Kimaris was one of the first ones out. He stopped on the sidewalk and turned to embrace one of the men with him. He said something that the microphones inside didn't pick up, clapped the man on the back, and started to walk down the sidewalk toward Kenzie and Priest.

"Oh, great," Kenzie said. "If he sees me out here he'll know something's up."

Priest said, "Drive."

"Too conspicuous. I'm sorry, but this is the only thing we can do." She reached across the seat and cupped Priest's face, turning her so they were facing each other.

Priest managed to say, "What—" before Kenzie kissed her.

Kenzie's tongue slipped into Priest's mouth as she shifted on the seat, angling over the console. Kenzie pulled back long enough to say, "Grab my ass." She smothered Priest's lips again, and eventually guided Priest's hands to her rear end on her own. Priest, unsure what else to do, squeezed. Kenzie arched her back and moaned into Priest's mouth.

Priest kept her eyes open throughout the kiss, wondering at the touch of Kenzie's tongue against her own, extremely aware of Kenzie's body through her clothes. Parts of her body woke and sent curious messages to her brain. It felt like worship, and she finally let her eyes close and met the thrusts of Kenzie's tongue with her own.

They grappled for a few seconds, Kenzie's hands exploring Priest's body before she broke the kiss and said, "Is he gone?"

Priest sagged against her seat, one hand dropping between her legs to rub absently at the ache there. She squirmed and finally opened her eyes. "What?"

Kenzie laughed. "Geez, Caitlin. Nice to know I still got the touch."

Priest jerked her hand away from her crotch. She looked around and saw that the street was indeed empty. "We should follow him."

Kenzie said, "You need a second to compose yourself?"

Priest opened the car door and got out to hide the fact she was blushing bright red. She was on the sidewalk when Kenzie joined her, shrugging into the jacket she'd pulled from the back seat. She was also carrying a gun. Priest eyed it, but didn't say anything as she tucked it into the back of her belt. "Maybe one of us should follow his people," Priest said.

"There are half a dozen of them," Kenzie said. "Just following one won't give us much, just where that particular man is. We follow Kimaris, and he'll eventually lead us to the others."

At the corner, Kenzie held up a hand to stop Priest as she checked to make sure Kimaris wasn't lying in wait. He was halfway down the street, hands in his pockets, walking calmly.

"I'll take the high road," Priest whispered.

"What does that mean?" Kenzie said. She turned in time to see Priest's shoes rise past her face. She recoiled, her brain deciding that she was about to get kicked, but she looked up and saw Priest grab hold of the fire escape railing. She clung to the outside edge of it briefly and looked down before she continued up.

Kenzie scoffed and shook her head. "Showoff."

Kimaris was nearly at the opposite corner when Kenzie started following him. She stayed in the shadows, moving quietly from one doorway to the next. She was confident that if she lost track of him, Priest would keep on his trail. Her biggest worry was that he would take the elevated train and she'd have no way to surreptitiously follow him. There was a station two blocks over, and that would be the end of the trail. Again, Priest would have to save her ass if that happened. She didn't consider the possibility of him having a car. Alexander Kimaris wasn't the kind of person who drove himself anywhere.

She was still trying to make sense of what Riley told her. Angels and demons, Heaven and Hell. She'd stayed up all night turning it over and over again in her mind but it was still hard to accept. She couldn't deny that it answered a lot of her questions, but accepting there were angels and demons was a lot different from processing the fact that she was following a demon with an angel as backup. She hadn't yet told Chelsea about Riley's revelation. She was struggling to think of a way to reveal it without sounding insane.

Kimaris crossed an empty parking lot not far from the el tracks. Kenzie kept walking and used one of the support beams to conceal herself. Kimaris held out one hand as he approached the door, and it flew open in time for him to walk through without breaking stride. Kenzie shook her head. "I guess that settles it. Either he's a demon or a magician."

"There are demonic magicians," Priest said.

Kenzie jerked away from the sudden voice behind her. "I'm going to have to hang a bell around your neck."

Priest nodded toward the building. "I got a look from above. The men who left the bar all seem to be approaching this building from different directions. Whatever is going to happen, it's going to start in there."

Kenzie took out her gun and said, "Well, it's nice of them to bunch together like that. Makes it easier to catch them all. What do you say we sit tight, let them all get inside, and go in to gather them up? Give Riley one less thing to worry about."

"Sounds good to me," Priest said.

Kenzie looked at the ground, littered with empty beer cans and objects that she couldn't and didn't particularly want to identify. "I hope Riley is enjoying herself more than we are."

Gillian let Riley undress her, her eyes closed as Riley's hands skimmed over bare flesh. Riley moved slowly. She touched Gillian's shoulder blades, the smooth and soft flesh above the back of her knee. When Gillian was down to her stockings and slip, Riley took her hand and walked her into the living room. Riley was still fully dressed, save for her jacket. She led Gillian to the couch and turned to face her. They kissed, and Riley guided her down into the seat. "Spread your legs," Riley whispered, her hand on one thigh to ease them apart. Gillian obliged, and Riley knelt.

Riley kissed Gillian through the slip, the curve of her breasts and the flat plane of her stomach. As she moved lower, she pushed her hands up Gillian's thighs. She lifted the hem of Gillian's slip and bowed her head, gently placing a kiss on each thigh above the tops of her stockings. She lifted Gillian's legs and let them rest on her shoulders as she licked her lips and breathed in.

"Is this what you wanted me to do in the restaurant?" Riley whispered. "With all those people watching?"

Gillian licked her lips. "Yes."

Riley kept her eyes on Gillian as she leaned down and placed a tender kiss on Gillian's labia. She stroked it with the flat of her tongue, and Gillian trembled.

"Do you think you could have kept quiet?" Riley said.

Gillian chuckled. "Not a chance."

"All those people would have known what we were doing." Another kiss, and Gillian whimpered. Riley rubbed Gillian with one thumb, stroking her clitoris until it appeared and then lightly brushed it with her lips. Gillian gasped, sighed, moaned, and Riley took it into her mouth. She used one knuckle to continue stroking as Gillian moved underneath her. She added a second finger, twisting them together before she eased them inside.

Gillian jerked and said, "Fuck, I'm..." Riley looked up and Gillian, with a laugh, said, "I'm so fucking glad you didn't try this in public."

Riley smiled and lowered her head again. Gillian laced her hands together behind Riley's head and moved her hips in concert with Riley's tongue, lips and fingers. Riley alternated between sucking Gillian's clit and sweeping her tongue over the sensitive folds underneath. She eased her free hand under Gillian's slip, running it up to cup her breast. Gillian arched her back and said Riley's name, her body trembling as she climaxed. Riley kissed Gillian's thighs and moved slowly up her body.

Gillian twitched a few times as Riley lay on top of her, and they kissed. She stroked Riley through her clothes, loosening a few buttons and touching the few spots of bare flesh that were exposed. "What are you doing?" Riley whispered.

"Touching you."

"Just making sure," Riley said. She kissed Gillian's cheek. "What are you going to do next?"

"Make love to you. Maybe in the bath."

Riley said, "I like baths."

Gillian said, "Good." She stroked Riley's breasts through her blouse, moving her hand down to her hip. She loosened Riley's pants and said, "So, are you going to carry me to the bathroom, or what?" When Riley didn't answer, Gillian looked at her face. Riley's eyes were closed, her lips slack with sleep.

Gillian kissed the corner of Riley's mouth. "I guess I'll have to wait to return the favor." She guided Riley's head to her shoulder and held her as she slept.

Kenzie checked the marks she had made on the post as the man crossed the parking lot. The door swung open as it had for Kimaris and the other men, and he disappeared inside. "Okay, that's all eight that were in the bar. You ready?"

"I am," Priest said. "But you're aware of the possibility that this is a trap."

Kenzie said, "I go into every situation assuming it's a trap. It keeps me on my toes. C'mon." She jogged across the parking lot with Priest coming up behind her. They took up positions on opposite sides of the door, and Kenzie tried the knob. She nodded to Priest and silently counted down from three.

As she mouthed "one," she twisted the knob and kicked the door open. Priest shouted, "Police! Everybody freeze, right now."

The interior of the room was a solid sea of black. A row of narrow windows just below the high ceiling let in meager blue light that did nothing to illuminate the ground level. Priest felt a darkness brush past her and tried to back up, but too late. The door slammed shut behind her and the lights came on.

"Finally," Kimaris said. He sounded exasperated, relieved that his wait was over. Kimaris was in the middle of the space, framed on either side by steel staircases. "Welcome, Detectives."

Kenzie suddenly yelped in pain, dropping to her knees. Her arms bent, and she twisted her arms around until her gun was pointed at her own head. The barrel scratched her forehead.

"What are you doing?" Priest said.

"I... I can't stop," Kenzie said. Her voice was strained, as if it physically pained her to speak. Her face was red and her arms trembled as she pressed the barrel under her chin.

Kimaris chuckled. "Well. That was much easier than I was led to believe. Lower your weapon, Zerachiel, or I'll have her pull the trigger."

Priest reluctantly did as she was told.

Kimaris stood in front of Kenzie. "I don't know how you found that bar, Detective Parra, but you could not have arrived at a more perfect time. You and your angelic friend are going to help me destroy Marchosias. And I'll ensure the loyalty of his followers by eliminating the city's champion for good once and for all."

Kenzie's teeth were clenched, sweat beading on her forehead. "I-I'm..."

"Shut up, Riley," Priest said.

Kimaris motioned to one of the demons standing by the door and he came forward to disarm Priest. "Can I release your partner now?" Kimaris asked. "Am I assured you won't try to do anything stupid? Because I think we've established I can make her do anything I want."

"Let her go."

Kenzie collapsed with a cry of pain, her gun dropping from her hand. One of the demons took Priest's weapon, while Kimaris gathered Kenzie's slumped form and supported her like someone helping a drunk to her car. He chuckled and said, "That's more like it." He slapped Kenzie's cheek and turned to Priest. "Now, we should probably get started. We have a very big night ahead of us."

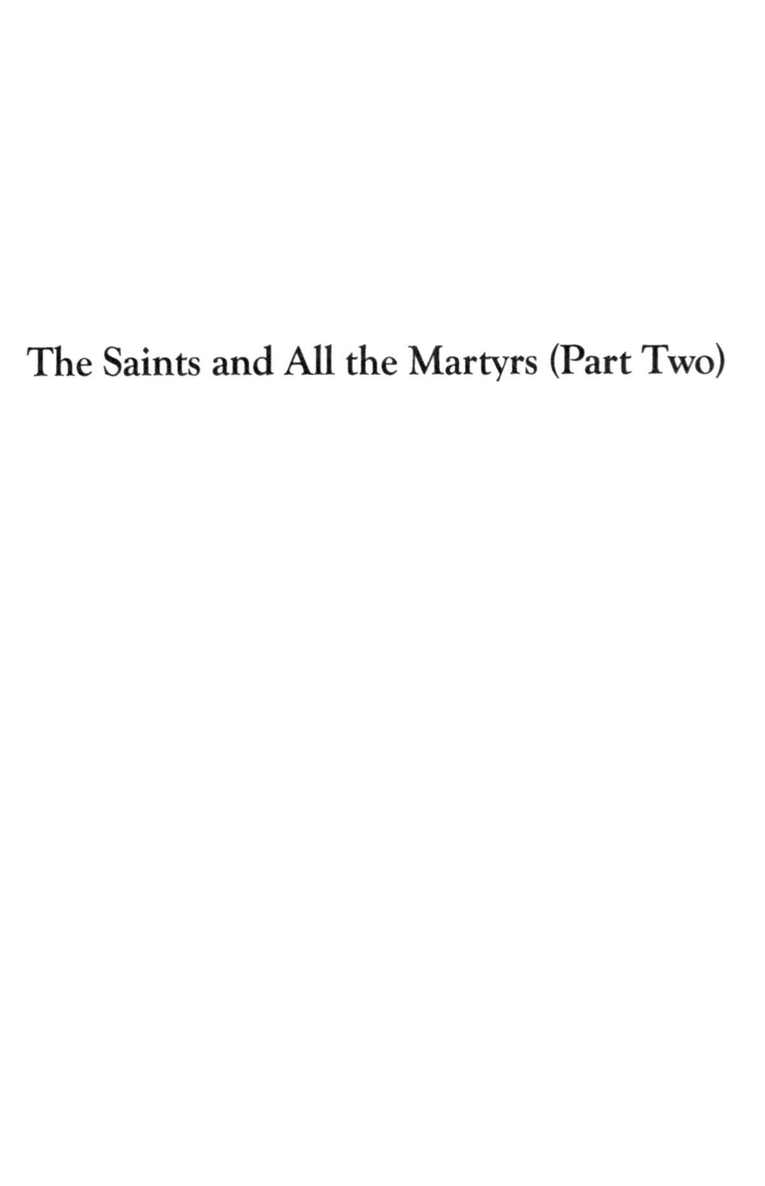

The Saints and All the Martyrs (Part Two)

Riley wasn't sure how long she slept before she was stirred by Gillian easing away from her. She clung to sleep, blissful and non-pharmaceutical sleep, as Gillian guided Riley to the cushions and rose from the couch. She vaguely remembered hearing a knock, but that might have been part of a dream. A blanket was laid over her body, tucked up by her shoulder, and she relaxed as she tried to slide back to unconsciousness. She'd been having a lovely dream recounting her evening with Gillian, and she kept replaying the last half hour of it over and over.

The light in the room changed, and Gillian whispered, "Do you know what time it is?"

A woman Riley thought she should recognize said, "I apologize. If I thought it could wait until morning I would have. Could I speak with Detective Parra?"

"No, you may not," Gillian said. "Detective Parra is sleeping. Whatever it is, I'm sure it'll still be there in the morning."

Riley reluctantly sat up. She knew the voice at the door, and it was useless to pretend she was still sleeping. "Jill."

"Christ," Gillian whispered.

"It's all right," Riley said. She fished around on the floor for her shirt before she realized Gillian was wearing it. She wrapped the blanket around her instead and stood up.

Chelsea Stanton was in the hallway, both hands wrapped around the top of an ornate wooden cane. Her trenchcoat was unbuttoned over a black suit, and she still wore the glasses Riley had seen during the short visit to her office. Riley stood behind Gillian, aware of her nudity under the blanket despite the fact Stanton probably couldn't see very well in the darkness.

"How did you get this address?"

"I still have a friend or two in the department," Stanton said. "I told them it was a matter of life and death, and I apologize for waking you, but I wouldn't disturb you at this hour unless it truly was."

"I find it hard to believe you have anything to say that I want to hear."

Stanton said, "My apologies. I assumed you would want to know that our partners seem to have gone missing."

Riley stopped in the process of grabbing the door to close it. "What?"

"Kenzie told me that your partner, Caitlin Priest, was joining her this evening for a stakeout. I didn't expect many updates during business hours, but Kenzie's shift at the bar ends at midnight. It has been three hours, and I haven't heard a word. She's also not answering her cell phone."

Riley had already returned to the living room to fish her phone out of her trouser pocket. She dialed Priest's number and listened to it ring endlessly in her ear. She hung up and sighed as she imagined Gillian's reaction. "Jill..."

"Just go," Gillian said. She walked past Riley, not looking up as she walked down the hall and into their bedroom. Riley closed her eyes and resisted the urge to curse.

Stanton, still in the doorway, said, "I'm sorry."

"Shut up. I have to get dressed. Wait for me out there." She shut the door and went to the bedroom.

Gillian was out of her shirt, sitting on her side of the bed. Riley said, "It's Priest."

"I know," she said without turning.

Riley went to the closet and took out the first thing she could get her hands on. She dressed quickly and said, "I don't want to fight. Not after the night we had."

"I'm not mad," Gillian said. She turned, and Riley saw her profile in the moonlight. It was heartbreaking to know she had to leave. "You were sleeping so peacefully. For the first time in ages. And now you're running out into the night again, into who knows what."

Riley took her gun from the nightstand, checked the load, and said, "I'm sorry, Jill."

"Just be safe. If you can. If you're even able."

Riley ducked her chin as she left the bedroom. She knew she shouldn't be mad at Stanton. It wasn't her fault that Kenzie and Priest were in trouble, but it was hard not to blame the messenger. Especially when the messenger was someone Riley already didn't trust.

Stanton was waiting patiently in the hallway, tapping her cane against the toe of her shoe. She looked up when Riley came outside and locked the apartment door behind her. "What's the name of the bar where Kenzie was working?"

"You don't think I'm going to send you there alone, do you?"

"I'm not going to baby-sit you," Riley said.

Stanton said, "You're not going into No Man's Land alone. Kenzie is my partner, and my responsibility. I'm going after her one way or another."

Riley sighed. She couldn't have a civilian going into the badlands by herself, especially a civilian with limited vision. "All right. Fine. But I'm in charge. I call the shots, and I decide when we back off."

Stanton chuckled.

"What?"

"Nothing. Relying on you to give the order to back off? I find that unusual given what I've read about you."

"Let's not discuss gossip, all right? Because whatever you've heard about me, I'll win that game. Got it?" Stanton pressed her lips together and nodded. Riley turned and led the way down the stairs. "Keep your mouth shut and follow my orders. Once we get our partners back, I never want to see your face again."

"I'll try to live with the disappointment," Stanton said.

Kimaris ordered two of his men to move Kenzie to the middle of the floor. They each hooked a hand under her arm and dragged her over the concrete, dropping her at the spot Kimaris designated. Kenzie's head was throbbing, but she somehow found the strength to push herself onto her back. The ceiling swam over her head, a maze of beams and light fixtures.

Kimaris appeared over her, tilting his head to look down at her. His lips spread into a reptilian approximation of a smile. "Hello. Brandi, wasn't it?" He set his foot on top of her hand, applying just enough pressure for her to know how easily her fingers could be broken. "I'm surprised at your patience. With the clues I was feeding you, I expected you to make your move much earlier. But I do appreciate you giving me the time to put everything in place."

Kenzie looked toward the door. One of the other men in the room had poured a line of sand around Priest, forming a circle. Priest met Kenzie's eyes and shook her head 'no.' There was calmness in her expression, and Kenzie tried to let it transfer to herself. But then she felt Kimaris' fingers inside her mind, and she knew that she was still in his power.

When the circle around Priest was complete, another man said something under his breath and held his hand out. The sand ignited and Priest was ringed by low blue flames. Kimaris rolled his shoulders and closed his eyes, like a man who had just sunk into his favorite recliner after a long day.

"Ah, that's a relief. I don't suppose Zerachiel told you about that little trick, binding angels with burning flax? No, why would she. The angels like to keep that a little secret. But I like secrets. Flax has been around for, oh, many more years than you could count. When it's prepared just right, ground to a perfect powder and ignited, it can hold an angel in check. Do you remember the story of Sleeping Beauty? The spinning wheel was a late addition. Originally the princess pricked her finger on a sliver of flax. The sleeping beauty was, in fact, an angel." He looked down at her and said, "Isn't telling stories fun? I bet you have all kinds of stories you want to tell me."

Kenzie swallowed hard. "I'm not a... very good storyteller."

Kimaris moved his foot from her hand and knelt next to her head. "That's all right, Detective Parra. I have other ways of learning what you know." He touched her temple and smoothed her hair back to expose the wounded side of her face. She tried to slap his hand away, but discovered that she was pinned to the ground. She never let people look at the burned remnant of her face, the scars created by a buried bomb in Afghanistan. She could feel his gaze on it, as intimate as if he'd actually groped her between the legs. "Quite a burn you got there. Did Marchosias give that to you?"

"Get your hands off me, you son of a bitch."

Kimaris sighed and withdrew his hand. Kenzie wanted to reach up and brush her hair back in place, but again her arms weren't obeying. It was as if gravity had increased several hundred times. She lay in the middle of the floor, exposed, as Kimaris stood up again.

"I wish we weren't doing this as adversaries, Detective Parra. I regret that I drew you here with subterfuge. You and I, and even Zerachiel, have the same goal. We want Marchosias gone. We want this war over and done with. It's possible. I have it all worked out. All I require are you and Marchosias to come to an agreement with me. In doing so, you will fulfill your goal as this city's champion. Everyone leaves happy."

Kenzie closed her eyes.

Priest said, "Leave her alone."

"Be silent, Zerachiel," Kimaris said, not bothering to turn around. "All that is required of you is non-interference." He undid the bottom button of his coat and checked his watch. "Do we have an estimated time of arrival?"

One of the men in the room said, "He has been located. He will be here when he can."

"He must arrive before dawn."

The man nodded. "He's aware."

Kimaris nodded and dropped to one knee next to Kenzie. "We haven't much time together, Detective Parra. So I apologize for the intrusion. But this is simply the fastest way I have of getting what I require."

He cupped her burn again, his fingers warm against the twisted flesh, and she managed to twitch slightly in response.

"Don't you touch me," Kenzie growled.

"Be silent. Aggression won't make this any more difficult on me, but it could have adverse effects on you. Just relax. It will be over soon." He closed his eyes and Kenzie thought she felt his fingers melting against her skin. And then, like she was pressing her head against cellophane until it broke, she felt his hand enter her head. Her body twitched against the concrete, the closest she could manage to a full seizure, as his hand pushed deeper into her head. She knew it wasn't a physical intrusion; his hand wasn't literally inside her head. But she could feel his fingers roaming, crossing her synapses, teasing through her consciousness as if it was a drawer.

He's going to find out who I really am. He won't hesitate to kill me. Oh, God...

"Please stop," Kenzie murmured.

Then she heard a voice. It filled her mind and seemed to come from everywhere at once. But she knew that it was meant for her and her alone. *Be silent. Be still.* Priest's words wrapped around her like a fog washing over a street. She closed her eyes and focused on Priest, across the room, and an image of Riley appeared in the darkness.

It will be all right. Focus on me.

She imagined a hand reaching for her and she imagined slipping her own hand into it. Priest squeezed, and Kenzie remembered their kiss in the car. Warmth and tenderness.

It will be over soon, Priest said.

He'll discover the truth.

No, he won't. Just relax.

"So much is blocked. Not just from me," Kimaris said. "From yourself. The war. You've seen things in a war that you don't want to remember. I apologize for this, but it must be done." Kenzie felt a pressure inside of her head.

A shopkeeper held his hand out toward their Hummer. He was bloody, beaten. They couldn't stop. Kenzie ordered the driver to continue and, as they passed, the shopkeeper cried out in Farsi. His hand exploded.

"No," Kenzie said. Her voice was hoarse. "No, stop it."

Dr. Gillian Hunt, eyes alight with demonic energy, lurched toward her.

Kenzie knew this was one of Riley's memories, placed there by Priest, and she was grateful for the reprieve from her own past. Kimaris pressed deeper, past even more guarded memories - *the commanding officer shoved her down. "Easy," she whispered as she undid the buttons on Kenzie's uniform pants, "I won't tell if you don't ask..." and Kenzie decided it was best to just lie back and -* digging through her consciousness. Priest's hand was still in her mind, and Kenzie focused on that. Her own painful memories combined with those Riley suffered was far too much for her to bear. She turned toward Priest, felt the fog envelop her, and drifted away into the oblivion Priest offered.

Riley parked in the alley behind Stanton's office and let her lead the way inside. The back door led directly into the greenhouse. Moonlight drifted in through the glass and lit their way down an aisle between flowerbeds. The roses were white, colored blue like everything else in the space, and Riley eyed them as she passed. "Nice flowers. You know they're not red, right?"

"Funny," Stanton said. She turned on the office light and gestured at the desk nearest the front door. "I'm sure you remember that Kenzie isn't the most meticulous note-taker. If there's anything to be found, it's on her desk."

Riley pulled out Kenzie's chair and sat down. She had a flashback to her time in uniform. Riley had a succession of small black notebooks that she wrote everything down in. She filled every page, front and back, with neat handwriting and started a new page for a new case. Kenzie, on the other hand, scrawled down whatever she could remember on scrap paper when they got back to the car. It looked like she hadn't learned any new organization skills in the military.

"So how does this work? Kenzie does the heavy lifting, you take the credit?"

"With my eyesight, I can't exactly go out into the field. Kenzie is my eyes, and she benefits from my years of investigative experience. Plus her face isn't quite as controversial as mine is. We complement each other."

Riley dug through the pile on Kenzie's desk. "When was the last time you tried to call her?"

"In the car," Stanton said. "I'll try again."

She put the phone on speaker and leaned back in her seat, looking at a random point on the wall as it rang. Riley took the opportunity to examine Stanton's body language; her lips were tight and, despite the relaxed pose, there was a lot of tension in her shoulders. It was more than worrying about her partner, even more than worrying about a close friend.

"You've reached Mackenzie Crowe. If you don't have the time to leave a message after the beep, then why the hell did you call?"

Kenzie hung up and said, "She never ignored my calls. Even if she has to answer them in character to protect her cover, she'll at least let me know she's okay."

Riley found a paper with Kimaris' name written on it. There were times, initials, scribbled explanations for why she was making a note, but none of it made much sense to her. She frowned and scanned the desk again. "We're not going to learn anything here that we don't already know. I have some contacts in No Man's Land. Let's hope they can help us out."

Riley stood and motioned for Stanton to follow her. Stanton shut off the lights and closed the door as Riley left through the greenhouse. "I've never even heard of this Kimaris guy before Kenzie brought him up."

"Of course you haven't. You've been dealing with insurance fraud and cheating husbands. He operates a few levels above you."

"I was once a cop, you know. Back in the days when dinosaurs roamed the Earth and No Man's Land was a fraction of the size it is now."

Riley said, "Yeah, I've been meaning to thank you for that."

"Thank *me?*"

Riley wanted to ignore the opening, but she couldn't. The truth was her ire had been building since she heard Stanton's voice on the phone, and now it wouldn't be denied. All those years of frustration boiled over and she spun around and got into Stanton's face. "It's because of cops like you that No Man's Land is the way it is. Cops who didn't give a shit. Cops who would rather take a payoff or snort something so things were easier to ignore."

"That's not fair," Stanton said. "Things weren't as simple—"

"I don't want to hear a sob story. I really don't. All I care about is finding Kenzie and Priest so I can go back to forgetting you exist. Come on."

Stanton shook her head as she followed Riley out of the building. Riley checked her phone again, in case Priest had tried to call in the last thirty seconds. She stuffed the phone into the pocket of her jacket and cursed under her breath.

When Stanton got in on the passenger side, she looked at Riley and said, "If I could make a suggestion without being insulted or cursed at?"

"What?"

"I gather Caitlin Priest is a competent detective. As good as you are, otherwise you wouldn't have sent her with Kenzie as backup."

Riley said, "Yeah. She's probably better than me in a lot of ways."

"So whatever happened to them, your being there wouldn't have prevented it. The only thing it would have changed is that you would be missing as well. Your absence made it possible for you to come to their rescue. You sat on the sidelines until you were called out to win the game. The woman I met at your home..."

"Gillian."

Stanton nodded. "Don't blame her for what happened. And don't blame yourself. Trust me, nobody wins in that game. When you go home after we find our partners, thank her for what she did for you."

Riley looked at Stanton. As much as she hated to admit it, Stanton had read her thoughts almost exactly. And her reasoning was sound. If someone had managed to take Priest out of the equation, then there was little to no chance Riley would have been able to escape. Who would have been able to come after them if she and Priest were both eliminated? She looked back down the alley and said, "You want to go to the bar first, or your office?"

Stanton said, "The bar. I want to see what Kenzie left behind."

Riley started the car and drove out of the alley.

Panic and fear overrode the pain. She was surprised how painless it was, at first. How she could smell the smoke and the burnt clothes. And something else. Cooking meat. She could feel the gurney shaking against her hand, or maybe it was the other way around. She was wheeled into a room and a medic in scrubs appeared over her. She was never able to remember what he looked like, but she did recall that his eyes were bloodshot.

"Crowe, Major Mackenzie Grace. Serial number..."

The medic quieted her calmly. He told her they already knew that information and said something to a nurse.

"My face," she gasped. He looked down at her. She felt tears, but only in one eye. "Do I still have a-a..." She couldn't finish the question. The medic touched her arm and pushed her into an operating room. She could hear other people screaming and crying and then the doctor appeared over her.

A light went on, blinding her, and then she was...

...once more on the floor of the warehouse. She could feel the sweat under her clothes, running down her face and dripping on the ground. Kimaris withdrew his hand and exhaled sharply. "We're making some progress. Chipping away at those walls. I'll get through soon."

Kenzie gasped. She gulped air like someone drowning, her lungs refusing to cooperate at first. Her arms and legs were tingling. She looked up and saw Kimaris looked about as bad as she felt. His face was pale and drawn, sweat beading on his forehead. He pushed himself up and scanned the room. "Where is he?"

Priest said, "Perhaps Marchosias didn't feel the need to waste his time on an associate of your stature.

Kenzie tried to smile. *Angel bitch slap.*

"You, silent," Kimaris said. He walked to the stairs and sat down with his feet on the bottom riser. "Perhaps we should take the time to get better acquainted. I would love to have you both on my side when Marchosias makes his grand entrance. And I do believe that is where we are. On the same side. We want the same thing. Peace. We want the war between angels and demons to end. Detective Parra, I know this wasn't what you had in mind when you started this mess. I'm sure you didn't intend for the angels to be losing already. My plan will bring an end to hostilities. The city will be calm."

"This city has never been calm," Priest said.

"Times change, Zerachiel," Kimaris said. "Leaders change. By the time people head to work in the morning, Marchosias will be gone. His reign will end, and a new leader shall take his place. You'll find my leadership style much different, I assure you."

"Marchosias is just going to hand No Man's Land over to you?" Priest said. "Do you think he is just tired of running things and wants to take a break?"

I think you're spending too much time with Riley, Kenzie said, in case Priest was still listening in. If she was, she ignored the comment.

"Believe me, I have everything sorted. I've been planning this for... ooh. A very long time. With the Angel Maker throwing the balance into turmoil, there is no better time to put things into motion." He rubbed his palms together and looked at Kenzie. "Everyone will get what they want. Including you, Detective Parra. You'll fulfill your role as this city's champion. You are the keystone to the entire plan coming together."

One of the men who had gone outside returned. "Milord. Marchosias approaches. He'll arrive within the hour."

Kimaris grinned widely and clapped his hands together. "Excellent. Perhaps Detective Parra and I will have some wonderful things to tell him." He stood and walked back over to her. Kenzie resisted the urge to recoil as he knelt and reached for her face again. She realized with dread that she couldn't have pulled back even if she wanted to. He was controlling her again.

"Stop..." she whispered.

"I will. Soon." He touched her head.

I'm so sorry, Priest whispered inside her head as the torture began again.

Riley parked behind Kenzie's car and scanned the area as she approached. Stanton let her lead the way and said, "An unprotected car on a dark street. Why isn't it cut apart for scrap metal by now?

Riley had thought the same thing. She felt something in the air, a static electricity that hadn't been there before. Maybe whatever Kimaris had planned was sending out a 'keep away' signal to the lower life forms. The door was unlocked, another bad sign, and she slipped into the driver's seat to examine the interior. She spotted the empty doughnut package on the dashboard and groaned. "Oh, Caitlin, don't tell me she got you, too."

She spotted two ear buds in the passenger seat and picked them up. "Did she have bugs planted in the bar? Maybe a recorder?"

"Yes, I think so. I'll check it out."

Riley continued her search while Stanton hurried off. She sighed and muttered to herself, "You really screwed this one up, Priest. It was just supposed to be a quick, simple surveillance." Headlights swept the street and Riley sank down in the seat so that she presented a smaller target. Her hand went to the butt of her gun as the car moved rolled slowly down the street and then stopped in front of the bar.

The headlights flashed twice, and Riley relaxed. She beeped the horn once and assumed a more comfortable position behind the wheel of Kenzie's car.

The other car parked and the driver unfolded himself from the front seat. He trotted to her car and knelt next to the open door. "Sweet ride, *mamacita.*"

"Spare me, Muse. What have you got for me?"

Muse rolled his shoulders. "Not a lot of time to get much," he said, "but you're an old friend so I worked some miracles. A couple of guys said there's been rumors of something that was going to happen soon, and apparently tonight's the night. Everything got real quiet around eleven. And quiet in No Man's Land is never good for nobody."

Riley nodded. "Any idea where this big something is going down?"

"Nobody's talking. I talked to a couple of guys who keep tabs on some blocks downtown. You know, private little fiefdoms. But nobody's asked to play in their backyard."

"Okay. I'm looking for a guy named Alexander Kimaris. You happen have any idea where he might be hiding?"

"First you want March, now you want Kimaris? Shoot. At least you're going the right direction. Kimaris is small-time enough you might be able to do something about *him*." He rubbed his chin. "He's got a couple of warehouses around here. He likes to use them to store things that are, shall we say, less than legal, if you catch my drift. You want to find him, those warehouses would be a good place to catch him. Lots of incriminating evidence lying around."

"Addresses?"

Muse laughed. "You call me with twenty minutes notice and expect the entire phone book, don't ya? I don't have addresses. All I know is they're near here. That, and your friend is across the street with a gun."

Riley looked past him and saw Stanton standing in the alley. She was obscured by shadows, but Riley could see that she did have her gun out. Riley reached up and turned on the dome light, then quickly turned it out again. She hoped Stanton understood the message that she was okay.

"She's not my friend. How'd you know she was with me?"

"Two white girls in No Man's Land after midnight and they ain't together? Please."

Riley said, "I'm Hispanic."

"Badge makes everyone white 'round here."

"Come on, Muse. Help me out. Anyplace that's usually vacant but is really busy tonight for some reason?"

Muse stroked his chin as Stanton crossed the street. "Near the el tracks," he said. "Couple of my boys said they had to move because it was a little too kicking there earlier. Can't narrow it down more than that."

Riley nodded. "Good enough. Thanks, Muse."

"Keep me in your Rolodex, Riley." He opened the door and climbed out of the car as Stanton approached. He held the door for her and said, "Nice to meet you, Riley's friend."

Riley waited until Muse was back in his car and had driven away before she turned to Stanton. "What did you find?"

Stanton held up a few jewel cases. "Some recordings on CD. I didn't have time to listen to them."

Riley took one of the cases and looked at the label. "Hopefully it'll be entertaining. Come on, let's go back to my car. Muse gave me a lead."

Priest stood in her prison, cursing the ring of burning flax that prevented her from going to Kenzie's aid. She kept her eye on the other men in the room, watching for an opportunity to present itself, but she wasn't holding out very much hope. They had been there for hours, and she was torn between hoping Riley would be arriving any second and fearing she would arrive too late. The torture Kenzie was enduring was bad enough; once Marchosias arrived, he would reveal the truth. She didn't hold out much hope for Kenzie's survival once that happened.

The only plan of action she had was entirely unacceptable. She could wait until Marchosias arrived, revealed Kenzie's true identity, and killed her. Then either he or Kimaris would turn on her. They would have to break the flax to even touch her, and she would be able to retaliate. It was a horrible plan, and she prayed that Riley would arrive before she had to implement it.

Kimaris was kneeling beside Kenzie, his hand on her face. Priest was fortunate that he had opened her mind the way he had. She was able to piggyback her own thoughts on his and prevent him from discovering anything incriminating. It was a dangerous balance, keeping Kenzie safe with a light enough touch that Kimaris didn't realize she was there. Unfortunately she wasn't able to protect Kenzie from reliving the thoughts and memories Kimaris unlocked. Painful things Kenzie had carefully set aside were dragging to the forefront, happening all over again in living color. All Priest could do was hold her hand during the process and hope it was enough.

"Milord."

Priest and Kimaris both looked toward the door as one of the lookouts returned.

"Marchosias has arrived."

Kimaris laughed and clapped his hands. "Finally. Gather around, friends. It's a momentous day for all of us."

Priest looked at Kenzie and met her gaze. *Come on, Riley,* Priest thought. *Time is short.*

They were nearly to the el station when Riley suddenly slowed and veered to the right. She bumped the curb with her tires and Stanton braced herself against the dashboard. "Maybe I *should* have offered to drive," she said.

Riley nodded toward the rearview mirror and slid down in her seat. "We have company."

Stanton looked over her shoulder and slid down as well. She could see bright lights advancing on them, four in a row. Her first thought was a drag race, but the cars were inching along at a snail's pace. Behind the advance cars, she saw more coming. She couldn't tell how many. She said, "Odd amount of traffic for this time of night."

Riley said, "An advance car, two more behind it, and two bringing up the rear. All surrounding a single car without headlights."

Stanton said, "Oh, good. I thought we might miss the annual No Man's Land midnight parade."

Riley waited for the cars to pass and opened the door. "It's a cortege. Come on."

"We're going to follow them on foot?"

"They'll notice the car," Riley said. "Besides, it'll be easy considering how slow they're going."

"Okay. But why, exactly, are we following them?"

"Muse said something was happening in a building near the el tracks. Here we have a mysterious car, running dark, driving toward the el tracks. Plus, our partners have disappeared. They have to be connected. Now are you coming or do you want to watch my car?"

"I'll come. But..." Stanton tried to hedge her true concern. "What if I can't keep up with you in the dark?"

Riley looked at her and considered the question. "Just try your best. I'm not leaving you here by yourself. Let's go." She got out of the car, leaving Stanton no choice but to follow.

Riley was parked near one of the supports for the el overpass. With her limited vision, the yellow security lights that lined each support beam became pale yellow halos above her head. Stanton climbed out of the car and followed Riley along the side of the road. The glasses she wore were mirrored to help improve her vision in normal situations, but they were a hindrance in the dark. She took them off and put them into her pocket as she followed Riley down an alley.

"The road the motorcade went down only has one possible outlet," Riley explained. "We can cut them off without being too conspicuous."

"Right," Stanton said.

Riley stopped at the mouth of the alley and pressed against the wall to check the street. The lead car had pulled up in front of a warehouse and the driver emerged. He buttoned his jacket, scanned the area, and walked to the closest door. "Looks like they've stopped. Warehouse is pretty lively for this time of night." She looked back at Stanton and said, "Kenzie didn't tell you anything at all about Kimaris?"

Stanton shrugged. "Just the typical information. Things you probably already know. His connections and his reputation. She told me that she was afraid of him."

Riley was obviously stunned. "Kenzie said she was afraid?"

"Not in so many words," Stanton said. "But she called you."

Riley pulled her gun and checked the load. She looked back out and saw the rest of the procession was arriving. The driver of the lead car was standing at the warehouse door like a guard, hands clasped in front of him. "Okay. Looks like the party is about to get started. Stay behind me. Anything happens, you and Kenzie are civilians."

Stanton nodded and they stepped out of the alley. Riley slipped her arm around Stanton's waist and drooped as if a weight had been dropped onto her shoulders. "Sing," she whispered.

"What?"

"Loud. And slur your words."

Stanton sang the first thing that came to her mind. "Tura-lura-lura..."

Riley said, "Yer a good friend, Tina. A real good friend." She let her right foot drag on the pavement behind her, scuffing on the asphalt as Stanton helped her up on the curb. "Just lemme, just lemme rest it off, I'll be fine. I'll be fine." She lolled her head toward the now parked procession. The man guarding the door stepped forward a few feet and watched their progress. Riley kept her head down, letting her hair cover her face in case it was someone who knew her.

"You ladies all right?"

"Just need to get her home. Let her sleep it off."

Riley tapped Stanton's elbow and nodded toward the stairs to the el station at the end of the block. When they were well enough past the warehouse, Riley pushed off of Stanton's side and started jogging. Stanton followed her, moving to the sidewalk where they could blend into the shadows a little better.

Stanton waited until they were on the stairs to the el before she spoke. "Where are we going?"

"I was hoping there would be a window around the side. There's no way we'll get onto that property from the ground level. They'll see us coming and stop us before we set foot on the driveway. We're going to have to find an alternate means of entrance."

The station platform was wide and vacant, with plastic benches along the outside edge. The wooden roof was equipped with three rows of flickering electric lights, giving Stanton enough light to see a little better. Riley stepped onto one of the benches and threw her leg over the waist-high barrier. She looked down and said, "All right. It's about five feet. Think you can make it?"

"Jumping?"

"Five feet," Riley said. "Come on. It's nothing."

Stanton hesitated and said, "All right."

"I'll go first if you need a hand." She lifted her other leg over the barrier and said, "There's a lip here just wide enough to stand on. She crouched, shifted her weight, and leapt. Stanton heard the double skipping step as Riley landed on the opposite roof. "Okay. Nothing to it."

Stanton hesitated. Even if she made this jump, there were three buildings between them and the warehouse where Kenzie and Priest were being held. How could she possibly make all those leaps in the dark?

"Stanton, I'll leave you here if you want," Riley said in a frustrated whisper. "Just make a damn decision."

Mackenzie is in trouble. She stepped over the partition and leapt to the building. She landed solidly, and Riley grabbed her hand and forearm to keep her from backpedaling. After a moment of vertigo, Stanton exhaled and nodded her thanks.

"Good?" Riley said.

Stanton patted Riley's arm. "Yeah. Let's go get our girls."

Priest felt Marchosias arrive, and she braced herself for his entrance. If Riley was waiting for the last minute, it was fast approaching.

Kimaris ordered two of his men to remain by the door, while the others moved back toward him. The door opened and two demons walked inside. They took position next to Kimaris' men. A few seconds later, Marchosias stepped through the door. He wore a black suit and shirt, the tie a deep blue. His face was brilliant red, the flesh scoured away to reveal wet muscle. He wore his hideous visage like a medal, reveled in the looks of shock and disgust it drew from people, even other demons. He eyed Priest as he walked past her, and then fixed his gaze on Kimaris.

"You've captured an angel. Well done. If that is all you wished to tell me..."

Kimaris said, "Hardly, milord. I'm certain you recognize the importance of this particular angel's identity."

"Zerachiel," Marchosias said. "She performs the farce of being Riley Parra's partner. Caitlin Priest. Capturing her was a truly impressive feat, but ultimately meaningless."

Kimaris could hardly contain his excitement. He kept his hands behind his back and said, "Perhaps this will change your mind. The reason I called you here at this late hour. I'd like to present you with a small gift. I will give you Riley Parra."

Kimaris ordered his men to move out of the way and Marchosias looked down at Kenzie. His eyes widened and he tilted his head slightly.

"Impossible." He walked forward and Kimaris practically danced along beside him as he crossed the room. Kimaris smiled smugly as Marchosias approached the prisoner and looked down.

Priest tested the limits of her prison. There was no escape. She looked at Marchosias, who was standing inches from Kenzie and staring down at her. Finally, he turned and looked at Kimaris. Priest couldn't read his expression, such as it was, and she flexed her wings experimentally. Shockwaves ran down the wings into her back and threatened to knock her down.

Marchosias looked at Priest, looked down at Kenzie, and began to pace. Kimaris kept his smug smile in place, ready to answer the inevitable questions.

"This is truly remarkable, Kimaris. Truly. How did you manage to capture the angel, by the way?"

Priest froze. Marchosias was looking at her, but speaking to Kimaris. There was no way Marchosias would have misidentified Riley.

Kimaris smiled. "Pure flax, from the Original Home. It's costly, but if one needs to capture an angel, it is the only method."

Marchosias stopped in front of Priest and slipped his hands into his pockets. "And Detective Parra?"

"Laughably easy. The rumors of her protection must be greatly exaggerated."

"Watch your tongue," Marchosias said, suddenly volatile.

Kimaris' smile faded. "Is there a problem?"

"The majority of information on Detective Riley Parra came from me. Are you implying I was unable to control her? That *you* are more adept at control than I am?" He turned to face Kimaris. "I asked you a question, Kimaris, and I expect an answer."

"I... did not mean to imply..."

"Have you ever heard of the burn on Detective Parra's face? The origin of it?"

Kimaris said, "I assumed it happened when she assaulted your stronghold. I have been attempting to probe her mind for further information, but it has been fruitless so far."

"Of course it has. The angel has been blocking your efforts." Kimaris looked at Priest, and she held his gaze.

From the corner of her eye, Priest noticed one of Kimaris' men look toward the roof. He muttered to the man standing guard next to him and then slipped silently out a side door. Priest had felt the arrival as well; Riley was very, very near.

Marchosias ignored that. "Tell me, Kimaris. Do you believe it's more likely that everything you have heard about Detective Parra is wrong, that every demon and every angel who has encountered her merely provided the wrong information, or did you stop to consider the fact that you... captured the wrong... fucking... person?"

Kimaris' eyes blazed and he looked at Kenzie. "That's impossible. The angel..."

"The angel lied to you, Kimaris, to protect her charge. The fact you were foolish enough to fall for it is nearly as embarrassing as the fact I actually came when you called." He turned on his heel and motioned to the men by the door that they were leaving.

Kimaris rallied his senses and said, "The identity of my prisoner doesn't change my main reason for bringing you here. Things are about to change, Marchosias. At dawn, Riley Parra will cease to be a problem and the war, the war that you are so eager to end, will be over. We will have been handed an unequivocal victory."

Marchosias stopped walking and slowly turned around. Kimaris produced a cell phone from his pocket.

"My men spent this evening planting explosive devices in various parts of the city. There are eight in total, concealed throughout the so-called respectable part of town. That small piece of real estate you've never quite been able to attain. All it will take is the press of one button and the devices will detonate. The city will be devastated. Crippled. There will not be enough resources to manage the destruction. People will die. And in the course of time, deprivation and ruin will spread like a plague. No Man's Land will march forth, and by the end of this year, there will be nothing else. I'm going to detonate the bombs momentarily. But I wanted to extend an invitation.

"In the aftermath, one of two things will happen. Either you become a joke and your followers drag you from your position kicking and screaming, giving me the mantle of ruler in your stead... or you will announce that I am your worthy successor. You will have a place in my court, naturally. One cannot ignore your years of dedication to the cause. But you will have no real power."

Marchosias said, "You're insane."

"No," Kimaris snapped. "Insane is waiting patiently, wasting decades and *centuries* waiting for the decay to occur on its own. Insane is entering agreements and playing fair. This nonsense of champions is ludicrous. It is time we took what we deserve."

"The difference is taking and *earning*," Marchosias growled. "What I have earned, the angels cannot simply steal back. Your plan is absolute madness. Do you believe our arrangement has only tied my hands? If you do this, you will unleash the full strength of Heaven's fury upon us. This war would look like a schoolyard spat compared to that. There's even a name for it. What you suggest would be firing the first volley in Armageddon."

Priest said, "I've heard that battle doesn't go well for you guys." She took advantage of their distraction to glance toward the roof. There was a skylight with frosted glass that had been turned milky white by the moon. A shadow crossed one of the lower quadrants and Priest had to conceal a smile. Her heart soared as she returned her focus to the demons in the middle of the room.

Kimaris waved the cell phone. "Play doomsayer all you wish. Time is wasting, Marchosias. Will you be dragged to Hell as a failure, or will you accept your place in my fellowship? I'm willing to decide for you, but I doubt you'll agree with my choice."

"There's only one way you're taking my throne, Kimaris. By holding my severed head for all to see." He unbuttoned his suit jacket and shrugged out of it.

Kimaris shrugged and returned the cell phone to his pocket. "As you wish."

Stanton had zip ties, and Riley used them to secure the demon that had come to investigate the noise they made jumping onto the roof. His tie was stuffed in his mouth, not that it mattered much. The piece of brick Riley used to knock him unconscious had left a deep gash on his forehead. She'd managed to stop the bleeding, but she wasn't holding out much hope for him surviving the night. Fortunately, she had seen his eyes before she hit him. Death to a demon was probably just a demotion, like going from salesman to the mail room.

She returned to the skylight where Stanton was waiting and listening. Stanton was still sweating from their dash across the rooftops, her hands scraped from where she had fallen. She turned away from the glass and whispered to Riley. "Kimaris believed he was holding you hostage. He was going to trade you to someone named Marchosias."

Riley felt a chill. If she hadn't taken the night off, she would most likely be Marchosias' property right now. She was definitely going to give Gillian a back rub when she got home.

"They keep calling your partner an angel."

"You should meet her," Riley muttered. She overheard Kimaris talking about an end to the war. She cupped her hand over the frosted glass, staying near the edge so she wouldn't cast a shadow, and squinted. She could make out vague shapes, but nothing concrete. She wondered if that was how Stanton saw everything all the time. She saw Priest near the door, surrounded by a low ring of blue flame. It looked like she was standing on the burner of a gas stove.

Kimaris explained his placement of eight explosive devices and Riley tensed. Stanton said, "Armageddon? These guys are pretty damned dramatic. But... God. He's right. The city doesn't have the resources to deal with something that big."

Riley looked across the roof at a tall water reservoir. Pipes ran from it, leading down into the building. She knew that Kimaris probably didn't pay the bills in all of his properties, but he wouldn't want them destroyed in a fire. She assumed he would have hooked the sprinkler system up to this reservoir as a preventative measure. The smoke from the fire around Priest's feet should have activated it by now, unless homeless people used the building for squatting. They built fires to keep warm in the winter, and most of them were savvy enough to disable the smoke detectors so they wouldn't get drenched.

"Did you hear me?" Stanton whispered.

"No," Riley said. "Stay here." She stood and ran across the roof at a crouch.

Stanton followed her. "There's going to be a fight. Kenzie is down there in the middle of all that. And why doesn't your partner just step over that fire?"

"It's complicated. Don't worry; I have a plan," Riley said.

She ducked under the reservoir and wished she had taken plumbing classes. All she knew was how to fix a leak in her own apartment, and even that would require a lot of trial and error. She could barely see the mechanisms in the dark, let alone begin to understand how to fix them. She needed to be able to see in the dark. Or...

"How much do you know about plumbing?"

"I helped install the water systems in my greenhouse. What does that have to do with anything?"

Riley moved to the side and said, "I need you to hook the sprinkler systems back up."

"What?" Stanton said. "What will getting them wet do, other than piss them off?"

"Trust me," Riley said.

Stanton scoffed, but she said, "I'll do my best. Where will you be?"

Riley took her gun from the holster and said, "I was apparently invited to this party. It would be rude not to make an appearance."

Kimaris delivered the first blow, his fist glancing off Marchosias' cheek. Marchosias wasn't slowed. He wrapped his arm around Kimaris' and wrenched it down. He drove his other elbow into Kimaris' face, and the erstwhile usurper dropped to his knees. Marchosias released the arm and punched Kimaris once, twice, three times until blood stained Kimaris' upper lip.

"Do you know how many people have tried to take my place? You arrogant gnat." He grabbed a handful of Kimaris' curly black hair and punched him in the face.

Priest saw movement across the room and looked away from the fight. Kenzie had rolled onto her side, struggling to get to her feet. She assumed the hold Kimaris had on her had weakened after the first blow. He had other things on his mind now.

Kimaris howled and punched Marchosias in the stomach. Marchosias released Kimaris' hair, and Kimaris lunged forward. He tackled Marchosias and began to pepper his midsection with fierce blows. Marchosias grabbed Kimaris' head and dug his fingernails into the flesh until blood began to flow in ten narrow rivulets down Kimaris' face.

A bell started to ring, but neither combatant paid it much attention. Priest looked at the ceiling as the downpour began. Streams of water cascaded from the sprinkler heads, pouring down on the entire ground level. She looked down and saw the blue flames being quashed and the flax diluted. She used the toe of her shoe to disrupt the ring further and she felt the energy holding her dissipate. She stepped forward and turned just as one of Kimaris' men lunged at her with his gun drawn.

Priest turned to face him fully and extended her wings through the immaterial restraint of her clothing. She flexed the wings once and rose out of her attacker's path, forcing him to change direction at the last second to avoid falling on his face.

Priest glided across the room, more of a long jump than flight, and touched down next to Kenzie. Kenzie looked up at Priest and her eyes widened. "Shit. You're really an angel."

"Can you run?" Priest said.

Kenzie said, "I can."

Priest helped support Kenzie and turned to face the room. Two of Kimaris' men were engaged in battle with Marchosias' escorts at the door, but the other four were quickly advancing on Priest and Kenzie.

"Okay. Forget running. Can you fight?"

Kenzie grunted. Her clothes were soaked from the downpour, her hair hanging down in front of her face to conceal her burn again. "I wasn't exactly confident on the running. I don't suppose you can call in for a miracle."

"Stay behind me," Priest said. She stepped forward and extended her wings to block Kenzie from the advancing demons.

An empty crate fell from above and landed on one of the demons. As he fell, the others turned their attention skyward just in time to avoid another rain of crates. Priest moved Kenzie to the safety of the wall and looked up. Riley was standing on the catwalk above them, using a handcart as a lever to dump the crates over the railing.

Priest beamed and grabbed Kenzie's arm. "You don't call in for miracles. They just show up when Riley's around."

Riley met her at the stairs. She took a moment to watch Kimaris and Marchosias fight and then said, "Don't even try the front door. Marchosias has men out there."

Priest said, "Kimaris has bombs set up in the city. There's no way to find them."

Kenzie said, "Yes, there is. He was going to detonate them with a cell phone." She was clinging to Priest. Her eyes were wide and haunted as she watched Kimaris and Marchosias battle. She swallowed hard and looked at Riley, expecting her to connect the dots.

"So?" Priest said.

Kenzie said, "Kimaris had one man plant each bomb. They didn't need to all be set at the same time if he was just going to wait until dawn to detonate. The man who planted the bomb also had a cell phone, and they used it as the detonator. The phones have to be active to receive the call, so we just find out where they were purchased and call for the tracking information."

"That's good thinking," Riley said. She put a hand on Kenzie's shoulder. "Are you okay?"

"Lot of... bad memories." She clung tighter to Priest and looked toward the door. "Chelsea."

"On the roof. That's how I got in. Access door. Priest, let's round these guys up. We need information if we're going to find those bombs."

Priest tried to pull away, but Kenzie's hand tightened on her blouse. "I..."

"It's okay," Priest said. "Go to the roof. Chelsea is waiting for you."

Kenzie nodded and reluctantly released her. She started up the stairs, and Priest joined Riley in gathering the demons. The sprinklers had soaked Riley's clothes, but she didn't even shiver as she dragged the demons to their feet. She pulled a handful of zip ties from her pocket and showed them to Priest.

"Will these hold them?" she asked.

Priest covered them with her hands and closed her eyes. "They will now."

As they secured their prisoners, Riley looked toward the stairs. Kenzie was already gone. She turned back to Priest and said, "What the hell did they do to her?"

"They made her remember."

Riley said, "I have never seen her like that."

Priest nodded. She couldn't bring herself to say anything.

Across the room, Marchosias bellowed in victory. His silk shirt was torn, revealing an inhuman mass of muscle on his chest. Kimaris was on the ground at Marchosias' feet, his face bloody. Marchosias locked his gaze on Riley and gave her a mock salute.

Riley moved her hand to her gun. There wasn't time to get to cover; she would have to fight and, most likely, lose.

Marchosias met her gaze for a long moment and then held his hands out to her. "We've all had a busy night, Detective Parra. It will be an even busier morning for you, I suspect." He lifted Kimaris' limp body and held him like a ventriloquist dummy. "For now, I have some managerial matters to discuss with my good friend here. Another day, Detective."

He looked at Kimaris' men and dragged Kimaris to the door. The demons that had been fighting at the door were all down. Marchosias and his men left the warehouse, but Riley didn't relax until she heard their cars drive away. She scanned the floor, the demons bound and unconscious, and then looked up at the ceiling.

"Think there's any way to..." The sprinklers shut off, and an alarm began to sound. Riley wiped the water from her face and flicked her fingers at the ground. "Never mind."

Riley stood at the back of the room while Priest let her associates into the building. The four angels looked like mafia hit men; designer suits, nothing but muscle, and piercing eyes that gave away nothing as they led Kimaris' men outside. Priest spoke with one of the angels and then walked across the room to where Riley waited.

"They'll get the information we need to stop the bombs. We can tell Briggs that they're in federal custody."

Riley nodded. "Sounds good to me. Not like we could have held them for very long anyway." Riley watched the angels leave and turned to look at Priest. She was in a rumpled dress shirt and vest, her sleeves rolled up to her elbows. "Are you all right?"

"I'm fine," Priest said. "Kenzie's the one I'm worried about."

"Yeah," Riley said. "Come on."

They went up the stairs to the access door, the lock Riley had broken with the butt of her gun still lying on the ground. The sky was starting to get color as the sun slowly rose in the east. Kenzie was sitting against the skylight with Stanton, pressed hard against her partner's side with Priest's suit jacket around her shoulders. She looked like a drowned rat when she looked up at Riley's approach. Stanton had one arm around Kenzie's shoulders, holding her close.

"Thank you," Kenzie said. "If you hadn't shown up..."

"Thank Chelsea," Riley said. "I wouldn't even have known you were missing if she hadn't come to get me."

Kenzie took Stanton's hand and squeezed. The last lingering doubts Riley had about their relationship were eradicated at that moment. She'd suspected when the legally blind woman followed her across several rooftops in the dark, but that grip could only mean one thing.

Riley said, "The cops will be here any second. Chelsea, why don't you come down with me?"

Stanton looked up at her. "What? Why?"

"We need a cover story. We can come up with something together... and you can tell it to the cops. It was your case, it's your bust."

Priest looked at Riley with an expression she couldn't read. Stanton and Kenzie exchanged a look.

"Come on. I'm feeling generous."

"Can I stay up here?" Kenzie said. "I just need to sit for a while."

Priest said, "I'll stay with her."

Riley raised an eyebrow. "Willingly?"

"What can I say? We went through a very difficult time together. She grew on me."

Sirens were coming closer, so Riley held out her hand. Chelsea took it and let herself be pulled to her feet. She looked down at Kenzie. "I'll be back as soon as I can."

Kenzie nodded and pulled Priest's coat tighter around herself. Stanton walked to Riley. "I'll need your help on the fire escape. I don't really trust..."

"I'll help you," Riley said. She threaded her arm around Stanton's elbow and helped her across the roof.

"Why?" Stanton said. "Why this sudden change of heart?"

Riley looked back at Priest and Kenzie. "She's in love with you. I didn't know for sure until I saw you together. But you're in love with her, too. And we were able to count on you when it mattered. That goes a long way."

Stanton said, "Thank you."

"Just don't hurt her," Riley said. "And don't make me regret doing this."

Stanton's smile faded. "I used to see how you and Kenzie looked at me in the station. When we'd pass on the stairs. And I remember the way you looked at me after... everything. I want that first look back. I know I have to work to get it, but... I'm willing." She saw the police cars arrive in front of the building, their lights flashing red and blue strobes into the alley.

"Nervous?" Riley said. "About them?"

"Yeah."

"Just think about Kenzie."

Stanton smiled. "Let's go."

Priest crouched next to Kenzie and said, "I am so sorry."

Kenzie frowned. "For what?"

"By using Riley's name, I prompted everything that happened afterward."

Kenzie chuckled. "If he'd known who I really was, he probably would have killed me outright. This, at least, I can recover from." She pulled Priest's jacket tighter around her shoulders and chuckled quietly. "I hope."

Priest chewed her bottom lip and looked toward the fire escape. "You should have been allowed to deal with those memories on your own terms. Having them dragged out like that will do permanent damage to your psyche. I've seen it happen before. The human brain is designed with fail safes. Yours were bypassed."

"So what?" Kenzie said. "I'm going to be a vegetable?"

"No," Priest said. "I can heal the damage."

Kenzie looked at a point on the ground, and a tear slid from her eye. "Well. I think... I would really appreciate it if you would."

Priest moved closer and straddled Kenzie's lap. She cupped Kenzie's face in her hands, tilting it up as she bent down and brushed their lips together. Kenzie's lips parted, and Priest tentatively explored with her tongue. Kenzie put a hand on Priest's hip, the other on her cheek. She gasped as a warm feeling washed through her, and the kiss increased in intensity. When Priest finally pulled back, Kenzie licked her lips and kept her eyes closed.

"Wow, seraphim," Kenzie whispered. Her voice was slurred, near sleep as she sagged against the skylight. "What was that for?"

Even with so few words, Priest could hear the difference in Kenzie's voice. The anguish was gone; the Kenzie she had grown to hate the last time they met was back. She smiled and touched Kenzie's hair, brushing it back into place to cover her burn. Priest rose and bent to gather Kenzie in her arms. She cradled the sleeping woman to her chest and carried her to the fire escape.

Riley saw Priest coming down the fire escape with Kenzie in her arms and nudged Stanton. They had just finished giving their statement to the responding officers and were waiting for Briggs to make an appearance so they could go through it all again. Riley started walking toward Priest, with Stanton broke into a run halfway down the alley.

"Kenzie. What happened to her?" Stanton demanded.

"She's fine," Priest said softly. "She just needed a little rest. I helped calm her down." She looked at Riley and nodded slightly.

Riley put a hand on Stanton's shoulder. "She'll be fine. Trust me."

"That's the second time you've asked me to trust you, Detective Parra. Kind of odd, considering that you don't trust me."

Riley shrugged. "I'm getting there. Go tell the police we're going to find someplace for Kenzie to rest more comfortably." Stanton nodded and went back down the alley with one last look at Kenzie's sleeping face. When she was gone, Riley said, "What did you do?"

"Kimaris didn't use any finesse when he raped her mind. I was able to follow the tracks he made and repair most of the damage. She still has the memories, but she'll deal with them when the time is right."

"Nice trick. Did it involve a lot of hocus pocus?"

"No," Priest said. "It only requires that I hold my hand against her skin for a few seconds and concentrate."

Riley said, "Sounds simple."

Priest gave her an enigmatic smile and said, "Sometimes I add embellishments."

Riley led the way out of the alley, with Stanton and Priest trailing behind her. They followed the el tracks, staying in the shadows so the press would hopefully not notice them. When they reached the block where Riley had left the car, she stopped and held up a hand. "Shit."

"What's wrong?" Stanton said.

"We have company." She put her back to the el support and looked around the corner as she pulled her gun from the holster. Marchosias was sitting on the hood of her car, and Kimaris was kneeling on the street in front of the bumper. Marchosias looked much better than the last time Riley had seen him, his wounds healed and his suit crisp and clean. Kimaris, on the other hand, looked a few pounds lighter and his thick black hair had been shaved to the scalp.

"This isn't right," Priest whispered. She had handed Kenzie to Stanton, who accepted her weight without hesitation. She moved next to Riley and scanned the street. "He's alone. He has to know we would see him."

"That's the point," Riley said. "He wanted us to see him."

Priest shook her head. "Riley..."

"I'm going out there."

"*Riley.*"

"It's all right. If he wanted me dead, he had his chance back at the warehouse. Just keep an eye on him." She holstered her weapon and stepped out into the open. Marchosias turned toward her and smiled. The expression caused revulsion so encompassing, Riley nearly had to turn away. "Fancy meeting you here."

"I was in the neighborhood," Marchosias said.

"You and your buddy seem to have recovered from the fight pretty well."

Marchosias plucked the lapels of his suit jacket and shrugged. "We've been... well. Somewhere else. Time is a little different there." He slapped the top of Kimaris' head. "Isn't it, Kim? Yes, it is." He chuckled and crossed his arms over his chest. "What happened tonight was an abomination. It was a child attempting to drive a car. It was sloppy, and it could have been disastrous to us both. I know Zerachiel is listening, so I'm extending this offer to the both of you. The angels will overlook the misguided events of this evening. I will not be held responsible for Kimaris and his plan. There will be no retaliation and no escalation in the war between us."

Riley looked at Kimaris. There were healed wounds on his face and neck, and his eyes were flat. "What do we get in return?"

Marchosias nodded at the man kneeling between them. "Alexander Kimaris. He's committed a hell of a lot of crimes even if you discount his demonic nature. He's been... conditioned. He's the same son of a bitch you know and loathe, but he's now subject to your mortal rules of punishment. Arrest, imprisonment, all those lovely things that make you feel safe when you tuck in your loved ones at the end of the day."

Riley looked over her shoulder and saw Priest standing at the corner. She nodded once, and Riley turned back to Marchosias. "Looks like we have a deal."

Marchosias slid off the hood and straightened his suit. "Fantastic." He looked at the sky. "It's been a long night. Do we have to go through the whole rigmarole of threats and warnings and portents of doom about how 'when next we meet, I won't be so cordial,' or can I just walk away?"

"As long as you do it quickly," Riley said.

Marchosias bowed to her, saluted to Priest, and walked into an alley. When Riley walked to the opening of the same alley, she saw that he was already gone. She took her handcuffs off her belt and walked back to where Kimaris was still kneeling. He kept his eyes on the ground, visibly seething as she pulled his arms behind his back.

"Alexander Kimaris. You are under arrest for kidnapping, attempted murder, eight counts of terrorism, and other charges to be named later. You have the right to remain silent..."

Riley and Priest spent another half an hour with Briggs. She was furious, but having Alexander Kimaris in custody took a lot of edge off her anger. She ordered Priest and Riley to both have a full report on her desk by the end of the day, and left to call the DA about Kimaris. Priest offered to stay with Kimaris until he was actually behind bars, just to make sure Marchosias wasn't setting them up, and Riley offered to drive Stanton and Kenzie home. Stanton asked to go to her office instead.

Riley parked in the alley and looked into the backseat. Kenzie was curled up, still using Priest's coat but now as a pillow.

"She looks too peaceful to move her," Stanton said.

Riley nodded. She looked at Stanton and finally asked what had been eating at her for years. "What happened?"

Stanton kept her eyes on Kenzie. "What do you mean?"

"You know what I mean," Riley said. "You were *the* cop. Every woman who set foot in the police academy knew your name. We idolized you. You showed us that it could be done."

"And you don't think that came with some pressure?" Stanton said. "I didn't ask to be the leader of a women's movement. I just wanted to be a cop."

Riley said, "So you were just crushed by the pressure?"

Stanton relaxed against the seat and looked out the windshield. "No. That was part of it, the stress. But..." She shook her head. "You're looking for some big revelation, right? My parents were killed by a mugger I let go, or I saw my partner get shot right in front of me. I'm sorry to disappoint you. I was the primary on a call that came in, two bodies in an apartment. Landlord heard the shots and called us. So I walked in, and there's a man lying in the kitchen minus his head. Woman was in the living room, on the couch. She was lying there peacefully. Just a little hole in the side of her head.

"She had a history at the local hospital. Bruises, broken bones, bloody noses. He didn't even bother to make sure the marks didn't show. He didn't care. She got her hands on a gun, and the next time he hit her, she hit back. And then she went to the living room, lay down, and killed herself. And I stood over her body and looked down at her, and I knew that I couldn't do it anymore. I couldn't stand over any more bodies. I couldn't hear one more goddamn sad story. So I got a little help. And then I got a little more help. And by then..." She took her glasses off and rubbed the bridge of her nose. When she opened her eyes, Riley saw they were the same brilliant ice blue that she remembered.

"You want to prevent yourself from becoming like me?" Stanton said. "Keep those partners of yours. Priest and..."

"Gillian."

Stanton smiled and nodded. "I remembered the name. I just like the way you say it."

Riley looked down and then looked at Kenzie in the backseat.

"I didn't have anyone like Kenzie to help shoulder the burden. I didn't have someone who would be mad because I ran out in the middle of the night. You're doing all right, Riley. Just remember that you don't have to do it alone."

Riley said, "Thanks."

"Any time. Will you help me get Kenzie inside?"

"Yeah."

They got out of the car, and Stanton gently took Kenzie off the backseat. Kenzie stirred and rested her head against Stanton's chest. Riley unlocked the office's back door and held it open for them to go past. Stanton directed Riley to a flight of stairs on the opposite side of the greenhouse and Riley went up to unlock the door to a spartan loft. Stanton went inside and deposited Kenzie onto a threadbare couch. Stanton smoothed Kenzie's hair over her burnt face, touched her lip with one finger, and then went back to the door.

"Thank you, Detective Parra. For everything you did tonight."

"She was my partner, too. Once." She smiled and held out her hand. She realized Stanton might not be able to see it and said, "I'm... um..."

"I see it. I just don't comprehend."

Riley smirked. "It's a baby step."

Stanton shook Riley's hand.

"Before you go," Stanton said, "I need to give you something."

Gillian's lower body was framed by sunlight from the window, her legs twisted under the sheet. Riley sat gently on the edge of the bed, careful not to disturb the mattress more than necessary, and touched Gillian's cheek. She trailed a light touch down over her jaw, to her throat, down her exposed arm and then back up. Gillian's eyes finally opened as the touch passed over her lips, and she focused on Riley almost immediately. She rolled onto her back, stretched, and looked at what Riley had been using to touch her. "Wow. That's beautiful."

Riley held it up and twirled the stem between her fingers. "A white rose. For you."

Gillian took it and smelled. "Mm. I'm still mad at you for leaving last night."

"I know."

"I know you had to. I know Priest and Kenzie were in trouble... are they all right?"

"Yes."

"Good. I know that you didn't have a choice. But I want to be irrationally mad."

Riley bent down and kissed Gillian's lips. "I love you for it."

Gillian touched Riley's face with the rose.

"I talked to Briggs this morning. I have to write up a report about everything that happened by the end of the day. I figure if I start sometime this afternoon, it should give me enough time. But until then... I think I'm going to sleep."

Gillian smiled. "Good girl."

"I need you here. So I called and got the day off for you. I hope you don't mind."

"You mean I don't have to get out of this bed, and go deal with death, *and* you'll get into the bed with me and stay until the afternoon? I'll cope."

Riley chuckled. She touched Gillian's shoulder and said, "I think I just need someone watching over me. I want you to be that person."

"I'll do my best."

Riley smiled and bent down to kiss Gillian. "I'll put the rose in some water and I'll be right back."

"Hurry," Gillian whispered, reluctantly letting Riley take the rose from her hand.

The clock changed morning to noon.

The white rose from Chelsea Stanton's greenhouse stood in a water glass, already angled toward the sun streaming in through the window. It cast a soft shadow on the bed where Riley lay on her side, limp with sleep. Gillian was curled against her back, head resting on Riley's shoulder, her hand occasionally brushing down Riley's side, to her hip, and then back up and around to her stomach.

Gillian didn't sleep the entire time, preferring occasionally to watch Riley sleep and listen to the sound of her breathing. Soon, she too drifted off with one hand lightly resting upon Riley's hip. They would sleep late, and Riley would miss her deadline to write a report for Briggs. Priest would cover for her. They would wake up, throw together a dinner with whatever they had in the fridge, and then go back to bed with the rest of the world. That would all happen later.

At the moment, Riley simply slept.

With a Broken Wing

Sometimes he just liked to stare at the blade. It was a beautiful blade, and the way it caught the light was almost unnatural. He turned his wrist, angled the blade down, cut at an unseen opponent. He reluctantly put the knife back in its sheath and hooked it on his belt. His sweatshirt covered it up, and he was already wearing a pair of black gloves in case he had to abandon the weapon. He didn't want to leave fingerprints; he was already making it far too easy on the police as it was. Not that they would catch him until he wanted them to.

He left his home through the outside entrance. The lights were on in the kitchen of his house, a deterrent to would-be robbers. Not that he believed anyone would dare infringe on his territory. He was untouchable.

He didn't ride the bus anymore. His friend told him that was too dangerous; the police would catch him too early if he kept up the schedule. It was disappointing, but he would cope.

There were a few cabs in the area. He considered taking one, but his friend said that it would be better to walk. This time, anyway. Next time might be different. It was hard to tell in advance just how the chips would fall. Each new adventure changed the playing field, just a little. That's what made it so exciting.

The sixteen block trip took him nearly to the center of town. The buildings were still nice here, and it was easy to forget how close No Man's Land was. He walked under the glow of streetlights, from one yellow spotlight to the next, his head down and his hands in his pockets. When he reached the bar, he went down a flight of stairs to the delivery entrance. The concrete walls rose above him on all sides. Like a tomb. His friend was in the shadows, in the corner, and he was happy to have an audience.

He wrapped his hand around the doorknob and found that it was open. He smiled, grateful for his friend's help. He slipped into the basement room and took out the knife. Cases of beer were stacked against the walls, looming on either side of him, forming aisles in the darkness. He loved the sound the metal made against the leather sheath. He moved quietly across the store room. He could hear music on the jukebox in the room overhead, even though the bar was closed. He wiped his hand over his face and balled his hand into a fist. He pressed it against first one eye, then the other, and calmed himself as he climbed the stairs.

He opened the door slowly. There was no need to rush. Rushing lead to mistakes. That's what his friend told him.

The bartender was sitting at a table with a ledger open in front of him. Money in a lockbox. The bartender jabbed the keys on a calculator and made some figures in his book.

The light from over the bar caught his knife again. He wouldn't be distracted.

David Bowie was playing on the jukebox. *Young Americans.* He liked that song.

He moved across the room slowly.

The bartender lifted his head just slightly, the animal part of his brain warning him that danger was near. But too late. Just a little too late. He wrapped an arm around the bartender's head and pushed his knife into the man's neck. After the first blow, he slashed the man's back before dropping him to the floor. It was messy, a dirty and wet mess, and he had to ignore the way his feet and hands twitched. The twitching disturbed him. Blood pooled around the bartender's head, his eyes staring wide and confused up at the ceiling.

He sheathed his weapon and knelt. He placed his hand in the blood and pushed it like a child finger-painting. He made the wide arc at the top and dragged his hand down, using the backs of his fingers to make the feathers. He took care to make sure the wings were perfect, adjusting the design as the victim continued to bleed. He made the second wing, forced to push a table out of the way with his hip to get the span right.

When he finished, he blotted his hands on the victim's shirt and stood up. He left the money on the table and went behind the bar. There was an old-fashioned push button phone, and he used a handful of bar napkins to pick up the receiver. He dialed using his knuckle so he wouldn't smear the dead man's blood on the buttons. His friend had told him the number, told him this was the next part of the plan. Still, it made him nervous. He trembled and looked down at his latest piece of work.

The phone was answered on the other end and a brusque woman identified herself. "Gail Finney."

"The Angel Maker claims another victim," he whispered. He gave the address of the bar and said, "If you hurry, you will arrive before the police even know about it."

He hung up the phone and stuffed the napkins into his pocket. He scanned the room to make sure he'd left nothing but the angel. He left the room as David Bowie stopped singing and the records began to shift to play the next programmed song. He was down the stairs and through the basement before it started to play.

His friend was waiting when he left, stepping from the shadows to follow him up the stairs. "Did you make the call?" His friend's voice was deep and dark. It reminded him of the evil tiger in the jungle movie he'd loved as a kid.

"Yes."

"Good. You did very well tonight."

He smiled. He made sure his sweatshirt covered his knife before he stepped out onto the street. He could hear an engine overhead and craned his neck to look for it. His friend stopped, too, and they watched as a small Cessna airplane flew between two apartment buildings. There was barely enough room for it, even tilted as it was. It was extraordinarily low.

His friend touched his shoulder. "Nothing to concern us. Go. We'll meet again soon."

He smiled. "I can't wait."

As he and his friend parted ways, the plane hit the ground with a sound like a giant tin can being destroyed. Soon, sirens filled the air.

"The next time you complain about me spending too much time at work, I want you to remember this." Riley slammed the car door and slipped the chain around her neck. Her badge fell to mid-chest, bumping against her as she walked toward the crime scene. Priest followed behind her, contrite. "I was out the door. Coat on, badge in the desk, actually physically walking to the door."

"I know," Priest said. "I apologize."

Riley said, "I'll let you explain to Gillian. I've been good for almost two weeks. I've been sleeping well, coming home on time, spending time with her, and now..."

"I'm sure she'll understand."

"Yeah," Riley said. She checked her watch and saw she was a half hour late for dinner. If she had been a little faster, or if she had ignored Priest's comment about their paperwork, they wouldn't have been there when Briggs came out of her office and told the first detectives she saw to gear up. She and Gillian could have been halfway through their meal by now. And that meant they could have been ten or fifteen minutes away from dessert, and that was really pissing her off. That, and the fact they were responding to a call that should have gone to the National Transportation Safety Board.

The street was blocked by yellow crime scene tape in both directions, and a crowd of spectators had gathered despite the lateness of the day. Two uniformed policemen were managing the crowd, while two more were standing by the wreckage of the plane.

The plane had impacted an el station on its way down, breaking all the glass and leaving the frame a twisted husk in its wake. It then took a quick nosedive toward the street. Riley guessed it was attempting an emergency landing on Madison Street. He didn't quite make it. The nose of the plane was crushed against the brick wall of a food bank.

One of the cops approached her. "Ma'am. We were the first ones on the scene."

"Why didn't you call the NTSB?"

"We did, ma'am, but they haven't arrived yet. We thought we would call homicide as well because... well..." He gestured at the plane and they followed him to the wreckage.

The pilot was slumped in his seat, obviously dead. Blood stained the front of his shirt and most of his face. The uniformed officer took out a flashlight and shone it at the windshield. "My partner noticed these."

Riley crouched and looked through the side window. The glass was cracked, but she could make out three distinct holes in the glass. She wasn't positive, but the way the glass had broken implied that the three holes came before the rest of the damage. She focused on the pilot and looked closer at his wounds. There was a wound above his right ear that could have possibly come from a bullet grazing his head.

She sighed and turned to look at Priest. "Get the ME down here. Looks like we could have a homicide. And the feds will be involved. Fun times."

Priest winced as she took out her phone. "Sorry again."

"Don't worry about it." She put her hands on her hips just as her cell phone vibrated. "Shit. That will be Gillian calling to..." She frowned at the display and flipped the phone open. "Detective Parra."

Briggs said, "Detective. I know you're already busy..."

"Yeah, kind of," she said. She turned to look at the plane. "It looks like the plane crash was really a homicide. We're waiting for the ME and the NTSB and the rest of the alphabet..."

"Riley," Briggs said. "It's the Angel Maker."

Riley tensed and looked back at Priest. "Don't tell me."

"Our boy is back. He got a third victim."

Priest had finished her call and was watching Riley. Riley angled the phone away from her mouth and said, "The Angel Maker is back."

Priest said, "Go. I'll take care of this."

"Are you sure?"

"It's my fault, right?" Priest said. "Go."

Riley said, "Boss. Priest is taking the plane crash. Where is the new victim?" She snapped her fingers at Priest, who produced a notebook from her back pocket and held a pen at the ready. Riley repeated the address Briggs gave her, and Priest wrote it down. "On my way. Fifteen minutes. Priest already has the on-call ME on the way. I want Dr. Hunt at the Angel Maker scene."

"Any particular reasons above the obvious?"

Riley stopped talking as she moved through the crowd, and waited until she was out of earshot to continue her conversation. "She was on the scene for the first murder. She knows more about this guy than anyone, other than me and Priest. If we're putting together a task force to catch him, Gillian needs to be on it." She didn't add the real reason; if Gillian was the medical examiner for the Angel Maker case, she and Priest could be upfront about their theories. It would make things a lot easier, not to mention more enjoyable for Riley, if she was officially involved.

Briggs said, "All right. I'll call her with the address."

"Thanks," Riley said. She tossed the cell phone into the passenger seat and checked the address before she pulled away from the curb.

Riley didn't recognize Fielder's Choice by name, but she knew it immediately as she parked outside. She had been there two or three years earlier with a flavor of the month, some brunette who was into baseball. They had a big screen on one wall, and the place was decorated with framed satellite photos of various stadiums. Riley's favorite was Fenway Park, and she'd been admiring it when a drunk blonde enticed her to leave the game and the woman she'd come in with. The idea was foreign to her; she had come a long way from the woman who would be that fickle about who she spent time with.

She ducked under the crime scene tape trying to convince herself that the location had nothing to do with her. If the killer wanted to make that kind of statement, there were far better places for him to choose. The front door of the bar was open and Riley walked past a car parked in front of a meter to get inside. She stopped on the sidewalk, looked at the meter, and waved one of the cops over. "Who does this belong to?"

The cop shook his head. "Not really sure. We assumed it was the bartender's."

There were fifteen minutes left on the meter. Riley looked at her watch and shook her head. "Not unless he put money in the second before he died." She bent down and looked in the passenger seat. A laptop case, stacks of notebooks, and loose pens littered the seat. She straightened and hooked a thumb at the car. "Have it put into impound."

"Yes, ma'am."

Riley went into the bar and took in the scene. The victim was in the middle of the floor, closer to the back of the room than the front. He wore black jeans and a white shirt, his apron still tied around his waist. Riley noticed that one of the tables had been moved out of the way to provide room for the artwork.

One of the cops had followed her inside. "We got in touch with one of the employees. He's on his way down. He said the owner, Mitchell Reese, stayed late on Friday nights to do the books. A couple of the surrounding businesses are still open, but no one noticed anything."

"Shit," Riley said. "It's Friday?"

"Um. Yes, ma'am."

She already knew that she would have to beg on her knees for forgiveness, but to miss an actual date night... Gillian was going to kill her. She sighed and walked into the room. The jukebox was on, but no music was playing. She looked at the spread on the table. "Money in the lockbox," Riley said. "Our boy doesn't care about robbery. No signs of a struggle. Why was the bar closed? It's seven o'clock on a Friday night."

"We talked to his bartender, 'cause it seemed weird to us, too." The officer pointed at the big screen TV. "Satellite went out. He decided to close than have people complain all night. They probably still complained, but he didn't have to hear it."

Riley frowned. She saw a door that would have been behind the owner if he was sitting at the table doing the books. "What's through there?"

"Basement storage room."

Riley went to the door and saw that the door wasn't latched well. She used the toe of her shoe to push the door open and peered inside. A narrow flight of wooden stairs led down to the basement. There was no banister, but she saw a light switch about halfway down. She held out her hand to the cop. "Light."

He handed her his flashlight and Riley switched it on. She went down to the switch, turned on the light, and crouched to get a better look at the basement. She saw shelves full of faded cardboard boxes that held glasses and napkins. She saw a door on the opposite end of the room and straightened to tell the officer to have someone check it out. Before she could speak, she heard movement at the far end of the room.

Riley held up a finger to keep the cop silent and drew her weapon. "I'm going to check that door." She nodded toward the corner where the noise originated and the cop nodded. He took his gun out as Riley started down.

She moved quickly across the floor, moving toward the shelves. Someone was definitely at the far side of the room. She knew it couldn't be this easy. The Angel Maker wouldn't get himself cornered in a damn basement. But that didn't make her any less excited as she moved down the rows of shelves. When she reached the far end, she stopped and said, "Let me see your hands."

Ten slow seconds passed before a pair of hands extended from behind the shelf. The hands were decidedly feminine, and Riley wondered if an employee might have witnessed the murder. Her hopes rose again, but she kept her guard up.

"I want you to come out slowly. Keep your hands where I can see them."

The woman stepped out of the shadows, not frightened or anxious as Riley would have expected. She wore a purple dress shirt partially buttoned over a white T-shirt and a black skirt, her blonde hair hanging in her face. When she looked up, Riley realized why the woman was so calm, but it ratcheted up her own anxiety a little. "Gail Finney, you are under arrest."

"Oh, come on," Gail said. "Do you want to put your gun down?"

"No. Trespassing on a crime scene," Riley said. "That's a good starting point."

Gail shook her head. "Look, I got a call. Some creep claiming he was the Angel Maker. I almost didn't even come down here, but I thought I should at least check it out. And I called the police as soon as I realized this wasn't just a joke."

Riley said, "And then decided to hang around and get an eyewitness account of how the cops screwed up? Put your hands on your head and turn around."

"I'll be out by midnight," Gail said, complying with Riley's instructions.

"I'm pretty sure all the judges you're friends with already went home for the weekend," Riley said. She fastened the cuffs on Gail's wrists and said, "You'll have to sweat it out until Monday." She made sure the cuffs were tight. "Piece of advice, don't be yourself. We might find you with a shiv in your back tomorrow morning. That's all kinds of paperwork."

Gail squirmed against Riley's cuffs. "Well, Detective Parra. I never knew you were into bondage. I mean, I'd heard rumors that you liked it rough..."

"Right to remain silent. Try it on for size." Riley turned Gail around and motioned for the cop to come forward. "Read this woman her rights. And use the card. Don't miss a single word or we'll hear about it."

"Who is she?" the cop asked.

"Gail Finney," Riley said. "The genius reporter who gave the Angel Maker his name."

Gail smiled as Riley handed her over to the cop. "And apparently he appreciated the attention. It kind of has a nice ring to it, don't you think?"

Riley resisted the urge to take one of the bottles off the shelf, although she wasn't sure if she wanted to drink it or use it as a blunt instrument. Gail Finney was a reporter and local radio show host who used her pedestal to antagonize the police. She frequently compared them to the Gestapo when she wasn't declaring them the Keystone Kops of No Man's Land. She was a piranha, and she delighted in making the police look like idiots, and she had just spent a good half hour walking around Riley's crime scene.

To the cop, Riley said, "Who cleared this building?"

"I-I thought... my partner said that he..."

"Shut up," Riley said. "Get her out of here."

Riley watched the cop go up the stairs with the police department's number one rival. She was going to catch hell for this. She pinched the bridge of her nose and left before the lure of the alcohol became too strong to ignore.

The crime scene unit arrived, and Riley left the bar so they could work. She spotted Gail Finney in the back of a cruiser and crossed over to her. A uniformed cop was standing guard, and Riley sent him away with a nod of her head. She got behind the wheel of the car and looked at Gail in the rearview mirror. "Have you given any thought about whether you'll be the husband or the wife when you get to jail?"

Gail said, "That depends. Which one are you?"

Riley smirked. "I might not know a lot about you, Gail, but I know a couple of things. You will not wear that outfit until Monday morning." Gail looked down at her blouse as Riley continued. "The same blouse, and the same underwear? You'll be going crazy by tomorrow afternoon. Not to mention that pretty blonde hair of yours. How long does it take you to wash that and dry it? You and I both know you're not going to spend the weekend in jail for a story."

"Don't underestimate my dedication," Gail said.

Riley shook her head. "One time only offer. I'm going to forget I found you here. But in order to do that, I can't be reminded of it when I open the paper tomorrow."

"You want me to sit on the fact I saw an Angel Maker body in the flesh?"

"No," Riley said. "But anything you got inside that bar is out. Pictures, details, everything gets held back. And I want the recordings."

"What recordings?"

Riley pointed at Gail's chest. "That undershirt has a pocket, and there's a voice recorder inside it. I want that, plus the recording of the call you received from the Angel Maker."

Gail reluctantly took the recorder from her shirt. "Were you checking me out, Detective?"

"I just know reporters too well," Riley said.

"The tape of the call is still at the office. I was planning to send it to you guys anyway, as soon as I got back."

Riley nodded. "Sure."

Gail said, "You know, it seems like I'm giving up an awful lot for two days of freedom."

"I'm not really in a position to offer you anything else."

"Oh, but you are." Gail leaned forward. "I want an interview with you."

"Not going to happen."

"Not tonight," Gail said. "When this whole Angel Maker thing is done. When the killer is caught and we can put this whole mess in perspective, I want to sit down and have an interview with you."

"You want to steamroll me and make me, and by extension the police department, look like an imbecile."

Gail shrugged. "Handle the case well and I won't have any ammunition."

"One interview, on my terms," Riley said. "And you don't print a word beyond what you would have gotten on the other side of the yellow tape."

"Agreed."

Riley got out of the car and opened the back door. Gail held out her cuffed hands, and Riley said, "If you print anything, and I mean one *word* beyond what we agreed, and I'll have you in jail for a lot longer than two days."

"Even if you have to fabricate charges."

Riley ignored the jab as she undid the cuffs and stepped back. Gail stepped out of the car and said, "The same goes for you. If you back out of the interview once the Angel Maker is in custody, I'll become your worst nightmare."

"Oh, you're already in the top four, Miss Finney. Don't go far, we're going to want to talk to you about why you got that call."

"Looking forward to it, Detective." Gail winked and walked to the crime scene tape.

Gail ducked underneath the tape as a blue van parked at the corner. Riley recognized it and groaned. "Out of one frying pan..." She moved to intercept Gillian, and they reached the tape at the same time. Riley lifted it and Gillian ducked underneath. "Hey. Sorry."

"Thanks," Gillian said. "And no, don't apologize. It's fine. Most couples go out to dinner on Friday night. Curl up on the sofa with a DVD. But no, I date Riley Parra, so I get called to drop everything and come look at a dead body."

"Sorry."

Gillian reached out and touched Riley's hip. "No, I'm sorry. I'm just venting a little. I'm not really mad. At least, not mad at you. How are you doing with all of this?"

Riley hadn't realized it until Gillian asked, but she could feel her rage reach the tipping point. Gail Finney was just the focus of it, at the moment. "He hit again, Jill," she said, her voice tight. "And he fucking bragged about it to *Gail Finney.* I want him."

Gillian moved her hand to Riley's shoulder and rubbed gently as they walked toward the bar. "You'll get him. You have a good support team."

Riley smiled and nudged Gillian. "As long as I don't run you away by constantly canceling dinner dates. I swear I'll make it up to you."

"You'd better. How bad is it?"

Riley looked toward the bar. "Same as the others. Owner was caught by surprise. I'm thinking the killer got in through the basement door, came in from behind him. He'd have to have a lot of inside information, though. That basement would have been pitch black, not to mention the fact he would have had to time it perfectly for the owner to have his back to the door. And who plans for a sports bar to be closed at six o'clock on a Friday night?"

Gillian looked back to make sure her assistant was still unloading the van. "Think his partner lent a hand?"

"I think his partner planned the whole thing out, start to finish."

Gillian stood in the doorway and sighed as she examined the scene. "Okay. Get out of here and let me work."

Riley let Gillian go into the bar and walked around to the alley. The officers had set up spotlights to illuminate the stairs that led down into a concrete cell. The edges of the space were lined with empty boxes and delivery pallets, almost completely hiding the entrance to the basement. A woman in a CSU jumpsuit was dusting the doorknob and Riley waited until she was done to ask her questions. "Found anything yet?"

"A few partials," she said. "But some of them are smeared. I think the guy wore gloves. The only matches we'll get are from employees and the victim. Maybe a couple of delivery guys."

"Don't discount anyone yet," Riley said. "The killer had a pretty good idea of how this place was set up. Could have been someone with inside information. Let me know if you find anything."

Riley turned and examined the rest of the alley. She walked slowly with her eyes sweeping the alley from one wall to the other. The spotlights threw unnaturally elongated shadows across the ground. An officer passed her going the opposite direction and Riley said, "There aren't any bus stops around here, right?"

"I don't think so," the officer said.

Riley resisted the urge to curse as she thanked the cop and continued walking. They had played their hand and let him know they were on to his pattern. He would stop using the bus to get to his victims. They were back to square one and it was because she jumped the gun. She resisted the urge to punch the wall as she reached the end of the alley.

Most of the businesses were closed for the night, their front doors and windows protected by pull-down grates. Riley realized they were only a few blocks away from the current edge of No Man's Land. Every year it was a little further in, another block taken over and forgotten. She wondered how long it would take before it had spread everywhere.

There was an el station nearby. Maybe the Angel Maker had only changed his method of mass transportation. The buses may be out, but he could have chosen the el or a taxi. She had a vague idea of where the first two murders had taken place in relation to the bar. She closed her eyes and pictured a map of the city. She added the bar to the pattern and saw a forty-five degree angle with a small tail angling to the northeast. No help, even if there was a pattern being made.

Riley turned and kicked a newspaper kiosk. It hurt her foot more than the machine, and she grimaced as she walked back to the crime scene. Even if Gillian hadn't found anything, it would calm her to be in the same room. The honest truth was that the Angel Maker would most likely have to kill again before they caught him.

Riley spent another hour at the crime scene interviewing witnesses and getting a wide range of statements ranging from "I didn't see anything" to "I didn't know anything happened until the cops showed up." Gillian had to perform the autopsy before she went home, so Riley returned to the station to fill in the new information to their murder board. She added Mitchell Reese's name to the list that already included Bernard Wright and Russell Stone. She added the bar to the list of locations and then plotted it on the map. As expected, there was no discernable pattern so far. Her theory about the locations being dictated by bus schedules was irrelevant now.

Briggs saw Riley through the window of her office and came out to stand next to her. She eyed the board and said, "Busy night. Anything useful?"

"Nothing on the Angel Maker, except we know we didn't scare him into stopping." She capped her marker and tossed it onto the desk. "Priest is taking care of the plane crash."

"She called to let me know she was on her way to the airport."

Riley smiled. "Her first solo case."

Briggs frowned and said, "I'm sure she had a couple before she transferred."

"Right," Riley said. "Of course she did. I don't know what I was thinking."

Briggs said, "Dr. Hunt is performing the autopsy?" Riley nodded. "Okay. We got in touch with Mr. Reese's wife, but she's out of the state. She's flying back in, but she won't be here until tomorrow. Get some rest, Riley."

Riley checked her watch and estimated when Gillian would be done with the autopsy. "I'll do my best."

She waited until Briggs was back in her office before she went to the morgue.

Gillian was standing over the body from the bar when Riley arrived. The pilot was on another slab, but the medical examiner working on him was nowhere to be seen. Riley knocked on the door as she stepped inside, and Gillian looked over her shoulder and nodded at the equipment table. "Gear up."

Riley put on a pair of rubber gloves, a mask, and a backless gown before she approached the table. She had seen several hardened cops turn green just at the thought of being in a morgue during an autopsy, but she'd never had a problem with it. She stepped up next to Gillian and looked down at the mutilated back of Mitchell Reese.

"We certainly have a weird relationship."

Gillian smiled behind her mask. "If I wanted chocolates and roses, I would date an elementary school teacher. I checked the knife wounds first. It's definitely our guy. He severed the spinal cord with his first blow, and then he slashed at the victim's back to cause the rest of the bleeding. It was quick. Judging from the way the knife entered, the victim's neck was extended. I imagine the killer put an arm around the victim's head, twisted, and then stabbed with the other hand. It makes him right-handed."

"Narrows down the suspect pool, at least."

"Yeah, I just eliminated ten percent of the population. That has to make you feel good."

"I'm giddy," Riley said. "No struggle?"

"No. No defensive wounds, anyway. I don't think he had any idea someone else was in the room until it was too late." She looked back at the pilot and said, "Caitlin is going solo?"

Riley chuckled. "Yeah. Airplane drops in the middle of the street, pilot is dead of a gunshot wound."

Gillian raised an eyebrow. "What is this, *Monk?*"

"What?"

"TV show. They always had weird... crime scenes. You know what, never mind. Have you heard from her?"

"Briggs said she was on her way to the airport to talk with potential witnesses."

Gillian raised an eyebrow. "That should be interesting. I wonder if it's possible for someone to lie to an angel's face."

"Sure. I lie to you all the time."

Gillian laughed. "I'm touched and offended at the same time."

"His wife won't be in until morning, so Briggs is sending me home. Do you want me to wait for you?"

"No, I'm going to be another hour at least." She turned her head and pressed her mask to Riley's. "Love you. I'll see you when I get there if you're still awake."

Riley said, "You can wake me." She backed away from the table and took off her protective gear. She waved goodbye to Gillian and went downstairs to the lobby.

The lights were all turned down low to conserve energy, but it made the place feel like a museum after visiting hours ended. Riley was almost to the front door when it swung open and Priest stepped inside. Riley smiled at her and said, "Hey, Z. How'd you get here?"

"An officer drove me. I like the squad cars." She smiled, but she looked exhausted. Her suit jacket was draped over one arm, and the top button of her blouse was undone.

"How is the case going?"

"Tedious. It's a very small airport, and the only people there when the victim took off were the air traffic controller and a man who said he was waiting for another flight. They both heard the gunshots right after takeoff, but both of them put it down to a car backfiring."

"Where was the witness?"

"In the terminal. The airport has a single common area where people can buy tickets and wait for their flights. It has a big picture window that looks out onto the runway."

Riley smiled. "Did you watch any planes take off?"

"I did. The floor shook a little when they were taking off and landing. It was amazing."

"Not quite as elegant as what you do, but still fun to watch."

Priest nodded and looked down at her notepad again. "I noticed the bullet holes in the plane came in from a downward angle. So the victim was already in the air when the gun fired, but not very high."

"I wonder why he didn't just turn around and set down when he'd been hit."

Priest shrugged. "I'll probably find out. I'm going up to get my preliminary report out of the way. Anything happening with the Angel Maker?"

"No. He changed his MO, like we were afraid of. He took advantage of about a half dozen coincidences, too. Bar closed early because the satellite was out, got into the building through an unlocked basement access door that's barely visible from the street, happened to enter the room while the bartender had his back turned... I figure the demon gave him the game plan."

"Stands to reason," Priest said. She looked at her watch and said, "I should head up."

"I feel like a slacker. You and Gillian are still at work and I'm going home to curl up in bed."

Priest smiled. "We're the ones who begged you to get more sleep. It serves us right."

"Right," Riley said. "Remember that."

She patted Priest on the shoulder as they passed each other, and Riley went outside. She looked down the street toward her car and suppressed a groan when she saw who was leaning against the front bumper. "Thanks for the warning, Caitlin." She slowly walked toward the car, resisting the urge to go back upstairs for her gun. She whistled and snapped her fingers. "Get your ass off my car, Finney."

Gail pushed away from the car and shrugged. "Hey, easy. I thought we were friends now."

Riley unlocked her car and dumped her things on the backseat. "We're not friends. We're reluctantly helping each other out. What do you want?"

"Fulfilling my end of the deal." She held up a CD case. "This is the recording from the newspaper. The Angel Maker's call, in high quality MP3. Should I give it to you or your boss?" Riley held out her hand, and Gail handed the disc over. "I've been thinking about our deal. I want to make a minor adjustment. It would be way too easy for you to back out of the agreement once everything is said and done. Once the Angel Maker is in jail, everything I have is old news. So I want something exclusive."

"You're cutting in to my sleep time," Riley said. "Out with it."

"I want to follow the case with you."

Riley laughed. "Not a chance."

"I don't mean follow you on calls or anything like that. I want regular updates. Interviews once a week, or once a month, until the Angel Maker is in jail. It would be a chronicle of your investigation from start to finish, but not one word would be printed until after the case is closed."

"You're dreaming," Riley said.

"All I want to do is give the police department exactly what they've been asking for: a fair look at how you do your work. You get all the articles before they're published so you can reject it if you don't like something."

Riley framed an imaginary headline and said, "*Police Censor Reporter's Words. What are they hiding?* Pardon me for not leaping at the opportunity."

Gail rolled her eyes. "Every reporter in this city wants exclusives on the Angel Maker. I have the inside edge and I'm not going to let it go without a fight. I'd hate for your boss to find out you found a reporter on your crime scene and then let her go. Especially one with my reputation."

"It sounds an awful lot like you're trying to blackmail me."

"Is it working?"

Riley said, "You get one interview when this is over. Count yourself lucky for that. Thanks for the disc. And as long as we're amending the agreement, the moratorium goes for your little radio show, too. I figure both your listeners can wait until everything's settled before you give them the story." She got into the car and slammed the door.

"You will talk to me, Detective Parra," Gail said, stepping up onto the curb. Riley was glad the opportunity to 'accidentally' hit her had been taken away from her. "That's a promise."

Riley pulled away from the curb without looking back.

Gillian got home a little past eleven to find Riley waiting with two TV dinners and a lit candle. They had a semblance of dinner before Riley took Gillian to bed and made love to her. As Riley was falling asleep, Gillian kissed her cheek and whispered, "That'll do for now." Riley kissed Gillian's temple and fell asleep with a smile on her face.

Riley parked outside of Priest's building the next morning at six. She started up the stairs, but hesitated when she heard the sound of singing from the church on the first floor. She had twice walked in on Priest 'enjoying' the worship, which was as close to masturbation as she thought angels could get. She didn't need to walk in on that again, so she turned around and walked down the block to the cafe.

She took a cup of coffee to a table by the window and reluctantly searched for Gail Finney's byline. The front page was dominated by a photograph of the crashed plane, with a small snippet about "investigating detective Caitlin Priest." Riley made a note to share that with Priest when she got back. She finally found a small story about the bar three pages in. It reported that Mitchell Reese had been murdered, but there was absolutely no mention of the Angel Maker's involvement.

Riley released the breath she had been holding and folded the paper. The only downside was that she now officially owed Gail Finney an interview. She checked her watch, saw that she had been waiting half an hour, and decided that would have to be close enough. She got a refill and a second cup for Priest, along with a bag of biscotti. She tucked the paper under her arm and walked back down the block to Priest's apartment.

She knocked on the door and waited for Priest to invite her in before she turned the knob. The first thing she noticed was that Priest had finally taken her advice and furnished the apartment. Thrift store furniture made up the living room, and a small television was mounted on an old desk. She smiled when she saw that the TV had a rabbit ear antenna and obviously had never been turned on.

She spotted Priest in the kitchen, sitting cross-legged on the floor. Her dress shirt was unbuttoned over a white T-shirt and untucked. She wore black trousers with her bare feet sticking out from the cuffs, her shoes and socks on the dining room table atop her neatly folded suit jacket. She smiled. "Good morning, Riley."

"Morning. I got you coffee, and a paper." She held out her hand and Priest took it. She levered herself up off the floor and Riley handed her the newspaper. "You're famous."

Priest unfolded the paper and read the first paragraph of the story. "Oh. That's embarrassing."

"Wait until they snap a picture of you walking the crime scene. It's never the dramatic, *CSI* type shot. You're almost always bending over or squinting into a light or something. Of course, knowing you, you'll probably look like a supermodel frolicking on the beach."

Priest blushed. She folded the paper and placed it on the dining room table.

Riley finally gave in to the urge and said, "So, did you rub one out or should I go back down to the cafe for a few minutes?"

Priest frowned as she put on her socks. "Pardon?"

"The worship." Riley nodded toward the floor. "Did you get your day off to a good start?"

"Oh! Yes." She rolled her shoulders and stretched. "It was particularly enlightening today. I had a long night."

"Redecorating?"

Priest looked into the living room and smiled. "No, that was a few weeks ago. Do you like it?"

"It's a good start," Riley said.

Priest nodded. She sat down to put on her shoes. "I spent last night following a few leads on the plane case. The pilot was killed by a shotgun blast, and the switchboard received several calls last night reporting a loud gunshot. I triangulated the origins of the calls and determined the gunshot came from the southwest corner of the airport's landing strip. No hunting is allowed within a hundred yards of the airport."

"So it looks like it wasn't an accident, and that's why he didn't land," Riley said. "Whoever had shot him was probably waiting to finish the job if he came back down."

Priest nodded as she followed Riley out of the apartment. "I found the next closest airport. He was heading straight for it when the plane started its descent."

Riley said, "Great work, Caitlin. You're almost to the point where I swoop in and take all the credit."

Priest smiled. She looked up into the sky as they left the building, and then looked into the front door of the church. Services were just letting out, and she nodded hello to a few of the women who left. "You seem to be in awfully good spirits considering the Angel Maker is back."

Riley hadn't realized it, but it was true. While she wasn't exactly in a happy mood, she was a far cry from the kiosk-kicking woman in the alley the night before. She shrugged and said, "A night with Dr. Gillian Hunt, the best medicine."

Priest waited until they were in the car before she continued the conversation. "I don't think it will be possible to find a pattern with this killing. The bus route was an anomaly, created specifically for you to find. If the demon who attacked you told the truth, the original pattern was just a way to get your attention. The only way we're going to stop him is to stop the demon controlling his actions."

"Yeah. Any idea how to do that?"

"It should be easier to find the demon than the man. Once we do, I may be able to release his hold on the Angel Maker."

Riley said, "Will it really be that simple?"

Priest looked out the window, deep in thought. Finally, she said, "The demon didn't create the murderous urge in the Angel Maker. The Angel Maker was likely on the precipice of violence when the demon sniffed him out and made his first move. Whispering in his ear. The closest approximation is a hypnotist. He can't make someone do anything they're morally opposed to. He can just make a suggestion."

"So he's a backseat driver."

"Essentially, yes."

Riley slowed and stopped for a red light. She ran her bottom teeth along her top lip and said, "How do we find him?"

"Once I close the pilot case, I'll go back and examine all the crime scenes. There may be a remnant, something I missed the first time around. And I haven't even seen the latest scene. Demons and angels both leave a sort of trail behind them. There's no way to prevent it. I haven't felt anything yet, but maybe we'll get lucky."

Riley sighed and drummed her hands on the steering wheel. "I don't like relying on luck."

"He doesn't appear to be giving us much else to work with."

The redhead was perched on the edge of a seat in the waiting area at the top of the stairs. One leg was bouncing and her eyes skipped from one surface to the next. Riley nodded for Priest to continue on to the office.

"Mrs. Reese?" The woman looked up hopefully, and Riley extended a hand. "Detective Riley Parra."

"Oh," she took Riley's hand. "The lieutenant told me I could wait for you at your desk, but I didn't want to impose..."

"That's fine," Riley said. She looked toward her desk and saw the Angel Maker whiteboard. If the news hadn't yet connected Mitchell Reese's death to the serial case, there was no reason to drop that bomb on the poor woman. "Why don't we talk in here?" She guided the new widow into an interrogation room and closed the door.

"I'm not a suspect, am I? I-I was in Toronto for a business..."

Riley smiled. "Not at all, Mrs. Reese. I just thought you might like some privacy. Please, have a seat."

"Thank you. Please, call me Elizabeth." She folded her hands on top of her purse and Riley saw that her fingers were trembling. "The woman I spoke to didn't tell me anything specific. Did you find the person who killed Mitch?"

"We have a strong lead," Riley said. "We just wanted to know a little bit more about your husband before we continued with the investigation."

Elizabeth nodded. "It was someone he owed money to, wasn't it?"

Riley remembered the full lockbox on the table. "Why would you think that?"

"Mitch had a 'system.'" She laughed sadly and shook her head. "He worked in that bar for about ten years before he decided he'd seen enough games to predict the winner of any game anywhere. He placed a few bets, got lucky, and decided he was untouchable. I'm sure you can figure out how that went. It never got so bad that bookies were threatening to break his knees or anything, but he got a few guys mad at him. When you called and said he was dead, I just... I assumed..."

"There was a lockbox near him," Riley said. "It was full of money. We don't think robbery was a motive."

Elizabeth frowned. "Oh. I feel terrible, but that's quite shocking. I was always so worried that he was going to cross the wrong person and that would be it. I guess I prepared myself to blame him. God, you must think I'm terrible."

Riley said, "Of course not. If you need some time to process the..."

"No," Elizabeth said. She wiped at her eyes and blinked rapidly as she leaned back in her seat. "Y-you said you had a suspect?"

"At the moment, we're keeping this information under wraps, but we have reason to believe that your husband was killed by someone that the press is calling the Angel Maker."

Elizabeth's eyes widened. "Oh, my God. So... it was just a random thing?"

"It appears that way. We need to know if there was anyone specific your husband was frightened of. Anyone who might have known how to take advantage of the vulnerabilities at the bar to get in unnoticed. A former employee or..."

"What vulnerabilities?"

Riley said, "The killer got into the bar through the basement entrance."

"That's not possible." Elizabeth shook her head as she considered what Riley had said. "There isn't a doorknob on the outside of that door. Are you sure it was the right place? M-maybe this is a mistake. Fielder's Choice."

Riley recalled the technician dusting the door for fingerprints. "There's no mistake. I was at the crime scene. I saw it myself."

Elizabeth frowned at her. "No. Mitch was always worried some drunk might sneak down there and rob him blind. So he had a door installed that only had a doorknob on the inside. He would have to go down and open the door himself for deliveries."

Riley's mind raced as she considered the possibilities. She looked at her watch and said, "Mrs. Reese, I apologize for running out like this, but if you're certain there wasn't a doorknob on that basement entrance..."

"I am absolutely positive."

"In that case, you may have given me very valuable information." She wanted to get on the phone as soon as possible, but she couldn't be rude to the widow of their victim. "I can arrange for you to identify your husband, if you would like."

Elizabeth started to say something and then just nodded. Riley walked around the table and put a hand on the woman's shoulder and said, "I'll send an officer in to sit with you until you're ready."

"Thank you, Detective."

Riley nodded and left the room. She spotted Priest at the stairs, just shrugging into her coat, and ran to meet up with her. "Hey, wait. I have a question."

"Okay." She held up a set of keys. "I got permission to use a squad car."

"Wow," Riley said. "Uh, listen. Could the Angel Maker's partner... create a different kind of door?"

Priest frowned. "What do you mean?"

"The widow of our latest victim swears the basement entrance to the bar didn't have a doorknob on the outside. The Angel Maker couldn't have gotten inside. But the door I saw had an exterior knob."

Priest stopped at the landing. "A demon wouldn't have let that affect his plans. He would have just knocked down the door or found another way inside that didn't require a door. There's a chance he could have transmuted the door to create a knob, but why would he?" She crossed her arms and looked at the floor as she thought. "He most likely would have physically replaced the door with a different one."

"Why go through all that trouble?"

"Perhaps it was important that the Angel Maker not be seen by his victim. He attacked Russell Stone from behind as well. We assumed it was necessary, to facilitate the wounds on the back, but perhaps he was worried about being recognized."

Riley bumped her fist against Priest's shoulder. "That's progress, Priest."

"Thank you."

"Good luck at the airport. I'll give you some advice, too. You decided the pilot didn't land when he got shot because the shooter was standing on the tarmac."

"Right."

"So why didn't whoever you interviewed at the airport notice someone firing a shotgun at a plane that was taking off?"

Priest raised an eyebrow and pointed at Riley. Riley winked at her and headed upstairs as Priest went to retrieve her car.

Riley scanned the crime scene photos that included the door. Now that she knew what she was looking for, the door was obviously new. The frame was weather-beaten, but the door itself didn't have a single mark on it. The door opened inward, which meant the hinges were on the inside. The demon would have had to already been inside to take it down. So why didn't it just kill the bartender and forget about the theatrics?

Because he's not the killer. The Angel Maker is.

It was important for the Angel Maker, the human, to actually do the crime. Riley assumed it was just another step in the corruption of the mortal. The demon was pushing the Angel Maker to damnation like Priest was helping Riley to be a better person. It made sense that the Angel Maker was her opposite, the champion of evil that her presence balanced out. All she had was the demon's word that it wasn't him.

The file had the phone number for other employees at the bar, and Riley picked up the phone and dialed one at random.

She went through four brief conversations before she found the bartender that had been on duty the night before. The man, James, was obviously still shaken, but he agreed to answer whatever questions he could.

"I still can't believe it. If I'd stayed, maybe he wouldn't have gotten killed, you know?"

"Believe me, sir. Your presence wouldn't have changed anything. We just want to know if anything unusual happened the night of Mr. Reese's murder."

"Other than the cable going out? Man, people were pissed off. Oh, God, I told Mitch that someone was going to kill him if he didn't get it fixed. Oh, shit."

Riley squeezed the bridge of her nose. "Did anyone suspicious come into the bar? Maybe they went down into the basement..."

"There was the water guy."

Riley perked up. "What water guy?"

"I don't know. He said there was a leak, a couple of buildings on the block reported their basements were flooded. So I got Mitch, and he showed the guy around down in the basement. There wasn't a leak."

"How long were they down there?"

"Fifteen minutes."

Riley thought about the basement. It was easy enough for Gail Finney to hide down there without being seen.

"Did you get a good look at this water guy?"

"Sure. He was wearing a blue shirt with the water company logo on it, and a baseball cap. He had some tools with him, too."

"What did he look like?"

"Kind of average height, I guess. Thin."

Riley resisted the urge to raise her voice. "Hair color? Did he have a thin nose, a sunken chin? Any identifying features?"

James thought for a long time until he said, "You know, I-I didn't really notice. I don't know. I guess I didn't pay very close attention to him, to be honest. He was the water guy."

"Did he find a leak?"

"Yeah. Mitch propped open the basement door for him so he wouldn't have to go through the bar. He fixed the leak and left."

Riley resisted the urge to slap the table. She thanked the bartender for his help before she hung up. She dialed the extension for the crime scene unit to tell them to retrieve the door, and then she had a lot of calls to make. There were only a handful of home improvement stores in town. She could only pray that one of them remembered selling a door to someone in the few days leading up to the murder.

A few minutes before five, Riley finally came out of the media room. Her eyes were blurry, and her back was stiff from hours of staring at the small flickering screen. She was halfway to her desk when Priest appeared at the top of the stairs and made her way over. "Riley. You solved the case."

"Fantastic. Doesn't feel like it."

Priest glanced at the whiteboard with their Angel Maker evidence. "Oh.

Sorry, not that case. The pilot." She pulled out her chair and sat down. Riley sat as well, issuing a groan as her back protested the change in posture. "Your clue about the witness at the airport. I checked him out and discovered he was in the middle of a divorce. He found out his wife was already seeing someone else."

"She was banging the now-dead pilot."

Priest nodded. "He said he was merely trying to scare the pilot. According to forensics, that's actually not hard to believe. They said it was a million to one shot that he actually hit the plane, and the shooter doesn't have any history of firearm training. He kept the shotgun for security, but there is no evidence he's ever even used it before. He's downstairs being booked now."

"He'll probably end up going down for manslaughter," Riley said.

"Most likely," Priest said. "How about you?"

Riley grunted. "The demon was at Fielder's Choice yesterday pretending to be from the water company. He claimed to have found a leak, and took the opportunity to change out the door. I got security footage from hardware stores in town and I spent the rest of the afternoon looking at them. Tedious, boring, dull. And most likely pointless. I mean, do I really think I'm going to find a demon on the cheapest security camera money will buy?"

"I don't think you're going to find him using traditional means," Priest said. "You have to feel him out. Eventually, you'll find him and stop him."

"In the meantime, people will die." Priest looked down at her hands. Riley leaned back in her chair and sighed. "Sorry, Caitlin. I didn't mean to bring you down after your first solo case. You did great. You're like a real cop."

Priest grinned and straightened the collar of her blouse and pushed away from her desk. "I'm going to get a cup of coffee. Want one?"

"Yes. Please."

Priest paused before she left. "You'll stop the Angel Maker, Riley. It's just another trial you have to endure."

"You guys have a set number of trials, right? Like I pass seven of them and I get a gold watch and retire?"

Priest pressed her lips together.

"Forget it. Make my coffee strong. I need to wake up after watching all that security footage."

Priest nodded and walked toward the break room. Riley laced her hands together and stretched, working the kinks out of her back. Another case that wasn't closed. Another notch in the Angel Maker's wall. She was getting damn sick of finding dead ends and following leads that went nowhere. She glanced toward the door and nearly cursed when she saw Gail Finney walking toward her. She stood up and turned the whiteboard so that it was facing the wall. She sat on the edge of her desk, arms crossed as Gail approached.

"Hey, Detective. Nice pose."

"How did you get in here?"

"I committed a murder and when the booking cops were looking the other way, I walked out." She pointed at Riley's desk. "You have my voice recorder. It's expensive, so I came to get it back. All I need is the machine; you can keep the tape."

Riley had already ejected the tape from the machine, so she took it from her desk and handed it over. "I had our tech guys look it over. Just in case you were trying to eavesdrop on the office."

"Damn, I didn't think of that. You must be more devious than I am."

"Don't sell yourself short," Riley said. "And don't let the door hit you on the way out."

Gail grinned and turned to leave. Priest came out of the break room with a mug in each hand, nearly colliding with Gail. They both took a step back, and Priest's eyes widened slightly as she barely kept from spilling the coffee. Gail smiled and said, "You must be the new partner. I'm Gail Finney." She held out a hand, realized Priest wasn't able to respond to it, and shrugged. "I've known Riley since the good old days of Sweet Kara. You have some big shoes to fill, missy."

Priest said nothing.

Gail waited and then turned to Riley. "Well, you're training them to shun me early." To Priest, she said, "I'm not as bad as she says. And I hardly ever bite." She winked and said, "Goodbye, Riley. Give my regards to the statue when she unclenches." She stepped around Priest and continued to the stairs.

Riley walked up to Priest and bumped her arm. "What the hell?"

"It's her."

Riley looked at the stairs where Gail was still barely visible. "What's her?"

Priest was deathly pale. "I can smell it all over her. She's living with demons, Riley. She's evil's champion."

"Gail *Finney?*"

Priest put the coffee down on a nearby desk, grabbed Riley's arm, and dragged her toward the break room. She shut the door behind Riley and said, "It fits."

"She's a newspaper reporter."

"You're a random police detective," Priest said. "Gail Finney is a reporter who spends the majority of her time badmouthing the police in print. She is a propaganda machine for the demons. Thanks to her, people distrust the entire department. She has a radio show where she can preach to the masses. And what does she preach?"

"Don't trust the cops," Riley said. She lowered herself onto the couch and clasped her hands between her knees. "How sure are you about this?"

"That she's your opposite? Positive. You don't get that... tainted by accident or by casual contact. But that doesn't mean she *knows* that she's being used. How well do you know her?"

"Too well," Riley said. "She's relentless. She smiles to your face so you're comfortable turning your back. Then she'll dig the knife in. She's your best friend until she buries you. If you say she's the one, then I believe it."

Priest crossed her arms over her chest and said, "Okay. So we accept she's the person we've been looking for. What do we do now?"

Riley looked up at Priest. "We stop her."

He had so many gloves. Gloves to wear during his activities, and another pair of gloves to wear after while he was coming home. He took one pair out and brought it to his face. He breathed deeply. He loved the smell of them. He put them on and walked back into his living room. His friend was waiting. "Tonight?" He was almost shaking.

"Not tonight. We don't have a victim."

"When?" He hated the neediness in his voice.

His friend stood and went to the window. "Patience. We will get more than enough blood on your hands before this endeavor ends."

He wanted to ask how it would end, but he was terrified to know. He just wanted to enjoy what was happening while it lasted. It was a joy. If it ended in his death, or in him being caged like an animal, he would accept that. Goodness and pain in equal measure, and he was getting so much goodness from their arrangement. So much joy. He could tolerate the consequences.

"Get some rest," his friend said. "We have a lot of big days ahead of us."

"Call me when we can have another victim."

His friend chuckled and nodded, silhouetted by the window. The front lawn was tree-lined, but some moonlight still came through. The streetlights on the corner were all broken. He turned and went back into his bedroom, flexing his fingers in the gloves. He would keep them on while he slept. He liked the feel of the leather on his palms.

A lot of big days ahead of them.

He couldn't wait.

Night Falls (Part One)

"I'm not going to lie to you, my friends. I'm afraid."

In No Man's Land, a bodega owner locked the front door of his shop. He really couldn't afford not to be open, but he also couldn't afford to be robbed every night either. He used a hook to grab the handle of the metal grating and stepped back to pull it down. He locked it, looked down the street at the kids gathered on the corner, and sighed as he slipped his keys into his front pocket. He picked up the little radio sitting on the ground next to him and turned it up. Gail Finney's radio show was comforting; it let him know that at least someone out there who cared about the way their world was going to hell.

"I'm afraid to leave my apartment at night. I double-lock my doors, and I'm sure you do, too. And it's only been getting worse. I don't want to live in a city where I'm afraid of my neighbors. I don't want to live in a city where I want to carry a gun when I go out to get the newspaper."

The woman looked nervously out the window at the sky. The sun was starting to set. She tapped her foot on the tile of the lobby and began to pace. She could hear Gail Finney's radio show playing over the security guard's radio as she moved in a wide circle. Finally, the elevator bell sounded and two men came out. She breathed a sigh of relief and tried to show them only irritation at their tardiness. The men moved to either side of her, and one held the door for her as they stepped out into the rapidly darkening day. They would walk her home and, more than likely, invite themselves in. She would sleep with them in exchange for getting home safely. And, to be honest, it would be nice to sleep peacefully knowing there were two tough men in the house with her. It was a small price to pay for security.

"How long do we have to wait for the police to do something? How many of you even remember that we have a police force in this town? The only people capable of making a living are criminals. The good people of this town have had enough."

The bell jingled over his brother's head, but the blood was rushing through his ears too loudly for him to hear anything clearly. He couldn't resist looking toward the counter at the old Arab sitting behind the cash register. His brother got a can of soda and carried it up to the counter. He would pay with a twenty, and when the old man opened the register for the change, they would pull their guns. He was shaking, and he heard that lady reporter talking on the radio behind the counter. He thought he heard the cash register open and pulled his gun, but it was too early. The clerk pulled his own gun. The clerk and his brother fired at the same time, and God, there was so much blood he didn't remember to empty the cash register before he ran from the store screaming.

"As if things weren't bad enough, this Angel Maker character is running around killing people. Apparently at random. The police certainly don't have any idea who he is or why he's killing people. So now in addition to everything else happening in No Man's Land, we've got to worry about some madman running up and sticking a knife in our backs."

The car rolled to a stop at the end of the street, and she approached cautiously. Never could be too careful these days. She heard the voice of that reporter lady on his car radio. That was kind of kinky, she thought, like they would have an audience. She slipped her hand into her purse, to the small gun she kept hidden there, as she leaned into the window. He was old, maybe fifty or so. He was nervous when he asked her for the price, and she was calm and considerate and put him at ease. He reached across the seat and unlocked the door. She slipped into the car and he drove into the alley. She remembered her birthday was coming up as he began to touch her. She'd be getting out of this business soon. Sixteen was just way too old to deal with this kind of thing.

"And for you who will ask me if I hate this town so much, why don't I leave it? To that, I reply with something we couldn't play over the radio. This is my town, folks. This is where I want to live, and I'm not going to abandon it because of the lazy sons of bitches who are wearing badges. I'm going to fight for my town, because I happen to love it. And if you love it, too, you won't stand idly by while the criminals and the drug dealers and the whores are taking over the street."

He kept the knife in his pocket as he left the building. The man in the courtyard behind him looked almost peaceful. His hands were at his sides, palm-up. A pair of red wings spread across the stone path as if they were sprouting from his back. The Angel Maker paused and looked up at the sky as the last traces of day faded and night took over. He smiled, crossed the street, and headed for home.

"This has been Gail Finney. I want to remind you to check out my reports every morning in The Ledger. Stay safe, folks. If you can."

Gillian picked up one of the newspapers on the table and almost immediately dropped it again. "Oh, God. Do you really need to bring that trash into the house?"

"Sorry," Riley said. She looked up from the article she had been reading and moved the paper Gillian had dropped. "Know thy enemy. I'm only reading up on her because Priest is positive she's my opposite number. The demons are using her to pull the town deeper into No Man's Land."

Gillian was still in her robe, her hair up following her shower. When she sat, the material draped and Riley was treated to an alluring peek at the curve of her left breast. She closed the paper so that Gail's article wasn't visible.

"I worry that you're poisoning your brain with this crap." She picked up a paper and flipped it open. "I can't even listen to her radio show for five minutes without wanting to punch her in the damn mouth."

"There's a fight I'd pay to see," Riley said. "I'm still trying to figure out how complicit she is in the whole mess. Is she saying these things because someone pushed her in the right direction, or was she already like this and the demons just latched onto her for their own purposes?"

"Does it matter?"

"If she's a puppet, there's a chance she can be saved."

Gillian nodded and flipped her paper to another page. "Ah, Garfield. Never controversial."

Riley smiled and pushed her hair out of her face as she read the rest of Gail's latest article. She reported on news stories, but she also had a small editorial space on the back page where she could rant to her heart's content under the freedom of the press banner. Riley didn't know why the paper wasted the space; her articles were full of backhanded comments and jabs at the police department. The department had sued on more than one occasion, but the cases only seemed to make her stronger and more popular.

Riley leaned back in her chair and rubbed her eyes. "Maybe you're right. Maybe I need a break."

Gillian put down her paper and stood up. She walked behind Riley's chair and began to massage her shoulders. "Maybe I could go make you a nice bubble bath. You could soak and I'll rub your feet. And higher, maybe." She bent down and kissed the top of Riley's head.

Riley turned her head and kissed Gillian's arm. "You know how amazing that sounds."

"But you need to research some more," Gillian said. There was no reproach in her voice. She knelt down and kissed Riley's neck and cheek. "All right. I'm going to bed. I'll see you in there in half an hour or I'm coming to find you."

"I'll be in soon, promise." She turned her head and kissed Gillian's lips. Gillian gave Riley's shoulders another squeeze before she walked away. Riley watched her go down the hall to the bedroom, already lamenting the loss of her combined bath and massage. But as appealing as it sounded, she couldn't just ignore Gail Finney.

Since discovering there was a champion working for the demons, the knowledge nagged at the back of Riley's mind. Everyone she met, everyone she read about in the paper, she couldn't help wondering if they were the one. Now that she knew who it was, she couldn't drag her feet. If she could prove that Gail was an unwilling pawn then there was a chance she could turn her into a double agent. She and Priest could show her what was really at stake, and turn her into a weapon for the good guys.

But if she already knew everything, Riley wasn't sure what the next step would be. She couldn't arrest someone for collaborating with demons. Even if she was sure the entire police department would back her up for arresting Gail Finney, she wouldn't fabricate evidence to do it. So what did that leave, murder? She wouldn't kill in cold blood, but if Gail discovered Riley was working with the angels it might come down to self-defense. She wasn't sure how she felt about that. She had killed in self-defense before, but the faces of those people - especially Sweet Kara - still haunted her daily.

She checked the kitchen clock and saw she had been staring into space for twelve minutes. She gathered her papers and put them into her bag, stretched, and turned out the lights in the kitchen. She locked the front door and undressed on her way to the bedroom, dumping her clothes into the hamper as she passed.

Gillian was curled on her side, and Riley slipped under the covers and spooned against her from behind. Gillian lifted her head from the pillow and said, "Good girl."

"What?" She kissed Gillian's shoulder.

"I said half an hour. That used to mean I wouldn't see you for forty-five minutes."

Riley put her hand on Gillian's stomach and pulled her closer. "I just had to remember what was waiting for me."

Gillian rolled onto her back and pulled Riley to her. They kissed, hands roaming under the blanket. Angels and demons and champions, Heaven and No Man's Land and Hell, none of it mattered. All that mattered was the woman underneath her. As long as she could keep that in mind, she would be just fine.

Gillian broke the kiss and brushed her lips over Riley's cheek. "So, is it too late for the bath and massage?"

"Never," Riley said. "I'll run the water."

Riley was standing in a basement, her clothes drenched from the downpour. She was walking in ankle deep water, gun in hand. She recognized the basement, but the dimensions were all wrong. It was the basement of Fielder's Choice, the bar where she had her run-in with Gail Finney a week earlier, but it was blown far out of proportion. The walls seemed to be a mile away, the water slowly rising up her legs. She moved toward the shelves where she had found Gail hiding in real life. The light coming from up the stairs shifted and changed colors. Darkening and brightening and then shifting from yellow to red to blue.

There was movement in the corner, just as in real life. Riley knew it was Gail even in the dream, but she wanted to believe it was the Angel Maker. She tightened her hands around the butt of her weapon, feeling the comforting texture of the plastic grip against her palm.

Gail was still in the shadows, a featureless silhouette. Then she smiled, and her teeth appeared floating above the darkness like she was the Cheshire cat.

"Do you think you'll get away with it?" Gail asked.

"I'm the police," Riley said. "I can get away with anything." She opened fire.

Gail's body was suddenly awash with the light from the discharge, thrown back against the wall. Everything was suddenly gunfire and blood, the water still rising around Riley's legs. She stepped forward and stood over Gail's corpse. She took aim again and emptied the clip into the reporter's crumpled form. Her gun didn't click empty for a long time, being a dream, and she was able to unload to her heart's content. When she finally dropped her arm, the room stank of copper and sulfur, and Riley smiled.

Riley jerked as something touched her face, recoiling away from the contact. It took her a moment to realize the water around her was from the faucet, and she was lying in the bathtub. Gillian was sitting on the edge, brushing the back of her hand over Riley's cheek. Riley closed her eyes and sagged against the smooth edge of the tub.

"Hey, it's only me," Gillian said softly. "You fell asleep."

Riley pushed her hands through her hair, smoothing it against her skull. "Yeah. Nightmare, I guess."

"I guess," Gillian said. "Want to talk about it?"

"No," Riley said. She could still see Gail's body jerk as the bullets entered it, and she remembered the satisfaction of pulling the trigger. It was far too vivid to revisit even with Gillian. "Help me out of here. Let's go to bed."

"Do you want me to towel you off?"

"Yes, please."

Gillian wrapped Riley in a towel before she bent down to drain the bath. When she straightened, Riley cupped her face and kissed her.

"Mm. What was that for?"

"For being there when I woke up."

Gillian smiled. "Well, I plan to earn more of those kisses."

"Good," Riley said. She kissed Gillian again, letting the kiss linger before she pulled back and said, "Let's go to bed." She put her hand in Gillian's and led her into the bedroom.

Riley spent the morning following up on witness reports from the previous Angel Maker murders. She was on the phone with Father Denis when she glanced up and saw Gillian crossing the room. Gillian's presence on their floor wasn't unusual in and of itself, but her expression gave Riley pause. Gillian caught Riley's gaze and she offered a wan smile before she gestured at Lieutenant Briggs' door. Riley mouthed, "Everything okay?" and Gillian shrugged.

Riley leaned back in her chair and watched Gillian knock on the door. Briggs called her inside, and Gillian ducked into the office and shut the door behind her.

When Riley finished her call, Priest said, "What was that about?"

Riley looked towards Briggs' office again. "I don't know."

The lieutenant's door opened and Briggs leaned out. "Parra. Priest." She hooked a thumb over her shoulder and went back into her office. Riley glanced at Priest before she stood up. Gillian was standing to one side of the desk with her hands clasped behind her back. She was in blue scrubs, her hair pulled back in a loose knot, and she looked like she had the weight of the world on her shoulders.

"We have a problem," Briggs said as she walked around her desk. She took a seat and said, "I'll let Dr. Hunt explain."

Gillian was sitting in front of the desk and turned in her seat to face the detectives. "A body was brought in last night, found dead in the courtyard of an apartment building. No one in the initial sweep of the building recognized him, and he didn't have any ID. Uniforms thought that it was a mugging, so it got sent to Robbery. I was doing the autopsy when I noticed something strange." She handed a file to Riley, their fingers brushing on the hand-off.

Riley flipped open the cover and looked at the autopsy report. "Cause of death was blood loss from multiple knife wounds."

"All the wounds were inflicted on the victim's back, despite the fact he was found face-up. No defensive marks." Riley looked up. "But no wings?"

Gillian shook her head. "The body was found at five-thirty this morning lying on a cobblestone path in the garden. Based on preliminary reports he had been dead for at least four hours. The building has lawn sprinklers set to go off at four-thirty every morning. The body and the entire scene got doused. It screwed up time of death determination for a while."

Riley said, "The wings may have been washed away."

Gillian nodded. "That's what I was thinking."

Briggs said, "I've asked Dr. Hunt to confirm the weapon is the same one used in the previous murders, and Robbery is transferring the case up to us. But far as anyone outside this office is concerned, this is *not* an official Angel Maker case. I'm sick of Gail Finney and her fucking radio show insinuating we're not doing our job protecting the people of this town."

"Insinuating?" Riley said under her breath.

"I want results, Detective Parra. We have four victims now."

"Yes, ma'am," Riley said.

Briggs said, "Dismissed."

Riley held the door for Gillian and Priest before she followed them out. She shut the door and said, "Results. It's not like we have any new information. The victim is a John Doe."

Gillian said, "I'm told the police are still canvassing the neighborhood. You'll get his identity eventually."

"Thanks," Riley said. She touched Gillian's elbow and said, "Great catch."

"All that time with you must have paid off. I'm Quincy now." She touched Riley's arm and said, "I should head back down. Stay safe."

"I'll see you later," Riley said. She watched Gillian go and then took her things off her desk. She motioned for Priest to do the same. Robbery Division was one floor down, just above the morgue. "Come on. Let's go see what the robbery guys have for us."

Priest followed Riley to the stairs. "I've been considering the situation with Gail Finney."

"Yeah, me too. I don't like our prospects."

"It can be difficult," Priest said.

Riley put up a hand to stop Priest on the landing. She lowered her voice and stepped closer to Priest so she could hear. "You've done this before, right? I mean, not you personally. But I'm not the first champion, and I'm sure Gail Finney isn't their first. Have the champions for good and evil ever gone head to head before?"

Priest looked toward the ground floor as if she expected help. "It's been known to happen. Usually they exist separately and never interact. They operate within set circles."

"Well, I don't think we can hope for that in our case. What has happened in the past?"

"They killed each other."

Riley blinked. "Every time?"

"Yes. In 1898, 1919, 1940, and 1971. The circumstances that bring two champions together are extremely volatile and usually coincide with great unrest on the physical plane. You set in motion a war the likes of which hasn't been seen in centuries. In 1919, the cause was the massive death toll of the flu pandemic. In 1940, it was the atrocities of the Holocaust." She sighed and leaned against the wall. "I admit I saw this coming as soon as you drove the car into Marchosias' building. I tried to..." She shook her head. "It's not use talking about it now. The important thing is to prevent an all-out catastrophe."

"I should just let it go?"

"I didn't say that," Priest said. "Focus on the Angel Maker. Focus on Marchosias. Maybe things will calm down. Just because you know her identity doesn't necessarily mean you have to do anything about it. If you manage to stop Marchosias their champion will be powerless. Cutting off the head kills the body."

"But if evil loses their champion, what happens?"

Priest shrugged. "Perhaps detente. But only if good loses their champion, too." She put her hands on Riley's shoulders. "If you're considering a sacrifice, it would be a stupid decision."

Riley brought her hands up and gently pushed Priest's arms away. "I'm not going to commit suicide. If I get backed into a corner and there's no way out, it'll be good to know something good can come from me dying. But I would never harm myself. For one thing, you'd be out of a job."

"It doesn't work like that," Priest said softly. "I just don't want to see you hurt. And if you think you're going to leave me behind to comfort Gillian..."

Riley said, "There. That's why you never have to worry about me killing myself."

Priest nodded and said, "Good."

Riley looked around to make sure no one had overheard their exchange. "Come on. The jerks down in Robbery are probably waiting for us."

Riley tossed aside the crime scene photos with disgust. She thought the other Angel Maker sites had been light on evidence, but this time the sprinklers had destroyed anything remotely useful. Halfway through reading the report, Gillian called up to let them know the knife wounds were a definite match. It was their boy, without a doubt.

Riley took the confirmation as an excuse to leave the report and visit the crime scene. She and Priest arrived a little before noon to find the crime scene tape was still blocking off the courtyard. The space was bordered by four walkways that opened out onto the garden through a series of stone archways. Paths of gray stone wound through the grass, circling rosebushes and willow trees. Riley ducked under the tape and walked to where the body had been found.

"Another public killing," she said. She pointed at the windows overhead. "Anyone could have looked down and seen him making his art."

"Robbery canvassed the building and didn't find any witnesses," Priest said.

Riley nodded and knelt to look at the stones. She couldn't see any blood between the cracks in the stones, but that didn't mean it wasn't there.

The north side of the courtyard faced the street. Riley assumed that was where the Angel Maker came in. It was strange that no one seemed to recognize their victim. If he wasn't a resident, what was he doing in the courtyard at one in the morning? The building didn't have security, but it was in a nice enough area that they didn't have to worry about drug dealers wandering through their garden.

"What do you think?" Priest asked.

"I think coming here to forget my frustration was a bad idea." She stood and stretched. "Are there any residents that the uniformed cops didn't get in touch with?"

Priest took out her notebook and checked. "Three on the first floor, and one on the third."

"Three on One and one on Three," Riley said. "I like the symmetry. Might as well check them out."

The foyer was dark, lit only by the windows on either side of the door. They crossed the black and white tile floor to the stairs, and Riley looked over her shoulder as they started up. "Just so you know, I might try to catch a nap in the break room when we get back."

"Aren't you sleeping well?"

"Not bad," Riley said. "But the past couple of nights, I've been having these nightmares."

"For how long?"

"About a week, in fact," Riley said. "Since you told me about Gail Finney. Why? Is that a symptom of two champions meeting?"

Priest hesitated before she answered. "How bad are the dreams?"

"I'd say a six, maybe a seven on the scale of the worst I've ever had."

Priest said, "I don't think so. I've never heard of a psychological aspect. It could be that it's just never been mentioned."

Riley looked at Priest's notes and went to the first apartment. "I'll keep you apprised. At the very least, it'll be good information for my replacement."

"I don't like those kinds of jokes, Riley."

"Yeah, but if I only did your kind of humor, I'd be stuck with knock-knock jokes. Do you have the picture of the victim?"

The apartment door opened and Riley showed the woman her badge. "Good afternoon, ma'am. We're investigating a murder that occurred here last night. We were hoping you could help us."

Riley changed into a pair of sweatpants and a light blue T-shirt with the number 8 on the back. She warmed up a glass of milk and drank it at the sink, staring at her reflection in the front of the microwave. She finished the milk, rinsed out the glass, and turned out the overhead light as she crossed to the bedroom. Gillian had called to say she had to do a rush autopsy for another case, so she was going to stay late. Riley reluctantly agreed, and even more reluctantly prepared to go to bed alone. It was far too familiar, reminiscent of the previous year when Gillian had left town. Riley didn't like remembering those nights.

She left the hall light on so Gillian would be able to see when she got in, and crawled under the blankets. She pulled Gillian's pillow to her chest and sighed, breathing in the scent of her lover. She hoped the smell would translate to her subconscious and bring nothing but good dreams, dreams about Gillian rather than the nightmares she had been having. She tossed and turned for a few minutes, turned on the radio so she wouldn't feel so alone, and finally fell asleep.

Gillian was dancing.

Riley sat on the edge of the bed in a dress shirt with the sleeves rolled up to the elbows, and watched as Gillian moved in the spotlight. The rest of the room was hazy, filled with smoke. Gillian wore a dress Riley had never seen before; it was pale blue, backless, and the movement of her muscles was hypnotic. When she turned, Riley saw that the gown was cut low in the chest and high on the hip. Her legs scissored underneath the material as she moved toward Riley. Her hips swayed. The music grew more raucous, a wild rockabilly song with guitars that sounded almost like screams as Gillian extended a hand to Riley.

"*Come on, Diablo!*" the singer yelled, and Riley was pulled from her seat. She held Gillian, their eyes locked, and they began to tango.

The dance was inappropriate to the music, but they didn't seem to care. Riley tore her eyes from Gillian and kissed her hard. Gillian returned the kiss with hunger, thrusting her tongue into Riley's mouth. Riley ran her hands down Gillian's bare back, and Gillian ran her hands over the crisp material of Riley's shirt.

One of Gillian's hands slipped between them, down to Riley's crotch. She squeezed and Riley suddenly became aware that she was wearing their strap-on. They didn't use it much, and Gillian always preferred for her to wear it. Riley groaned as Gillian's hand traced the shaft through her pants, and she thought she could actually feel the touch on flesh. Of course, since it was a dream, maybe she could...

Gillian moved her lips to Riley's ear and nipped at the lobe. Riley began to lift Gillian's gown, the rational part of her mind wondering if Gillian would want to recreate the dream when she got home. She could see herself explaining every detail, right down to the color of stockings Gillian was wearing in the dream.

Gillian pressed her lips against Riley's ear and whispered in a low, throaty voice: *"Did you think it would be that easy?"*

Riley smiled. "Do I have to work for it, sweetheart? Do you want me to beg?"

"Not that," Gillian said. Her voice was odd, sultry but at the same time like nails pressing against the base of Riley's skull. *"Your angel. Did you really think she was that powerful?"*

Riley leaned back. Gillian's hand was still on her crotch, rubbing, pushing her arousal to the edge. Gillian held tight, didn't let her retreat. Her eyes were dark, but at the same time seemed to glow from within. She smiled, and Riley was inexplicably sickened by the sight of it. Blood red lips pulling away from gleaming white teeth.

"Did you think she could just kick me out of such a perfect body? Did you think I would let her?"

"You're the Duchess," Riley hissed. She wanted to get away. Wanted to run.

Hands tightened on Riley's body, keeping her from escaping. *"I want you to call me that when you fuck me."*

Riley struggled, but the demon's grip was too strong. Riley realized her hand was on Gillian's hip, the flesh warm under her hand, but she couldn't seem to pull it away.

"I went away to learn how to be her. To learn how to fool everyone. And it worked. None of you, not even your pathetic angel, knows the truth. And your tattoo! You thought you were protecting me. It was all I could do not to laugh in your face. When you branded me with that mark, you locked me inside. You locked me inside your girlfriend. Forever." She bit Riley's earlobe until blood trickled down Riley's neck. *"What are you going to do about it?"*

Riley managed to get away when Gillian, the demon, the Duchess, and howled in pain and anger and frustration. The body was so familiar, but suddenly the eyes were completely inhuman. The mess of red hair looked like flames, tangles rising up like horns above her inhuman yellow eyes. Riley's body was electric, her muscles throbbing. She stepped forward, took a handful of the Duchess' hair, and yanked her head back. She kissed her hard, thrusting her tongue forward, and forced the Duchess to her knees.

"Give her back to me," Riley growled when she broke the kiss.

"Take her from me."

The blue dress ripped when Riley pulled it, and she used her superior weight to pin the Duchess to the floor. She managed to get her trousers open and she gripped the hot flesh inside. The Duchess spread her legs, her eyes wild, and she lifted her head to return Riley's kiss. She bit down, and blood flooded both of their mouths. Riley shoved the Duchess' legs apart and growled as she thrust inside and began to fuck her.

Riley woke just before gravity pulled her off the edge of the bed. She was trembling, freezing, and she rolled onto her hands and knees seconds before the first convulsion came. She went to the window and fumbled with the lock, pushing it up just before she threw up. Tears burned her eyes, her body trembling as she clutched the windowsill. She hung half out of the apartment, her eyes locked on the fire escape as she emptied her stomach and then began to dry heave.

She dropped back into the apartment and pressed herself into the corner. She drew her knees to her chest, pressed both fists against her eyes, and trembled, sobbing.

Riley heard sounds outside the bedroom door, but she didn't react to them until she heard footsteps in the hall. She crossed her arms over her knees and pressed her face into the crook of her elbow. Snapshots of the nightmare scrolled through her mind and she started crying again.

"Honey, I'm home," Gillian said. The last word was punctuated by Gillian's bag hitting the floor with a hollow thud. Then she was on her knees by Riley's side, holding her, rocking her back and forth, whispering into her hair until the crying stopped.

Riley sat at the kitchen table and stared toward the window. Her fingers were still tapping against the tabletop when Gillian set a cup down in front of her. "I found some ginger ale. It'll settle your stomach," she said softly. She brushed Riley's hair and pulled a chair over to sit beside her. Riley turned her head toward Gillian's hand to brush her lips over her palm, and wrapped both hands around the cup.

After a few minutes, Gillian said, "Do you want to talk about it?"

"No," Riley said. "I can't."

Gillian nodded. She took one of Riley's hands and held it, running her hand across the knuckles. After a moment, Riley squeezed her hand.

"Must have been a bad one."

"Yeah," Riley said. She took a sip of the ginger ale and licked her lips.

Gillian leaned in to kiss her, but Riley pulled away at the last second. Gillian withdrew and looked into Riley's eyes. "Was it about me?"

"No," Riley lied. "I just need a little time."

"Okay," Gillian said. "Do you want me to stay up with you?"

Riley shifted in her seat and said, "No. I'm not going back to bed tonight."

"Riley..."

"I'm sorry, Jill. But if I close my eyes, I keep seeing..." She shuddered and involuntarily squeezed Gillian's hand. "I'm sorry. I need to go talk to Priest. I need to get my head on straight."

Gillian brought Riley's hand to her lips and kissed it. "I understand. Do what you have to do. But if you come back, don't just crash on the couch. I want to see you."

"You need to sleep, too."

"I'd rather know you're okay." She stood up and kissed Riley's temple. "Go see Priest. Feel better. I've never seen you like this, and it scares the hell out of me."

Riley turned toward Gillian and hugged her around the waist. "I'll be fine. I just need a little time. I think I'll take a walk and clear my head."

"Okay. Call me if you need a ride or any... just call me."

Riley stood up, slipping both hands into Gillian's. She kissed her lips, tentatively at first but with growing passion. Gillian held Riley's hands and returned the kiss, eyes closed though she knew Riley's were still open. When they parted, Riley pressed her cheek to Gillian's and said, "I may be doing that a lot in the next couple of days. Just to forget."

"Anything I can do to help," Gillian said. She kissed Riley's earlobe and tried to ignore the shudder that ran through Riley's body. She pulled back and said, "I mean it. Anything."

Riley touched Gillian's face and nodded before she turned and left the kitchen. Gillian saw that Riley's mostly full glass of ginger ale was still sitting on the table. She took a drink herself and put the rest in the fridge for in the morning. When she turned off the kitchen light, she heard the front door open and close as Riley went out into the night.

Riley didn't walk directly to Priest's apartment. She meandered down side streets, trying to rid the images of her nightmare from her brain. She saw people on the sidewalk, silhouettes cut away from the shadowed alleys. Twice, she heard footsteps falling in behind her and twice she casually took her gun from her belt and noisily cocked it. Both times her tails quickly disappeared, absorbed back into the night while they waited for an easier target.

Riley remembered walking the streets of No Man's Land when she was a kid. It was a miracle she survived those reckless excursions.

The church Priest lived above was quiet, and Riley tried to remember if she'd ever seen it closed before. She was under the impression they were on some kind of perpetual worship mission. She walked past the dark storefront and went up the dark stairs. The shadows in Priest's building felt different than those outside, somehow less ominous. She felt at ease there, despite the fact it was even darker than the streets she had just walked. Probably a benefit from having an angelic tenant.

She knocked on Priest's door and stuffed her hands into her pockets. The memory of her dream still weighed on her mind and on her soul. She knew the Duchess had been exorcised. There was no doubt in her mind that the woman she loved wasn't an imposter. She looked down the stairs, paced in a tight circle, and then knocked again. She knew Priest had taken the plunge and bought furniture. Maybe she was trying sleep as well.

Riley was about to knock a third time when she heard movement inside. The door opened without the delay of a bunch of locks being undone and Priest stared out at her. Her hair was wet, and she wore a faded Wonder Woman T-shirt and sweatpants. Riley was stunned by the sight; she'd never seen her partner looking quite so... human.

"Riley. Are you okay?"

"Not really," Riley said. "I need to talk."

Priest nodded and leaned against the doorframe. "Okay. Sure."

"Can I come in?"

Priest hesitated. "I don't..."

"I'm not in the mood, Caitlin," Riley said. She pushed the door open and brushed past Priest. The apartment was immaculate, as always, and Riley shrugged out of her jacket. "I really need some... I don't know. Guidance or an explanation." She tossed her jacket on the couch and noticed that another jacket was already lying there. Riley frowned at it and slowly turned to face Priest. "Who's here?"

"What? No one." Priest crossed her arms over her chest and inadvertently glanced toward the bedroom.

Riley looked down the short hallway and then back at Priest. "What's going on?"

"Nothing. Maybe we should go somewhere else to talk. There's an all-night diner..."

Riley put Priest's wet hair, tossed-on clothes, and delayed response to the door together. She looked at the Wonder Woman shirt and realized why it had been so odd to see it on her partner. "That's not your shirt."

Priest looked down at herself and, while she was distracted, Riley walked down the hall to the closed bedroom door.

"Riley, wait. You shouldn't..."

Riley opened the bedroom door and stepped inside.

Priest had a queen-size bed on the opposite wall from the door, flanked on either side by night tables. The sheets and blankets were a tangled mess, two of the pillows lying on the floor. Riley had expected to see Kenzie Crowe lying on the mattress, since she remembered the T-shirt from their time as a couple, but seeing Chelsea Stanton spooning behind her was a complete shock. Both women were undisturbed by Riley's entrance, and Priest gently pulled Riley back into the hall. She shut the door and guided Riley back to the living room.

"What the hell?" Riley hissed.

"It isn't as it appears."

"The phrase is 'it's not what it looks like.' And it's pretty hard to misinterpret."

Priest sat on the back of the couch and said, "I am not physically involved with either of them. A few weeks ago, when Kenzie asked for our help with Kimaris, I overcame my animosity for her." Riley scoffed, but Priest ignored it. "Something I never told you was that she and I... were intimate during that time."

"You were..."

Priest hushed her and glanced toward the bedroom. "We kissed. Twice. The first time was merely subterfuge during the stakeout. But I enjoyed it immensely. I had never been kissed before. I was curious. So I kissed her again, on the rooftop while you and Chelsea were speaking with the police. After that, we met twice for coffee. She told me she had finally admitted her feelings to Chelsea following the ordeal in the warehouse."

Riley shook her head. "This is unbelievable. How does that end with them naked in your bed?"

Priest blushed and looked toward the window. "I was curious. I've been curious for a while about human sexuality. I see the way you are with Gillian, and it's so radically different from how you are with anyone else. It intrigued me. So I... I asked if... I could... watch."

Riley suddenly wondered if she was having another dream, but she didn't think she would ever have come up with something as bizarre as this. She rubbed her temples and shook her head as she brushed past Priest. "All right. Forget it. I still need to talk to you."

Priest took a long coat out of the closet and pulled it on over her T-shirt and sweats. Riley left the apartment, halfway down the stairs before Priest came outside after her.

When they got to the street, Priest looked both ways as she buttoned her coat. "Where did you park?"

"I walked. This way."

They started walking, Priest hanging back to let Riley lead the way. When they reached the corner without saying anything, Priest touched Riley's arm. "I want to apologize. Kenzie is your former partner, in both senses of the word. I should have consulted you—"

"Just shut up, Z, okay? There's no need to apologize," Riley said. "I'm just having a really bad night."

"Are you sure? You look very pale."

Riley said, "That has nothing to do with what happened back there. I dreamt..." She found she couldn't even say the words. "Nightmare doesn't even begin to cover it. Night terror comes closer."

"In Latin, night terrors are called *pavor nocturnus*."

"That fits better," Riley said. She exhaled and said, "I don't want to tell you what it was about. But I have to know if the demons are capable of affecting me this way. Can they affect dreams?"

"Perhaps," Priest said. "It would take a concentrated effort, though. And your protection, even dampened by sharing it with Gillian, would likely make it extraordinarily difficult for them to influence you."

"What about Gail Finney? Could she have helped them get a lock, or whatever?"

Priest said, "No. Unless you willingly took her personal property and held it for a prolonged period." Riley stopped walking and Priest turned to look at her. "What?"

"Finney. When I caught her at the crime scene, she had a little voice recorder. I took it from her."

"Oh," Priest said. "That's a bad thing. How long was it in your possession?"

"Less than a day," Riley said. "It was in my desk most of the time."

Priest shook her head. "That doesn't matter. You took it from her willingly. It was enough to create an imprint on you." She lifted her chin and seemed to be looking at the rooftops for a moment. After she had a chance to think, she looked back at Riley. "The mara locked on with that."

"Mara?"

"They're creatures of folklore. It's where the original phrase nightmare originated. They were believed to be the bringer of bad dreams. In reality, they're service demons. They have little to no cognitive ability of their own. They live to follow orders. Someone, I'm assuming whoever is acting as Gail's handler, locked onto you using her voice recorder."

"All right, so how do we stop it?"

"The imprint will wear off in a week or two," Priest said. "The easiest—"

Riley said, "No way. There's no way I'm suffering through a week of this."

Priest said, "If you know they're dreams..."

"I raped and killed Gillian," Riley said, barking the words. Her hands were trembling as she said the words, the bile rising in her throat. "I can't get it out of my head, Caitlin. I can't possibly go back to sleep knowing that the memory is there, and knowing that whoever is playing with me is going to try again. And they'll only get worse, right?"

Priest looked down at her feet. "I am so sorry, Riley. I had no idea."

Riley turned away from Priest, She could feel tears in her eyes as she scanned the street. "I could barely look at her. She was trying to comfort me, and all I could see was that..." She trembled and closed her eyes. "I need to make it stop."

"It would require killing the mara that has you in its thrall," Priest said.

"Good. Fine. Let's go find the bitch and kill it. Could you find it?"

Priest looked like she wanted to lie, but she said, "Yes, theoretically. They like water, and they would need a large space for their hellhounds to roam. Any of the abandoned buildings on the waterfront would suffice. But it's not as simple as finding and killing it. The mara are protected by hell-hounds. They are ghastly abominations who have torn angels to shreds for sport. There's a chance you would be successful if you caught them off-guard, but it's comparable to attempting to drive through the base of a tornado. Theoretically possible, but suicide in practice."

Riley rubbed her temples. Something Priest had said about the water-front rang a bell, but she couldn't put it together. Her mind was too noisy, too occupied with trying to avoid remnants of the painfully fresh dream. "I can't do this, Priest. If I have to wait out fourteen nights of this, I'll... put a gun in my mouth by the weekend."

"Riley..."

"Never mind. Sorry I bothered you with this. Go back to your orgy." She turned and started walking away. She shoved her hands into her pockets, ducked her chin against her chest, and refused to look back to see if Priest was following her.

Riley pushed aside the gate marked with the sign for Mara Properties and left her car on the driveway. She had her gun, and she'd gone home to change into something more appropriate to what she was going to do. The leather jacket buttoned at the throat, and she wore a bulletproof vest on top of it. She checked her gun, a Glock 18 with a 33-round magazine. She had two more magazines in her back pocket.

The building loomed in front of her, the moonlight turning the few unbroken windows into pools of quicksilver. She could smell the waterfront as she crossed the cracked pavement, her muscles tight and ready to take ac-tion. She couldn't take another dream like the one that was still clawing at her mind.

She heard movement from above and immediately dropped into a de-fensive position. She brought the gun up and followed the movement as Priest landed effortlessly a few feet away from her. She had changed into a dress shirt and slacks, but there was no tie and her top button was undone. She kept her wings visible, stretched wide as she looked up at the building. Her face was drawn with anger, her movements quick and precise as she checked her own Glock. She looked up at Riley and said, "You're insane."

"It has to end tonight," Riley said. "Thank you for backing me up."

"I'm not backing you up," Priest said. There were tears in her eyes as she moved toward the building. "If you insist on doing this, then I'm the only hope you have of succeeding here." At the door, she turned to Riley and said, "I want you to know something before we go in there. I love you. Everything I do, I do it for your benefit and because of that love."

Riley wanted to return the sentiment, but she'd never felt the kind of love Priest was talking about. Her father was barely a person in her life, and she'd never known her mother. Fortunately, Priest didn't seem to expect any kind of reciprocation. They moved to either side of the door and waited until Priest nodded that she was ready. She took a steadying breath and then tried the doorknob. It was unlocked, and she pushed the door open. She had a flashlight in one hand, bringing it up to shine the beam alongside her gun. When nothing stepped out to rush them, she nodded at Priest.

Priest flexed her wings and pulled them in just enough to fit through the door. Riley followed her into the darkness. Her beam played across the furniture of a prefabricated office, the thin walls erected to cut the space off from the rest of the warehouse. After determining the office was empty, Riley nodded for Priest to continue through the door to the main office. Riley caught a glimpse of Priest's weapon and a thought occurred to her.

"Why didn't you bring a sword? Samael and the others, they all have swords."

"Hellhounds and Mara are trained against angelic swords. They are more vulnerable to human weapons," Priest whispered.

"Convenient."

The warehouse was deathly still. The windows let in enough light for Riley to see the outline of stairs stretching toward the ceiling, and the hulking forms of machinery all around them. They were nearly to the middle of the room when Priest stopped walking. Her wings seemed to be illuminated, each feather casting a halo around her.

Priest suddenly tensed, her head rising a fraction as she scanned the room around them. There was a tremor in her voice when she spoke, not bothering to stay quiet now. "Riley. Run."

"I'm not going—"

Priest spun, true anger in her eyes, and yelled, "Riley, my job is to keep you alive. Even at the cost of my own life. You'll get a new angel to protect you. This is what I was sent to do. So *run*, Riley, please."

Before Riley could argue, a black shape separated itself from the rest of the darkness and launched silently at Priest's back. She turned at the last second and fired twice, her bullets digging trenches deep into the creature's face. Its charge halted, it fell to the ground in a tangle of limp muscles. The creature looked nothing like a dog, as Riley expected from the name, but more like a Brahma bull with a bulldog's face. Priest flexed her wings to their full span as two more of the massive hellhounds appeared.

"Priest..." Riley said.

"Go, Riley!" Her voice echoed off the corners of the room.

"Take this!"

Riley threw her gun, and Priest caught it without looking. With a gun in each hand, the glow from Priest's wings seemed to intensify. It created a spotlight effect in the middle of the room, shining a white light on the machinery near Priest's position. The hounds shied away from the edge of the light, but Riley knew was only a temporary deterrent to their attack.

Riley turned and reluctantly ran from the building. She slammed her shoulder against the door of the office, shamed with her retreat even as she shoved through the outer door and ran into the brisk night air. Her feet sounded like hollow slaps as she ran back to her car, heart pounding in her chest, her body breaking out in a cold sweat. She threw open the car door and got inside. She gripped the wheel and stared at the building.

The windows flashed with the light of each fired gunshot and Riley wondered how many rounds Priest had left. Their two guns had thirty-three rounds each, so she must have been getting close to empty on one. The extra magazines pressed against her ass, useless in the back pocket of her jeans. She remembered Priest saying the hellhounds and the mara were both vulnerable to human weapons and opened the trunk.

The AR-15 rifle had become something of a golden fleece among the department detectives when it was donated by a former Gulf War veteran. Riley had coveted the weapon as soon as the man brought it in. Somehow, through favors paid off and more promised for the future, it ended up in her hands. She was one of the few detectives willing to go into No Man's Land, after all, so the brass agreed it made sense to equip her accordingly. She took the gun and slapped the magazine in, feeling its weight as she slammed the trunk lid down. She had only used the weapon on firing ranges, but it was time for the demons to get a taste of what she could bring.

She raced across the lot, Priest's gunfire still echoing inside the building. Now Riley could hear the baying of the hounds, the barks and growls as the beasts attempted to overtake her. Riley ran back inside, through the office, and brought the gun up as she entered the main room. The sight that greeted her was so horrifying that she didn't depress the trigger immediately.

Priest was standing with a hellhound hanging from one arm, its teeth digging into her flesh. Both of her sleeves were torn, and bright red blood ran down her arms in multiple streams. Blood streaked her face and blouse. She fired point blank into a hound's face, then turned and fired at the one trying to tear her arm off.

"Priest!" Riley shouted.

"God damn you, Riley," Priest howled. "I told you to *go*."

Riley opened fire and the dogs were thrown back like grass clippings being hosed away. Priest stumbled and spun to face her. "Riley, get out of here!"

"I won't leave you."

A hound pounced on Priest from behind and threw her to the ground. Its paws, thick and ursine, pounded into her back between her wings, and its claws tore at the material of her blouse. Riley clenched her jaw and said, "Get off of her, you fucking mutt."

Before Riley could fire, she was knocked to the side by the sweep of a mighty arm. For a moment she thought someone had knocked her over with a baseball bat, but then one of the hounds dropped down onto her chest. It was unimaginably heavy, its weight pushing the air from her lungs. Riley struggled to raise the rifle, but she couldn't get the angle right. She looked toward Priest and saw the hellhound bring up a bloody claw to swipe at her back again. Blood spattered across the concrete floor.

The hound holding Riley down parted its lips to reveal horrific, yellow teeth. It dropped its head faster than she could react and clamped its jaws around her throat. She felt the incisors digging into her flesh and braced herself for the inevitable, waited for it to tear her throat out with one twist of—

Riley was wrapped in something. She struggled against it, twisting her body and kicking her legs in a futile attempt to escape. "Stop, stop," she panted, drenched with enough sweat that she wondered if she had been out in the rain. Strong hands cupped her face and she focused on Gillian's face. She realized she was on the couch in their apartment, the window bright with dawn. She blinked, her breath still coming in ragged huffs. "I-I don't... Priest. We have to save Priest..."

"You've been shouting her name for the last fifteen minutes," Gillian said. "It's all right. I've called her." She smoothed Riley's hair, touched her clammy cheek, and said, "She's on her way, Riley. Please, relax."

Riley looked down and saw a sheet wrapped around her torso. It was pulled tight, pinning her arms to her sides. "What..."

"I got sick of you punching me."

Riley cringed. "Jill..."

"I know. It's okay." She kissed Riley's forehead and said, "I'm okay. I'm worried about you. I didn't think I would be able to wake you up."

Riley's heart finally began to slow down, her tremors subsiding. "My throat. Touch..."

Gillian ran her hands over the smooth column of Riley's throat, revealing it to be completely intact.

"Priest said you came over to talk to her. You guys had a fight?"

"Not really," Riley said. "Maybe. Please untie me." Gillian loosened the sheet, which wasn't really tied, and rubbed Riley's arms. Riley looked for bruises on Gillian's face or her exposed arms. "Are you sure you're okay?"

"I'm fine," Gillian said. "I've been hit harder."

The door opened and Priest came inside without knocking. Riley was relieved to see she was completely intact. "What happened?"

"Another nightmare," Riley said. "I was right. They're getting worse."

Gillian said, "Do you know what's causing them?"

Priest explained to her about the mara, and then shook her head. "But I have never heard of attacks of this magnitude."

"Could it be because of who I am?" Riley said. "Have mara ever targeted champions?"

"That's probably it," Priest said. She chewed her lip and said, "You were right last night, Riley. You can't continue like this. I'll see if I can track down the mara tonight, and—"

Riley had a flash of Priest's back, the streak of blood between her wings, and she said, "No. Don't... don't do it. *You* were right. It's way too dangerous."

"We can't continue like this," Gillian said. She stroked Riley's hair and said, "She nearly took my head off. If it keeps getting worse."

"Take me somewhere they can take care of me," Riley said. "Commit me."

Priest and Gillian both stared at her.

Riley chuckled. "Jill, you had to tie me up so I'd stop hitting you. I'm a wreck even when I'm not asleep because those dreams are..." She pressed the heel of her hand against her eye and shook her head. "Put me in a mental institution. Tell them to put me in solitary confinement until this wears off."

Priest said, "Riley... your career would be over."

"Right. The way to protect my job is to go in like this. We can tell Briggs I need a few mental health days. She'll understand. The Angel Maker and everything that's been going on, she'll understand."

Priest rubbed her eyes. "She'll take you off the case, Riley. Do you really think anyone else has a chance of solving it?"

"We don't have a choice," Riley said. "You have to lock me up."

Priest looked at Gillian. Finally, she nodded. "Okay. But it won't be an asylum. I'll isolate you at my apartment."

"It's not secure."

"It will be," Priest said. She looked at Gillian. "I need to prepare. I'll let Briggs know that Riley is incapacitated. Will you be all right with her here?"

Gillian said, "Yes, of course."

Riley watched Priest leave and then pulled Gillian to her for a hug. "God."

"Can you tell me what happened in this one?"

"Priest was slaughtered," Riley whispered against Gillian's shoulder. "I watched her get torn apart."

"God," Gillian said. She kissed Riley's cheek and said, "And you still can't talk about the first one?"

"No," Riley said. "I'll never... I can't. I'm ashamed, and horrified by it. It's bad enough I have to live with the memory..."

Gillian nodded. "Okay. I understand. Do you want to take a bath while we wait for Priest to come back?"

"Yes."

Gillian helped Riley stand and walked her to the bathroom. Riley let Gillian undress her as the tub filled, wiping away the dry sweat with a towel before she guided Riley into the water. Riley relaxed against the curved edge of the tub and, remembering that she had fallen asleep the night before, said, "Keep me awake."

"Okay," Gillian said. She sat next to the tub and held Riley's hand. "What should I do?"

"Just... talk."

Gillian nodded and ran her fingers over the palm of Riley's hand. "I want you to think about our date. The date we had a few weeks ago."

"I remember it well," Riley said. "Especially the end."

Gillian blushed slightly as she chuckled. "Well, I've been known to revisit that night in a few dreams. That's all we have to do. We have to get you focused on the good dreams and just push the bad ones out."

The bathroom door opened and Riley looked up, expecting Priest. Her eyes widened when she saw who it really was.

Sweet Kara smiled down at her, checked out Riley's body, and gave an approving nod as she leaned against the sink. "Always knew you had a great body, Riley."

Riley couldn't respond, could only gawk at the specter that Gillian was ignoring. The side of Kara's head was bloody, as if the wound was fresh rather than over a year old.

"Don't worry about me being a vengeful spirit," Kara said. "I stopped blaming you for what happened a long time ago. Remember, it was all my fault. I don't know what I was thinking, getting involved in affairs of angels like that. Only a complete buffoon would get themselves in over their head that far." She gave Riley a coy smile and then winked. "Oh, and you can talk to me. Dr. Hunt won't hear. You're just dreaming."

"I didn't fall asleep."

"Yeah. Sitting in a warm tub with your lover stroking your hand. What's relaxing about *that?*" She rolled her eyes. "Speaking of, thank *God* you finally got together with her. It was like high school every time we had to go look at a body. There was a pool going for a while about when you guys would finally get together. I actually chose 'not in my lifetime.'" She thought about it and then smiled. "Hey. Guess that means I won."

"Get out of here," Riley said.

"You're grumpy. I don't remember that." She sighed and pushed away from the sink. "Don't worry, Riley. I'll be around."

Riley suddenly jerked, sloshing the water around her into a series of small waves. Gillian was perched on the edge of the tub, her hands on Riley's shoulders and her blouse wet up to the elbows. "Thank God," she said. "Are you okay?"

"What? Yes."

"I went to get a towel, and when I came back you were underwater."

Riley wiped her hand over her face and said, "I... I'm fine..."

Gillian's bottom lip quaked and she said, "No, Riley. You're not." She pulled Riley to her and hugged her tightly.

The ride to Priest's apartment was a blur. Gillian found a hard rock station on the radio and turned it up loud enough to shake the windows, a weak attempt to keep Riley from falling asleep. When they parked, a few of the women coming out of the church cast a judgmental gaze on the car and Riley's hoodie and jeans. Riley had put on a pair of sunglasses during the drive; the morning sun was way too bright and her sleep had been anything but restful the past few nights. Her head was killing her.

Gillian put an arm around her waist and guided her to the stairs. "It's okay, Riley. Caitlin will take care of you."

The apartment door was open and Gillian led Riley inside. She had a flash of the night before, the scene she'd walked into in the bedroom. She pushed it out of her mind. Maybe that was all part of the dream, too. Gillian guided her to the couch and she sat down, taking off her sunglasses and tossing them onto the table. "Caitlin?" Gillian said. "Are you here?"

"I'm in the spare room," Priest said. She came out a moment later and said, "I'm just making preparations."

Riley patted Gillian's arm. "I'm here, I'm safe. Go to work."

"Are you out of your mind?" Gillian said. Riley scoffed, and Gillian ducked her head. "I didn't mean..."

"No, it's true."

Gillian said, "Either way. I'm not leaving you."

"No. There's nothing you can do here but worry."

Gillian said, "Yeah, imagine how useful I'll be at work."

"Go. Please, I'll be fine here with Priest."

Gillian looked past Riley at Priest, and then reluctantly gave in. She kissed Riley's lips and said, "I'll call to check up on you. I love you."

"I love you, too."

To Priest, Gillian said, "You call me if anything happens. Don't try to protect me, and don't let her talk you out of it."

"Yes, ma'am," Priest said.

Gillian kissed Riley one more time before she finally stood up. She left quickly, obviously hurrying so she wouldn't be tempted to stay. Priest followed Gillian to the door and closed it behind her. She turned to Riley and said, "All right. Let's go tour your home for the next two weeks."

Riley pushed off the couch and followed Priest down the hall. "Can I ask you a question?"

"Of course."

"If you wanted to see human sexuality in practice, why didn't you ask to watch me and Gillian?"

Priest paused at the door of the guest room. "Would you have said yes?"

"No. Probably not."

Priest nodded. "I'm not sure why. It never crossed my mind. Mackenzie and Chelsea have a new relationship. What you have with Gillian feels more... sacred."

Priest opened the door to the guest room and Riley stepped inside. The room had been stripped of amenities, left with just a cot in the far corner and a small radio on the floor next to it. The window was covered with plywood and the walls were covered with cryptic runes.

"Don't touch the walls," Priest said. "The ink isn't quite dry."

"Thanks," Riley said.

"The room should offer you protection from outside influence. I don't think it will block the mara's influence entirely, but it should at least let you get a little restful sleep. I hope."

Riley nodded. "I'm willing to try anything. Thank you, Caitlin."

Priest said, "'Caitlin'? Now I'm really worried."

"At least I didn't call you Zerachiel."

Priest smiled and said, "I'll check on you throughout the day. Call me if you need anything."

Riley went into the room and Priest closed the door behind her. Riley, for some reason, expected to hear a key in the lock and bolts being thrown. She walked to the cot and stretched out, toeing off her shoes and crossing her feet at the ankles. Her entire body felt battered, and her brain felt like it was in a vice. She rubbed her temples to try and quiet the encroaching headache, but it didn't help. She rubbed her throat, still sore in the aftermath of the hellhound dream. It was bad enough that she had to relive the dreams in memory; if she was going to start having physical reminders, she would be done.

She tried to sleep, but her mind refused to cooperate. She could hear traffic outside, singing through the floor, and Priest moving around in the rest of the apartment. Riley could tell she was trying to be as quiet as possible, but apparently even angels could have club feet.

After a while, she dozed. The dream she had was actually more of a hallucination, a fantasy where she was a princess locked up in a tall castle tower and protected by an angel. She imagined wide, rolling fields outside the castle, the beauty ringed on all sides by a dark and dead forest. Demons and monsters lived in the forest of No Man's Land, and the darkness was spreading. Grass and flowers refused to grow near the border of the forest, and that only increased its reach. The branches of the tall, black trees seemed to be almost reaching for her.

Riley woke easily. She rubbed her face and cursed the fact that *that* was what counted as a good dream for her. She sat up, placed her feet on the floor, and tried to look at the runes Priest had painted on the wall. Any of them she looked directly at seemed to reject her gaze, forcing her to slide her eyes away. And as soon as she looked away, she couldn't remember the exact shape of the rune.

She stood up and stretched, paced the perimeter of the room, and finally took off her hoodie. She dropped to the floor and began to do push-ups. She didn't count, but she could tell when she reached the end of ten. She counted out seventy before she stopped and moved onto her back. She did another seventy sit ups, touching each elbow to the opposite knee before dropping back down.

Riley heard Priest talking in the living room of the apartment and she stood up. Her muscles ached from the exercise. It was a good ache, but not enough to make her tired. She opened the bedroom door to ask for a glass of water and paused when she recognized Gillian's voice.

"We'll have to tell her eventually."

Priest said, "Give me a chance to smooth it over. For now we can just tell her it's vacation time. It's not exactly a lie."

"I don't like it, Caitlin."

Riley came into the room and said, "I don't like it either. Why don't you tell me what's going on?"

Priest and Gillian both looked at her, Gillian's expression full of guilt while Priest just looked ashamed. "I thought you would call out if you needed something. You should stay in the room, the protection—"

"Just tell me what's going on. Now."

Gillian looked at Priest and said, "Lieutenant Briggs suspended you."

"*What?*"

"I was going to tell you," Priest said. "The fourth body was identified. Briggs wanted us to follow-up immediately, but I told her that you needed a few days to recuperate from recent stresses. She reassigned the case to Logan."

Riley resisted the urge to punch the wall. "That's bullshit. Logan is too close-minded. I'm amazed he's survived this long as a detective. He needs every damn thing lined up for him before he can come to a conclusion. He's..."

"Calm down," Gillian whispered.

Riley stepped up to Priest. "How could you let her take the Angel Maker away from us? That's our case. No one else will have our information. No one else will be able to close it."

"I'm lending my assistance to Logan. I'll make sure he follows the right path. When you're better, we'll talk to Briggs. She'll give us the case back and everything will be fine."

"I'm not going to go on like this," Riley said. "If we just sit it out and wait for the effects to wear off, they'll just do it again. They'll have a weapon they can use to get me out of the way two weeks at a time. We might as well just bend over and wave the white flag."

"Riley, I told you. The hellhounds that protect the mara..."

"Right," Riley said. "I saw it in living color in my dreams, remember? But there has to be something we can do. Why can't we set fire to the building that the mara is in? Shoot whatever comes crawling out."

"The mara aren't vulnerable to fire."

"You said they were susceptible to human weapons."

Priest frowned. "I did?"

"Yeah. In..."

"In your dream?" Gillian said quietly.

Sweet Kara stepped out from behind Gillian. "They're all out to get you."

"Oh, Christ," Riley said. She rubbed her eyes with the heels of her hands.

"What's wrong?"

Riley looked at Kara. She was still standing beside her, glaring at Priest and Gillian. The ground no longer felt solid under her feet. "Nothing. I... nothing is wrong. Except that I'm going to lose both of my jobs if I sit here and do nothing."

"Both..."

"Champion and cop," Riley said. She grabbed her coat and headed for the door. "I can't just sit back there and twiddle my thumbs. I have to do something."

Gillian followed Riley to the stairs. "What about your third job?"

Riley turned and looked up at her.

"My partner," Gillian said. "What will you do to keep that job?"

"Don't make me choose," Riley said. "That's not fair."

Gillian said, "It's not fair to make me keep waiting, Riley. If you leave, if you go out there with your mind the way it is, then... I'm done. I won't stand by and watch you kill yourself."

Riley met Gillian's eyes before she turned and continued down the stairs. She stepped outside and squinted at the bright sun. She felt nauseated, weak. She put on her sunglasses, slipped on her suit jacket, and walked to the corner. She wasn't sure where she was going, wasn't sure if she had a plan. All she could think about was moving forward. She wasn't going to sit in some damn room and *wait* for the bad guys to win. She was embarrassed Priest had suggested it, ashamed she had so eagerly accepted.

She wanted to storm into Briggs' office and demand the Angel Maker case back. She wanted to punch Logan in his damn fat face for even trying to take it from her. She wanted to rant, scream, yell, fight. She wanted to do anything except lay down her arms.

Riley boarded the el train and rode without paying attention to the stops or the neighborhoods it ran through. Normally she liked when the train was going slow enough to look into the buildings they passed. Snapshots of normalcy, of real life, of people who weren't dead or killing each other or fighting. Dinners on a dining room table, a family doing dishes, the occasional intimate moment after work... today she couldn't even focus on the buildings.

An idea began to form in her mind. The images were clear, the logic sound. It grew until it blocked her vision, kept her from paying attention to anything but the beauty of her idea.

Sweet Kara was sitting next to her. "It would certainly feel good, wouldn't it?" she said, obviously aware of Riley's plan. "And it's inevitable anyway, right? So why not?"

Riley rode the train to the appropriate stop and then followed the flow of people out the door. She barely registered the fact that they were giving her a wide berth. She wondered how bad she looked. Sleep deprived, sick to her stomach, pissed beyond belief... she would probably have stayed away from herself, too.

She had a vague idea of the directions, but she took a few wrongs turns along the way. The sick feeling in her stomach only increased the more she walked. She had to get rid of this damned mara, and there was only one safe way she could think of to do it. She pushed through the glass door, her palm leaving a smear as she dragged it away. She walked directly toward the stairs.

A security guard rose from the desk, a blur in the corner of her eye that wasn't worth turning to face. "Excuse me..."

Riley pulled her badge out of her pocket. Briggs hadn't gotten that yet, at least. She took the stairs two and three at a time, sweating by the time she reached the right floor. A receptionist looked up and began to stop her. "Where..." Riley flashed her badge, and the woman backed down.

She breezed past the desk, the security guard and receptionist now both following behind her. Her gun was in her belt, hidden by the tail of her shirt, within easy reach.

Gail Finney looked up from her desk as Riley approached. She arched an eyebrow and leaned back in her seat. "Well, Riley Parra. Come to do the first part of our interview?"

The first shot hit Gail above the right eyebrow and painted blood and gore on the wall behind her chair. Gail was tossed back into her seat, expression one of shock, her lips parted in a wide oval as she slumped in the leather seat. Riley squeezed off three more shots and Gail Finney's body danced with each impact. Riley resisted the urge to laugh, aware it would sound like an insane giggle.

The security guard hit Riley from behind and knocked her to the ground. Her gun skittered across the floor and landed against the trash can.

If Gail Finney had summoned the mara, then her death would cut its ties. Logical. Not that Riley was holding out much hope for things to be fixed now, since Gail was only dead in a dream. The security guard wrenched Riley's arms behind her back and she felt zip ties tightening around her wrists. She wondered how long it would take Priest and Gillian to wake her up from this one. Not that she was in a hurry. She could see Gail's body on the floor, separated from her by a desk. She was bloody, and quite indeed dead. It was finally an image she *wanted* to keep with her after she woke up.

"Wake me up," she whispered.

Someone checked Gail's pulse, but it was a futile gesture. People were screaming. Crying. She could hear people running around the room, fleeing to the stairs and elevators. The security guard was kneeling in the small of her back. She thought he had a gun, but she wasn't sure. He was muttering something in another language. A prayer, perhaps.

"Wake me up," Riley whispered. "Wake me up."

Sirens filled the air, coming closer. Riley's breath became rough, harsh.

"Wake me up...

"Wake me up...

"Jill, please, wake me up..."

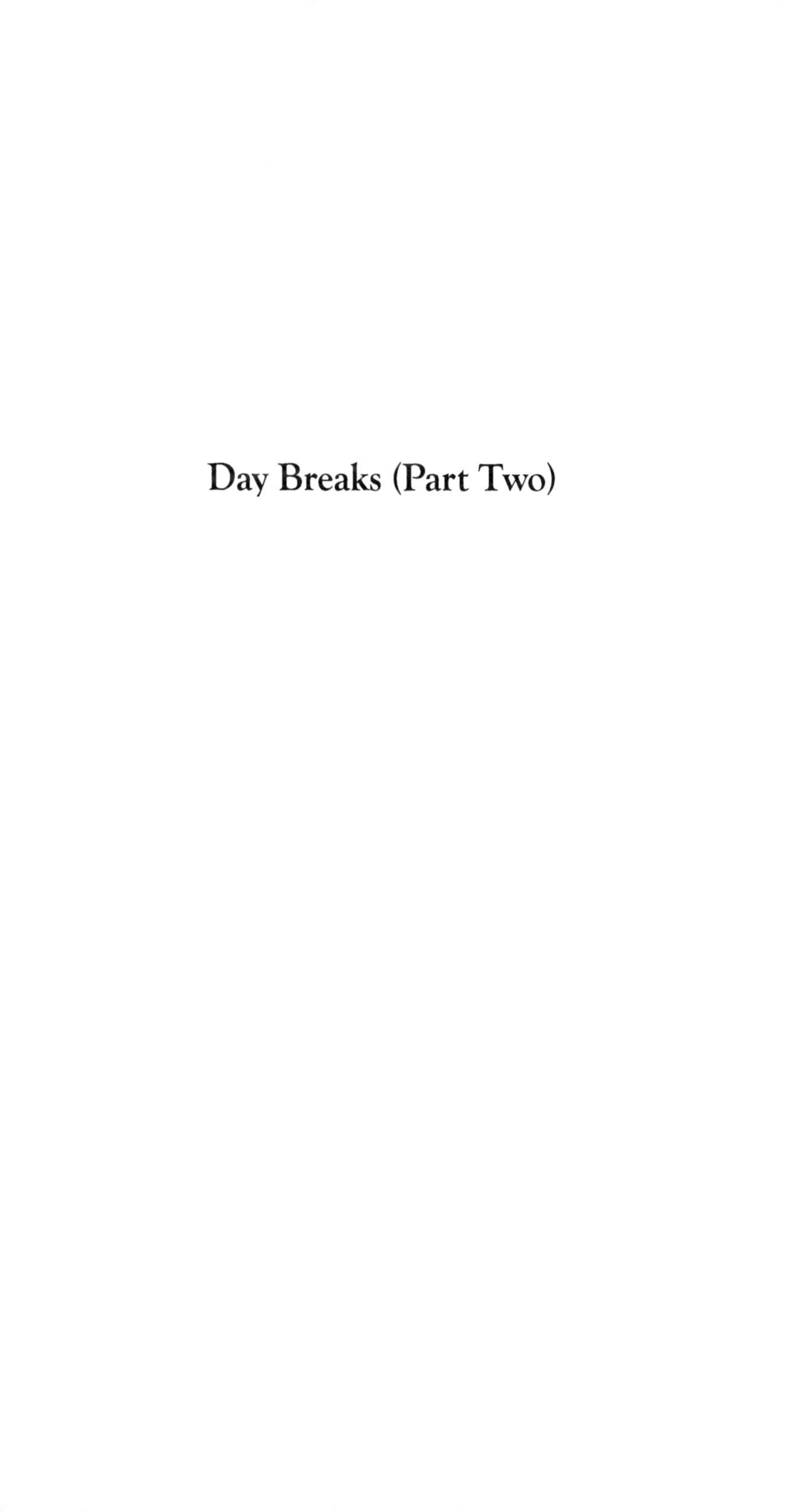

Day Breaks (Part Two)

Riley didn't remember the police arriving. She only had a vague recollection of being shoved into the back of a cruiser and the zip ties being exchanged for steel handcuffs. The booking process, which she had done so many times that the procedure had become rote, barely registered. Of course, she was usually on the other side of the process. Mug shots, fingerprinting, and they made her change into a white T-shirt and a blue jumpsuit while they booked her clothes and possessions into evidence.

Finally, she was led into a private cell reserved for VIPs and the occasional arrested police officer. The cop who escorted her down the hallway stepped back and put his hand against the cell door before he closed it. "We all know who the victim was, all right? This here is all just, like, a formality. The only people mad at you are the ones who are pissed you did it first. You need anything, you let us know. You did everyone in this building a favor."

"Shut up," Riley said, too exhausted to even argue with him. She sat on the edge of the cot and buried her face in her hands. It had seemed so logical in her head, forming the plan, acting it out. She was so sure it was a dream. Now she didn't know what to believe.

She could still feel the righteous anger burning in her veins as she left the train and chose the fastest route to the newspaper offices. Even as she had pulled the trigger, it felt so *right*. But it had also felt so much like a dream. No consequences. Just a big reset button at the end of all your wildest fantasies. But the longer it lasted, the less likely it seemed that she would wake up and everything would be back to normal.

She wasn't sure how long she had waited before the guard returned. "Parra. You have a visitor."

Riley looked up, expecting to see Gillian. Instead, the guest was Priest, dressed for work in a suit. "Riley. Are you all right?"

Riley was thrown by the fact that Priest's first question was about her well-being. She felt tears burning at the corner of her eyes as she walked to the bars. The guard stepped out to give them privacy, and Riley shook her head. "I don't know. I don't know what happened. My head was... I couldn't think straight. Where's Gillian?"

Priest said, "The commissioner is already involved on the case. He requested that the ranking medical examiner take over Gail Finney's autopsy."

"Does he know about our relationship?"

"Gillian told him when he called. He didn't care as long as she remained impartial. It's not like she can say you didn't do it. There were at least a dozen witnesses."

Riley put her arm against the bars and rested her head against it. "Jesus, this is all so wrong. What did Briggs say?"

Priest winced. "We should focus on what our next steps will be."

"So I'm fired."

Priest looked down at the ground and said, "Yes."

Riley stepped away from the bars and laced her fingers at the back of her head.

"We'll work this out, Riley."

"Work it how? How, exactly, will we work it out, Caitlin? Let's just sit Briggs down and tell her, 'Look, I know this is hard to believe, but I killed Gail Finney in cold blood because she's working with demons, and I know because I'm working with angels and they told me so.'"

Priest said, "Everything you've done for this city..."

"Does not matter," Riley said. "I killed someone, okay? I had intent. It doesn't even matter that I'm fired, because I'm going to prison for the rest of my life."

Priest closed her eyes and said, "I should have just gone with you to stop the mara."

Riley remembered Priest's bloody body lying underneath the hellhounds. "No. That wouldn't have worked out any better. Trust me." She gripped the bars with both hands. "Tell Gillian I'm sorry I walked out. Tell her..." She looked toward the wall. "What does it matter? Our relationship is over anyway."

"No. She'll forgive—"

"She deserves more than a conjugal visit at the end of the month. Forget what I just said." She wiped her hands over her face and forced herself to stay calm when she said, "When you leave, go tell Gillian that we're done. I don't want her to visit, or write. I don't want to see her again. I don't... care." Her tears finally began to fall and she pressed her face against the shoulder of her jumpsuit. "Tell her I don't... want to see her."

Priest said, "I won't do that, Riley."

Riley sagged. "Then tell her I love her. And that I'm sorry."

Priest nodded and put her hand on top of Riley's. "That message I will pass along. Do you need anything?"

"No. But if I have to spend the rest of my life in jail, I want Marchosias gone. If that means I have to hand over my status, then so be it."

"Riley, there will be demons in prison. Demons who know who you are. Just because you're not the champion anymore..."

"I won't be doing the city any good in jail," Riley said. "I want to pass it on."

"Have anyone in mind?"

Riley said, "Kenzie. She deserves it, and she'll do a good job. But ask her. Don't... I don't want her to be forced into something like this."

"I'll ask. And I'll do what I can about making the transfer of powers. It's not as easy as just waving a hand. Stay strong, Riley."

"Yeah. Thanks, Priest."

Priest squeezed Riley's hand before she walked away, knocking on the door to let the guard know she was ready to go. Riley watched her until the door closed again and knocked her head gently against the bars. She pictured herself in a prison jumpsuit, blood spilling from a shiv in her back. Beaten in the laundry room. Her corpse found dangling from a knotted sheet in her cell. She was going to prison for the rest of her life, but that didn't mean she'd be there long.

She pushed away from the cell door and turned to go back to the cot. Lieutenant Nina Hathaway was standing a few inches in front of her, so real that Riley jumped back and slammed into the bars. "Jesus fuck..." Riley snapped.

"You made a bad decision, kid," Hathaway said. Her blouse was soaked with blood, the bullet wounds that had killed her still visible in the material. Blood spatter was on her chin and neck, fresh and glistening as she walked to the cot and sat down.

"You should have stayed with me. Given me some of that nice protection so that this," she gestured at her chest, "would never have happened. Then maybe I would still be around to cover your sweet ass when something like this came up. And all I'd ask in return is a little head now and then. Is that such a big deal? Did you hate going down on me in the office after you killed Sweet Kara?"

"I didn't kill... Those were different circumstances."

"Seems the same to me. Angels and demons. Kara was on the wrong side, and you blew her brains out. I saved your ass then, and I could have saved it now. 'Detective Parra was working on an intensive investigation into Gail Finney, during which she uncovered damning evidence. Detective Parra confronted Ms. Finney with these allegations and, when Ms. Finney seemed to be reaching for a weapon, Detective Parra responded with appropriate force.'"

"Appropriate force," Riley repeated. "I emptied my gun into a woman sitting at her desk with her hands in plain view. In front of a dozen witnesses. You really think you could spin that?"

"I could spin anything," Hathaway said. "Given the right incentive."

"You're the kind of cop who gave Gail Finney her ammunition. You were a bad cop, Nina."

"I never went to jail."

Riley walked to the opposite end of the cell and leaned against the wall. She slid down, rested her elbows on her knees, and pressed the heels of her hands against her eyes. She was exhausted, but she didn't dare close her eyes in case she fell asleep and had a dream worse than her current reality. "I want to go to sleep. I just want to sleep."

She sat with her hands over her eyes, listening to her heartbeat over the sounds of the building. It was as familiar to her as anything, the next best thing to home outside of Gillian's apartment. But now it felt alien. Every shout was menacing, and the knowledge she couldn't walk out the front door was petrifying. She could hear sirens outside and focused on them. She pictured the street in her mind, the cars coming and going like worker bees flitting around a hive. The sound was a comfort to her; she was one of the good guys, and that sound meant she was doing her job.

She would never wear a badge again. Even if by some miracle she didn't end up in jail, her days as a police officer were over. How would she even survive? Go to work at Stanton's private investigation firm? Forgiveness was one thing, but Riley doubted she could spend more than a few hours in Chelsea Stanton's presence.

The exterior door opened and Riley looked up as Briggs walked in with the guard. Riley pushed herself up and steeled herself for the worst.

"I assume your partner already told you our decision," Briggs said.

"Yes, ma'am."

"Regardless of that fact, we're not going to abandon you. The department will assist in your legal fees if you wish, and we've assigned you an advocate. You'll most likely be declared non compos mentis. Your actions on the train this afternoon will go a long way in proving that to be true."

Riley shook her head. "But I didn't do anything on the train."

Briggs said, "Several passengers called 911 to report a crazy woman with a gun. The description matches you perfectly. Apparently you kept checking and rechecking to make sure it was loaded. The entire time, you kept muttering about angels and demons. The demons were out to get you, and if the angels wouldn't help, you would have to help yourself."

"This is insane," Riley said.

"I'm glad you recognize that, Detective. If it comes down to it, a hospital is better than a prison cell."

Riley walked to the cot and sat down. "Frying pan and fire, boss. And I'm not a detective anymore. You don't have to call me that."

"Right," Briggs said. "I want you to have a complete once-over. I've... I've asked Dr. Hunt to take a look at you. Make sure you're all in one piece. She'll be down when she's finished with... when she becomes available."

"Thank you."

Briggs turned to leave, but she stopped at the last moment. "You could have picked worse, Riley. You really could have."

Riley gave a distracted nod and stretched out on the cot. She wished people would stop praising what she had done with one hand while using it to destroy her life with the other.

Riley tried to sleep, but she couldn't stop panicking about her situation. She wasn't a cop. She wasn't a citizen. She was a prisoner. The best she could hope for was being committed to a mental hospital. She remembered suggesting that route to Priest earlier and almost laughed at the absurdity of it. She lay on the cot, one arm thrown over her face, and tried to silence her mind. She imagined a gray cloak dropping over her thoughts, fine-boned hands smoothing out the material until it was all just a fog.

Through the door, she heard a flurry of activity and voices raised in anger. She sat up as the door was thrown open and Briggs stormed up to the bars of her cell. "Explain," Briggs said. Her face was flush, her nostrils flaring with each intake of breath. Priest came in behind Briggs. She wore an expression of shock and stared at Riley as if she was a stranger.

"Explain?" Riley said. She thought the situation was clear enough. She licked her lips and shook her head. "I-I don't know. I didn't even realize I was going to the newspaper until—"

Briggs grabbed the cell door and shook it. "Don't play fucking games, Parra."

"The *knife*, Riley," Priest said. "What were you thinking?"

Riley looked at Priest and then at the swarm of cops standing in the corridor behind her. "What knife?"

"Tell me you found it in the course of your investigation and just neglected to tell your partner. And that you were just *stupid* enough to take it home with you."

Riley said, "I don't own a knife. What knife?" She locked onto something Briggs had said. "Wait, you searched my apartment?"

"Your behavior has been worse than erratic lately," Briggs said. "Dr. Hunt gave us permission, since the apartment is still in her name. We found the knife in the front closet in a bag that Dr. Hunt confirmed belonged to you."

"That's my gym bag. Why would I put a knife in my gym bag?"

Priest said, "Riley. Where did it come from?"

"I have no fucking clue what any of you are talking about."

Briggs slapped a crime scene photograph against the bars. Riley recognized the bag serving as a platform in the photo; it was hers, and she could see her running shoes tucked alongside. She didn't recognize the ornate weapon lying on top, its blade carved with a series of designs. The handle was black with an ivory inlay, and it had what appeared to be dried blood on the hilt. Riley shook her head and recited the words she had heard so many times. "That's not mine. I've never seen that before. And no, I've never believed anyone who said that, either. What does a knife have to do with anything?"

Priest's voice was meek. "It's the Angel Maker's."

Riley gripped the bars with both hands.

"Dr. Hunt confirmed," Briggs said.

"No." Riley tightened her grip, as if she could break the metal through sheer force. "No, Caitlin. Boss, this isn't right."

"Twenty-four hours ago, I would have called you a lunatic if you told me my best detective would be in jail for murder. So now I have to ask. Riley Parra, are you the Angel Maker?"

"No," Riley shouted. "No, boss. I swear to you. Priest, you have to know this is a set-up."

"The... bad guys couldn't have gotten into your apartment, Riley. The door. Was locked."

Riley remembered Priest laying protection down over Gillian's apartment. No demon could set foot in the apartment. But that didn't mean anything. The Angel Maker was human, he was just being used by a demon to do his dirty work.

"I've never seen that knife before."

"Then *explain*," Briggs said. "Explain how it got into your apartment, and explain why your fingerprints are all over it."

Riley suddenly understood the Angel Maker's plan. There was no rhyme or reason to the murders because the murders weren't the important thing. The important thing was the *murderer*. And now all the evidence was pointing her as that murderer. She sagged against the bars and said, "Why would I do this? Why, boss?"

"I don't know. I don't know what happened to you when you were abducted earlier this year, but I know you came back scarred. Physically, you've healed, but... I was never quite sure about mentally. The Angel Maker murders started right after you went back on duty. I guess now we have our answer. Give me a good explanation for why this knife is in your apartment. Tell me that your sudden fascination with demons has nothing to do with the fact this killer draws angel wings with the victim's blood."

Riley looked at Priest and gave in to the inevitable. "Because the demons want me to look insane. They want you to lock me up, because I'm the only hope this city has."

"Is that so?"

"I didn't want this. I didn't ask for it. I was chosen as the champion for the angels, and I have to fight demons now." A tear rolled down her face. "The demons are trying to kill me, boss. They won't let me sleep."

A cop at the back of the room muttered, "Jesus Christ," and stepped out into the corridor.

"Do you have any evidence of this?"

"Priest," Riley said. "She's an angel. Her name is really Zerachiel. She has wings. I've seen them. She... she can fly."

Briggs looked at Priest and shook her head slightly. She turned and left the room, ushering the other cops outside as well. Priest was the last to go. She placed her hand on the knob and then looked at Riley over her shoulder. She mouthed an apology, dropped her head, and closed the door behind her as she left.

Riley heard someone shouting around midnight. Another prisoner in another cell, someone alternating between fury and fear. Their voice broke on every other word. Riley tried to block it out, but trying to ignore it just made the crying louder. There was a time, between one and two in the morning, when she thought it might have been her. But the voice was wrong, and it was too far away. Every time she started to fall asleep, she would inadvertently jerk herself awake. Exhaustion was preferable to whatever nightmare was waiting to attack her. It was getting harder and harder to distinguish between the nightmares and reality anyway. Best to just stay awake.

"There used to be nights when you couldn't wait to get into bed."

"Not her," Riley groaned. She closed her eyes and squeezed the bridge of her nose. "Come on, have a fucking heart."

Christine Lee, Riley's first real lover, touched Riley's thigh as she sat on the edge of the cot. "That's not a very nice thing to say. I've missed you, Riley. You hardly ever think about me anymore."

Riley didn't look, left her arm across her eyes. Hathaway and Kara had both still carried the wounds that killed them. She didn't want to see Christine post-car accident.

"Because I hate you. And I love you. What you did to me."

"What did I do to you?"

"*This*," Riley growled. "You put me here. You gave me this... mark. But you were my first lover. And when I think about how you died, and that you died because of me..."

Christine scoffed. "I made a conscious decision. Like you did with Gillian."

"I wasn't dumb enough to give it all away. What the hell were you thinking?"

"I watched you. I knew you would need all the help you could get. So I gave it to you."

Riley dropped her arm, but she kept her eyes closed. "Why did you give me this responsibility?"

"Not me, Riley. You were chosen when I met you."

Riley frowned. "No. The... tattoo marked me."

"The tattoo helped. It sealed the deal, as it were. But you were chosen when you were born, Riley. Why do you think the demons took your mother?"

Riley's face burned. "What?"

"The man you lived with was not your father. He was a lackey for the demons, sent to keep you from achieving your destiny. You were stolen, and your mother was driven mad. The demons have known about you since before you were conceived, Riley."

"Then who is my father?" Riley said. "Because the way things are going, you'll tell me it's Marchosias or Samael."

Christine chuckled, and the sound tore Riley's heart out. She remembered that laugh, the sound of it like wind chimes. It was the first beautiful thing she'd ever heard in No Man's Land.

"Your real father is just a man. And your mother was just a woman. Same as everyone else."

"So what made me so special?"

"Time, circumstance, location, the arrangement of the stars. Ours is not to question why, as they said."

Riley rubbed her throat and said, "So my job was to start Armageddon and then get executed by the state. Some job."

"Things have a way of working out, Riley. Don't lose faith."

"Right," Riley said. "Faith is something I have a surplus of."

Something hit the bars and she jumped. When she looked toward the front of the cell, she saw Christine was gone, but the guard was standing on the other side. "Talking to yourself ain't gonna help your insanity defense. Go to sleep and shut up."

Riley lay back down and listened for him to retreat back to his post. She wondered if Gillian was still awake, if she was still in the building. Of all the faces she had seen that day, Gillian's was the one she longed for. Why had she tried to push her away? She prayed Priest hadn't decided to give the first message.

"Gillian," she whispered to the darkness. "I'm sorry. Don't leave me, Gillian. I can take everything else. Not that. Please, Jill." She fell asleep pleading. Her cell faded into a dark stage, the walls retreating until there were no borders. She saw Gillian in the kitchen, her hair down. She had changed into an oversize T-shirt, her legs bare. She was furious, and Riley saw why as the rest of the apartment came into focus.

The police who had searched left the apartment a shambles. Gillian's carefully chosen art prints lay against the wall, the cushions from the sofa tossed carelessly aside, and the drawers all stood open. Gillian finished heating her tea and carried the cup into the living room. "I still don't like it. It feels wrong."

Priest lay on the floor in front of the couch, in her underwear. Riley bristled at the site as Gillian straddled Priest's waist and sat down.

"It had to be done to get her out of the way."

Gillian put her hand on Priest's stomach and brushed her fingernails up to the cups of her bra. "Still. Committing those murders and pinning them on her. There had to have been a more decent way to get rid of her."

Priest smiled, a sickening grin that made Riley's flesh crawl. "But not as fun."

Gillian laughed. "Definitely not as fun." She bent down and kissed Priest passionately. Riley railed, screamed, kicked and fought against the image as Gillian stroked Priest's body. Priest's hands slid under Gillian's shirt and Riley swung at her.

The impact of her fist against the concrete wall woke her. She pulled the hand to her chest, biting her lip to keep from crying out in pain. After a few minutes, when the first waves of anguish passed, she flexed her fingers. The middle finger was a bit out of whack, but the rest weren't broken. She wrapped the hand in her blanket and stared at the ceiling.

There was no way she would survive two weeks.

She didn't sleep at all the rest of the night. At five the next morning, four guards arrived to transfer her to the courthouse for arraignment. Her wrists and ankles were shackled, the chains attached to another that wrapped around her waist. The locks were checked before the guard escorted her out of the cell. There were two in front of her and two behind, and she was extremely aware of the weapons on their belts. Each officer also carried a Taser. She'd been hit by one before and while it was definitely preferable to being shot, she wasn't eager to repeat the experience.

Cops were posted at every door she passed, fingers hooked casually on their belts. They all stared at her with coldness and disgust. She saw officers who had been on crime scenes with her. The same guard who had praised her for killing Gail Finney now looked like he wanted to take a crack at her. She ignored them as she passed. She didn't want to think how she looked; exhausted, unwashed, beaten down, dragging her feet. She probably looked as bad or worse than any punk she had ever sent down to the cells herself. All it had taken was twenty four hours to turn her into one of them.

When they reached the end of the corridor, one of the guards spoke into his shoulder-mounted radio before he opened the door. The transfer area was familiar to Riley; she had acted as security several times during transfers when she was still in uniform. The door led out to a driveway flanked on either side by tall concrete walls. The driveway rose at a steep angle and wrapped around the back of the police station. There were two places where people could stand and gawk, one on either side, and today that space was filled with reporters. They immediately crushed against the railing, shouting questions and snapping photographs.

"Detective Parra, *are* you the Angel Maker?"

"Were you acting on orders from your superiors to eliminate Gail Finney?"

"Is it true that you and Gail Finney were in a relationship? Was her murder the result—"

Riley tuned them out and started to duck her head for the rest of the walk to the bus. Something caught her eye and she scanned the crowd until she realized what it was.

Marchosias stood amid the scrum of reporters, his arms resting on the top of the barrier. His face, normally a fright mask of exposed musculature, was covered by a tight mask that mimicked human skin. He smiled when he saw that she had noticed him, and he offered her a curt salute. Riley resisted the urge to flip him off. He raised one hand, pointed at her chains, and snapped his fingers.

The chains relaxed, and fell from her with a sound like glass breaking. The guards stopped mid-step and turned toward her. Riley immediately raised her arms to put her hands on her head, ready to surrender, eager for them to know that she wasn't trying to escape. "I didn't do this," she said, "I didn't—"

Before she could finish, the gunfire started. Riley felt the breeze of a bullet that barely missed her head and she went on instinct; she went for cover. She ran past the guards and crowded between the bus and the concrete wall, her heart pounding as the gunfire continued. The angles were impossible; it was almost as if someone was standing on top of the bus and firing straight down at her. She had to walk sideways, her back rubbing against the concrete and her hands flat against the side of the bus, but she finally reached the other end.

Riley didn't have the luxury of stopping to think. Her chains had fallen off, and she had run. She couldn't even be certain anyone else had heard the gunfire. As soon as she took one step, she was a fugitive. She pushed away from the wall and sprinted toward the chain link fence that separated the police station from its northern neighbor. She leapt at it, hooking her fingers in the metal and planting one foot to propel her upward.

"Stop right there!"

Riley reached the top of the fence and flung herself over. She landed heavily, the impact sending a tremor up her calves. She ignored the pain until she had a time to feel it, taking a route that led her away from the police station. Already a plan was forming in her mind. She would get in touch with Briggs and tell her everything. Angels, demons, the whole mess. She would provide evidence if necessary. She would make sure that Briggs believed her. Then she would find the Angel Maker. She would walk him through the police station and hand-deliver the bastard as she turned herself in.

Marchosias stepped into the mouth of the alley, and Riley couldn't stop herself without falling. Instead, she picked up her speed and swung out when he was within arm's reach. Her fist cracked off his jaw, throwing his head back and knocking him out of her way. He lashed out with one arm, grabbed her bicep, and swung her into the wall. The wind was knocked from her as he pinned her to the wall like a suspect who was under arrest.

"Nice move, asshole," Riley growled.

"Now, now, Detective. I didn't go through all the trouble of freeing you just so you can be recaptured immediately. When the police fail to recapture you, they'll realize that somehow they managed to neglect this street on their search." He released Riley and stepped back. "The thought of you rotting away in a prison cell, awaiting trial, waiting for the appeals to run out, waiting for them to finally kill you... I'm just far too impatient for all of that. And someone like you shouldn't end that way. You need to go out in a blaze of glory, Detective Parra."

"You're a prince."

"Actually a marquis. Hence the name." He grinned and said, "Besides. I looked at your situation and I thought, 'how could I *possibly* make things worse for her?' How did I do?"

"I give it a solid A-plus."

Marchosias clapped once, bowed, and said, "Now, if I were you, I'd find a quick way out of here. We're going to meet again, Riley. And trust me, you will meet an end worthy of your stature." He turned and walked casually down the street, his hands in the pockets of his coat. Riley watched him go and, as the sirens began to fill the air, she chose a direction and started running.

As a kid in No Man's Land, Riley had quickly discovered that the worst place to hide was usually the best place to run. She once shoplifted some food and, when the clerk chased her, she ran to the back of the building and climbed the drainage pipe to the roof. She had lay flat, totally still, and waited. The police arrived and the owner told them that she had just vanished into thin air. Another time, she slid underneath a dumpster and stayed there until the kids chasing her got tired and went home.

So rather than venturing into the city and trying to escape the inevitable roadblock and manhunt, Riley ran in the logically wrong direction. She went to the back of the police station, avoiding the flood of cops who were leaving the building through the front and the main garage. There was a second garage at the back, one few people liked to think about. It allowed for loading and unloading of bodies, and featured an elevator that went up to the morgue.

The access door was locked, but Riley didn't necessarily need it. She knelt down by the side of the garage door and peeled the rubber molding out of the way. She could just barely fit her hand inside to feel the roller wheel and, with sweat stinging her eyes, popped it out of the track. She repeated the move on the other side and pressed on the bottom of the door. It gave her a gap just wide enough to slip beneath, squirming on her back with the metal lip of the door scraping down her body.

Once inside, she put the wheels back into the tracks and looked around to make sure no one had seen her entrance. She brushed off the back of her jumpsuit and went to the emergency stairs. She twisted the knob, unlocked, and pulled the door open a crack to make sure Gillian was alone. The access door was just beyond Gillian's office, with a limited view of the main morgue. Riley could hear someone moving around but had no way of seeing who it was. She was about to retreat until it was safer when Gillian crossed from the morgue to her office door. She had a file in her hand, intent on the photograph inside.

"Jill."

Gillian jumped at the sound of her voice and looked up, her eyes widening behind the protective lenses she wore during autopsies. She crossed to the door, taking off the glasses and tossing them and her file onto the first horizontal surface she passed. She pulled Riley into her arms, holding tight as if afraid of being torn away from her.

"What the fuck are you doing here?" Gillian whispered against Riley's neck.

Riley put her hand on the back of Gillian's head, eyes closed as she clung to the last sane thing in her world. "I didn't have anywhere else to go."

Gillian kissed Riley's forehead and pulled back to look at her. "Why did you run?"

"Marchosias set it up," Riley said. "I didn't have a choice. Once I got away from *him*, I couldn't exactly explain why I had run away. So I just kept going. Jill, I am *not* the Angel Maker."

"I know," she said. "Even when they pulled that knife from the closet... I never doubted you. Not for a second, Riley. You have to know that."

"I know," Riley said, and she kissed Gillian.

They held each other for a long moment until Gillian broke the kiss and touched Riley's cheek. "You should probably go. Briggs could come down here at any moment." She looked down and said, "Wait a minute. I have something for you." She disappeared into her office and, a moment later, returned with an armful of folded clothes. "My street stuff. You can't run around in that jumpsuit. I'll just wear scrubs home."

Riley took the clothes and said, "Thank you, Jill."

Gillian kissed Riley. "Be safe."

"I will."

Gillian held Riley's hand and squeezed. "Will I see you again?"

Riley's answer caught in her throat. She cleared her throat and looked down at Gillian's hand. "I don't know. I hope so."

Gillian pulled Riley back to her. She hugged her tightly and whispered in her ear, "I love you, Riley. Whatever happens from now on, I want you to remember that."

"I love you," Riley said. "More than I've ever loved anything in this world."

Gillian kissed Riley's neck and said, "My cell phone is in the pocket of the jeans. As far as anyone knows, I left it at home today. It won't hold up long, so you might want to dump it as soon as you can. Do you need the car?"

"No," Riley said. "Thank you."

"Don't say good-bye."

Riley nodded. She said, "I love you," and stepped back into the stairwell. She took the opportunity to shed the prison jumpsuit, exchanging it for Gillian's sweater and jeans. She picked up the jumpsuit and carried it with her down the stairs. She unlocked the outside door and, taking a quick look to make sure no one had thought to reconnoiter the station itself, stepped outside. She took the phone from her pocket and dialed a number she never thought she would have to use in this situation.

After one ring, the call was answered. "Legitimate Businessman, LLC, may I ask who is calling?"

"It's me, Muse," Riley said. She walked quickly down the alley, tugging at her borrowed jeans. She and Gillian were pretty much the same size, but her jeans were loose around Riley's hips. She glanced over her shoulder and stepped into the first doorway she found. "I need some help. A ride. I need to get somewhere with a cooler climate."

There was a moment of silence before Muse said, "You know how hot you are right now? The dumbest punk on the street wouldn't touch you with oven mitts and a nyoprene suit."

"I think you mean neoprene, and I don't think it's what you think it is," Riley said. "But you've got both of those, right, Muse? You can handle the heat."

Muse was silent. Riley tapped her head gently against the wall, mouthing, "Please."

Finally, Muse said, "I must be the dumbest punk on the street."

"You've got a heart of gold, Muse."

"Same difference. Where you at?" When she told him, he nearly dropped the phone from laughing too hard. "Auguste Dupin woulda been proud, Riley. I'll come and get you myself."

"It'll be too hot for you to get me here. There's a laundromat at the end of the street. I'll be watching for you."

Riley sagged against the wall as she hung up. She had no idea what she was going to do, where she was going to do, or how she was going to even begin to find the Angel Maker on her own. What she knew for certain was that there was only one place for her now: She belonged in No Man's Land.

Riley stepped into the street as the old Chrysler pulled up in front of the laundromat. The sky had opened up while she was waiting and fat raindrops were beginning to create puddles along the sidewalk. She opened the back door and slid inside before the car had a chance to pull to a complete stop. There was a hoodie in the backseat and Riley pulled it on, flipping the hood down over her head. Muse reached over the back of the seat and handed her a pair of wraparound sunglasses. "You stylin' now, Riley," he said as he rounded the corner and headed back toward No Man's Land.

"You don't have a problem aiding and abetting a murderer?"

"Ain't been convicted yet," Muse said. "Plenty of people I know been *charged* with all kinds of things."

Riley slumped in the corner and tried to look inconspicuous. It seemed like there was a squad car on every corner. She pulled Gillian's cell phone out of her pocket and passed it over the seat. "That belongs to Gillian Hunt. Can you make sure she gets it back?"

"Sure, sure," Muse said. He took it and slipped it into his pocket. "Like I ain't done enough for you already."

"I owe you, Muse."

Muse said, "You say that a lot, you know. Ain't seein' a lot of action on your part."

"I'm not really in a position to grant favors right now."

"I know, I know. Just keeping you aware that your debt keeps on growing."

Riley nodded. "Might as well add one more thing to the list, then. I need to get in touch with my partner, Caitlin Priest. Can you do that?"

"A cop? I don't know..."

"You know *I'm* a cop, right?"

"Yeah, but I'm immune to *you*." He sighed. "I'll see what I can do. I'm not exactly as magic as you think I am, you know."

Riley said, "You're close enough to magic for what I need."

She allowed herself to relax as they crossed the unspoken border of No Man's Land. It was odd, considering she usually had the opposite reaction to the bad part of town, but she couldn't deny her odds were better here. She began to see fewer police on the streets, and the chances of her being spotted by someone who would turn her in dropped drastically. She waited until they were several blocks in before she said, "All right. Stop here."

Muse leaned forward over the steering wheel and eyed the street. "You sure? You got your gun?"

"No. I'll be fine."

Muse leaned down and reached under the seat. He pulled out a gold-plated Mark XIX Desert Eagle and held it out to her. "I'll put it on your tab."

"Put that down."

Muse chuckled. "You ain't a cop anymore, Rye-rye. Even worse, you're an ex-cop in No Man's Land."

"How legal is this thing?"

"'Bout as legal as you are right this minute. You get caught, having this in your belt will be the least of your problems. Take it or I'll never rest easy again."

Riley reluctantly took the weapon. The barrel glinted in the dim light, and she had to admit it was a comfort to have it in her hand. "Nine rounds?"

"Yep. Fully loaded, and I got an extra magazine, too." He handed it over the seat and Riley took it as well. "Point five-oh Action Express. Appropriate, right? Five-oh, like the cops?" He winked. "I'll try to get in touch with your partner. Both of 'em."

"Tell Priest I'll be at Midway at noon. If she's not there, I'll come back at six. After that, I won't see her again."

"Got it."

"Thanks, Muse." Riley climbed out into the rain and stepped immediately into an alley. She tucked the gun into her belt and watched Muse pull away.

The rain was still falling and she took refuge under an overhang for an abandoned grocery store. She wanted to find and stop the Angel Maker to clear her own name. She needed a clear head to do that, which meant she had to stop the mara. She considered the warehouse in the dream where Priest died and figured the odds that there was really a warehouse like that near the waterfront. She cursed herself for not asking Muse when she had the chance.

She waited for a break in the rain before she crossed the street. She moved via alleys and side streets, the hood and glasses from Muse's car still obscuring her features. She kept one hand on the butt of her gun. She stalked through places she had once walked with her head held high, her protection destroyed so that she was just another potential victim. When she had been a kid, she'd walked the same streets with the same target on her back. It felt like a million years ago and she needed to learn how to feel confident without the police or angels to back her up.

The foyer of the building seemed infinitely smaller than she remembered, but it otherwise was unchanged. She crossed to the ratty sofa at the far end of the ground floor, nestled between a soda machine and the wall, and sat down. More than once, she tried to tell herself to leave and that she wasn't doing herself any good by sitting and watching the door. Her mind kept listing the things she had to do, none of which involved this damn building that she had spent so long trying to get away from.

She had been there for an hour when the front door opened. A man came in out of the rain and Riley tensed. After all these years, she still recognized her father's posture. He had gained weight and his shoulders were slumped as if carrying a heavy burden. He didn't have an umbrella, but his head was covered by a loose cap. He shuffled to the wall of mailboxes next to the stairs and fumbled with a key. Riley watched him take out two pieces of mail and mutter as he read who they were from.

He glanced toward her and then away without recognition before he went up to his apartment. She heard his footsteps on the stairs, the apparently reluctant upward climb to his little home. She had eighteen bullets. It wasn't like he was really her father; he was just a warden that demons had thrown her to. She didn't have a father, and she'd lost her mother without ever really knowing her.

She touched the butt of the gun and rested her head against the wall. She visualized her desk at the police station. Gillian's apartment. Gillian's bed. That was her real home. That was her true family. She pushed herself off the couch and walked to the door. She had put her past behind her a long time ago; this was just a final farewell.

Her first stop was a shop well-known around No Man's Land for providing all sorts of unusual weapons. The main business of the shop, according to the owner, was selling medieval replicas; swords, maces, chain mail and that sort of thing. But everyone on the wrong side of the law knew that, for just a few dollars more, the shopkeeper would provide you with a real weapon. The owner of the shop, Fisher, was a contradiction in terms. He didn't like the idea of people getting hurt with something he made, but he wasn't fulfilled making duds with dull blades. Those weren't real weapons, they were toys, and if he could get paid good money to make the real thing, he was willing to shut off his conscience.

Riley had discovered the side business the hard way when she was a teenager. A boy threatened her with a knife unless she did whatever he wanted. Fortunately, her boot between his legs ruined his plans, and she took the knife and ran. A few questions to other kids on the corner had led her to the Dolorous Stroke. When she confronted Fisher, he apologized profusely for his part in her assault. As penance, he gave her a knife of her own so that she could fight back the next time.

The weapons he sold were illegal, but the police department was more concerned with handguns and assault weapons than knives. When Riley became a cop herself, she left Fisher's business alone providing he kept her informed on unusually large purchases. Fisher was happy to accommodate. He liked making the knives, but the thought of allowing anyone to come to harm was a burden on him. He just liked making beautiful pieces.

She walked into the shop, greeted by a full suit of armor that stood next to the door. Fisher was behind the counter, bent over a recreation Excalibur. He was grayer than she remembered, and the ring of hair around his bowling ball was now completely white. He overwhelmed the poor stool on which he sat and was currently squeezed into an argyle sweater. He looked over the rims of his magnifying glasses as she walked in, straightened and stretched, and said, "Detective Parra. What can I do for ya?"

Riley heard renaissance-style music coming from a CD player behind the counter. "Hey, Fish. Heard the news lately?"

"I don't listen to that nonsense. I want to hear people call each other Communists and Nazis I'll just go to a family reunion. But I did hear you were on some big case. Angel Maker."

"Yeah," Riley said. "I need to know if you made a certain knife. I don't have a picture, but I can describe it to you."

Fisher reached under the counter and came back with an order form. "You seem to be missing a lot of stuff. The picture, your partner..."

"She took the only copy to ask other places. And we have so many cases to cover... people don't stop killing each other just because there's a serial killer out there." She picked up a pen and drew a close approximation of the knife she had seen in Briggs' crime scene photo. She figured the correct length, although she had only barely noticed the ruler placed next to the weapon when she was shown the photo.

Fisher watched while she drew and whistled. "That is a bad boy."

"The handle had an ivory inlay," Riley said. "And there were carvings all over the blade."

"Words?"

"Symbols," she said. "I can't remember exactly what they were. Look familiar?"

Fisher rubbed his thumb against his chin and looked at the paper. "I know I didn't make it. But that doesn't mean I can't point you in the right direction. Can you give me a couple of days to ask around?"

"Fish, how long have we known each other? A knife like this didn't just fall out of the sky. If it got made in No Man's Land, it was in your hands at one point or another. The hilt, or the blade, or carving the designs on the blade. Whatever it was, you have a part of this knife."

Fisher pressed his lips together and reluctantly pointed at the handle. "I may have done work like this, but the blade wasn't part of it. I make a lot of hilts like this."

"Do you remember who ordered it?"

"You think the fella I made this for is the Angel Maker?" Fisher said as he pulled out a ledger. "I'll grab a knife and go after him myself if that's the case."

Riley said, "We have enough vigilantes out there chasing this guy. Just whatever you have on him."

"Got a name and an address," he said.

Riley perked up and said, "That's amazing, Fish."

"This *is* a business. Got a pen?" Riley picked up the pencil she had used to draw the knife. He recited the address and Riley wrote it down. "Thanks."

"I didn't see you pull up," Fisher said. "You got a car?"

"I'll walk it."

Fisher said, "It's pouring out there."

Riley said, "Then I'll take the el. Thanks, Fish. You're a prince."

He waved her off and she stepped back out into the deluge. She flipped the hood back up and kept close to the building so that they would protect her from the majority of the downpour. She was aware of someone walking alongside her, but she shut them out of her mind. She knew that walk, knew the movement, and she knew that Sweet Kara couldn't possibly be there.

"We did this before, Riley. Remember? The swords. It was right before you killed me, so you may have blocked some of it out."

"You're not real," Riley said. "So shut up."

"Oh, I'm real," Kara said. "Just because I'm a hallucination doesn't mean I'm not real. Or... maybe I'm a waking dream. I like that better than hallucination. Such bad connotations with that word."

"I'm going to find the Angel Maker, and then I'm going to find the mara and kill it. And then you're going to go back to wherever you came from."

Kara said, "Oh, Riley. Didn't you miss me? I'm hurt."

"She doesn't miss any of us," Christine Lee said. She was now walking on Riley's right. "She just uses us and moves on. It's what she's always done. Priest and Gillian are just going to be tossed aside..."

"Shut up."

Hathaway said, "At least you got to have sex with her. Do you know how long I lusted after her before I finally got—"

"Shut up," Riley said. "All of you just..."

Riley stopped in her tracks, refusing to believe what she saw ahead of her.

Gillian, dressed in the same scrubs Riley had left her in, was standing on the street corner. Her forehead was burnt, and blood trailed down either side of her face as she turned to look at Riley. "Latest in a long line," she said. "They came after me when they couldn't find you. The demons. I wouldn't tell them where to find you, so they took it from me. They're coming, Riley. They're going to catch up with you and kill you. I'm sorry."

Riley reached out and touched Gillian's face, stifling a sob when she actually felt flesh under her palms. Gillian's blood flowed over her fingers.

"You're not real," Riley said.

Gillian smiled. "You can believe that if it helps you sleep better."

"You can believe we're all alive," Kara said. "We just moved to a farm upstate."

"Stop," Riley gasped. The pain of seeing Gillian was too much, and she couldn't bear the sticky feel of blood on her fingers. She desperately wanted to hold them out in the rain, let it scour the blood away. She pulled violently away, spinning to get Gillian out of her sight. She faced Hathaway, whose blood-spattered face loomed before her. Riley backed up and ran between Hathaway and Kara, not caring where she was going as long as it was away.

The truck seemed to materialize out of the rain, headlights shining like twin suns. Riley lunged at the opposite sidewalk, barely avoiding the truck as she hit the asphalt and rolled. The horn blared as the truck sped past her close enough to soak her with water. She landed on her stomach, panting, her face bleeding where it had scraped the pavement, and she looked back across the street.

Kara, Hathaway, Christine and Gillian were all gone. Riley crawled to an alley, not trusting her legs. She pressed against the wall and tried to catch her breath.

There was still a chance it was all just a dream. Maybe the angels and demons and everything that had happened to her since waking up two years ago was all some insane nightmare. Maybe she was insane. She rubbed her throat, rolled her neck on her shoulders, and pushed away from the wall. She had an address. All she had to do was find the killer, the real Angel Maker, and her name would be cleared. For that, anyway. She decided that, when she turned herself in, she wouldn't fight the other charges. She would do her time for killing Gail Finney, and for running.

She checked to make sure she still had the gun and the spare magazine, checked the street, and started down the sidewalk at a run.

The Angel Maker lived near the center of No Man's Land, only a few blocks from Marchosias' stronghold. When Riley turned the corner, she saw angels in armor doing battle with black-clad demons, flaming swords clashing against black axes. Riley stopped in her tracks. While she had seen signs of the apocalyptic battle, she had never actually witnessed the front line. She assumed it was taking place on another plane, invisible to human eyes. She watched while a demon swept a sword away from its throat and swung its axe. The blade dug into the angel's chest and it screamed in agony as it fell. Another angel, wings spread in a magnificent display of lustrous feathers, swung a sword and lopped off the demon's head.

Riley skirted the edge of the battle and entered the building Fisher had pointed her toward. The foyer smelled rank, full of blood and other bodily fluids, and Riley held her breath as she climbed the weathered stairs. Every surface in the building reeked of mildew, as if the roof had been withdrawn for every rainfall in the last century. She avoided touching the banister unless absolutely necessary.

When she reached the appropriate floor, she pulled the Desert Eagle from her belt and braced herself. She wiped her palms on her jeans, rolled her shoulders, and kicked the apartment door open. She stepped inside before it could swing shut again, sweeping her gun across the wide space of the living room. Across from the door was a wall of windows, looking down onto the battle below.

The only piece of furniture was an old wingback chair placed in the very center of the room and turned to look out the window. Riley said, "Hands up. I'll shoot you through the back of the chair if I have to."

"Finally."

Riley froze.

Priest rose from the chair and stretched. She wore a red dress that left her shoulders and back bare, a slit running far up on her thigh to expose her whole right leg as she turned. "It's about time you found me."

"No. This is wrong."

Priest smiled. "Do you want to know the amazing thing? I swore up and down that you would *never* trust an angel again after what Samael did. When I was sent, I told them it was a fool's errand. I didn't reveal my true nature to you because I knew that you would probably have just put a bullet between my eyes without a second thought. You surprised me, Riley. And not in a good way. In a 'the good guys must be very disappointed' way."

"You can't be the Angel Maker."

"No," Priest said. "I'm not the actual murderer. I had a friend for that." She gestured toward the kitchenette, and Riley saw a pair of legs lying on the floor. The pool of blood told her she shouldn't bother to go check on him. "He outlived his usefulness. I just sort of guided him along. All for this moment, right here, and that stupid, stunned, betrayed look on your face."

Priest took a step forward and Riley steadied the gun on her. "Stop."

"Oh, Riley. If you were going to shoot me, you would have done it by now. This is the last part in our little dance. You die. I kill you. You played your part so well. Gail Finney is dead, so now your only mission is to die. New champions will come in. The dance will begin again. If I'd known it would only take one little mara to make you crack, I would have pulled it out years ago. I just never thought you'd be so weak."

Riley fired, and Priest deftly avoided each bullet. "You'll have to do better than that, Riley. I'm an angel, remember? Albeit, not a very good one. You've corrupted me something fierce. Zerachiel was pure, but the second he became Caitlin Priest... something changed. Human emotions are the most dangerous drug I have ever seen. And trust me, I've tried a couple since I got my body. You never even knew. You just saw sweet, pure, Priest. That's why you were so easy to defeat."

Riley had started with nine rounds in the gun. She had fired five times at Priest, the evidence in the cracked glass of the window behind her. Riley began to circle, and Priest moved to stay away from her, exchanging their positions. "So this whole thing has been a lie. All the times you saved my life."

"Subterfuge."

"You're such a fucking bad liar," Riley said. "I don't know who you are, but you're not Priest. Those visions down on the street aren't Gillian or Kara. You just want... me dead." She narrowed her eyes. "But it's not that simple, is it? You wanted me to give up my protection."

Priest's expression darkened and she moved forward. Riley fired, and this time hit her in the shoulder. Priest growled and backed up, clutching her now-bloody arm. Two bullets left. Riley resisted the urge to rub her throat. It felt like she was trying to choke on something. She twisted her neck to loosen the collar of her T-shirt.

"You wanted me to willingly give it up so I would be vulnerable. And then what? You would have just slaughtered me in my cell?"

"I was going to hand you over to Marchosias. After we had a bit more fun with you, of course." Riley fired again, hitting Priest's other shoulder.

Priest howled. "You bitch!"

One bullet left, Riley thought. *Gotta make it count.* She was standing in front of the window now.

"So this is how it ends?" Riley said. "I die, Armageddon comes to an end, new champions are chosen, and the whole thing cycles around again? And how far does No Man's Land grow without me here to protect it?"

"Endlessly," Priest said. If there was any doubt in Riley's mind that this wasn't Priest, it was erased when she saw that feral smile. "How many bullets do you have left, Riley? Do you remember how many it took to kill Samael? I don't suppose those bullets are blessed, either. Do you really think you can win this with one bullet?"

"There's a way," Riley said. She brought the gun up and jammed the barrel into the soft flesh below her own chin. She backed up toward the window. "What happens then? Hmm? What happens if I die before I pass on my protection?"

"Don't," Priest said.

Riley's throat was killing her. She swallowed, and it felt like fire. Had she hurt her throat? She thought back as she stared Priest down. The only injury she could remember had been in a dream... she narrowed her eyes at Priest and moved her gun forward. It was aimed at a forty-five degree angle in front of her face, the single bullet destined to go up into the ceiling.

"What the hell are you doing?"

"Figuring the angles," Riley said. She adjusted her aim slightly and pulled the trigger.

The explosion was deafening, and the force of the blow knocked Riley back. She fell through the window weakened by her earlier shots, the glass shattering around her. She couldn't hear anything but the ringing in her ears, the awful aftermath of the gunshot deafening her as she tumbled out of the building and...

...the light faded...

...she was lying on her back...

...the mara was a bloody torso lying on top of her, its head blown away by the blast from Riley's Desert Eagle. She looked at the weapon she had received in a dream, trying to wrap her head around its existence in the real world as she grabbed her throat. The blood there was tacky, partially dry, and she rolled onto her side.

She was back in the warehouse. Mara Industries, with the hellhounds. She swung her empty gun around, but fortunately the dogs seemed to have died with their master. Riley got to her knees, trembling as she tried to find the strength to stand. It had all been a dream. A fucking epic nightmare. None of it after the hellhounds had been real. Which...

She turned and her heart broke.

Priest lay a few yards away, battered and bloody. Her clothes were ripped, the pale flesh underneath stained red with blood. Riley managed to run to her, dropping to her knees and pulling Priest's ravaged body onto her lap. She stroked Priest's hair and said, "No, Caitlin, no..."

Priest's right eye opened and slowly focused on Riley's face. She smiled weakly. "You won. I knew it."

Riley pulled off her jacket and balled it up, pressing it against the wound in Priest's stomach. Priest grunted and arched her back. "Ow. That... that hurts. I saw the mara holding you down. That level of contact, no one breaks through that." Tears rolled down her cheeks. "I am so proud of you, Riley."

The weakness in Priest's voice scared the hell out of her. She saw the blood on her pants and her arm, and she said, "Can you walk?"

"Don't... think so."

Riley slipped her arm under Priest's legs and lifted her. Priest groaned and put pressure on Riley's coat to slow the blood. "Just leave me here. You'll get a new angel."

"Screw that," Riley said. She was still weak from her ordeal in the nightmare, but somehow she found the strength to get Priest across the room. She nearly stumbled a few times, ignored the blood spreading across her shirt from where Priest touched it and the growing ring dripping from her own throat. She was lightheaded when she finally reached the car.

She placed Priest in the backseat and cupped her face in bloody hands. "If you die after this, I'll never forgive you."

"I'll do my best," Priest said. Her voice was weak, her skin deathly pale. Riley ignored the warning signs, knowing full well that she wouldn't be able to function if she let them take over. She got behind the wheel of the car and pulled out, going as fast as she dared without tossing Priest around in the backseat. She could hear Priest muttering a prayer and, as she rounded a corner, added her own voice to the mix.

"Barachiel," Priest said.

"What?"

"I'll request Barachiel to be your new angel. It will... be an upgrade," Priest said. "He's very good. He knows I want him... to take my place."

"Caitlin?"

"Mm?"

"Shut up."

Priest laughed, and it devolved into a coughing fit. Riley gripped the wheel tightly with one hand and pulled her phone out of her pocket with the other. She dialed a number without taking her eyes from the road, spoke a quick message, and then tossed the phone onto the seat. The sun was just starting to come up, brightening the sky to their right. "You're going to be okay, Zerachiel. I had a fucking demon poisoning me, clawing my throat out, and I got through it okay. You're not going to let a little dog bite take you down."

"I don't regret coming with you," Priest said. "Better me than you."

"God, will you shut up," Riley gasped. "Just shut up."

"I love you, Riley."

"I love you, too, Caitlin," Riley said. Tears burned her eyes and she tried to fight them, tried to choke them back.

She hit the brakes, one tire bumping against the curb. She climbed out and a woman on the sidewalk recoiled from the sight of the blood soaking Riley's clothes. "It's okay, I—" She remembered that she was back in the real world. She grabbed the badge off her belt and held it out in front of her, brandishing it like a talisman. "I'm a cop. I need help."

The woman and her friends came forward and looked into the backseat as Riley opened the door. One of the woman gasped and said, "Caitlin! Oh, Lord."

"Help me get her inside."

"This woman needs a hospital, young lady."

"Trust me. She's at one. Help me, please. Hold that jacket there."

One of the women held the jacket in place. Riley put Priest's arm around her shoulder, while another woman got under the other arm. Together, they carried her into the church below Priest's apartment.

The reverend paused mid-hymn as they entered, every head turning to face them. "Don't stop," Riley said. "You're going to have to trust me on this, but please. Just keep singing."

Riley and the women guided Priest into the back pew and gently lowered her. Riley sat next to her and whispered her thanks to the women as they slipped back out into the aisle. Riley applied pressure to the coat as Priest leaned heavily against her.

"It hurts," Priest whispered. "Oh, God."

"I know," Riley said.

The singing had resumed, and Riley looked toward the pulpit. The words to the hymn were displayed on an overhead projector, glowing on the wall next to the wooden cross. Riley cleared her throat and began singing. "All the saints adore Thee, casting down their golden crowns around the glassy sea; Cherubim and seraphim falling down before Thee, who was, and is, and evermore shall be..."

The door opened and Gillian came rushing in. She had only thrown on a coat over her pajamas, and her messy hair was gathered with a plastic clip. Riley said, "Jill."

Gillian turned and dropped onto the pew. "God, oh, God," Gillian gasped. She put her hand on top of Riley's. "What happened?"

"Long story. Just sing."

"What?"

"She needs worship. She's dying." Gillian looked at Riley's bloody clothes. "It's mostly hers. I'll be fine."

Gillian reluctantly looked toward the front of the church and they both began singing. "Only Thou art holy; there is none beside Thee, perfect in power, in love, and purity."

Priest rested her head on Riley's shoulder. "If I die, I need you to forgive me. Please."

"I will," Riley said. "But don't. Okay?"

Priest said, "Not just for dying. For everything."

"You haven't done anything," Riley said. "Be quiet. I need to sing."

Priest said, "You sing well."

Gillian snorted, but didn't miss a note. Riley ignored them and continued singing. The rest of the worshippers occasionally looked back toward them, but most of them stayed focus on the hymn. Gillian looked at Priest and tightened her hand against Riley's. "How long should it take?" she whispered.

"As long as it takes," Riley said.

Gillian nodded. She slipped her free hand around Priest and touched Riley's hip with it. Riley reached down and laced their fingers together as they continued to sing the hymn.

Mockingbirds

"Hush, little baby, don't say a word..."

Gillian no longer startled awake when she heard the song in her head; she had gotten past that during her time in Georgia. But as soon as the words entered her mind, she was usually awake for the day. She opened her eyes, adjusted the pillow so that she was resting on a cool spot, and listened to the sounds outside the window for a few minutes to see if she could fall back to sleep. The garbage truck rumbled out of the alley and moved on to the next street with a hiss of hydraulics. A car alarm started to blare, silenced seconds later with a double-beep of a remote.

After ten minutes, she resigned herself to wakefulness. She rolled onto her back to see if Riley was awake as well. Riley lay on her back, one arm tucked under the pillow. She was turned toward Gillian, but she was definitely asleep. It had been three weeks since Gillian got the middle of the night call from Riley, begging for her to come to the church under Priest's apartment. And what she saw when she got there...

She gently touched Riley's throat with her fingertips. The wounds there had started healing almost immediately, and Priest explained that they would vanish completely within a few weeks. Mara didn't leave many physical traces once they were killed. Hellhounds, on the other hand, seemed to have no trouble leaving their marks behind in the physical world.

Riley and Gillian spent most of that first day with Priest, sitting in the last pew of the church and praying that Priest was just asleep against Riley's shoulder. When Priest finally let them move her upstairs, Gillian examined and dressed her wounds as best she could. One of the wicked cuts on her back had come within centimeters of severing Priest's right wing. Gillian only had her memory of the first angel she'd examined to make sure she wasn't crippling Priest when she sewed up the wound.

She closed her eyes and remembered the sight of Priest, bloody and bandaged, lying facedown on her bed with both wings extended. It was a magnificent sight, despite the damage to Priest's body. After a very careful procedure, after which Priest confirmed she still had a full range of motion,

Priest ordered Riley to the hospital. Gillian was more than happy to support that decision, but she left Priest with a promise to call her if she needed anything.

Riley was examined at the local emergency room and her neck was bandaged. After a week, as Priest promised, the wounds were barely noticeable.

Also barely noticeable was the Angel Maker. Since claiming his fourth victim, the John Doe whose wings had been washed away by sprinklers, the killer hadn't made a peep. Riley discovered the newest victim's name was James Graham, a former cab driver who was fired after several complaints were filed against him by female passengers. He was accused of driving them off the main drags and then making sexual advances toward them. He never graduated to rape, but the uniformed officers in his area figured it was only a matter of time before he made the leap.

With the new information about his background, the fact he was lurking in a dark courtyard in the middle of the night was more than a little alarming.

Gillian finally slipped out of bed and padded barefoot to the kitchen. It was only a little past four o'clock, but she knew she wasn't going to get back to sleep. She wanted coffee but she knew the smell would wake Riley, so she settled for a glass of milk.

"Hush, little baby, don't say a word..."

Gillian shuddered and rubbed the bridge of her nose. She just had to wait it out. By the time she showered, dressed, and left for work, the seven little words would be out of her head and she'd be fine. It was only at night when she had to worry about it, when it came creeping back.

She had just finished her drink when she heard footsteps in the hallway and looked up as Riley appeared in the kitchen doorway. "Hey," Riley whispered as she leaned against the corner of the cupboard. "What are you doing up?"

"I couldn't sleep. Go back to bed."

Riley walked into the kitchen and held out her hand. "Come with me."

Gillian took Riley's hand. "I'll just keep you awake."

"Who says I'm planning to go back to sleep? Come on."

Gillian let Riley pull her up. She put her arms around Riley's waist and kissed her. She felt Riley's hand sliding under her tank top and decided it had been far too long. She broke the kiss and whispered, "Let's go."

They walked back to bed, and Riley lay on top of the covers. Gillian stretched out next to her, one hand on Riley's neck to pull her in for another kiss. She pushed up Riley's T-shirt with her free hand, curling two fingers and slipping them under the waistband of her shorts. Riley spread her legs and lifted her hips to meet Gillian's hand, moaning as Gillian parted her lips with the tip of her tongue.

"You're aggressive tonight," Riley whispered.

"Is that okay?" Gillian said.

"Very okay," Riley said. She kissed Gillian's chin and ran her hands up under Gillian's tank top. "Take this off."

Gillian withdrew long enough to raise her arms and let Riley peel the cloth away from her body. Riley pushed the tank top up, and then smoothed her palms down Gillian's arms, down her flanks, to the curve of her hips. Gillian lifted her leg and settled on Riley's thigh, cupping her face for another kiss. Riley held Gillian against her, and Gillian began to rock her hips gently. She pressed herself against Riley's thigh and broke the kiss with a groan. Riley ducked her head and licked Gillian's throat, her collarbones, and her breasts. She sucked one nipple into her mouth, flicked it with her tongue, and flattened one palm in the small of Gillian's back to pull her closer.

Gillian pulled at Riley's T-shirt and Riley retreated just long enough for it to be removed. Gillian put a hand on Riley's shoulder and pushed her back, letting her hands move down to Riley's breast when she was on the mattress. Gillian pressed her thigh against the crotch of Riley's underwear and began to thrust her body in a slow, steady rhythm.

"Oh, Jill," Riley grunted.

Gillian teased Riley's nipples as she moved, Riley's body rising to meet her with each move. She felt her orgasm building and kissed along Riley's jaw to nibble on her earlobe. She whispered, "I'm close." Riley dug her fingers into Gillian's hips and she moaned inarticulately. Gillian licked Riley's neck and held onto her as she came, bucking her hips as Riley climaxed underneath her.

She lifted her head and kissed Riley's lips, easing her body down onto Riley's. She let Riley cradle her head to her breast and listened to her breathing and the slowing drum of her heart. Riley kissed her hair and Gillian closed her eyes. She felt more than loved, and tried to choose the correct word. Cherished, adored. She kissed Riley's chest.

"What time do you have to be in at work?"

"I was going to leave around six-thirty," Gillian said. "Why?"

"Enough time for a shower. Unless you want to try sleeping again."

Gillian said, "That depends. Will you be showering with me?"

Riley chuckled. "That can be arranged."

They climbed out of bed and went to the bathroom to shower. While Riley was shampooing Gillian's hair, during a break after her third orgasm of the morning, both of their pagers began to vibrate on the nightstand. Riley answered the call while Gillian dressed and laid out Riley's clothes for her. Riley spoke to Briggs and, when she hung up, thanked Gillian for the clothes.

"Big?"

"The Angel Maker," Riley said.

"Shit."

Riley nodded and pulled on her underwear.

"Who was it?"

"They haven't been identified yet."

Gillian frowned. "They?"

Riley said, "The Angel Maker killed two people this time."

An intern from the medical examiner's office volunteered to drive the van to the scene, so Riley and Gillian rode to work together. The first body was lying at the bottom of the stairs that led up to the station, and it was naturally the first one found. The police discovered the other body while they cleared the scene. It was hidden better, nearly invisible underneath the wooden support frame of the el tracks.

Riley parked amid the sea of black and white cruisers and led Gillian to the first taped-off area. A civilian in a suit grabbed Riley's arm as she passed. "How long is this going to take? If I miss the next train, I'm going to be at least half an hour late to work."

"Just walk to the next station, sir," Riley said. "This is going to take awhile."

"Unbelievable," the guy said. "Look, you know who it is, and wasting time here isn't going to help you catch him any faster. I mean, if you're too incompetent to have caught him by now..."

Riley twisted and the man's hand fell from her arm. "Walk to the next station. Walk all the way to work for all I care. Just get out of here."

The guy muttered something under his breath as he stormed off.

Gillian said, "Continuing recruitment for the Riley Parra fan club."

"The only member I need or want shampooed my hair this morning."

Gillian grinned and ducked under the tape with Riley. The body was lying with its head resting on the bottom step, with barely enough room even for the small wings the Angel Maker had given him. Gillian's assistant was already kneeling by the body and Gillian crouched next to him to observe his findings. There were two stab wounds in the man's chest, which was different from the killer's usual MO, but Riley knew it wasn't a copycat; she was practically a patron of this particular artist, and she could tell him by the way he painted. It was their guy.

A patrolman came up to them and nodded a greeting before began to speak. "Early bird nearly tripped over the first one on the way up to meet the six-oh-five. He called the cops, who showed up on the scene fifteen minutes later and closed off the scene. In the course of clearing the area, we found a second body hidden under the tracks."

"They were most likely killed the other way around," Riley said. "Guy under the tracks was killed first. Can I see him?"

Gillian stood up. "I'll come with you. I have to see him sooner or later."

The cop escorted them into the shadow of the tracks. "Your idea is pretty much what we were figuring. Angel Maker killed this guy out of sight, and got spotted trying to leave the scene of the crime. So he stabbed the other guy and decided to make it a double-or-nothing sort of thing."

"Do you have ID on either of them yet?"

"Both. We got Allan McDade back there in the stairs, and Sidney Lee is down here."

Riley said, "He's never killed a woman before."

"Oh. He still hasn't... apparently it can be a boy's name, too. It's spelled with an 'I.'"

Riley said, "An I? Where?"

"After the S," Gillian said, and she spelled it.

"Oh. I was picturing it at the end. Didn't fit." Riley stepped down into the concrete ditch that ran underneath the tracks. Piles of garbage lined both sides, either blown there by the wind or tossed there by uncaring passerby.

The cop pointed up ahead. "Body is down there. We're lucky we saw it."

Riley and Gillian continued on without the cop. The trash had been cleared away so there would be enough room for the body and the wings. "It's a pretty isolated place down here," Riley said. "Seems kind of an unusual place to stage the body, though."

"Maybe he wanted to make sure his artwork wasn't destroyed like last time," Gillian said.

"Maybe. But if it had rained, this whole thing would have been flooded. We would have found the body out on the waterfront in a couple of days, been forced to rely on your amazing forensic skills to find out it was an Angel Maker corpse."

"Fresh," Gillian said.

"I try," Riley said. She looked up at the train tracks overhead, and the wooden framework all around them. "Also, it's so secluded. Part of his artwork is in the display. The church, the middle of the street..."

"The bartender wasn't public," Gillian said. "That could have gone hours without being found."

"And that's why he called Gail Finney to let her know he'd struck again. He's not shy." She looked around to try seeing what was visible from the crime scene. There were two chain link fences put up, most likely a futile attempt to keep kids out of the drainage ditch, and a sliver of the nearby intersection. "Maybe this is the best place to find the victim by himself. Or maybe this victim meant something different. Either way, it's worth noting."

Gillian said, "Or... he knew how secluded it was, and the body at the stairs wasn't a death of convenience. Maybe that was his marker to make sure we found this body."

"That could be." Riley looked at the cop. "Is this your regular beat?"

"Pretty regular. People come down here a lot more than you'd think, Detective. Kids, mostly, to smoke and drink and fu—" He caught himself and rubbed the back of his neck. "You know. Teenager stuff."

Gillian crouched next to the body, a few feet to Riley's left, and examined the dirty clothes and stubble on his cheeks.

Riley moved next to her, watching Gillian exam the body. After a while, she said, "So he was homeless?"

"No, look at the hands," Gillian held one up and indicated the fingers. Riley saw that the fingernails nails were clean and trimmed. "The rest of the outfit is hobo chic. Teenagers dressing up to look homeless."

Riley scoffed. "God, that's what's cool now? I would have been the coolest kid at school."

Gillian smiled. "You should see the mall. I've given change to a couple of kids hanging out in the food court." She looked at the victim's face and said, "Still, that's mostly a teenage thing. This guy has a couple of years on them."

"We know him," the cop said. "He's a dealer. He dresses and acts ten years younger than he is because he wants the kids to relate to him."

Riley said, "Okay. You good here, Jill?"

"Yeah, Mr. Lee and I have a lot to go over."

Riley patted and squeezed Gillian's shoulder before she stepped away with the cop. "Let me know when you have something."

"Will do." Gillian watched them walk away and then turned back to her patient. She sighed as she looked at the wings painted over the cracked and dirty pavement. "Let's see what you can tell us about our killer, Mr. Lee." She sighed and began her preliminary examination of the corpse.

Gillian had changed into a pair of scrubs when she arrived at work, leaving the work of preparing the bodies to her assistant. When she returned to the main room, she examined his work and thanked him for his help transporting the bodies. She had just begun her in-depth examination when the doors opened and Riley came in. "Hey. I didn't see you when you left the scene."

"Hi. You were interviewing witnesses. I didn't want to disturb you."

"Have you found anything interesting?"

"Just that you were right."

Riley smiled. "I love when you say that."

Gillian raised an eyebrow. "Because it's such a rarity? In this case, I was referring to the times of death. Sidney Lee was indeed the first victim. His wounds are precise, placed with clear intent. McDade, on the other hand..." She turned to face the other body. "The wounds are haphazard. Frenzied, almost. There was no planning whatsoever in this murder. The Angel Maker was probably covered in blood from Lee's murder, the commuter saw it, and the killer made sure he kept quiet. I did notice one interesting thing on Mr. McDade. See this wound?"

Riley looked at the diamond-shaped cut in the man's chest. "Not a back wound."

"Nope. And it's incredibly shallow. Barely an inch. I think the Angel Maker was in such a frenzied state that the knife slipped in his hand. Hopefully he cut himself on the blade and some of this blood will turn out to be his. It doesn't mean much without something to match it to, but it's something."

Riley kissed Gillian's cheek. "Let me know when you have anything else."

"You'll be the second to know," Gillian said. "Will I get another kiss if I find something good?"

"We'll see. We'll take it on a case by case basis. Do I get a kiss if I find anything out during interviews with the family?"

Gillian grinned and said, "Case by case basis."

Riley kissed Gillian's cheek again and said, "All right. I'll let you get to work. Lunch?"

"I'll probably work through. Dinner?"

Riley nodded and waved good-bye as she left the morgue. Gillian clicked on the voice recorder and began to record her progress as she examined the bodies in the order they were killed. She had finished Sidney Lee and moved on to Alan McDade when the door opened behind her. She paused the recorder and turned to see the last person she would have expected.

"Caitlin. What are you doing up?"

Priest smiled. "Do I really look that bad?"

"No, actually. You look amazing."

It was only a small lie; Priest was in a T-shirt and jeans rather than her usual suit, and the clothes made her look ten years younger. She wasn't wearing makeup and her unwashed hair was pulled back in a ponytail. Her flesh was pale, and she was leaning heavily on a cane. But considering the shape she had been in after the hellhound attack, it was amazing that she was even able to stand upright. And even given the circumstances, Priest was distractingly beautiful. The phrase 'angelic' came to mind before she realized the irony of the word.

She stepped away from the table and quickly gave Priest a visual examination. "How do you feel?"

"Pretty well, considering. It's an unusual thing to be prepared for your own death and then wake up the next morning."

Gillian started to flash back to the bad time she'd had a year earlier, but she forced herself to remain in the present. "Did Riley call you?"

"She wanted to tell me the Angel Maker struck again, but she's taking the investigation on her own. I was just a bit thrown by the fact that... there were two victims?"

"Right. The apparent target and someone who was in the wrong place at the wrong time."

"I thought I should get filled in, since I will be back on the case eventually. This is a fairly... fairly big change in his modus operandi."

Gillian nodded. "Uh-huh. Caitlin, are you sure you're all right? Do you want to sit down?"

"No, I'll be fine. I just want to check this out and then I'll go rest in the break room to gather the strength necessary to return home. May I?" She gestured at the table and Gillian stepped back so she could approach. Priest looked down at the bodies and then said, "Which of them was killed first?"

"The blonde fellow," Gillian said. "Sidney Lee. Cops knew him as a drug dealer. He was killed under the el tracks. Riley thinks the other victim was an early commuter who happened onto the scene as the Angel Maker was leaving. The killer panicked and lashed out. The wounds back up that theory. It wasn't planned."

"But the Angel Maker still took the time to make the wings?"

"Right. It could mean the artwork is a compulsion with him."

Priest nodded and closed her eyes suddenly. Gillian assumed even the minor motion had triggered a headache, and decided that was enough.

"Okay, show and tell is over. I'll fill you in on everything when you get back, but right now you need to rest up."

Priest smiled weakly. "Are you my doctor now?"

"I saw you half naked and sewed you back together. You better believe I'm your doctor now. You may not be mortal, but this body might need another bandage or two if you keep hanging around my girlfriend."

"You have a point. Tell Riley I'll be in the break room if she comes back."

"Will do."

Priest left, and Gillian went back to her report.

Riley was still out trying to find Sidney Lee's common-law wife when Gillian finished her report on both bodies. She carried the files upstairs to hand deliver them to Lieutenant Briggs, glancing toward Riley's empty desk as she passed. Her favorite part about having to come upstairs was getting a chance to spy on Riley at work. The door to the break room was open, and she spotted Priest asleep on the couch as ordered.

She knocked on Briggs' door and waited for the response. She hadn't spent much time with the new lieutenant, but she knew Riley trusted her. And anyone was better than the former lieutenant, Hathaway. Gillian always suspected something had happened between Riley and Hathaway, but she didn't want to pry. Riley would tell her anything pertinent when it was necessary.

She was about to give up on Briggs when she heard an invitation from within. She opened the door and saw a uniformed officer standing in front of the desk. The man's hands were clasped casually behind his back, his head held high, eyes focused on the wall behind Briggs' desk. Gillian immediately started to step back out. "Oh, I'm sorry..."

"No, it's fine," Briggs said. She looked flustered, confused, and waved Gillian forward. "I could use a breather."

Gillian held up the reports. "I just wanted to drop these off with you. My report on the bodies found this morning."

"Thank you, Doctor."

Gillian placed the folders on the desk and glanced at the officer. His eyes met hers, and Gillian felt something tug at the back of her brain. Like a piece of piano wire had been attached to her cerebellum and this man was tugging on it. She tore her gaze away from him, her skin exploding in goose-bumps as she tried to keep her breathing steady.

Briggs finally noticed Gillian was still standing beside her guest. "Doctor?"

"I believe the lieutenant excused you," the officer said. His voice raked against Gillian's bones and she couldn't stop herself from shuddering violently at the sound of it. She braced herself against the edge of the desk, moving to one side so she wouldn't have to stand next to the creature anymore. He was a demon. Somehow she knew. She could feel it inside the cop's body.

"*Is* there anything else?" Briggs said. She looked more concerned than angry.

"N... yes," she said. "Do you have a Bible handy?"

Briggs blinked. "No..."

She could see the computer monitor from where it stood, and saw that Briggs was connected to the Internet. "Could you do me a favor and look something up online? Go to the Gospel of Mark." The cop had taken a step back as Briggs typed, but Gillian locked her eyes on his. "No. You can stay. This will only take a second." She looked at the screen, trying to work some saliva into her suddenly dry mouth. Briggs found the page, and Gillian scrolled down to the chapter she had read so many times during her self-imposed exile.

"And when He was come to the other side into the country of the Gadarenes, there met him two possessed with demons, coming forth out of the tombs, exceeding fierce, so that no man could pass by that way."

The cop hissed, "Stop it."

Briggs tore her eyes from the screen at the man's gruff tone, and frowned at Gillian. "Doctor, what..."

Gillian ignored them both and continued to read. "And behold, they cried out, saying, 'What have we to do with thee, thou Son of God? Art thou come hither to torment us before the time?'"

The cop shot out one hand, resting it on top of the computer monitor. "I said *stop*." His fingers curled and the plastic cracked.

Briggs recoiled from the deep, inhuman voice.

"Read," Gillian gasped.

Briggs looked at Gillian and then they both began to read aloud. "Now there was afar off from them a herd of many swine feeding. And the demons besought Him, saying, 'If thou cast us out, send us away into the herd of swine.' And He said unto them, 'Go.' And they came out, and went into the swine: and behold, the whole herd rushed down the steep into the sea, and perished in the waters. And they that fed them fled, and went away into the city, and told everything, and what was befallen to them that were possessed with demons."

Briggs reached into the collar of her blouse and pulled out a cross necklace. The demon flew back from it, hitting his shoulder against the doorframe. Gillian shouted Priest's name as the demon turned and ran from the office.

The door to the break room opened and Priest stepped out. The demon recoiled from the sight of her. Priest didn't seem to need an explanation. The fingers of one hand tightened around the head of her cane and she lifted the other. She spread her fingers and said, "Go no further."

The demon skidded to a stop.

Briggs said, "Everyone, to the stairs. Out of the building, now."

The detectives and officers in the room hesitated for only a second before they made their way for the stairs. Briggs pulled her gun and aimed it at the back of the officer's head. Once the room was empty, Priest moved cautiously forward.

"Identify yourself," Priest demanded.

"Vinea," the demon said.

"What is your business here?"

Vinea slowly turned to face Briggs. His eyes burned green and Briggs muttered a curse under her breath. The room was clear now, but the energy Priest expelled caused the lights to flicker and cast unusual shadows across the familiar space.

"It was my mission to infiltrate Riley Parra's hierarchy. To possess her superior and use my position to destroy her."

"What is going on here," Briggs said in such a quiet voice that Gillian assumed she was talking to herself.

Priest said, "You have failed in your mission."

"My primary mission, perhaps," Vinea said, turning to face Priest again. "My secondary mission can still find success." He lifted his hand and the air in the room seemed to tremble. Priest gasped in pain and pools of blood began to form against her shirt.

"Leave her alone, you bastard," Gillian shouted.

Priest bared her teeth and hunched her shoulders. Her wings extended out from the center of her back, rising up and out before they spread in a divine show of pristine white feathers. Even in the dim room, as the lights had finally given up the battle to stay on, each feather seemed to be illuminated along their center shafts.

Briggs drew a trembling breath. "Holy Mary, Mother of God..."

Gillian reached out and touched Briggs shoulder, drawing her away from the display. Gillian felt something warm against her hip and reached back to brush whatever it was away. As her fingers crossed the tattoo, she realized that it was the source of the heat. She lifted the hem of her scrub top and twisted to look at the design Riley had given her. She covered it with her palm and felt the tips of her fingers tingling as if she was standing too close to a live wire.

Gillian brushed past Briggs and weaved between the desks to where the demon stood. It almost made her physically ill to be so close to him, but she stood her ground. She flattened her right palm against the tattoo and raised her left hand. "Leave her alone," she said.

Vinea turned and Gillian pressed her hand to his face. The power that shot through her body threw her off her feet. She hit the side of a desk and fell to the ground, her limbs shaking with the remnants of the energy that had coursed through her. She recovered enough to see that Vinea was retreating toward the stairs, and Priest was slumped in the break room doorway.

Briggs had a phone in her hand, barking orders. "...no one else in or out of the building without my say-so."

"Except Riley," Gillian said as she struggled back to her feet.

Briggs looked at her for a moment and said, "Scratch that. Detective

Riley Parra is allowed inside when and if she arrives. Anyone else, we are under a lockdown."

Gillian crossed the room to where Priest was slumped. She put her hand on Priest's shoulder, cupping her face with the other. "Caitlin, look at me. Are you all right?"

"I just popped some stitches, I think," she said. Her hair was covering her face, but Gillian could hear her struggling to draw breath. "No new injuries."

"You have wings."

Gillian and Priest both looked up to see Briggs standing a few feet away. "Lieutenant," Gillian said.

"She has a pair of damned wings coming out of her back," Briggs said, her voice one note away from hysteria. She looked at Gillian. "And what the hell did you do to Officer Taylor?"

Priest said, "That was no longer Officer Joseph Taylor. It was a demon called Vinea. I know this is a lot to throw at you all at once, but you must keep your wits."

"So that makes the two of you angels?"

"No," Gillian said. "Just her."

Briggs looked at Priest. "Is Riley an angel, too?"

"She's mortal, like me," Gillian said, feeling a bit crazy as the words left her mouth. "Only Priest is an angel."

"And it looks like she's hurt. I'm guessing these injuries weren't caused by a car accident like you said when you asked for the sick leave."

"I'll be fine," Priest said.

Gillian said, "She's a *stubborn* angel. Look, we can get you patched up, call Riley, and figure things out from there. Vinea is gone..."

"No. He's not. He has a second plan. He won't leave here until he succeeds with that. Phone, please. I need to call Riley. I need her to pick some things up before she comes to join our little party."

Gillian went to the desk and pulled a phone down to the floor. A uniformed officer appeared at the top of the stairs and he stopped to examine the tableau. Priest had lowered her wings down so he couldn't see them.

"Report," Briggs barked, and the officer jumped.

"Uh, the building has been cleared. Officers are standing guard outside until you give the all-clear. All access to the holding cells has been cut off."

Briggs said, "Good job. Go outside and wait."

The cop made a hasty retreat. Priest had the phone and was dialing, and Gillian nervously scanned the entrances to the room to make sure Vinea wasn't circling around on them. Priest turned the speakerphone on and slumped against the wall as it rang.

"Detective Parra."

"Hey. Riley," Priest said. She smiled weakly at Gillian and chuckled. "If you don't hurry, you're going to miss all the fun."

Briggs helped Gillian carry Priest to the elevator. As they moved her, it became apparent the extent of damage Vinea had done to her. The blood was spreading across her T-shirt, one pool stretching to meet others. Gillian had checked the wounds before she even thought of moving Priest, but the wounds seemed to be minor enough at the time. She was already starting to regret her decision given the amount of red marring Priest's T-shirt.

Briggs sighed and leaned against the wall of the elevator once the doors were closed. "I'll say one thing; I am definitely looking forward to this briefing. But right now, I'll settle for the Cliff Notes version."

Priest exhaled. "Riley was chosen to stand as champion for the city against the forces of evil. Namely demons under the command of a demonic lord named Marchosias. I was sent to act as her guardian angel."

Briggs looked at Gillian. "And who are you?"

Gillian shook her head. "I'm just Riley's girlfriend."

"Well, thank God for a bit of normalcy." Briggs exhaled and said, "So this Angel Maker guy..."

The elevator doors opened and they helped Priest out.

Priest grunted and continued her explanation. "He's a mortal, but he's under the influence of a demon. That's the reason Riley and I have been so determined to keep the case for ourselves. No one else will be able to catch this killer because they don't fully understand what he is."

Gillian moved them toward an empty examination bed and motioned for Briggs to help Priest up onto it.

"Okay. So why is it a good thing that this... Vanya is still in the building?"

"Vinea," Priest corrected. "And it's only a good thing in the short term. If we know where he is, then we can stop him and maybe ensnare him. But in the long run, he's here to cause damage. I believe he intends to destroy the building somehow. By trapping him here, we're only giving him time to put his plans in motion."

Gillian eased Priest's T-shirt up over her stomach while she was talking. The bandaged wounds were soaked with blood, smears of it spreading across the too-pale skin of her abdomen. "Your stitches definitely popped. Lieutenant, would you mind—"

"Tell me what you need," Briggs said, shrugging out of her blazer.

Priest closed her eyes as Gillian removed the dressings. The wounds were mostly healed, so they weren't nearly as bad as that first night after the hellhound attack. Briggs sucked in a breath through her teeth when she saw the damage, but she didn't say anything. Gillian removed the ruined stitches and spoke quiet directions to Briggs when she needed something cleaned or moved out of her way.

Briggs said, "What do you know? You're good with the living, too."

"I'm only dangerous to houseplants," Gillian said. She looked up at Priest and saw her eyes were closed. "Cait? I need you to stay awake."

"Sorry. It's just painful."

"I know, honey."

Briggs took Priest's hand and squeezed it. "Talk to me, Detective. I need to know what to expect with this demon."

"Don't take his appearance for granted," Priest said. "The building was evacuated quickly, but there's still a chance he found a new host. Officer..."

"Taylor."

"Yes. He might be wandering around, confused and unsure of what's happened."

Briggs said, "Someone can be possessed by a demon and walk away without any ill effects?"

Gillian cleared her throat. "I wouldn't say *no* ill effects..."

Briggs looked at her and sighed. "For God's sake."

"It was before your time. Don't worry," Gillian said. "Priest, stay with me."

Priest nodded, but kept her eyes closed. "I'm trying. Holding him back like that... took a lot out of me."

Gillian said, "I know. I'm almost done. Tell me about the stuff you told Riley to pick up at your apartment."

Priest licked her lips. "Palm branches, incense, candles and holy water. They're sacraments of the church. If we place them near the entrances and exits, Vinea won't be able to cross them."

Briggs said, "And just so I'm clear, we do *want* this crazy, evil demonic cop trapped in here with us?"

"For now," Priest said.

Gillian said, "Don't worry. Riley's great at this sort of thing."

"She damn well better be."

Gillian redressed Priest's wounds and said, "How does that feel?"

"A lot better," Priest said. She slowly sat up, pulling her T-shirt back down over her abdomen. "Where would he be most likely to go if he wanted to destroy this building?"

"Explosives on the parking level would damage the building's structural integrity," Briggs said. "I doubt he'd want to play it safe, though. I imagine there will be bombs on every floor if he can manage it."

"He has nothing but time," Gillian said. "How long until Riley gets here?"

"She was about fifteen minutes from my apartment when I called." She looked at the clock on the wall and shrugged. "Figure another ten minutes to get everything loaded up, ten more to get here from there. It's been twenty minutes since we called her, so another fifteen."

Gillian said, "You've driven with Riley before, right? Considering I'm in danger, and you're in here with me."

Priest said, "Five minutes?"

"At the outside," Gillian said.

Priest accepted that. "Vinea won't leave until he's sure the building is wired to blow. And he won't blow it unless he knows the three of us are inside. If he can't control Riley, he'll want to cripple her."

Briggs said, "I didn't know I meant so much to her."

"You're actually not that important," Priest said. She suddenly realized what she had said. "Um. Boss. I just meant—"

Briggs smiled. "I know what you meant, Detective. I'm her immediate superior. So what do we do?"

"I can feel him. Vaguely. All I know is that he's above us, so somewhere on the fourth, fifth or six floors. He can feel me, too. He'll know if we head for the exits, and he'll come to stop us to make sure we're still inside when the bomb goes off."

Gillian nodded. "And then we pull the bait and switch? Reveal he's locked in?"

"Sure," Priest said. "I'm making this up as I go along."

Gillian took a steadying breath. "I'm starting to wish I had a gun."

Priest looked at the instruments beside the bed and picked up a scalpel and a syringe. She wet the blade of the scalpel in the blood Gillian had cleaned from her, and she used the syringe to draw more blood. "These will be more effective. The blood of the seraphim is like poison to a demon. Once it's inside them, it doesn't come out. It'll stop him long enough for you to get away."

Gillian took the syringe and scoffed at the idea of using it as a weapon. "Tools of the trade," Gillian said.

"What?" Priest said.

"I don't know," Gillian said. "I just said it to be saying something."

Priest looked confused, but she let it drop. "Boss, are you armed?"

Briggs pulled the gun from the back of her waistband. "Grabbed it as soon as things started to get hot up there. It's not every day one of my people asks me to recite from the Bible."

Priest said, "Which verse?"

"Matthew 8. The chapter about Legion."

"Very nice choice. Demons hate that chapter."

Gillian smiled and slipped her weapons into a fanny pack so she wouldn't accidentally jab herself with them. Briggs helped Priest off the table, and Priest was able to walk to the elevator under her own power. When they got to the elevator, Gillian glanced at the two women standing to her right and chuckled.

"What?" Briggs said.

"A medical examiner, an angel, and a police lieutenant. Hunting demons in a locked-down police station. This is a fucking Quentin Tarantino movie."

Briggs grinned as the elevator arrived. "Lock and load, bitches."

Homicide was located on the fourth floor, one floor above the morgue. The elevator doors opened and Briggs took the lead, leading with her gun as she inched from the car. Priest followed, her gun drawn but her focus more on staying upright and conscious. Gillian remained behind, aware that she was a civilian in this situation but still feeling useless. Briggs finally confirmed the room was clear and motioned for her to exit.

Priest said, "He's still above us somewhere."

"Do you have any idea where he would plant the bombs?" Gillian said.

Briggs considered and scanned the room. "There's any number of places that would be devastating. We don't have time to check them all."

"We'll just have to make him tell us," Priest said.

Briggs said, "I have a zip drive in my office with back-up files of pretty much all of my detectives. If Vinea does manage to detonate, we'll only lose a day or two worth of work."

Priest said, "I'll watch your back. Go."

Briggs crossed to the office and Priest moved to keep an eye on the stairs and the elevator both. Gillian checked her watch for what felt like the tenth time and again wondered where Riley was. She focused on Priest, who seemed to have most of her color back. "How are you feeling?"

"It's been a bad month," Priest said. "But I'll be okay. Thank you."

Gillian looked at the elevator indicators, which were dark for the moment. "What will we do when we find Vinea? Do you think you'll be able to exorcise him?"

"No," Priest said. "In my condition, it would be suicide. When Riley gets here, we'll have him restrained. All we have to do after that is decrease the size of the binding until he fits into a prison cell. We'll figure out what to do with him after that."

Briggs came out of her office with a small steel box. "Can't you call down some of your buddies to deal with him? I doubt you're the only angel in this town."

"Things are hectic right now," Priest said. "The fact that a pack of hellhounds could be kept in the city limits without anyone noticing is a sign of how splintered our attention is. There's a battle raging in No Man's Land."

"That doesn't surprise me a bit," Briggs said. "Angels and demons are to blame for that?"

"Technically, Riley is to blame," Gillian said. "There was a kind of detente before Riley poked the beehive."

Briggs considered that and said, "I'm sure she had a good reason."

Priest smiled. "Benefit of the doubt?"

Briggs exhaled and shook her head. "I just found out my lead detective is a major player in Armageddon while managing to, for the most part, play by the rules and close cases. I think I owe her an apology for some of the shit I've been giving her. If we get out of this, I'm going to give her a bit more leeway."

Gillian cleared her throat. "That's great, but... maybe Riley doesn't have to *know* you're going to be more lenient with her."

Briggs smiled. "Just to keep her on the straight and narrow."

"It wouldn't be a *bad* think," Gillian said.

Priest pushed away from the desk. "The elevator is moving."

They saw the indicator that said the elevator was going down. Priest and Briggs both took position in front of the elevator, guns drawn. Priest extended her wings and Briggs looked over at them. "I won't be able to get used to that. Dr. Hunt, take cover."

Gillian moved to hide behind a desk, one hand on her fanny pack to make sure the syringe and scalpel hadn't fallen out. When she looked up, she saw furtive movement on the stairs. She looked toward the elevator. If it was a distraction, then Vinea would be able to get the jump on them from behind. But if she called out and broke Briggs and Priest's concentration when Vinea was actually coming down on the elevator...

She ran across the room at a crouch, hoping the desks provided her enough cover, and pulled the scalpel from her pack. It felt bizarre to be handling a scalpel with dried blood; it was unsanitary for one thing, but she knew that infection was the least of Vinea's worries if he was cut by it. She reached the stairs just as the stealthy newcomer arrived. Gillian brought up the scalpel and said, "Don't move."

An arm shot out, knocked the scalpel from her hand, and Gillian swept her left hand against the other person's face. She heard a grunt, gasped, and suffered a blow to the gut. Gillian wrapped her arms around the other woman and breathed, "Riley!"

"Jill? God... are you okay? Oh, God."

The elevator continued past their floor, and Briggs relaxed her stance. "Dr. Hunt?"

"Fine. I'm fine." She clung to Riley until she got her breath back. "Nice left hook."

"I'm so sorry," Riley said. She helped Gillian across the room to rejoin Priest and Briggs. She eyed Priest's extended wings and then looked at Briggs. "So. The jig is up."

"I would say you have a lot of explaining to do," Briggs said, "but this actually explains a *lot*. I guess you weren't captured by gang members last year?"

"No."

"Demons?"

"Angels, actually."

Briggs frowned.

"It's complicated," Riley said. She put her hand on Gillian's stomach where she had hit her, rubbing gently. "Fill me in."

Priest said, "First, the supplies. Did you get them?"

"Yeah. I have uniformed officers placing candles around every exit to the building, and there's a perimeter of holy water being poured as we speak. The palm branches are being wrapped around the door handles."

"Perfect," Priest said. "The incense?"

Riley pulled a package from her jacket. "I figured we could use them in here."

"Good," Priest said.

"How on Earth did you explain all of that?" Gillian said.

"I told the officers that we were dealing with a practitioner of voodoo, and the mere sight of the ceremonial bindings would keep him inside. They bought it, I guess. Or they think I'm crazy. Either way, it's done."

"Well done," Gillian said.

Riley said, "Okay, tell me what we know."

Priest said, "The demon is Vinea. His original plan was to possess Briggs and use her to control you. When Gillian stopped that—" Riley looked at Gillian and squeezed her hand in gratitude. "—he changed his plans. He's going to blow up the building instead. We have to keep him in here until we find the explosives and disarm them."

Riley shook her head. "He's not going to give that up very easily."

"We'll have to be very convincing," Briggs said.

Priest was watching the elevator. "He's on the ground floor. Only a matter of time before he discovers that he's locked in. He'll come looking for us."

"How are you holding up?" Riley asked Priest.

"I'm fine, all things considered. I'll be happy when we end this so I can get to a church."

Briggs looked curiously at Riley, who explained, "She soaks up worship. It's like recharging a battery."

"Ah."

Priest suddenly trembled and stumbled, catching the edge of a desk before she fell over. She exhaled and said, "I think Vinea just discovered he couldn't leave. He's pretty mad."

"How do you know?" Briggs said.

"Emotional shockwave. You know how you can just tell when someone you're spending time with is in a bad mood? It's the same thing. Humans tend to shrug it off, but angels are more sensitive to it. Especially when a demon is the source. He's coming to find us."

Riley said, "Should we split up?"

Priest shook her head. "No. We're more effective as a group. Individually, he could pick us off without much trouble."

"Okay, where do we go first?"

"He was just on the upper floors," Briggs said. "There are a couple of places he could have set bombs, but it will be more dangerous if he managed to plant something in the parking garage. There are all kinds of load-bearing walls and support beams he could have sabotaged. If he set a bomb down there and even one of them goes off, the entire building could collapse on top of us. And going down there would let us keep on the move while keeping away from him."

Riley said, "Or we could let him fool himself. He's expecting us to be running scared. So we go to the garage and we act cornered. Priest is too weak to fight, Gillian and Briggs aren't equipped for this kind of enemy, and he doesn't necessarily know I'm even here. He'll be cocky when he comes after us. We can use that to our advantage."

"There's only one problem with that," Gillian said. "Priest *is* nearly too weak to fight, and Lieutenant Briggs and I *are* unequipped for this kind of battle."

Priest said, "You have your syringe and scalpel. Those might not stop him, but he most likely won't even expect you to fight back. Riley is right. Vinea will be pissed off and arrogant, and he expects to find three weak women cowering in a corner. We can use that to our advantage."

"I'll be your secret weapon. Once he realizes I'm here, he'll be cornered. Then it's four against one."

"More like two against one," Briggs said. "Dr. Hunt and I don't exactly belong to the same level as you and Detective Priest."

"Right," Riley said. "I was counting Priest as two."

Priest chuckled and Briggs smirked.

"All right. Let's go before he comes to find us." They started for the stairs and Riley again touched Gillian's stomach. "Are you okay? I'm so sorry I hit you."

"Don't be," Gillian said. "You didn't see what I was planning to do to you."

They trekked downstairs with Riley in the lead. Gillian was behind her with Briggs, and Priest brought up the rear. Riley was careful to keep track of Vinea's progress on the elevator. He was traveling up, pausing to search each floor to look for them.

They paused on the third floor landing above the entrance to the morgue. Riley said, "Priest? Where is he?"

"I think he's still here. I can feel him very nearby."

Riley checked her weapon. "Okay, I'll go take a closer look."

"No," Briggs whispered. "We can't afford to lose you if you're spotted. You stay here, I'll go recon."

Riley started to argue, but she saw from Briggs' expression that it was pointless. She nodded and moved toward the wall as Briggs started down. She paused at the foot of the stairs, peered around the corner to make sure Vinea wasn't coming, and darted across the hall. Riley scooted down next to Gillian and said, "Looks like you guys had things pretty well taken care of before I showed up."

"We were faking it," Gillian said. She took Riley's hand and squeezed. "I'm glad you're here. Even if you did punch me in the stomach."

"I'm going to pay for that, aren't I?"

"No," Gillian said. She put her head on Riley's shoulder and squeezed her hand. "Not that I'm complaining, but why doesn't Vinea just blow the building anyway? He'll get caught in the blast, but... I mean, he can come back, right? Demons can't die."

"Of course they can," Priest said. "Once a demon or angel manifests in a human form, they are as vulnerable as anyone."

"Samael didn't stay dead," Riley said.

"Samael fell," Priest said. She chewed her bottom lip. "When an angel comes into being, it is granted divinity. It's what makes us what we are and what separates us from mortals. When I became Caitlin Priest, I took on the same vulnerability. When the mortal form of an angel dies, the divinity is violently expelled from their body."

"Can an angel survive without divinity?"

"Technically," Priest said. "The loss of divinity is usually the death throe for an angelic being. If I had died from the wounds inflicted by the hellhound, Caitlin Priest would have died and Zerachiel would cease to be. My divinity would have dissipated. I could have chosen to come back as an angel, but I would never be Caitlin Priest again."

"So what's the alternative?" Gillian asked. "If you chose not to come back?"

"Oblivion," Priest said. She smiled. "It's not as bad as it sounds."

Briggs returned and motioned for them to come down. Priest went first and made a point to stand near Briggs before she let the lieutenant anywhere near Riley or Gillian in case Vinea had captured and jumped into her. Priest gave a subtle nod that it was indeed Briggs before Riley and Gillian came down.

"Vinea is back in the elevator," Briggs reported. "Going up. We've got a clear shot to the garage."

"Let's go," Riley said. She led the group down the remaining flights of stairs. Priest cut away from them at the lobby and limped to the front doors to check the placing of the sacraments. She caught up with them again as they entered the garage. She had retrieved a jug of holy water from one of the policemen outside and reported, "Everyone outside seems to think this is some huge practical joke."

"I'll take the blame for that," Briggs said. "Better than being blamed for the building getting destroyed on my watch."

The first rows of cars near the door were all official police vehicles, black and whites, with personal cars along the outer walls of the building. Riley gestured for Briggs and Priest to take the far side while she and Gillian went straight ahead. She whistled when she saw a bundle of explosives tied to the base of a concrete support beam. Briggs whistled as well.

They continued until they found a total of five explosive devices. They regrouped in the middle of the space. Briggs said, "I don't suppose any of you did time on the bomb squad."

Priest said, "The bombs are demonic in origin. There's a chance I could disable them, but there's a better than good chance that my interference would just cause them to detonate."

Briggs said, "The demon answered every question you asked when you had it... bound or whatever. Is there a chance you could do that again and ask it how to disable the bombs?"

"You saw what it did to her last time," Gillian said.

Priest said, "It might be our only shot."

"The host is aware of everything the demon does," Gillian said. She was aware that Riley turned to look at her when she said that, but she ignored it. "If we could speak to him, maybe he could tell us how the bombs were designed and where they are all planted."

"You mean an exorcism?" Priest said. "I don't have the energy to bind a demon, let alone expel one."

Gillian finally met Riley's look. "What if he left voluntarily?"

"No goddamn way," Riley said.

Briggs glanced at Riley and then looked at Priest. "What's she talking about?"

"She means offering Vinea a more appealing host," Priest said. Her voice was low, and she shook her head. "It's an admirable suggestion, Dr. Hunt, but it won't work."

"Anyone else would be immediately incapacitated, but I've been through it before. I know what to expect."

"That doesn't mean you'll be able to do anything about it," Riley snapped. "This is not happening. We'll find another way to defuse the bombs."

Gillian said, "I'll let Vinea possess me." Her voice cracked and she shook her head. "Even if I'm not able to tell you what you want to know, the previous host should be. I should be able to hold off Vinea's control long enough for you to trap him in a circle of holy water or something."

"And then what?" Riley said. "We kill you?"

"If we have to, we wait for Priest to be well enough to exorcise him."

Priest said, "I don't like this plan, Riley..."

"Join the club."

"...but we're kind of low on options."

Riley turned to face her. "I'm not letting that *thing* in Gillian. How could it even be possible? She has a tattoo. She's protected."

"It doesn't matter if she invites it in willingly," Priest said softly.

"Then *I'll* do it," Riley said.

Gillian said, "Riley, no offense, but you have no idea what to expect when a demon takes over your mind. The fight for control would be over before it started and we'd be in worse shape than when we started."

Riley grabbed the collar of Gillian's scrub top. "I'm not going to risk your life."

"No. I am."

"Priest's blood."

Everyone looked at Briggs. She gestured at Gillian's fanny pack and said, "What would happen if you injected a demon with that?"

Priest considered it and said, "The blood would be like poison to the demon. It would flee as soon as possible. It would look for another host, so Riley and Lieutenant Briggs would still be vulnerable. Riley, the incense?" Riley remained where she was. "Riley. The incense."

Gillian opened Riley's jacket, keeping eye contact as she took the package out of the inside pocket.

"We don't have much time to prepare," Priest said.

Riley turned from Gillian and walked down the row of cars toward the far end of the garage. Gillian watched her go and then looked at Priest. "Get it set up. I'm ready when you are."

Gillian found Riley in the far corner of the garage, knees drawn up and her arms resting across them. She approached and, when Riley didn't say anything, held out a stick of incense. "Priest said to light it when the demon comes in. It'll protect you once Vinea is out of the current host."

Riley took it. "Don't do this."

Gillian sat down next to Riley and said, "I have to do it. The current host is already too far gone. I'll be able to get all the information you need."

"What if it doesn't work?" Riley said. "I won't fight you."

"Priest..." She looked across the room. "You won't have to fight me."

"She said she'd kill you?"

Gillian put her hand on Riley's arm and rubbed it. "When I was a little girl, I didn't like going to sleep by myself. I still don't, really. Never grew out of it. The only person that could get me to fall asleep was my mother. She would come into my room and sit on the edge of my bed. A half hour, forty-five minutes of her night, every night, was spent sitting in the dark. She would hold my hand, and she would sing to me so I'd know she was there and that I was safe. 'Hush, little baby, don't say a word. Momma's gonna buy you a mockingbird.'" She smiled. "Even when I was nine or ten and Daddy said I was too old for it, she would still come in just to make sure I was okay. I'd always make her sing.

"That night, after you left... when I was trying to nap. I kept hearing the first part of the song. I thought it was you. I couldn't remember when I had told you the story about my mother, so I got up to come find you. The apartment was empty. So I looked in the hall to see if you had come back for something and I'd just missed seeing you. She was waiting for me.

"Do you know when you look down at your shirt, and you see a spider crawling on you? That's how it felt. Everything in me seized. It was an animal fear. She took me over. It was the most terrifying thing I've ever experienced. I can still remember everything she said, and everything she made me do. It's *crystal* clear, Riley. It's so unfair. I have memories that fade. The first time you and I made love. The first girl I ever kissed. They're still there, but blurry on the edges. But everything the Duchess said to me, and everything she showed me to keep me from fighting... I can see it like it's on a movie screen in front of me."

"Then don't put yourself through that again. We'll find another way."

Gillian said, "I have to, Riley. I need to *win*. Last time, you and Priest defeated the Duchess for me. That's why I can't let it go. Those mornings when you find me in the kitchen making breakfast at four-thirty, or the times you find me lying on the couch watching the early news. Those nights, I wake up with the sound of that lullaby in my head. The Duchess stole that memory of my mother from me. And if I can stand up to a demon and defeat him, then... maybe I can get the memory back."

Riley took Gillian's hand in hers.

A minute or so later, Briggs made her way over. "Doctor. Detective. Priest says Vinea is on his way down. We need to make sure everything is ready."

"Okay," Riley said. She pushed herself up and helped Gillian get to her feet. "If you want to back out, just say the word. Priest and I will put two bullets in Vinea's head and we'll find another way to disarm these bombs."

Gillian nodded as they crossed back to where Priest was waiting.

"Lieutenant Briggs, Riley and I will be behind a protective line of incense. Vinea may sense it, but it won't seem out of place. He'll expect us to be defending ourselves. When he's in the room, Dr. Hunt will feign panic and make a break for the stairs. Vinea will take the opportunity to fulfill his original plan by taking her over. Lieutenant Briggs, you will get Vinea's current host to safety. Riley and I will restrain Vinea and hopefully Gillian will be able to tell us where the bombs are and how to defuse them. Once we have the information, or if it becomes clear we won't get anything from him, we'll inject Gillian with the angel blood. Is everyone ready?"

"As ready as I'll ever be," Riley said. Priest and Briggs began lighting the incense circle they had formed, and Riley turned to Gillian. She kissed her tenderly and whispered, "I love you."

"I love you, too. Remember last time this happened? It was the first time you told me you loved me."

Riley said, "This won't be the last."

"Better not be."

"Riley," Priest warned.

Gillian and Riley got behind the incense barrier. They were hidden from the door by three rows of cars. Gillian's heart was pounding, and she blotted her palms on her scrub pants. Riley had the syringe full of Priest's blood, and Priest had her plastic jug of holy water. After what seemed like ages, the door to the main building was blown open with an explosive force.

The women ducked, and Priest put a hand on Gillian's shoulder to prompt her to run.

Gillian pushed herself up and ran. "Oh, God, God, no..." She weaved blindly through the cars, vaguely aware of the demon in a dark blue police uniform standing a few yards away from her. The skin of his face was pulled tight over his skull, and he was deathly pale. There was no mistaking his demonic nature now.

She didn't have to fake the panic, but the random flight was hard to pull off. She rounded the end of a cruiser and skidded to a stop when she saw Vinea in front of her. "No, no, no. Riley! Riley, help!"

She heard the scuffle of shoe leather on concrete, and she had a mental image of Priest and Briggs both holding Riley down. She regretted her choice of words as she turned and tried to run for the exit.

"No, no, no," Vinea said. He grabbed her from behind and pulled her back toward him. "A dumb move," he shouted. "You should have gotten your girlfriend out of here while you had the chance."

His grip tightened, and Gillian's panic rose. They hadn't considered what would happen if he took her as a hostage. She was aware of a dull throb in the small of her back, and she realized that her tattoo was trying to protect her. She calmed somewhat; Priest mentioned she had to allow Vinea into her. Maybe she was subconsciously preventing the protection from doing its work. She could let it go and burn the demon any time she wanted. She swallowed and said, "Please. Please, don't take me."

Vinea turned his head. She could feel the stubble on Officer Taylor's cheek as he considered her words. "Well. The idea was for the boss. I guess it depends on who wears the strap-on in your relationship." He chuckled and bit her earlobe. Gillian retched, and Vinea tightened his hold on her. "Why not? Let's see if I can hit a double."

The cell had stone walls.

There was a window high above. Too high to see through. She could smell horrible things through it, however, and the sky was dark.

She was naked. Dirty. Wet. Something was in the cell with her.

Gillian closed her eyes and pushed at the walls of the room with her mind. Slowly, surely, like filling a balloon with air, using her mind, ignoring everything but the room. The walls breathed. The gaps between the stones became wider. Wider. She pushed harder. Her breath was coming raggedly now, sharp pants between her teeth, nostrils flaring. She held out her hands and felt one wall against each palm. She shoved outward with all her strength.

Blood spurted from her nose. She could taste it on her upper lip as she dropped to one knee and stumbled forward. Priest was directly in front of her, and Riley was kneeling by her side. But not too close. Gillian saw a ring of water on the concrete around her. She coughed and blood spattered the ground. "More water," she said, and her voice sounded inhuman. Priest splashed some more water onto the ground to reinforce the ring.

That bitch whore the Duchess was here, she heard a voice say in her head. *She likes using human bodies to fuck. Did she make you fuck someone while she was riding you? I bet you loved every second of it.*

Gillian focused on the voice and envisioned it in her head. She saw the demon as a dark shape against a velvet background, barely visible but definitely there. She imagined herself using the bricks from her prison to surround it, using its own trap against it. The demon laughed as she dropped bricks, her mind racing and jumping from one thought to another. She couldn't focus. She felt like there was a rope around her ankle and she was dangling above a deep, dark pit.

The world swam around her. Solid lines weren't, and gravity seemed erratic, and sometimes the floor became a wall and she felt like she was going to fall. Gillian drew a deep breath. "Sixth floor. Sex Crimes. Lieutenant Stanson's office." She swallowed. "Fourth floor, homicide, Detective Parra's desk. Third floor, morgue, Gillian Hunt's chair." She swallowed hard, her throat raw, barely aware that she had just spoken her own name. "Five in the garage. That's it. That's it. That's it."

"Jill..." Riley's voice cracked and she put her hands on Gillian's shoulder.

Gillian slapped them away and recoiled from the touch. "Fucking get your fucking hands off of me, you whore, you bitch. If you ever want to taste my pussy again you'll keep your fucking hands to yourself, you hear me?"

Riley tightened her grip on Gillian's arms. "Vinea, shut the hell up. Jill? Are you there?"

It felt like razor wires were wrapped around her brain, flexing and tightening with each breath she took. Gillian gasped in pain and focused on the woman in front of her. "Riley."

"How do we defuse the bombs?"

Gray brick walls tried to constrict around her, but Gillian felt them coming and held them back. A fresh flow of blood washed down her chin. "Grey. Box. On the devices. Separate it from the main device and they will be impossible to detonate. Oh, I love you, Riley."

"I love you, too."

"Bomb squad... will do the rest. They'll be duds without the boxes. Oh, God, Priest, I want you to fuck me hard, you angel cunt." She parted her lips and lewdly wagged her tongue at Priest before her body jerked as if from a physical blow. "What the fuck are you bitches doing to me? I'll kill you all, cut you, drink your blood." She laughed maniacally, but it cut off and turned into a groan. "Riley..."

Suddenly Priest crossed the distance between them and grabbed Gillian. She moved faster than Gillian would have thought possible, her arm around Gillian's neck in a half nelson. Gillian's right arm was stuck straight out. "Do it. We have what we need."

Riley pushed up Gillian's sleeve, slapped the crook of her elbow with two fingers, and pressed the syringe into the exposed vein.

"No, stop, fuck, I'm good, I'm fine, I have it under control, stop, it burns, Riley, it's not my blood type, stop!"

It felt like Riley had touched a live wire to her arm, and the heat spread up toward her shoulder and down to her fingers. It felt like she was being washed in it, covering her all at once like being doused in water. She closed her eyes and pictured the darkness on velvet again, the demon, Vinea, struggling for an exit, infuriated by another loss. She pictured her body in the darkness, folding it around the small blot, crushing it inside herself as the warmth spread. What had felt like fire now felt like a comfortingly warm breeze, a summer gust of wind.

The demon wailed and the razor wire in her head tightened. But Gillian only tightened her own grip, refusing to give an inch no matter how badly it hurt.

Priest released her, and Gillian spun around. Strong arms - Riley's arms - wrapped around her. She grabbed Riley's collar and pressed her face against the smooth material of Riley's blouse.

The laundry room at her building was large, but it always felt cramped to her.

It was almost ten at night, so no one else was there. Two machines were running. Gillian took Riley's clothes out of the dryer and folded them while the second load finished. She smoothed her hand over the material, the clothes that Riley would wear tomorrow, or in a few days, or sometime in the future. She smiled.

Gillian's body jerked. Riley cupped her face and whispered to her. Tears and blood dripped onto Riley's blouse.

"Hush little baby," Riley whispered. "Don't say a word..."

Gillian seized, her heels kicking at the floor as she struggled to stay in control.

"Momma's gonna buy you a mockingbird. And if that mockingbird don't sing, momma's gonna buy you a diamond ring. And if that diamond ring don't shine... Momma's... gonna take it to a private eye."

"Turns brass," Gillian said. Her throat was dry and it was painful to speak.

Riley bent down and kissed Gillian's forehead. "If you say so."

"Vinea."

Riley looked up and listened to someone speak. Gillian could hear her, but couldn't make out the words. Riley blinked and said, "We... didn't capture him."

"Oh, God..."

"No, Priest said... Jill. You destroyed him."

Gillian said, "What?"

"The angel blood. The strain you had him under trying to take control, the angel blood eradicated him. He left you and it was like... it was like smoke in front of an industrial fan. You killed him. You got your win, baby."

Gillian's eyes drifted closed. "I win."

"You bet you do." Riley pulled Gillian's head to her chest and rocked her as Priest and Briggs left the garage to disarm the remaining of the explosives.

They thought she was asleep. They had taken her up to the morgue to clean away the blood, and she asked if she could stay on the bed to rest a little. Riley kissed her lips and promised she would be nearby. Gillian dozed, but she could still hear them talking; to each other and to the EMTs that were making sure she was okay.

Briggs. "...Taylor is being taken to Intensive Care. They think he'll pull through. He's not exactly sure what happened... as far as anyone is concerned, Officer Taylor inadvertently came into contact with an unknown psychotic agent and the rest was out of his control. It's out of his system and he's fine now."

Priest, a few minutes later. "Stop doting on me, Riley. The battle is over. I'll go to a church once everything here is settled. But thank you."

At one point she did fall asleep. When she woke, Riley was sitting beside her bed. Her hand was wrapped around Gillian's, her head resting on Gillian's hip as she slept. Briggs and Priest were nowhere to be found, and half the morgue lights were turned off to make the room feel like twilight. Gillian brushed her hand through Riley's hair with her free hand and fell back to sleep.

Gillian bent down and pulled the blouse from the dryer. She had just started to fold it when she saw two diamond-shaped blood stains next to the row of buttons. She rubbed them with her finger, annoyed at herself for not treating it before the cycle. She was about to toss it aside when she realized where the blood had come from. It was hers, and it had gotten there when Riley held her. She ran her fingers over the stain again, smiling this time. She hadn't won that day. She had helped Riley and Priest win. And with their help, she had defeated a fucking demon. Destroyed the motherfucker.

She folded the blouse carefully. She would do her best to remove the blood later, but even if it was set in the material, she wasn't going to be in a huge rush to throw it away. That blood had special meaning.

She bent down to finish unloading the dryer. As she folded, she began to hum without thinking about it. She began to tap her shoe against the floor as she folded, moving her hips as she began to sing a blues version of her mother's song. "I'm gonna buy you a diamond ring. If that diamond ring don't shine. I'm gon' take to a private eye. If that private eye can't see... he better not take that ring from me..."

For the first time in a year, the song reminded her of more than the Duchess. It was more than her mother's song, too. It was the song Riley sang to comfort her, to calm her after her literally hellish ordeal. As she danced in place and folded their clothes, she continued to sing. Sometimes she would make up verses, and she would add risque items to the list of purchases. It didn't matter, no one was there to see her. The song no longer belonged to the Duchess; it was Gillian's song again, and it was Riley's song, and it was her mother's song, and it would never be anything else.

Matchstick Men

Riley left the car running at the curb, not bothering to close the door behind her. She was on the sidewalk and through the front door before Priest was even out of the car. Riley had her gun in one hand, her badge in the other as she ran for the stairs. The elevator might have been theoretically faster, but she couldn't stand still.

Priest called up to her from the lobby. "Third floor, apartment C!"

Riley didn't slow down to acknowledge the information. She took the stairs three at a time and reached the third floor before the elevator could have. She pounded her fist against the door under the golden 3C and said, "Leah Mason, this is Detective Riley Parra. I need you to open the door." She waited for a five-count, pounded again, and then stepped back. She placed a kick next to the doorknob and the lock shattered.

She was inside the apartment before the door could swing shut on her. She smelled something burning on the stove, but she didn't have time to deal with it. She scanned the living room. Shoes in front of the couch, radio on, but no sign of the occupant. "Leah Mason?" Riley said again, her voice echoing off the walls of the narrow hallway. The three doors in the hall were closed, and she took the time to give each room a cursory check before she moved on.

The last door was a bathroom, and she knew she'd found Leah. The door was locked, and Riley slammed her shoulder against it twice before the lock gave way.

"Riley?" Priest asked as she arrived in the apartment.

"Check the kitchen," Riley called. It wouldn't be good if they saved Leah just to have the apartment burn down around them. The bathroom was white tile and filled with light gray steam. Riley crossed to the bathtub, which was full to the brim. The brunette was huddled against the edge of the tub, waves lapping against her legs and hips, her knees drawn up to her chest as she stared at her wrists. The razor blade was dull in the fog of the room, but there was no doubting the sharpness of its edge.

"Ms. Mason?" Riley said, softening her voice. "Put the razor blade down."

She didn't look up. Riley holstered her weapon and took a careful step closer to the tub. She heard Priest come into the room behind her.

"We're here to help you, Ms. Mason."

Leah finally looked up at met Riley's eyes. Her gaze was unfocused, her lips slack. She looked down at her wrist and applied pressure with the edge of the blade.

"Leah," Riley snapped. "Look at me."

"I..."

Priest came into the room. "Leah, don't do it."

"I have to."

Riley said, "No, you don't. You're safe now." She reached carefully out. Leah didn't react as Riley took the razor from her and handed it back to Priest. She scanned the room and found a terrycloth robe hanging on a hook next to the tub. She picked it up and said, "Come on. Let's get you out of here."

She helped Leah out of the tub, covering her nudity with the robe. Leah let Riley put her arms in the sleeves, but then tied the belt herself. She walked out of the bathroom with Priest on one side and Riley on the other, her feet dragging on the tile. When they stepped out of the bathroom, she put a hand to her forehead and swayed on her feet.

"Ms. Mason?" Priest said.

Leah looked up at Riley, looked at Priest, and clutched at the collar of her robe. "What the hell are you doing in my apartment? Who are you?"

Riley held up her badge. "We're the police, Ms. Mason. Detective Riley Parra, this is my partner Caitlin Priest."

"What are you doing here?"

"I'm sorry, but there was just an attempt on your life." She nodded at Leah's wrist, and Leah finally noticed the trickle of blood running down her forearm.

Leah pressed two fingers to the wound and looked at Riley again. She pressed her lips together and said, "I think maybe you should start at the beginning, Detective."

Riley and Priest waited in the living room while Leah got dressed. Riley wandered the living room and examined the framed photographs that shared the wall behind the TV. Leah in a business suit, Leah posing on a snowy mountain with ski poles, and several pictures of Leah in front of the courthouse. Riley never got to see Leah in action as a DA, since she worked mostly with the organized crime division, but she knew her reputation was harsh both in and out of the courtroom.

When Leah rejoined them, she wore a pair of sweatpants and an old T-shirt. Her hair was up, and Riley caught a glimpse of a fresh bandage on her wrist. It was no surprise why she was such a good lawyer; despite the bizarre situation, she looked composed, for the most part. Riley, however, could detect a hint of uncertainty behind her expression as she walked into the living room and tried to think of a good place to start.

Leah looked at Riley and said, "You look familiar to me."

"Maybe I testified for a case."

Leah said, "I do mostly organized crime. Still, I know you're not some con artist trying to hoodwink me. So, Detective." She sat in the armchair facing the couch, her elbows resting on her knees. "Why don't you tell me what happened here tonight?"

"It has to do with the Alexander Kimaris trial," Riley said.

"It starts tomorrow," Leah said.

Riley nodded. "And what would happen if the DA was found dead the night before?"

"They would assign a new DA to the case," Leah said. She kept her voice steady, but she was visibly shaken by the idea. "The case would just be delayed."

"How many lawyers would have to die before the State's Attorney bowed to the pressure from Kimaris and his friends?" Riley said. "Or, alternatively, how long before they got to one that Kimaris could buy?"

Leah started to answer, but she shook her head. "Okay, let's say Kimaris *is* trying to kill me. How, exactly, did he do it?"

Riley glanced at Priest. They had decided it would be too farfetched to tell the truth, so she went with a slightly more believable cover story. "There was a drug in your coffee at the office. It made you easily suggestible. All they had to do was plant the idea in your head and you were powerless against it."

"Hypnotism?"

"No, more powerful," Riley said. "We've got the guy who... drugged you, but Kimaris has far too many associates for us to keep an eye on them all. I want to ask you to consider protective custody."

Leah scoffed and stood up. She walked to the front hallway, prepared to escort them out. "Listen, I prosecuted Joseph Raum when you were still walking a beat, okay? You think he didn't send some people after me? I can deal with threats."

"Not these threats," Priest said. "You don't know what you're up against."

Leah stood up. "I think I can handle it."

"You had a razor blade to your wrist," Riley said. "What do you think would have happened if Priest and I hadn't been here? This isn't a case of willpower. If you try to fight them on your own, they'll win. Every time."

Leah was looking at the remnants of her door. "I'm not going to walk on to my home turf with bodyguards all around me."

"We'll find a way to make it work," Riley said. "But saving face doesn't mean anything if you're dead."

Leah sighed. "All right. What's the plan, you have a safe house set up for me?"

"Not exactly. The best way to make sure you're safe is for the two of us to keep an eye on you. You'll stay at my apartment, and Priest and I will take turns staying with you."

"What makes your apartment any safer than mine?"

Riley looked at Priest again and considered her response. "It's hard to explain. Basically, my apartment is safer because it's a tertiary location. It's not someplace you've frequented, and it's not a place where anyone would expect you to be. If the bad guys can't find you, they can't try this thing again. Priest and I will keep an eye on you through the trial. When Kimaris is sent to the state pen, he'll be powerless once he's that far away."

"*If* he's sent away. There's still a chance he'll be found not guilty. He's weaseled out of worse charges than these in the past."

"Not this time," Riley said. "We have him dead to rights, and we've got him cut off from his bosses. He's not going to get out of it this time. The only people still loyal to him, the ones coming after you, are the low-rent thugs. They won't bother with revenge; they'll just get absorbed into a larger group."

Leah shrugged. "Okay, even if he does go to jail, he's still not out of reach. Maybe you've heard of telephones. The internet? Cons can reach out from prison if they really want to."

"I hate to say 'trust me' when you don't know me from some random woman on the street, but once Kimaris is outside city limits, you'll be safe."

"So I'm just supposed to pick up and leave my apartment on a moment's notice and go with you to God knows where?"

"Do you want to call our boss and confirm our story?"

Leah sighed. "No. That's fine."

"Priest and I can stay the night here if you need time to get things together before we go."

"No, I'll just throw some things in a bag. Give me fifteen minutes."

Priest waited for Leah to go back into the bedroom before she turned to Riley. "We got very lucky."

Riley breathed a sigh of relief and nodded as she leaned back on the couch. Priest had to give a deposition in the murder of the airplane pilot, and Riley went along for moral support. They were on their way out of the building when Priest noticed a demon loitering outside the building. Riley and Priest kept their eye on him and watched as he stopped Leah and spoke to her briefly before he casually walked away. They followed him, and Priest cornered him in an alley. It hadn't taken much persuasion before he revealed his plans, but it was still almost too late.

"Think the protection you've put on my apartment will be enough?"

"It should," Priest said. "The things you told her are true. The demons can't target her if they can't find her. You and I should escort her to the courthouse every day."

"Briggs already signed off on the protection detail. It's a lot easier now that I don't have to lie to her."

Leah came back out of the bedroom rolling a small overnight bag behind her. "All right. I'm about as ready as I'll ever be."

Riley nodded. "Priest, can you take care of the door?"

"I'll do my best."

"Thanks. Come on."

Riley escorted Leah downstairs. When they reached the lobby, Leah said, "How did you know I was in danger?"

"My partner recognized the guy who spoke to you at the courthouse. Do you remember him? Tall, thin, with blonde hair and dark eyes?"

"The last thing I remember clearly is being in my office. Then bits and pieces until you showed up in my bathroom."

"Don't worry, I didn't try to sneak a peek," Riley said.

"I think I'm offended."

Riley smirked and put Leah's bag in the trunk. Priest arrived and said, "The door is in place. It should hold."

"What are you, a carpenter in your off-hours?"

"No, but I am very good friends with one."

Riley smiled at Priest over the top of the car before they got inside. "I'm going to drop Priest off before we head to my apartment. She'll take over in the morning."

"All right," Leah said. She was already on her cell phone. "Yes, this is Leah Mason. I need to forward my calls for the rest of the night."

Riley looked at the clock on the dashboard and saw it was nearly eight. Priest whispered, "How many calls can she be expecting in a single night?"

"I think we're going to find out," Riley muttered. "I hope Gillian is in a good mood."

Leah put a hand over the mouthpiece of her phone. "What was that?"

"Nothing," Riley said. "Just thinking out loud."

Leah went back to her phone call and Riley pulled away from the curb. "Yeah. It's going to be a long night."

When Priest got out in front of her building, Leah moved from the backseat into the front. Priest leaned down and looked at Riley through the window. "Call me if you need any backup. I'll be there as soon as possible."

"Thanks, Priest. Sweet dreams."

Priest waved goodbye and backed away from the car. Once Riley was back on the road, she glanced at Leah and saw she was rubbing the bandage on her wrist with two fingers. "You okay?"

"Yeah," Leah said. "I guess I owe you my thanks."

"Don't worry about it," Riley said. "Part of the job."

Leah said, "Still. I know I was all bluster and bravado back there, but I just couldn't believe that my mind was so blank. I only remember bits and pieces of my night. That kind of thing scares me. Not knowing."

"I know the feeling."

"So thanks. I'm glad you were there."

Riley said, "You're welcome. Just do what I say, and don't take any stupid risks over the next few weeks of the trial, and you'll be fine."

"Weeks," Leah said. She shook her head and sighed. "I don't know if you'll want me as your houseguest for that long. I'm not really good with the chores."

"Hopefully we won't need you in protective custody that long. Caitlin and I are going to see what we can do about neutralizing Kimaris' gang. If we convince them it's in their best interest to leave you alone, we shouldn't have to worry about another attempt."

"Here's hoping."

They drove on in silence until Riley arrived at her building. Leah glanced at the front of the building as they pulled into the parking garage. "You live here?" she asked.

"Yeah," Riley said. The neighborhood was relatively nice, upscale. Better than she had ever lived in. "What's wrong with it?"

"Nothing. No, nothing."

They parked and Riley took Leah's suitcase from the backseat and handed it to her. Leah said, "You're sure that whatever happened to me is done? I feel fine, but if it's still in my system..."

"Don't worry," Riley said. "The effects of the drugs fade after the initial burst."

"I've never even heard rumors of a drug like this."

Riley pushed open the door to the lobby. "It's rare and expensive. No one on the street have access to it."

"Nice to know there are things even the bad guys can't afford."

"Yeah," Riley said. "Now and then we get lucky."

They started up the stairs and, at the second landing Riley realized Leah had stopped following her. She turned and saw Leah staring at her. "What is it? Everything all right?"

"Uh, yeah," Leah said. "I just remembered where I know you from."

"Good memory or bad?"

Leah smirked and shrugged. "Depends on which side you were on. Go on up."

Riley continued up. She unlocked the apartment door and led Leah inside. "Gillian?" she called.

"In the kitchen."

Riley shrugged out of her jacket and told Leah, "You can leave your suitcase by the door." She went toward the kitchen entrance, her view of Gillian blocked by cabinets. "Hey. We have some company."

"Priest?" Gillian said. She kissed Riley hello and then looked past her into the living room. Her demeanor immediately changed. "Leah?"

Leah had her hands in her pockets, her head ducked and her shoulders hunched as if expecting a blow. "Hey, Jill."

Riley bristled at Leah using her nickname for Gillian so casually. "You guys know each other?"

"You could say that," Gillian said. "Leah and I... we dated."

Leah said, "That's where I recognized you from, Detective. I don't blame you for not remembering; you were pretty beaten up at the time."

"I don't..." Riley suddenly recalled the woman's face. The night after her first ill-advised assault on Marchosias' building. Something had drawn her to Gillian's apartment and, when she arrived, Gillian had a guest.

She was on the couch, the pain somehow continuing to get worse now that she could focus on it. Gillian had walked away for a moment and intercepted a woman coming out of the bedroom. The woman had obviously dressed hastily, and hadn't had time to comb her hair. Gillian said, "Hey, can we talk for a second? Just wait." They moved into the hallway for privacy, but Riley could still hear Gillian's hushed voice. "She's someone from work. She's hurt. I don't know. Just stay, all right? No, it– Fine, all right, go."

The woman stormed out of the apartment and slammed the door behind her. When Gillian returned, her lips were pressed tight together in anger. She knelt in front of Riley and continued to clean the wound.

Riley said, "Damn, I'm sorry. I didn't... I didn't think that you might be..."

"Don't worry about it. That wasn't about you."

"Are you sure about that?"

Gillian nodded and chuckled without humor. "Oh, yeah. You're just her latest excuse. Her last excuse."

Riley remembered very little of that night besides her pain and the fact it was her first night in Gillian's bed. The same night Leah Mason had apparently left it for the last time. "Oh."

"Yeah," Leah said. "Look, I can just go..."

"No," Gillian said. She looked at Riley, who easily translated her meaning. She knew that if Riley had brought Leah to their apartment, there had to be a good reason for it. "We're all adults here. I mean, it might be a little awkward, but we'll cope. Right?"

"Right," Riley said. She kept her eyes on Leah and her hand on Gillian's hip.

Leah cleared her throat and said, "So. I guess I'll be taking the couch?"

Leah went to take a shower, her appetite destroyed by her episode in the bathroom. Gillian led Riley into the kitchen once Leah was gone and tried for casual conversation. "So I picked up some Chinese. I was just serving it up when you came home." She handed Riley a bowl.

"Thank you." She took it and said, "I can move her to Priest's apartment."

"No, that's... no. You brought her here for a reason."

Riley smiled. "I knew you'd understand."

Gillian smirked and carried her dinner to the dining room table. When Riley sat next to her, she spoke in a low voice. "Okay. What do you want to know?"

"Start to... well, I know the finish."

"You saw the last scene of the movie," Gillian said. "Doesn't mean you know how it ends." She stirred her rice with the tines of her fork. "I did the autopsy on a mobster that was found on the waterfront. I testified that the cause of death was a blow to the back of the head rather than the four gunshot wounds in his back. The defendant was trying to cover up the true killer; his son. So the guy got off."

"You let a mobster off the hook?"

Gillian said, "I kept a man from doing time for something he didn't do. Did he deserve to go to prison? Yes, absolutely. But I wasn't going to commit perjury or risk future inquiries to my work. I told the truth."

Riley touched Gillian's hand. "You're right. I'm sorry."

"That's what I told Leah when she confronted me outside the courthouse. She accused me of being paid off by the family, said that I was a toady for the mob. She was screaming in my face and then... she started to cry. I was stunned."

"I saw the mood swing myself," Riley said. "Once that shell comes down, I guess it comes down with a crash."

"Yeah," Gillian said. "So I held her. The case was the culmination of months of hard work and late nights, and I had thrown it all out the window. She told me she wasn't mad at me, just that she had been too gung-ho to look at the information herself. I asked her out to dinner and she said yes. After that..."

"You can spare me the details," Riley said.

Gillian smiled. "I was going to say after that, we would meet for coffee and dinner every now and again. That turned into overnight stays."

"How long were you guys together?" Riley said. "I never even knew you were dating anyone."

"Ten months," Gillian said. "Off and on. She didn't want our relationship to become common knowledge just in case I ever ended up in court with her again. The defense would kill to cross-examine a prosecutor's lover. So we kept quiet."

"Until I showed up in a bloody heap on your doorstep."

Gillian shook her head. "We were done a long time before that. We kept breaking up and getting together for 'one more dinner' or 'one more...'" She cleared her throat and Riley shifted uncomfortably in her seat. "We were just afraid to cut the cord entirely. When you came in that night, it was just another ill-conceived attempt to keep the relationship alive. The next day, I spoke to her. I told her we were over."

"We weren't even..."

"I know," Gillian said. "But I knew we would be."

Riley looked down at her food.

"So why did you bring her here?"

"Thanks for the segue," Riley said. "Priest saw a demon talking with her at the courthouse. We ran him down and got him to talk. She's representing the State for the prosecution Alexander Kimaris. The trial starts tomorrow, and one of his thugs decided to take her out of the equation permanently. Priest and I are going to see if we can get his gang to hang him out to dry." Riley heard the water shut off in the shower and said, "Are you really okay with her being here? She would be just as safe with Priest."

"It'll be fine. I better go get linens to make up the couch."

"I'll do it," Riley said.

Gillian smirked. "Worried about me making the bed for an ex?"

"Not at all," Riley said as she pushed her chair back. "But I'll make the couch up."

Gillian chuckled as Riley left the kitchen. There was a blanket and an extra pillow in the hall closet, and Riley pulled them out as Leah came out of the bathroom. She had taken her suitcase into the bathroom with her, so she was dressed in a T-shirt and a pair of sweatpants. She and Riley both froze where they were for a moment before Riley gestured with the folded sheets. "I was just going to make up the couch for you."

"You don't have to do that. I'm pretty good at making up couches."

"Fine by me," Riley said.

They walked back into the living room, Riley leading the way. She put the linens on the couch and stuck her hands in her pockets. She looked toward the kitchen and saw Gillian was pouring herself a drink with her back to the door. "Listen. Jill doesn't have a problem with this, so I don't, either. I just want to make sure we're all on the same page."

"I don't know how much she told you about us, but we were on the way out before you showed up. That was just the final nail in the coffin.

Trust me, we're fine."

"Glad to here it. Um, TV, radio... remote is there."

"Thanks. I think I'll just crash."

"We'll try to keep it down."

Leah smiled and said, "I'd appreciate that."

"Oh... God. I didn't mean..."

"I know. I'm just messing with you."

Riley rolled her eyes. "Goodnight, Ms. Mason."

"Goodnight, Detective." Riley started toward the kitchen, but Leah said, "Detective Parra? Thanks for saving my life tonight."

"It was my pleasure."

Riley undressed and slipped into bed just as Gillian came in from the shower. Her hair was up, and she wore a tank top that was just barely long enough to cover her panties. Riley watched her cross the room, resting against the headboard as Gillian performed her nightly ablutions in front of the vanity mirror. When she finally crawled into bed, she kissed Riley's shoulder and said, "Want to have sex really loud so she knows how it is?"

Riley smiled and pulled Gillian closer. "No. Having sex really loud should never be used for evil purposes."

They kissed for a while, hands roaming under the covers, before Gillian said, "Well, if we're going to be considerate, we should probably just go to sleep."

"Right," Riley said. "I don't trust myself to be quiet."

Gillian settled on her side of the mattress and fluffed her pillow before she lay down. She nodded to Riley, who reached up and turned off the bedside lamp. Riley rolled onto her side and looked at Gillian's profile in the moonlit darkness. "How are you doing?"

"Hmm?"

"The whole possession thing."

"Oh," Gillian said. "I don't know. Maybe it's a bit of 'hair of the dog,' but I think it solved a lot of what I've been going through. The loss of control and the fear that it'll happen again and you and Priest won't be there to save me. The nightmares have stopped."

"Thank God for that," Riley said quietly. She brushed Gillian's stomach through her shirt.

"How is Briggs dealing with everything?"

Riley chuckled. "Better than I did. But hey, everyone did better than me. You, Kenzie, Chelsea Stanton... Briggs told me she spent some time in church after all was said and done. She told me that I had a little more leash for my outside investigations, but I shouldn't go crazy."

"That'll be a relief," Gillian said.

"We'll still have to come up with something to put on the official report. But if we ask for a little time off, or if we come in with our arms and legs broken, we won't have to come up with some lie off the top of our heads. That will take some of the pressure off."

Gillian's eyes were closed, and Riley stroked her cheek. Gillian stirred and said, "Mm. I'm awake."

"Go to sleep," Riley whispered.

Gillian moved closer and put her head against Riley's chest. Riley held her and looked at the ceiling. A yellow triangle from a nearby streetlight glowed in the far corner of the room, and Riley stared at it. Every now and then it seemed to expand and send a shot across the room, an optical illusion caused by headlights going around the corner. Riley heard water running in the pipes and tensed before she remembered they had a houseguest.

She was impressed with how Leah was handling the change. She remembered how she felt when she found out Kenzie was dating Chelsea Stanton. There were no lingering romantic feelings for Kenzie, and Riley would never choose Kenzie over the woman currently sleeping in her arms, but she had still felt a little punch. She wondered how love could fade when jealousy remained just as strong as ever. And she couldn't even begin to imagine what it would be like to be exiled to the couch in Gillian's apartment.

Riley kissed the top of Gillian's head. "Are you awake?"

"Almost," Gillian said.

Riley put her finger on Gillian's chin and lifted her head. Gillian started to open her eyes, but closed them when Riley kissed her. Gillian shifted her weight and settled on top of Riley. Riley's tongue slipped into Gillian's mouth and the kiss deepened. Gillian hooked her thumbs in Riley's boxers and pushed them down a bit. Riley spread her legs, and Gillian straddled one and lowered her weight gently onto one thigh.

"I thought you said you couldn't be quiet."

"You'll have to bite my tongue," Riley said.

Gillian chuckled and covered Riley's mouth with her hand. "I'll gag you with something. Maybe there's something down here." She reached under the blankets and shifted her weight. Riley kissed Gillian's palm. "Stop that."

Riley licked. "That *tickles*. Stop." She pulled her panties out from underneath the blankets and pressed them against Riley's lips. Riley obligingly opened her mouth and let Gillian push them in. "Good?"

"Mph," Riley said.

Gillian grinned and kissed Riley's chin. "Good." She kissed Riley's throat and moved down under the covers. "Now that we have that taken care of..."

Riley closed her eyes and brought one hand up to grip the headboard. Gillian's lips brushed her thighs, her tongue slid up from the curve of her knee and all the way up to her crotch, and then she pulled the boxers down and out of her way. Riley closed her eyes as Gillian made love to her, biting down on the lace in her mouth. Her cheeks occasionally puffed out with the force of her exhalations, her fingers clawing at the headboard as she moved against Gillian's lips and tongue.

Riley put her free hand on top of Gillian's head, holding her in place as she came. Gillian took her time coming back up, kissing a trail up Riley's body through her shirt. She kissed each breast, kissed Riley's cheeks, and then took the panties from her mouth.

"I think I bit through them," Riley whispered.

"That's okay," Gillian said. She kissed Riley, their tongues twisting and thrusting as Gillian moved her hips between Riley's legs. Gillian broke the kiss and brushed her fingers down Riley's face. "Only you. No one else. Ever again."

"Good," Riley whispered. "And... ditto."

Gillian chuckled and kissed Riley. Riley rolled until she was on top, and Gillian yelped quietly. "Do I need to put the gag back in?" she asked.

"No," Riley said. "My mouth will be otherwise occupied." She licked her lips and went under the covers to give Gillian her turn.

Six faces stared down on Riley's desk. She leaned back in her chair and met all twelve eyes.

Bernard Wright was a recovering alcoholic who worked for St. Isidore's Church. He was a handyman, and he was actually killed by a blow to the head from a petty thief. The kid wasn't to blame, though. The demon helping the Angel Maker had screwed with the kid's mind and caused him to lash out violently. The Angel Maker was as much to blame for Bernie's murder as any of the others.

Russell Stone was killed crossing the street in the middle of the night. According to all accounts, he was a lousy husband. He beat his wife, showed up for his job whenever it was convenient, and managed to sweet talk the police every time they showed up on domestic disturbance calls.

Mitchell Reese was killed in his sports bar, and was one of the most confusing deaths on her board. A door that had been replaced to allow access through the alleyway. The Angel Maker hadn't bothered to take anything from the cashbox, which proved his intent was only in the murder and the artwork he left behind.

James Graham was a cabbie who was found in the courtyard of an apartment where he didn't live. Their investigation had turned up the fact he had been fired for multiple complaints by female passengers. A budding rapist, no love lost there.

Then the twofer; Sidney Lee, a drug dealer, and Allan McDade. The second victim was only guilty of being in the wrong place and seeing the wrong thing. Sidney Lee, on the other hand, was a regular customer of the revolving door at their holding cells.

Riley tapped her pen against her bottom lip and remembered something Russell Stone's wife had said. When Grace Stone was told that her husband was a random victim, she had said, "Well, at least they picked the right person." Riley picked up a marker and stood in front of the board. Under Russell Stone's name, she wrote, 'Wife-beater.' She moved to Mitchell Reese. His wife had mentioned a gambling problem. She wrote 'Gambler' under his name.

James Graham was a rapist waiting to happen, if he hadn't crossed that line already, and Sidney Lee was a drug dealer. Riley stepped back and eyed the board. Allan McDade didn't fit the pattern, but he wouldn't have if he was just a witness who had to be taken out of the equation. He wasn't planned. Riley moved back to the first victim, Bernie Wright. Could his alcoholism be enough of a crime to loop him in with the others? She sat down at her desk and pulled the keyboard closer.

Priest came into the bullpen behind her and looked at the new marks on the board. "What's this?"

"Trying to find a pattern," Riley said. "Bernie Wright screws it up, though. If James Graham fit the bill as a *budding* rapist, then maybe Bernie fit because he was an alcoholic. Recovering, but..."

"Recovering isn't the same as incipient."

"Yeah," Riley said. She looked past Priest to the stairs. "Where's Leah?"

Priest said, "She went upstairs to Organized Crime. She wants to use one of their offices to call her secretary and make sure everything is set for today."

Riley nodded. "What time does the trial begin?"

Leah was escorted into the room just then, the uniformed cop assigned to keep an eye on her walking a few paces behind. "We should be there at nine, so we should probably get a move on." She glanced at Riley's victim board. "Angel Maker?"

"Yeah," Riley said. She stood up and began to erase the crimes she had given each victim. "Thought I was on to something."

Leah stepped forward and said, "Who is the first victim?"

"Bernard Wright. He was found murdered in the church where he lived and worked."

Leah said, "May I?" Riley took the photo of Bernie Wright down and handed it to her. Leah stared at the face for a long time before she said, "Do a search for Barney Worth."

Riley frowned and bent over the keyboard to type the name in. A few seconds later, she had an arrest report. "Vehicular manslaughter," she read.

"Barney Worth is a piece of scum," Leah said. "He was busted no less than ten times on DUI charges. About fifteen years ago, he was driving drunk when he slammed into a car in an intersection. The driver and passenger got cuts and bruises, but the little girl in the backseat died. She was six. Worth went to prison, but he got out after five years due to good behavior and overcrowding."

Riley remembered talking with Father Denis about Bernie Wright. The one comment that stood out was *"Bernie had a past when he came here."* The man had seemed anxious during their talks about Bernie's past. Riley had a feeling she had just found out why. She picked up the marker and wrote "drunk driver" underneath his name. She stepped back and looked at the row of crimes.

"Think that's it?"

"Hard to say," Priest said.

Leah said, "As much as I hate to admit it, even if you had ten victims with criminal records, it could be counted as a coincidence in this town. Did you do a full background check on Allan McDade, the bystander? He could be the exception that proves the rule."

Riley nodded. "The only crime he's guilty of is being insanely dull. Pays his taxes on time, hardly ever misses a day of work, happily married with two kids."

Priest said, "We can focus on it later. Right now we should probably go on to the courthouse."

Leah looked at her watch. "Shit. Just as hanging around the two of you was starting to get interesting."

The parking garage was guarded, but Riley wasn't going to take any chances. She rolled down the passenger side window as they drove through the gate, and Priest gave her a subtle shake of her head. No demons masquerading as garage attendants, then. Riley parked as close as she could to the doors and climbed out, one hand on the butt of her gun as she scanned the area. "All right. Come on."

Leah got out of the car and adjusted her suit jacket. She smirked as she followed Riley to the elevator. "I have to say, it's kind of nice to have a bodyguard."

"If you start singing Tina Turner songs, I'll shoot you myself."

The elevator took them to the fourth floor. Priest left the elevator first and motioned for them to step out behind her. She stepped close to Riley and said, "Only one, and I know who it is."

"Kimaris is here?"

"Of course."

Riley said, "Okay. Priest will stay here with you to keep you safe, and I'll see if I can flush out his people and convince them to take the target off your back."

Leah said, "This case is open and shut. Everyone knows that Kimaris is a criminal. Small-time, maybe, but still a criminal. His defense doesn't stand a chance. The only complication would be if he tried to make a deal and flip on his boss, but if he hasn't done that by now, he's not going to."

"Yeah. I think he's more afraid of his boss than anything else right now," Riley said. To Priest, she said, "Call me if you need anything. I'll let you know what I find."

Riley turned to leave and saw Alexander Kimaris coming out of a side room with his lawyers. His curly black hair was shaved, the dark circles under his eyes enhanced by the pallor of his skin. He spotted Riley and managed a devious smile. She stopped, unwilling to retreat from the man's gaze. "You look good in orange," Riley said. "The shackles might be considered a little gaudy, but you pull it off."

"Make your jokes, Detective Parra. Your time is coming."

"Sorry, but I'm not going to waste my time being afraid of someone who kidnaps the wrong person."

Kimaris let his lawyers shuffle him away, down the corridor to the courtroom. Riley met Priest's gaze and nodded toward Kimaris. *Keep your eyes on him.* Priest nodded that she understood and Riley continued to the elevator. She hated leaving; she wanted to be there if Kimaris or his goons made another attempt on Leah. But she needed to end the threat once and for all, and the only way to do that was on the street. If she couldn't protect Leah herself, then Priest would be the perfect substitute.

Chelsea brought out a pitcher of ice tea and set it down on the edge of the desk. "Please, help yourself."

"No, thanks," Riley said. "Not much of a tea drinker."

Chelsea nodded. "Then would you mind pouring me a glass? It's... kind of a bad day." She gestured at her glasses, and Riley obligingly poured her a glass. "Thank you."

Riley settled back in her seat and said, "You're sure Kenzie isn't around?"

"She could get here in about half an hour if you'd rather wait." Chelsea smiled. "But since you have to spend the time here anyway, you might as well get the information and leave as soon as possible."

Riley shifted uncomfortably. She hated that Chelsea had so easily seen through her, no pun intended, and that she was petty enough for what she said to be the truth. She sighed. "Sorry. It's just that I'm more accustomed to dealing with Kenzie. Nothing personal against you."

"Well, I've gained Riley Parra's forgiveness. And to think all it took was a kidnapping and a little late night roof jumping."

Riley smiled. "I need what you know about Alexander Kimaris' organization."

"They're scattered," Chelsea said. "Once he went to prison, his people got absorbed into other groups. I think the largest contingent went with an up-and-comer named Alyssa Gremory. Have you met her, by the way? You might find her interesting."

"I have enough interesting in my life, thanks," Riley said. "Are there any of his lieutenants who might still be loyal to him? Anyone who might want to keep him out of prison and help him retake his former position?"

"There *is* no former position," Chelsea said. "I've done some investigating since you and Priest filled me in on what really goes on here in No Man's Land. Your pal Marchosias would never let Kimaris back in. There are two options for him; he can go to jail, or he can come out and let Marchosias send him back to Hell for being disloyal. There's no middle ground."

Riley said, "Maybe we've been going about this all wrong. Maybe it's not someone loyal to Kimaris; maybe it's just someone who would rather see him dead than in prison."

"That would increase your suspect pool by about ten thousand."

"Yeah," Riley said. She stood up and said, "Thanks for your help."

Chelsea stood up and leaned on her cane as she walked Riley to the door. "I wanted to thank you for bringing me and Kenzie into the loop. It really gave us an edge with some of our investigations."

"If you or Kenzie ever need help again, you know where to find me."

"I appreciate that," Chelsea said. "And... ah." She licked her lips and said, "Say hello to your partner for me."

Riley read the tone in Chelsea's voice and winced. "Thanks a lot. I was pretending that was all part of a bad dream I had."

"Sorry," Chelsea said. "Mac thought it would be fun."

"'Mac'?"

"It's my pet name for her. She said she likes it."

Riley started to say that Kenzie didn't like *anyone* calling her Mac, but she caught herself. If Chelsea had gotten away with it even once, then Kenzie must be all right with it. Riley said, "Well. All right, then."

"Let me know if you need any help flushing out whoever went after Ms. Mason."

"Will do. Love to Kenzie."

Riley left the building and ran through the possibilities as she went back to her car. When Kimaris left the confines of the city and became imprisoned, he would be completely cut off from Marchosias. He would be just another inmate. Maybe someone was taking advantage of his vulnerability to remove him from the equation entirely. It couldn't be Marchosias; he had an opportunity to kill Kimaris, but he handed him over to the police. There was no reason for Marchosias to try and get at him now.

The simple fact was that Chelsea was right. They had far too many suspects who might want Kimaris dead instead of in prison. If she couldn't find the culprit and make them stop, then the only alternative was to keep up the protective detail on Leah Mason until the trial ended. The thought of that was almost unbearable to consider. Of course, if Leah was right, the case wouldn't last much longer. She might not have a houseguest for very much... the dominoes started to fall in place, and Riley didn't like the picture it was creating.

Someone wanted Kimaris dead. They most likely didn't care how they did it, as long as he was gone. They tried to get him by removing the DA and getting the case thrown out, but that failed and the trial was starting as planned. Leah was sure the trial would be a cakewalk. If it was a short trial, then whoever wanted Kimaris dead would have to strike at the courthouse as soon as possible. If the demon was willing to kill Leah to get what they wanted, then an entire courtroom - or maybe the entire courthouse - wouldn't pose much of a hindrance.

Riley pulled away from the curb without bothering to fasten her seatbelt. Her tires protested with a loud squeal as she spun the wheel around to go back the way she had come. She pulled her cell phone from her pocket and dialed Priest's number.

There was a delay during which Riley imagined Priest standing up and moving to the back of the courtroom. She would do what she could to keep Leah in her line of sight, but Riley didn't know any judge that would allow a cell phone conversation in their courtroom. After an agonizing amount of rings, during which Riley started to worry the demon had already struck, Priest finally answered.

"This is Priest."

"Priest, I talked to Stanton. She doesn't think anyone is loyal enough to Kimaris to try to get him out of jail. I think the attempt on Leah's life was a way to get Kimaris freed so that the demons could take care of him their own way. We kept that from happening so their next plan..."

"They'll hit the courthouse."

"They may be setting it up now."

Priest said, "I'll look around and see if I can find anything. Leah..."

"Leah isn't the target anymore," Riley said. "Last night's attempt was just a means to an end. Whoever is doing this is after Kimaris."

"Okay. Are you on your way?"

"No. I'm going to have a word with our friend from last night."

Priest said, "Good luck."

"You too," Riley said. "We're both going to need all we can get."

The church had been in foreclosure for years. The windows were boarded up, covered with graffiti from the more sacrilegious punks in the neighborhood. The front and side lawns were overgrown with weeds that hid broken beer bottles and other accumulated garbage. Riley parked in the gravel back lot and bypassed the broken concrete steps of the back door. The cellar was held closed by a chain, secured by a shiny new silver lock. Riley took the key from her pocket and opened the door.

The concrete walls were covered with sigils and protections, all meticulously drawn by Priest the night before. The Cell was an experiment, a way to hold the various demons they encountered in their investigations. Sometimes exorcising them immediately left them without a source of information. Riley came up with the idea after their encounter with Kimaris, but she wasn't aware Priest was actually working on the idea in her spare time.

At the bottom of the stairs, turned to face the demon she and Priest had seen influencing Leah's mind the night before. "Hey there, Markus. You lied to us."

"And I feel just terrible about it. After how well you've treated me. I've not received a meal yet, if that's something you would like to address before we speak."

He was standing in the center of a containment sigil, glaring at her.

"Leah wasn't the real target. Whoever sent you to put the whammy on her really wants Kimaris. Leah Mason's death would have been a means to an end. It didn't work, so you won't go after her again. My question is what is the alternate plan? What does your boss have up his sleeve?"

"Mayhem." The demon put his hands behind his back, at a parade rest and staring forward despite the fact Riley had moved to his left.

"Is he going to take out the entire courthouse? No. He wants Kimaris to himself. If he wanted Kimaris to just be one victim among many, he could have done it any number of times before now. But it's important that it happens before he goes to prison. So this is his last shot. So maybe he has something big planned. Something a demon can survive, but would kill every human around him. Poison in the air vents? Fire?"

Markus smirked and said, "There's nothing you can do. You might as well sit back and enjoy the show."

Riley said, "Tell me what the plan is, and I'll let you go."

He raised an eyebrow. "Why would you do that? You're not stupid."

"No. I know that one more mediocre demon running around isn't going to make that much a difference. And if you being free can save some lives, then fine. I'm willing to make that trade."

Markus pretended to consider it. "And what prevents me from ripping your limbs from your body the second you let me go?"

"My tattoo."

"Right," Markus said softly, almost disappointed. "Very well. You release me, and I will tell you everything you need to know before I go running off into the night."

Riley looked at Markus' profile and said, "Hm."

He turned to look at her. "What?"

Riley said, "I'm just thinking. Kimaris is probably happy to be heading to prison. Even though it means he's stripped of everything that made him powerful. He's basically a demon trapped in a human shell, forced to spend the rest of his life in prison, and he probably doesn't mind going. Know why? Because he crossed Marchosias. And anything is preferable to facing Marchosias and taking his punishment. I bet demons have a punishment far worse than our legal system."

"What is your point?"

"You're not scared of your boss. You walk out of here, you have to deal with the fact that you not only failed, you sold your boss out to the cops. Why doesn't that worry you?"

Markus said, "I'm weighing my options."

"You're trying to get me to release you so that you can make another attempt on Kimaris. There *is* no boss. You put all this together yourself, and now you're trapped. As long as you're inside this little trap, you don't have a chance in Hell of getting another shot at him. Literally."

Markus turned to face forward again.

"So all I have to do to keep the people in that courthouse safe is... nothing."

"Are you willing to bet all those people's lives on that, Detective Parra? A hunch that I am some Machiavellian mastermind?"

Riley turned and walked back to the stairs. "Thanks for the information, Markus. Someone will be with you shortly to send you back to Hell."

"Wait!" Markus shouted. "Let me out of here! I'll tell you everything you want to know! I'm not the only one lying to you, Detective. Let me out of here. You'll definitely want to hear what I know about some of your so-called friends..."

"Hey, Markus," Riley said, raising her voice to be heard over his yelling. He stopped, and Riley said, "I'll see you once Mr. Kimaris is on his way out of town."

Riley shut the door on Markus' shouting after her.

When Riley returned to the courthouse, she found Priest pacing the hallway outside the elevators. She looked up when Riley appeared and said, "The building seems secure. No signs of demonic activity other than Kimaris, and even he is low-level. Still leashed by Marchosias, thankfully. If there's a trap here, I can't find it."

"That's because we already stopped it," Riley said. "Markus was the mastermind. When we captured him, he pretended to be a lackey so we would have to use him for information."

"Smart," Priest said. "And good that you caught it."

"I got lucky," Riley said. She gestured toward the courtroom and followed Priest down the hall. "That Cell of yours will hold him until the trial ends, right?"

"It won't fail," Priest said. "I was a bit weaker than I would have liked when I set it up, but even the weakest sigil in there is strong enough to hold a demon for months. He won't get out unless we let him out."

"Good," Riley said. "How's Leah doing?"

Priest said, "Very well, not that she could really screw it up. The judge seems to be treating the entire thing as a formality. Leah has been listing the charges against him since the session began. His defense seems to have already given up."

"He went against the family. Marchosias and his cronies are the ones who protected him. When Kimaris tried to take over, he cut himself off from that protection. They dropped him."

"I guess that's why this trial is happening so fast."

The courtroom doors opened and Leah came out, nearly stumbling over Riley and Priest. Riley stepped back and said, "What's going on?"

"Adjourned for the day," Leah said. "We'll reconvene tomorrow so the defense can put on whatever puppet show they have planned. Hopefully they'll rest their case so the judge can issue his verdict before the weekend. How'd your end go?"

Riley said, "Turns out we already caught the guy we were after. It was a small-time hood named Markus, the guy who... drugged you. There's no conspiracy to kill you, Markus just wanted Kimaris out of jail to deal with him personally."

"And this Markus is in jail?"

"In a manner of speaking. It's complicated."

"A lot of what you do is complicated," Leah said. She kept her gaze locked on Riley for a long moment before she looked at Priest. "So I guess the two of you won't have to guard my body any more."

Riley said, "All good things and all that. C'mon. We still have to get you home."

Before they could move very far, Kimaris and his lawyer stepped out of the courtroom. Riley locked eyes with him and Kimaris smirked. "I'm getting to know your face pretty well, Detective," he said. "I won't make a mistake next time."

"If you come back into this town during my lifetime, Marchosias will tear you limb from limb. Sorry if I'm not watching over my shoulder every night when I get into the car."

"I could have had you," Kimaris said.

His lawyer said, "We don't have time for this, Alexander."

"Yeah, Alexander," Riley said. "Run along. Get used to spending your days in a tiny gray cell. Seeing the world through bars."

Kimaris straightened his shoulders and faced her. "I was never a true threat to you, Riley. And yet, look how close I came. With a little more planning, imagine what I could have accomplished. You've taken great pleasure in mocking me. But consider this. If I am such an inconsequential man, just know there are so many more above me. People will more power and ingenuity. People who will be coming for you, Riley. Your friends can't protect you forever. You will fall. And I am guessing it will happen soon."

"Thanks for that prediction," Riley said. "As for you, I predict your cellmates will trade you for cigarettes on a nightly basis. Try not to tense up, it'll just make things hurt more."

The lawyer tugged on Kimaris' arm, and this time he went along.

Priest said, "I'll make sure he gets to the car without incident."

Riley said, "We'll meet up in the garage." Priest nodded, and Riley waited until she was gone before she led Leah to the elevator.

"Well," Leah said. "That was intense."

Riley shrugged. "If all the bad guys liked me, I wouldn't be doing my job very well."

Leah said, "I guess you have a point there. Listen, while we have a second to ourselves. I never once thought of Gillian as a long-term partner. She never struck me as someone who even wanted to settle down. But then I saw her with you, and I realized she was just not interested in settling down with *me*. You guys go well together."

"When did you see us together?"

"After you had dinner, sitting in the kitchen to talk. I was just pretending to be asleep. You know, you're not a very good detective."

"I was focused on Gillian. I rest my case, counselor."

Leah grinned. "An acceptable defense, Detective. No further questions."

They stepped into the elevator and Riley pressed the button for the garage.

"That doesn't mean we're going to hang out or double-date or anything," Riley said.

"God no. Friends with a cop?" Leah shuddered.

"What about me, friends with a DA? I deal with enough scum at work. I don't need to see one when I'm off-duty."

"Although it might be fun to see Gillian squirm if we did start hanging out."

Riley laughed. "Hey, you don't have to live with her."

"Have to?"

"Get to."

"That's what I thought." She sighed. "Well, even if my death was just a means to an end for whoever was going after Kimaris, you still saved my life. So thank you, Riley. For keeping me safe."

"I think that's the first time you've called me by my first name."

Leah shrugged and looked down at her shoes, obviously uncomfortable.

"It was my pleasure, Leah. Thanks for..."

"Leaving Gillian when I did?"

Riley smirked. "Yeah. Thanks for that."

The elevator doors opened and Leah said, "She didn't belong with me. I just moved out of the way so fate could take its course. But if you have any ex-girlfriends and feel like returning the favor, I'll leave you my card." She looked across the garage and bit her lip. Priest was waiting by Riley's car, leaning against the trunk as she watched the street. "As a matter of fact... that partner of yours. Is she seeing anyone?"

Riley chuckled. "Two people, actually."

"Oh?"

"Yeah. She just watches."

"*Really?* Kinky."

Riley shrugged and said, "I'll put in a good word for you." Priest pushed away from the car as Riley unlocked the door with the remote. "Come on, Priest. Let's get the DA home. Maybe we can even go out for dinner afterward."

"I thought you had plans with Gillian," Priest said.

Leah said, "That's too bad. Guess it'll just be the two of us. I'm feeling like Italian."

Priest frowned at Riley over the top of the car.

"Get in the car, Caitlin," Riley said, unable to stop herself from chuckling.

"Apparently they're still at dinner. Priest keeps texting me about etiquette."

"I'm surprised you set them up," Gillian said. They were walking up the stairs to their apartment after dinner, Gillian's shoes dangling from two of Riley's fingers. "If they hit it off, you'll have to deal with my ex-girlfriend hanging out with your current partner."

"It's not the worst thing in the world," Riley said. "Leah's a really sweet person." She tucked her cell phone back into her pocket as they approached the apartment door.

Gillian said, "Yeah, unlike all those troglodytes I usually date."

Riley put her arm around Gillian's waist and pulled her close. Gillian took out her keys and unlocked the apartment door, ushering Riley into the apartment. "I like to think that," Riley said as she shrugged out of her coat. "I'm the aberration. The one nice girl you finally managed to find after decades of kissing toads."

"Decades?" Gillian said. "How old do you think I am?"

"Fifty-six," Riley said. She pulled Gillian close and kissed her neck. "Maybe fifty-seven."

Gillian embraced Riley and untucked her blouse. "You just want to check for gray hairs."

"Mm," Riley said. "There's an idea."

They moved toward the couch as they kissed, and Gillian pushed Riley down onto the cushions. She pulled her skirt up over her knees and straddled Riley's legs before she sat down. Riley slipped her hands over Gillian's thighs. Riley's cell phone buzzed and Gillian groaned.

"I'll let it go to voice mail," Riley breathed.

"Could be important."

"Priest. Wants to know if the salad fork can be used for other food." She lifted Gillian and flipped her, pinning her to the cushions.

"Could be work."

Riley pressed her hand between Gillian's legs. "Want me to check?"

Gillian closed her eyes and moaned inarticulately. She licked her lips as Riley began to move three fingers in slow circles over her underwear. She moved her hips against Gillian and kissed her neck. Gillian held Riley, moving slowly against her. "Gonna give me a chance to repay this?" Gillian asked. "Before you answer your call and go running off?"

"Of course," Riley said.

"Just checking," Gillian said. Riley lifted her head and kissed Gillian hard. When they parted, Gillian said, "Does this have anything to do... with the fact Leah slept on this couch last night?"

"Completely forgot about that," Riley said. She was breathing hard. "Come for me."

"Admit you're marking your territory," Gillian groaned.

"Come for *me*," Riley said.

Gillian arched her back, her nails dragging along Riley's back and leaving marks even through her blouse.

Riley settled down on top of Gillian, who kissed her temple and stroked her body through her clothes.

"Undress me?" Riley whispered.

"Check your phone first," Gillian said. "It might really be important."

Riley groaned and pulled her phone out. "It's from Priest." She read the message and turned the phone so Gillian could see it.

"'The purpose of a date must not be food,'" Gillian read aloud. She was struggling not to laugh. "'We must speak so I cannot eat, and she wants to hold my hand so I find it awkward to hold cutlery. How is someone supposed to eat during a date?'"

"Poor Caitlin," Riley said. She kissed Gillian's forehead.

Gillian flipped Riley's phone shut and put it on the table. "She'll figure it out on her own. Just like everyone else in the world. Now, you said something about putting clothes on you? Right?"

"You're close..." Riley said, guiding Gillian's hands to the buttons of her blouse.

Riley slipped out of bed a few minutes past eleven. Gillian rolled away from the now-empty part of the bed and pressed her face into her pillow. Riley waited to make sure she wasn't awake before she left the bedroom. She poured herself a glass of milk and sat in her usual seat at the dining room table.

Gillian arrived a few seconds later. "I think I can feel when you leave me," she said.

"Sorry," Riley said.

"It's okay. I like the feeling." She went to the sink and poured herself a glass of water. She yawned as she sat down and crossed her legs. "What's on your mind?"

"The Angel Maker."

Gillian nodded.

"He has a pattern. Criminals, bad people. I keep thinking about it."

"What's tripping you up?"

Riley said, "We know there's a demon involved. He's the one pulling the strings for this mortal killer. So why these victims?"

"Why not them?"

"A demon would want to use the Angel Maker to cause terror," Riley said. "He'd aim for elementary school teachers, or nurses, doctors, cops. I keep going back to what Grace Stone said about her husband being killed. She said the killer was 'making good choices' in who he murdered."

"That's an awful thought."

"Yeah," Riley said. She rubbed her face. "Even if the demon somehow decided he was going to kill only these bad people, he couldn't have known..." She stared at the lip on her glass of milk and reordered her thoughts.

"Riley?"

"Nothing," Riley said. She swallowed and pushed the glass away. "I have to go out for a little while."

"It's the middle of the night."

"It's important, Jill. Trust me."

Gillian hesitated and Riley was afraid she would argue. Instead, she stood up and kissed Riley's lips. "Be *careful.*"

"I promise," Riley said.

Priest reached the landing before she realized Riley was standing under the security light next to her door. "Riley. Hello. Are you checking on how the date went? I sent you a text message…"

"I'm not here about that, Caitlin," Riley said. "I've been doing some thinking tonight, and I needed to bounce some ideas off of you before I do anything drastic."

"Okay."

Riley kept her hands in her pockets and began to pace in front of Priest's door. "I was thinking about the Angel Maker and the demon pulling his strings. And I've been thinking about the pattern we have. All these victims have been tied together with their criminal histories, but that kind of makes things worse. Because that doesn't fit. These aren't victims a demon would pick. So I started thinking about who *would* pick these victims. It's not a very long list, because whoever it is would have to know about the criminal records in the first place.

"The person giving the Angel Maker his list of victims would most likely be an angel, and they would need to have access to the police computers."

Priest remained where she was, her head bowed so that the security light didn't reach her face.

"All I want to know," Riley said, her voice low and angry, "is how long you've been working with the Angel Maker." Priest was silent until Riley slammed her fist against the apartment door. "Damn it, answer me."

Priest raised her head, her eyes wet with tears. "I've been working with him from the beginning, Riley."

Darker With the Day

Then

Terrence Charles Bishop liked the way his full name sounded. His mother called him Terrence, and most people at his work called him Terry. But he always signed all three names, even though someone at the clinic once told him that only psycho killers did that. James Earl Ray, Lee Harvey Oswald, John Wilkes Booth, Mark David Chapman. He didn't care. He thought it made him sound more impressive than he actually was.

He was at his favorite diner, eating a ham steak with two over easy eggs with a tall glass of milk. He'd been there for an hour already taking up valuable counter space, but the waitresses didn't rush him along. They thought he was slow. He didn't mind that, either. If they thought he was slow, then they treated him nicer and called him sweetie.

The other man slipped down onto the stool next to him with a groan. Terrence didn't look up. He avoided eye contact which avoided conversation which was just fine with him. But the other man spoke first. "It's a hell of a thing, isn't it?"

Terrence pretended to assume the man was talking to a passing waitress and cut another piece off his ham.

"Terrence Charles Bishop, I'm speaking to you."

His knife hovered over the plate and he risked raising his eyes to meet those of the man sitting beside him. The man had strong features and looked like a news anchor, with smooth skin and perfectly coiffed hair. He extended a hand. "My name is Aiperos, but you can call me Cain. How do you do?"

"Why are you talking to me?"

Cain smiled and folded his hands on top of the newspaper. "That's an amusing question, Mr. Bishop. I'm here because you need me. I've been sitting over there listening to you think." Terrence frowned, but Cain held up a hand. "Allow me to finish. I was listening to things you weren't aware you were thinking at the moment. The things you only allow yourself to think about in the dark of your bedroom."

Terrence felt the blood rising in his cheeks and turned away. He looked at the waitress on the other side of the counter as she refilled someone's drink.

"Don't worry about her," Cain said. "She will only hear me if I want her to." He looked at the woman and said, "I think you should pick up this knife and slit your throat. Make sure to get it deep." He paused and then said, "Sweetheart, could I get an orange juice while I work on the menu?"

"Sure can," the waitress said.

Terrence swallowed. "She can't hear you because you're not here. You're just one of the people I pretend."

"Is that what they tell you at the clinic?"

Terrence hated that people knew about the clinic, and his pills. He twisted his lips and focused on his food even though his appetite was gone. The waitress brought Cain an orange juice and quickly hurried off.

"I know what you want to do. I know that you resort to medication to keep you from giving in to those urges. But what if I told you there was a way I could help? What if I could help you submit to your darkest urge without fear of retribution?"

His palms were sweating so he had to put down his silverware. The fork rattled against his plate and he realized he was trembling.

"I'll give you everything you lack. Confidence. I will cloak you in darkness so that the police will never be able to identify you until we choose. And you will finally get to feel a blade slicing through a living body and know what it is like to have warm blood pour over your fingers."

Terrence said, "Why?"

Cain smiled. "You ask excellent questions. I knew you would; I didn't select lightly. All I ask in return, Terrence, is that you use your... experiments... to send a message for me. I know the school when you were a boy, the place you were sent, used finger painting. That's all I want you to do. Just a little painting."

"When I can start?" He couldn't resist blurting out the question; it had been on the tip of his tongue since this man started speaking.

"Unfortunately, you can't start immediately. We need time to get to know one another before we can work together. Besides, the audience I require is... absent without leave, as they call it in the military. So we will prepare, and then you will go to work. Do we have a deal, Mr. Bishop?"

Terrence tried not to look too eager when he nodded, but it was difficult.

Cain patted him on the shoulder and said, "Goodbye, my friend. I'll be in touch about when we can begin our work. Enjoy the rest of your breakfast."

Terrence turned to watch Cain leave, but he was nowhere to be seen. Terrence exhaled, closed his eyes, and eagerly finished his breakfast. He couldn't stop thinking about the possibilities of finally just *giving in* to his urge. How good it would feel. How relieved he would be when his fantasies finally became reality.

He slid off his stool and paid for his breakfast. He gathered his things and hurried from the diner into the warm mid-morning sun. It was going to be a hot day, but he still wore a coat; he liked the pockets. So many more pockets than his pants or any of his shirts. He walked to the curb and looked for a cab.

"Mr. Bishop?"

He started at the voice; how did so many people know his name today? He turned and saw a blonde woman standing between him and the diner entrance. How had she gotten there without him seeing her? She wore a suit and tie, the jacket missing and the sleeves rolled up. Oh, God, someone *had* heard Cain talking. Or, more likely, heard him talking to an empty bar stool. They called the police to come and take him back to that place. He opened his mouth to speak, but his lower lip just trembled.

"Don't be afraid. I'm not going to harm you." She stepped forward and the hair whipped across her face. "My name is Caitlin Priest. I need to talk with you about the man you just met."

Now

Priest unlocked her apartment door and Riley stormed inside. She stuffed her hands into her pockets to keep herself from lashing out violently, pacing in a wide circle around Priest's living room before she turned to face her partner. She snapped, "You want to explain, start."

"You were in Georgia with Gillian, recuperating from the wounds from your trial. The war had only just started, and demons were becoming bold. They were testing their limits. An angel named Michael was monitoring them, just in case their reach extended too far. He discovered one demon, Aiperos, was planning to use a mortal as a tool of violence. We weren't allowed to intervene directly, so we chose a different path."

"You gave him a hit list?"

Priest still refused to look at Riley. "Of a sort, I suppose. The killer was on the edge of taking the step himself. He would have been wandering the streets and murdering randomly even if the demon hadn't intervened. That was why we couldn't just remove the demon from the equation. Terrence Charles Bishop was—"

Riley kicked the coffee table and sent it askew. "You knew his fucking *name*. From the beginning of this?"

Priest lowered her eyes.

"Son of a bitch," Riley said.

"With the demon guiding him, we had justifiable cause to control his actions as well. I couldn't prevent him from killing, but I could make sure that he didn't kill innocents. I used the police computer to find an appropriate list of names."

"Give it to me."

"I will."

"No, I mean right *now*, Zerachiel. Hand over the list."

Priest walked into the small room off the kitchen and returned with a printout. Riley snatched it from her and read the list. Russell Stone was the first name on the list, followed by four names that were unfamiliar before she reached Sidney Lee. The others were all lower on the list. "This isn't in order."

"No. I just gave him the information. Terrence or his handler chose the victims depending on... ease. I believe they chose to kill Bernard Wright first because of the symbolic nature of his crime scene."

Riley folded the paper and said, "I can't believe you would do this."

"I did what I thought was best, Riley. No matter what my involvement, the Angel Maker would have been out there killing. Would you have preferred he chose his victims randomly? Or worse, allowed a demon to pick for him? Random people he passed on the street, the waitress who served him breakfast, the mailman. I didn't create the Angel Maker. All I did was—"

Riley said, "You just aimed him. The demon loaded the gun, and you aimed it, and... what, the mortal gets blamed for pulling the trigger? Seems like a pretty good deal you guys have worked out. You should have told me. Immediately. The fact that you didn't... I mean, were you even trying to help me out on this, or was that part of the game? Were you supposed to keep me running in circles until he hits his quota?"

"No. That wasn't my plan."

Riley shouted, "Then fill me in, God damn it."

"It was exposure," Priest said. There was some anger in her voice now, but it was tempered with her compassion. "You're trying to save this city single-handedly, Riley, and you don't have a chance. You've said it yourself; you're just a random cop. The Angel Maker is your chance to become famous. And with that fame, you can do actual good in this city. You can finally present a challenge to Marchosias. When you end the Angel Maker's killing spree, you'll be on the front page of every newspaper. You'll have the platform to finally turn the tide of this war and maybe loosen the hold of No Man's Land."

Riley shook her head and started for the door.

"Wait, Riley..."

"No," Riley said. She stepped to one side so Priest couldn't reach her. "This is... beyond the pale. You should go to prison for this, you realize that? I should tell Briggs what you did, and you'd be placed under arrest. Instead, I'm going to take this list to her, and I'm going to lie about where I got it. You'll be covered. But you're done. We're done. This is twice you've screwed me over, Zerachiel. You left me defenseless for Samael last year, and now this." She held up the list. "You had the name of a killer for *seven months* and you didn't tell me. So that's it. Ask for a transfer, hand in your badge, I don't care. We're not partners anymore. There's nothing you can do to make me trust you again."

"Riley..."

"Save it." She turned and walked out of the apartment, leaving the door open behind her as she went down the stairs. She pushed the door open and stepped out onto the sidewalk, taking a deep breath of fresh air. She closed her eyes and waited for Priest to come after her. When a few minutes had passed and she was still alone, Riley looked down at the list in her hands. There were twenty names, and she could cross off five of them. She folded the note and walked to her car, trying to quiet the raging voice in her head as she pulled out her keys. She didn't have time to mourn the loss of a good friend and a partner, and she didn't give a damn what happened to Priest or Zerachiel. She focused on the name, Terrence Charles Bishop, and the list of fifteen names in her hand.

Her cell phone rang as she got into the car and she pulled it out, flipping it open without checking to see who it was. "Hey. I was about to call you."

"Hopefully it wasn't anything important."

Riley tensed. Lieutenant Briggs calling her this late at night could only mean one thing. "Boss. Sorry, not who I expected. What's going on, as if I don't know?"

"He got another one."

"Do you happen to have a name?" Riley asked as she smoothed the paper over the steering wheel.

Briggs hesitated. "Um, yeah. Hold on." Riley heard her speaking to someone and then she said, "Last name was Dixon, first name…"

"Gordon," Riley said, finding the name on her list.

"Yeah. Did you know him? Where are you?"

"I'll explain when I get there."

Briggs gave her the address and said, "I'll let Priest know—"

"Priest is off the case," Riley said. She tried to keep the venom out of her voice, but it was difficult. "Personal reasons."

"Okay. You can explain that when you get here, too." She gave Riley the address, and Riley scribbled it down on a spare piece of paper. "It's the usual mess, but this time there are witnesses and a crowd for you to wade through."

"At this time of night?"

Briggs said, "Apparently there was some kind of party downtown. It ended a few minutes before the murder happened, so there were about fifteen people on the street. They called the police and ten of them stuck around to give statements."

"Fine," Riley said. "See you there." She disconnected the call and dialed Gillian.

"Hey. Everything okay?"

Riley started to speak but found her voice failing her. She looked out the window and said, "No. Priest."

"Did something happen to her?"

"She did something. Unforgivable."

Gillian said, "Okay. Do you want to talk about it?"

"I can't. The Angel Maker struck again."

"God. Hell of a night."

Riley nodded. "It's his last one. I have his name."

Gillian was quiet for a moment. "You what? Whose name?"

"The Angel Maker," Riley said. "I'll explain it all when we have some time. I should go. Briggs is waiting at the crime scene."

"Yeah. I'll probably be getting a call soon, too. I'll see you there."

"Yeah. Love you," Riley said.

"Love you, too."

Riley put her phone back into her pocket and took the opportunity to look up at Priest's apartment. The light was off, and Riley wondered if Priest was still up there. Maybe she had called her superiors and they flitted away with her. Maybe Zerachiel was back up in heaven and the shell of Caitlin Priest was lying there waiting to be discovered. Either way, Riley was done with her. She would work by herself until Briggs assigned her a new partner. And her new partner *would* be a cop, and a mortal. She'd had her fill of angels.

Apparently the witnesses hadn't just called the police. Riley saw two television news vans parked at the end of the block and she prepared her best 'no comment' expression before she got out of the car. She was almost to the crime scene tape when she heard a familiar, unwelcome voice behind her.

"Detective Perry! Detective Perry, do you have a moment?"

Riley's resolve crumbled and she gave in to the urge to turn and face Gail Finney. "Parra. It's not that hard. Maybe you'd be better in the comic pages if you can't get something that simple right."

"Sorry, brain fart," Gail said. She held out a small recorder, the same one that caused Riley so many problems, and said, "I'm doing a story on why it's taking the police so long to capture him."

"We're not even certain this is the Angel Maker."

Gail said, "So a copycat? Two killers the police can't catch?"

Riley turned and walked away from her.

"It's Parra with two Rs, right? I want to make sure I get it right in the story."

Riley looked at Gail and said, "I liked you a lot better last time I saw you. With a hole between your eyes."

Gail blinked, speechless, and Riley took the opportunity to duck under the yellow tape. She saw Briggs standing halfway down the block. Her hair was up, her Asian features enhanced with just enough makeup so that Riley almost didn't recognize her. She wore a sparkling green dress with a borrowed police jacket covering the top of it. She broke away from the officers she was talking to when she spotted Riley. "I didn't know you were one of the partiers," Riley said.

"I wasn't," Briggs said. "I was looking for a way out of an excruciatingly boring party with some of our bosses higher up in the department. I would have preferred the stomach flu. The commissioner says hello, by the way." She led Riley toward the body. "Tell me how you knew the victim's name."

"Long story," Riley said. "I got a list of potential victims from a confidential informant. I also got the Angel Maker's name."

Briggs grabbed Riley's arm and stopped her. "Where did the CI get this information?" She paused and said, "Or can I not ask that?"

"Suffice to say it came from someone we can't bring in and leave it at that," Riley said.

Briggs looked around and stepped closer. "Is this a higher power situation?"

"Something like that."

Briggs sighed heavily and shook her head. "This will all be brought up at the trial. You can't just produce a list of victims and a name and say you'd rather not say where you got it."

"We'll burn that bridge when we get to it," Riley said.

"Fine. Tell me what you know."

"According to the new information, the Angel Maker's name is Terrence Charles Bishop. Gordon here was on the list about halfway down. What did the witnesses see?"

"No one saw the actual attack. Someone screamed, and when the people on the street turned around, they saw someone kneeling on the ground making the angel wings. They were afraid of ending up like Allan McDade, innocent bystander turns into victim number eight, so they stayed back until he was done. Killer then got up, ran down the street, and disappeared into the shadows. One of the witnesses is a doctor, so he checked to make sure the victim was dead."

"Any description?"

"Just a dark figure," Briggs said. "Possibly wearing a windbreaker, possibly colored black or dark blue. Two people said he was wearing a trenchcoat, and one said it was a woman."

"Gotta love civilians," Riley said with a sigh. "I talked to Gillian before I came in. She's on her way."

Briggs nodded as they approached the body. Gordon Dixon lay face-up, as the others had been. His wings were sloppy, however. The blood had continued to pool after the killer left and it spread out along the edges of the design. Riley absently noted that Dixon was the first African-American victim, his skin now a pallid gray.

"Looks like more of the same," Riley said. "Have you checked him for priors?"

"I remembered your pattern, so I dug around a little. Assault and bat-tery and weapon possession, plus there's a sealed file he built up before his eighteenth birthday. I have someone working on getting it open for us."

"Records don't get sealed without good reason."

"I want to know how Bishop got into these files in the first place," Briggs said.

Riley felt her anger rise again, but she bit back on it. If she gave Priest up, there would be no going back. Instead, she shrugged. "Criminals are loudmouths. They brag about what they've done to whom, how they got away with it... word spreads. There are no secrets in No Man's Land. Who knows how the Angel Maker got hold of his information. What's important is that we stop him now before he gets the other fourteen people on his list, criminals or not."

Briggs said, "I've put it off long enough, Riley. I'm sorry, but I need to put together a task force and get–"

"No," Riley said. She took Briggs arm and guided her to the side of the road. "I've played by the rules with you as much as I could. But now you know the magnitude of what I'm dealing with. We can't bring in anyone else, any other cops, because they'd be walking into a hell storm. Literally. They wouldn't be prepared and they would be slaughtered."

Briggs said, "Who do you suggest we take?"

"Me, you, Jill, Kenzie... Stanton."

"Chelsea Stanton? You'd be willing to work with someone like her?"

Riley said, "She saved my ass. More importantly, Kenzie trusts her. That's all I need."

"All right." Briggs looked down the street as the medical van pulled up on the other side of the tape. "What about Priest? What happened with you two?"

"It's not important," Riley said. "She's out. And we're only taking Gillian as a medic. She doesn't fight."

"With only five of us against a demon, she might not have much of a choice."

Riley refused to argue the point, but she would go to great lengths to keep Gillian at a safe distance from any fighting. Gillian made her way to the crime scene and said, "What's going on? You have the Angel Maker's name?"

"Yeah. Long story. I need to get to the office and do some research."

"Okay. I have my friend here to keep me company. I'll see you at the morgue."

Riley walked with Briggs back to her car. "Need a ride to the office?"

"Yes, thank you. I took a cab from the party and I expected to catch a ride with one of the uniformed officers."

When they got into the car, Briggs pulled out her phone and dialed. "This is Lieutenant Briggs. I need you to get as much information as you can on a..."

"Terrence Charles Bishop," Riley said.

"Did you get that? We're on our way in now, should be about five minutes. I want a preliminary report by the time we get in."

Riley pulled away from the crime scene and used a nearby driveway to turn around. Briggs hung up her cell phone and said, "You're going to use the drive to tell me everything that happened with Priest."

Riley shook her head. "No, I'm not. She's saved my life too many times for me to completely turn my back on her. All you need to know is that she's on the outside now."

"Just like that?"

"Yeah," Riley said. "Just like that."

When Priest opened her front door, Michael was the first one she saw. He wore his fatigues, the armor of God always being updated to keep with the times. Before he could say anything, she noticed that the stairs were lined with other angels. She recognized Gabriel, Raphael, Sealtiel and Jegudiel, but the others had taken new forms since the last time she saw them.

"Don't you have a war to be fighting?" The anger in her voice was outweighed by the tears. She resisted the urge to wipe her cheeks before Michael and the others.

"There are portents," Gabriel said. "Something of grave importance is building. We must be prepared."

"Bigger than your little war?" Priest said.

"*Our* war," Michael said. "I think you have forgotten whose side you're really on."

Priest stepped back into her apartment. "No. I'm on Riley's side. Always Riley." She slammed the door in their faces.

Riley had spent many nights at the station, but it still felt weird to arrive in the middle of the night. The skeleton crew wandered hallways only partially lit, half the overhead lights turned off to save money.

Briggs went into her office when they arrived and emerged an impressively short time later in a completely new outfit. Her dress was gone, replaced by a pair of jeans and a white V-neck blouse. Riley was at her desk and motioned for Briggs to join her. "I checked some of the names on the list. This guy, Stanley Cooper, was accused of killing his mother and cashing her social security checks. We didn't have any hard evidence, so we had to let him go. Nathan Calloway did twelve years for killing his neighbor in a dispute. The rest probably are just as bad."

"We still have to set up protection for them. We usually have a couple days between killings, but we can't take the risk. If Bishop knows we're onto him, he may escalate and try to take out as many as possible before we take him down."

"Not protective custody," Riley said. "Pulling these people in won't help us find Bishop. We call this a list of suspects to let them know they're in danger, and we'll have officers sit on them in case Bishop shows up."

Briggs said, "That could work."

"I also looked at the information the desk sergeant found on Mr. Bishop. We don't have a record on him, but I did find his fingerprints on file. He's a regular guest of some of our finer shelters, when he's not hanging out at the free clinic. He's been picked up a couple of times and got thrown into the drunk tank. That's about it. No driver's license, no permanent residence listed..."

"He has to have someplace," Briggs said. "The shelters don't exactly love us, but they would report if someone was regularly coming in with clothes soiled in blood."

"Not to mention his knife. He keeps that with him, so we can rule out shelters. He's definitely staying somewhere."

Briggs said, "Give me the list of victims. I'll assign some officers to sit on these people until we have Bishop in our sights."

Riley handed over the list and leaned back. She stared at the computer screen and typed Bishop's name into the search engine. She found the drunk and disorderly complaints that caused him to end up in their custody. Each report had the area where he'd been picked up and Riley made a note of them on her pad.

Briggs returned and said, "Every scumbag on that list will have a pair of uniforms shadowing them tonight. It'll be interesting to see if the crime rate drops as a result. What are you doing?"

"The spots where Bishop has been picked up by our guys. Every report says pretty much the same thing; he was walking down the street shouting at himself and occasionally pounding his fist on the side of his head."

"Any of these arrests happen after the Angel Maker murders started?"

"Not a one. Maybe he found someone he could talk to."

Briggs said, "What you told me in the car, about the devil on his shoulder. I kept thinking about it. In the cartoons, there's always a devil on one shoulder and an angel on the other."

"Those are cartoons," Riley said, bristling at how close Briggs was to the truth.

"Right," Briggs said. "I have two questions that you refuse to answer. What did Detective Priest do that was so unforgivable, and where did you get the Angel Maker's name. I think I can put those two questions together and get a pretty reasonable answer. Don't you?"

Riley pulled a map from her desk drawer and started marking locations. "If I say yes, then you'll have to arrest her for aiding and abetting a serial killer. So I have no idea what you're talking about."

"But you're done with her."

Riley looked up into Briggs' eyes for a moment before she took out a blue pen and made different marks on the map. "Aren't you?"

Briggs said, "I've been going over this whole thing in my head ever since you, Priest and Dr. Hunt filled me in. I never thought that Heaven and Hell were quite as cut and dried as they were presented in church. This world is filled with shades of gray, Riley. Everyone makes compromises, and everyone has to sometimes make decisions they otherwise might not. All I'm saying is consider all the circumstances before you condemn someone who cares an awful lot about you." She looked at the marks Riley was making on the map. "Are you listening to me?"

"Yes," Riley said. "And I promise you, I will think about what you've said. But right now, it's all I can do not to punch Priest in the face."

"That's understandable. If she walked in here, I would be hard-pressed to stop you."

"I'm going to change the subject." Riley pointed at the map. Her marks were clustered in a group that covered about two square miles with an occasional stray out in the borders. "Angel Maker crime scenes are marked in red. The locations of Bishop's arrests are in blue. I don't have the bus schedule memorized, but we should input the locations of the stops. It'll give us a place to start searching."

"Nicely done, Detective," Briggs said. "I'll get some gear for us. You call Kenzie Crowe and Stanton. We have a killer to catch."

Stanton was waiting at the door when Riley parked in front of the agency. She stepped forward as Riley and Briggs got out of the car. "Looks like we're even. I disturb your sleep..."

"Sorry about that," Riley said. "Chelsea Stanton, Lieutenant Zoe Briggs."

Stanton's smile widened and she said, "Lieutenant. I knew you had it in you."

"Nice to see you again, Chelsea," Briggs said. Her voice was formal, stopping just short of friendliness.

"We knew each other on the force," Stanton explained to Riley. "Zoe was a few years ahead of you and Kenzie. She was in the first group of female detectives to follow in my footsteps. They were probably the most affected by what I did. Hope you can forgive me."

"I overcame the stigma," Briggs said. "Riley tells me you're reformed. Drug-free."

"One hundred percent," Stanton said.

Briggs gestured for Riley to lead the way inside. The lights were all on, and Kenzie was slumped in the chair behind her desk. Her hair was a mess, but still swept forward to disguise the burns on the side of her face. She eyed Briggs as she walked in and then looked at Riley. "New partner?"

"For tonight, at least," Riley said. "Sorry if I woke you."

"No," Kenzie said pointedly. "You didn't wake either of us."

Riley said, "Then I'm even sorrier."

Kenzie smirked and held her hand out to Briggs. "Mackenzie Crowe."

"Lieutenant Zoe Briggs."

Riley said, "She knows everything, pretty much."

Stanton said, "That'll make things easier. Fill us in."

Riley sat on the edge of Kenzie's desk and said, "What I say doesn't leave this room." Everyone nodded, but Riley was only interested in Briggs' response. When she nodded, Riley continued. "The Angel Maker has been working with a demon from the very beginning. What we didn't realize was that he also had an angel working with him."

"And Priest didn't know?" Kenzie said.

"It *was* Priest."

Stanton leaned back. "Whoa. I know I don't know her very well…"

Riley shook her head. "She thought she was helping me. She wanted to make me into some kind of a hero by bringing down a killer."

"That's fucked up," Kenzie said.

"Yeah," Riley said. "Moving on. When I found out Priest was involved, she gave me a list of victims along with the killer's name. Terrence Charles Bishop. We had another murder earlier tonight, but if he figured out we're onto him, he may go into overdrive. We have officers watching the potential victims. Meanwhile the four of us here and Gillian will spend tonight trying to find out where Bishop is hiding out between murders."

Briggs said, "Riley narrowed down the search area." She handed the map to Kenzie. "We'd have to get pretty lucky to find his rabbit hole, but it won't be impossible."

"Gillian is back at the office doing the preliminary exam on the latest victim. The four of us should split up and see what we can find. Kenzie, you want to ride with me again?"

Kenzie said, "Can't wait."

Briggs looked at Stanton. "Don't worry, Lieutenant," Stanton said, "if you want to go alone, I'll stay here and coordinate everything."

"Don't be silly," Briggs said. "I was just wondering if you had a car."

Kenzie took a set of keys from her desk drawer and tossed them to Briggs. "Take my car. Just be careful with her."

"I'm an excellent driver."

"The car is a boy. I was talking about Chelsea."

Riley said, "Speaking of. Stanton, can you help me out? I have some supplies in the car."

"Sure," Stanton said. She followed Riley out of the apartment and was halfway down the stairs before she spoke again. "What's the real reason you pulled me away?"

"I need a hand," Riley said. "Vests are heavy."

"And you asked the blind woman you don't like to help you? The truth, Detective."

Riley stopped at the bottom of the stairs. "That's why. I wanted to ask you privately if you were up to this. There's a chance we'll have to do some fighting in close quarters, in the dark. I don't want you to be a liability. So if you want to bow out, let me know. I'll take the blame, I'll say it was my choice."

Stanton sighed. "I'm not entirely blind. I use the cane when I get tired and my eyes have problems focusing, but I *can* see a limited amount. My problem is with detail and eye strain. Even if I'm standing in a dark room, I can tell the difference between a hat rack and a person. And I can tell the difference between someone in a police vest and a demon trying to kill me. I've spent years on the sidelines, Detective Parra. If I have a chance to make amends for my past sins, then I'm going to take it. I won't be a liability, and you won't have to take care of me."

Riley listened intently and then nodded. "Okay, then. I just had to make sure. Now come on. I really do need help with those vests."

Gail Finney dropped her briefcase and jacket on the chair, undoing the buttons of her blouse as she crossed the apartment. She had a view from the balcony of the el train and the waterfront. When the light was right, it looked like the train was skimming across a pool of liquid silver. She opened the balcony door and let the cool breeze blow the curtains apart. It reached into her open blouse like a cloud of fog and she closed her eyes, sighing as it washed over her.

She finished undressing and took a long shower. She couldn't get Riley Parra's voice out of her head. *"I liked you a lot better... with a hole between your eyes."* She didn't want to focus on what the words meant, and she hated that Parra might have seen how much the words shook her. The simple fact was that Riley Parra should have been a dribbling idiot after the whammy they had laid on her. The mara should have been the end of her.

Gail got out of the shower and toweled herself off as she walked into the bedroom.

"Stop."

Gail froze where she was and dropped the towel onto the foot of the bed. She could see movement from the corner of her eye, red hair and pale flesh in black silk. She kept her eyes straight ahead, her hands at her sides as she was circled from behind until the intruder was in front of her. A blood red fingernail touched Gail's bottom lip and she sucked it into her mouth.

"You saw her tonight."

"I did."

The hand slid down her shoulder, down to her stomach to the sunburst around Gail's navel, the mark that revealed her as evil's champion in the city. A single blade-like nail drew circles around the mark and then retreated.

Gail swallowed and wet her lips.

"May I speak?"

"Of course."

Gail focused on the touch of her lover. "I thought you would have been here earlier. When I came home."

"Did you miss me?"

"Yes."

Scarlet lips part in a grin wide enough to reveal the sharpened fangs. When Gail first saw them, she had asked if she was a vampire. The answer had been negative, with a quiet laugh. Gail had felt those teeth on her body quite often, but they'd never pierced her flesh.

"I'm sorry, darling. It's a busy night. All hands on deck."

Gail's expression hardened. "Parra."

"Mm-hmm. Big night."

"Do you have to go immediately?"

The demon smiled and backed up to the bed. "I could do with a bit of worship." She sat down and unfastened her trousers. Gail dropped to her knees and bowed her head.

The houses in the neighborhood were all dark shapes set at the back of unkempt lawns. The decrepit buildings were silhouettes that joined with trees and broken down cars to create an illusion of monstrosities waiting in the darkness. Riley drove slowly, flashing back to her time on patrol when she and Kenzie were both in uniform. She paused at an intersection, the pole on the corner missing its stop sign, and said, "You and Stanton must be getting pretty good at this demon-hunting stuff by now."

"Actually, a lot of our work is pretty mundane. Stolen property, cheating spouses. I spent four days last week watching a man who claimed he was too destitute to pay child support."

"What was the verdict?"

"He was definitely destitute. Buying that plasma TV and the basketball tickets probably wiped him out."

Riley smirked.

"So what are we looking for here?"

"I'm not really sure. He would need a place where he could go to ground between killings. Maybe he has a place he calls home, but I don't think he would risk any of his neighbors spotting him in his blood-soaked clothes. Allan McDade saw him and ended up dead for his trouble. He has to have a place where he can turn back into a law-abiding citizen."

Kenzie said, "Like a Batcave."

"If that helps you," Riley said.

Kenzie grinned. "Chelsea told me that you know about, uh... our little thing with Priest."

"God. If there's a way we can *not* talk about that..."

"It's the elephant in the car. It's just something that sort of happened. I was attracted to Caitlin when I met her last year, and they went into overdrive during the whole Kimaris thing. But I've had feelings for Chelsea since we started working together. I don't think I would ever have considered it before, but with Caitlin, yeah. I felt it would be okay."

"You call her 'Caitlin'?"

"Yeah. You don't?"

"Sometimes. Rarely."

Kenzie said, "Oh, that's right. You don't like first names."

"What?"

"Priest, Briggs, Stanton... you've never liked calling people by their first names. Even with me, you call me Kenzie."

"You wanted me to call you that."

Kenzie shrugged. "Special circumstances. Do you actually refer to anyone by their first name?"

"Gillian."

Kenzie chuckled. "Okay. She's enough, I guess."

Riley paused at the next corner and glanced at the shadows on either side of the street. Something caught her eye, but it took her a moment to realize why. She pointed over the wheel and said, "Look at that."

Kenzie looked until her eyes made out the shape of the building against the darkness. It was a squat Victorian house set in the back quadrant of a huge lot. A turret rose from the back, rising just slightly higher than the roof to look out over the rest of the block. They couldn't see many features other than the covered porch that wrapped around one corner of the house and their headlights reflecting in the few windows that still had glass.

"Why that place?"

"No light inside," Riley said. "No homeless campfire, no cigarettes flaring, I don't see a stack of beer cans a mile high on the porch. People are staying away from it, even though it's obviously abandoned. Look at the trees."

Kenzie looked. "What about them?"

"They're growing away from the house."

Kenzie looked again and saw a pronounced angle in the branches. It looked as if a powerful force had erupted from the property and forever altered the growth of the trees. Kenzie unfastened her seatbelt.

"That's it, then. Let's go."

"No," Riley said. "If he's in there, he'll still be on a high from his latest killing."

"And if he hasn't arrived yet, we can be in there waiting for him. And if he's in there, and we wait, he might have a back way out and we'll lose him."

Riley looked back at the house. "If we hit him now, in the middle of the night, the demon helping him will be at the height of his power. We should wait closer to dawn when Bishop is tired and the demon's power is diminishing."

"Demons get weaker at dawn?"

"Stands to reason, right?" Riley said. "It sounds like something Priest would say."

Kenzie shrugged. "Okay, how about a compromise. I stay here and keep an eye on the place, and I'll let you know if Bishop or his buddy hightail it somewhere else."

Riley reluctantly nodded. "I'll head back to your office and join up with Briggs and Stanton." She said, "I can't call Briggs by her first name because she's my boss. And Stanton was my elder, so I'm in the habit of..."

"Let it go, Riley," Kenzie said. She laughed and started to open the car door.

"Wait," Riley said. "How far are we from your office?"

Kenzie looked around to get her bearings. "The main road is about three blocks north of here, and then two blocks west."

"I can handle that. You keep the car, in case Bishop decides to go somewhere else and you can't follow on foot."

Kenzie said, "You're going to walk five blocks in No Man's Land after dark by yourself? You picked a hell of a night to piss off your angel."

"I still have protection." Riley pulled the Desert Eagle from the back of her belt and Kenzie's eyes widened.

"Where the hell did you get that thing?"

Riley turned the weapon over in her hands. The light was meager, but somehow the gold of the weapon still managed to reflect brightly back at her. "I'm not entirely sure. Someone gave it to me in a dream, and it was still there when I woke up."

"Maybe you didn't really wake up."

Riley shuddered. "Don't even joke about that, Kenzie. Stay safe, and stay in contact with us. Cell phone?"

"Got it."

"Call Stanton and Briggs, tell them what we found. We'll regroup at your office. We'll call when we're on the way back."

Kenzie saluted and climbed over the center console to drop into the driver's seat. Riley walked around the car to the sidewalk. Kenzie drove the car away from the intersection in search of a better place to set up surveillance on the house. Riley checked to make sure she was alone, listening for the telltale sound of sneakers on pavement that would tell her someone was trying to sneak up behind her. It was only then that she noticed how deathly quiet the street was. No dealers positioned on the corners, no lookouts trying to look busy while they kept their eyes out for cops, and no winos weaving down the sidewalk. It was like being in the forest without any birdsong; something was off about the block.

She looked at the house one last time before she started walking. She kept her hand on the butt of her gun, tuned in to the sounds of the street for even the slightest change that would signal she wasn't alone. When she spotted the first drug dealer, a gangly black teen who looked at her before shuffling off into the darkness, Riley made a note of the spot and turned to look over her shoulder toward the house.

Two and a half blocks of emptiness that the local wildlife didn't dare step into. There was definitely something wrong with the house she had seen. Riley could see the turret over a stand of trees that marked the edge of the property and knew without a doubt that it was where the Angel Maker would be found. She continued toward Stanton's agency, moving a little faster now.

Riley was sitting on the floor behind Kenzie's desk when Gillian arrived. It was a few minutes after midnight, and the headlights washed over the front door when she pulled in. Riley pushed herself up off the floor and went to let her inside. Gillian greeted her with a kiss and a quiet hello, and Riley locked the door behind her before leading her to the small nest she had set up for herself. There was a sleeping bag and two pillows up against the wall, nestled in next to the filing cabinet. A laptop was sitting open underneath

Kenzie's seat.

Gillian sat down with her back to the wall and Riley sat next to her so that she could see the front door and the greenhouse windows.

"What's with the computer? Surfing porn at a time like this?"

"Nothing that fun," Riley said. "I'm reading about exorcisms. Without Priest, we may need to have an ace up our sleeves when it comes to fighting a demon."

"How are you doing with that?"

"Latin is hard," Riley said. "How about you? Did you find anything worthwhile?"

"The latest murder was definitely the Angel Maker. I confirmed the knife wounds were identical to the other victims. I still have to do the paperwork but I thought that could wait. How are things here?"

"Everything's kind of on hold right now. Kenzie is keeping an eye on the place we think Bishop is staying. Stanton called her a few times for updates, but then she headed up to bed."

Gillian said, "Briggs?"

"Stanton offered her the couch. I stayed down here to watch the door. And to let you in. I made a little space..."

Gillian kicked off her sneakers and stretched her legs out. "I got the stuff you asked for, by the way. It's out in the trunk of the car."

"Good. Thank you." She looked around and said, "Sorry about this. I know you'd probably rather spend the night at home, and this isn't exactly the Hilton."

"No, it's fun. Kind of reminds me of lock-in."

"What's that?"

"It was this thing we did in high school. A group of seniors got to spend the night at the school after prom. We had music and all kinds of games. Spent the whole night running around in the school. Some of us had sleeping bags. Mine..." She chuckled and looked down at her hands. "I put my sleeping bag behind my English teacher's desk. I had such a huge crush on her and... I don't know. I guess my eighteen year old brain thought it was like sleeping with her."

"Did you ever tell her how you felt?"

"Oh, no, never. She was married, two kids. She liked me, though. Not... I mean, she liked me as a student. She thought I was an excellent writer."

"You write?"

Gillian shook her head. "Silly stuff in high school. I didn't really have a passion for it."

Riley nodded. "Are you okay? Do you need water or... Kenzie has a mini-fridge over by the greenhouse door."

"No, I'm fine."

Riley rested her head against the wall and Gillian stretched out to put her head on Riley's lap. Riley stroked her hair and stared across the dark office. Someone shouted down the street and Riley heard glass breaking. She knew she had bigger problems to deal with, but it took effort to keep from rushing from the office with her gun drawn.

"Does it bother you that I don't call people by their first name?"

"What?"

"Priest and Stanton and..."

Gillian said, "You call me by my first name."

"We're partners."

"You've always called me that. Or Jill." She rubbed Riley's calf. "I like it when you call me Jill. But you've never called me Hunt, even when we were just coworkers."

Riley looked down at her. "I haven't, have I?"

"Dr. Hunt, sometimes. When you have to be formal. But that's kind of hot."

Riley smirked and rested her hand on Gillian's shoulder. "We're going to head out around four in the morning. Gives us a couple of hours to rest up and then regroup before we go after Bishop. Get some sleep, Dr. Hunt."

"I'll try, Detective Parra."

Riley rested her head against the wall and closed her eyes, although she knew it was a lost cause trying to sleep. Eventually, she heard Gillian's breathing slow and become steady with sleep. She took her phone from her pocket, careful not to disturb Gillian's sleep, and connected to the internet. Riley continued to stroke her hair, reluctant to break contact with her. Despite the effort she made to block the thoughts out, she wondered where Priest was. Either she would respect Riley's wishes and stay away, or she wouldn't be able to resist lending a hand at the last minute. She wasn't sure which one she was hoping for.

Gillian murmured in her sleep. Riley heard someone cross the floor upstairs and then the rush of water in the pipes.

A year ago, she would have been crippled by the loss of Priest. She would have been forced to ignore what Priest had done so she would have a shot at succeeding. But now, she had other partners. She had people she could count on. Terrence Charles Bishop may have a demon in his corner, but he was still just one man. One man with one undeniable weakness.

He had no idea what was coming for him.

Riley bent down and kissed Gillian's cheek to wake her. "It's time."

Gillian sat up and stretched. Stanton and Briggs were across the room at Stanton's desk, dressed in dark clothes. Riley helped Gillian to her feet. "You probably have time for a quick shower while we gear up."

"No, might as well get it over with," Gillian said.

Riley nodded and didn't mention the fact they all might need to shower again after their work was done. She led Gillian out from behind the desk and said, "Stanton just spoke with Kenzie. Bishop showed up at the house about an hour ago and he's been inside ever since. That gives him enough time to get nice and comfortable. He may even be asleep now."

"And the demon working with him?" Briggs said.

"He'll be bright-eyed and bushy-tailed, but Gillian took care of that. She brought the sacraments Priest told us about during the lockdown. There's holy water in the car, and we have a couple of jars of holy oil," Riley said. "I've spent the past hour rubbing down our weapons with the oil."

Briggs said, "Holy oil is different than gun oil. Um. Right?"

"I assume so," Riley said. "I just coated the outside of the weapons; I didn't strip them and coat every surface. It should be enough."

Stanton said, "Let's hope so."

Briggs said, "There are bulletproof vests in the backseat of Riley's car. For tonight's purposes, Stanton and Kenzie are temporarily deputized. You both have the same training Riley and I do, so it shouldn't be a problem."

"What about me?" Gillian said.

Riley slipped her Desert Eagle into the back of her belt. "You're not going in."

"The hell I'm not."

"Don't blame Riley, it was my idea," Stanton said. "If we're going into this place, odds are good one of us is going to get hurt. We're going to need a medic. It'll be better if you're safe."

Gillian looked at Riley. "I don't suppose you fought this idea very hard."

Riley met Gillian's eye. "Why the hell would I fight that idea?"

Gillian held Riley's gaze and then slowly nodded. "Fine. I'll stay outside. But if you need backup, I'm not going to hesitate to come running."

"I can live with that," Riley said. "Are we all ready?"

Everyone agreed, and Riley took her coat off the floor. Stanton and Briggs were the first out the door, with Gillian and Riley bringing up the rear. Riley hooked her hand on Gillian's elbow and whispered, "If anything happened to you..."

"I know," Gillian said. She touched Riley's hand before they stepped outside.

The sun was still down, but the sky was slightly brighter than it had been when Riley left Kenzie. Briggs and Stanton were waiting by the car, but they were looking at the storefront across the street. "We have an audience," Stanton said. "Even I can see them."

Riley looked and saw a row of winged creatures standing along the rooftops of the buildings. Some were obscured by signage, while others stood silhouetted against the dark clouds. They were lined up like crows on a power line, shuffling and occasionally flexing their wings as they observed the scene below. Riley looked above, at the roof of Stanton's agency, and saw more angels there.

"You'd think they'd have bigger things on their plate," Briggs said.

"The champion of good is going after a demon in No Man's Land," Riley said. "They wouldn't miss this." She walked to Gillian's car and unloaded their supplies. Gillian took a black bag loaded with something light and let it dangle from her hand as she followed Riley to Briggs' car. "Ignore them. We have other things on our plate without these bastards distracting us."

Riley and Gillian sat in the backseat for the drive to pick up Kenzie. At the stop sign where Riley had first spotted the Angel Maker's lair, Briggs flashed her headlights. She received an answering flash from halfway down the block. Riley's car was backed into the loading dock of an abandoned business. The road sloped down to a pair of garage doors, and Briggs parked next to Riley's car.

Kenzie climbed out of the car and tossed the vests onto the roof of the car. Riley took them and handed them out.

Kenzie gave a theatrical shudder as she joined them. "Thank God I won't have to do this again. This place is fucking creepy. And I don't know if you've noticed, but we have an air traffic control problem in the area."

"Yeah," Riley said. "It's the hot ticket of the night, apparently. We can assume the demon using Bishop has been tipped off."

"Battle plan?" Stanton said.

Riley looked at Briggs. "The, uh, lieutenant should..."

"I'm going to defer to your experience in this situation, Detective. But don't get too used to giving the orders."

Riley nodded. "Lieutenant Briggs, you take the back door. Kenzie and Stanton, you two are together at the north corner of the building. Keep an eye on the doors and windows to make sure Bishop doesn't try to make a break for it. Jill, you can watch the front from here. If you see anyone but us coming out, lay on the horn. We'll come running."

Gillian pulled out the bag she had taken from her trunk and said, "I was kind of embarrassed about including these, but..." She took out a small gun made of green plastic.

"I can't see very well in the best of conditions, but I think it's particularly bad right now. Are those water guns?" Stanton said.

"Filled with holy water," Gillian said. She handed one to Riley and said, "Shoot it in the demon's eyes. Anywhere you hit him it'll be like a dart."

"She's right," Riley said. "That's brilliant, Jill." She took an orange gun and tucked it into her belt. Stanton, Kenzie and Briggs each took one as well. Riley looked around and said, "Are we all ready?"

"Let's go," Briggs said.

Riley led the way up the ramp to the road. Gun drawn, she led the way across the street to the overgrown lawn of Terrence Charles Bishop's house. Briggs was right behind her, with Kenzie and Stanton bringing up the rear. Riley brought her hand up and motioned for them to split up to their positions. Kenzie and Stanton crossed the front yard and followed the gravel driveway around the corner of the house. At the front porch, Riley pressed against the wall and Briggs continued forward. She moved at a crouch, staying below the levels of the window as she ran to the back corner.

Riley waited until she was in position before she moved to the first broken window. She dropped to a crouch next to the window and peered inside. The window looked into a room full of broken furniture. The interior walls were painted with indecipherable sigils that looked black in the darkness. When she determined the room was empty, Riley climbed over the windowsill and entered the Angel Maker's home.

Kenzie checked the backyard. The grass was taller here, at least up to the knees, and the alley was blocked by a dilapidated fence. She could see the back porch, a slab of concrete placed underneath a screen door that swung free in the breeze. She saw Zoe Briggs on the other side of the house and motioned to her. Briggs nodded and Kenzie pressed against the wall. "Backyard is clear."

Stanton said, "I hear something. In the grass."

Before Kenzie could turn to look closer, an arm wrapped around her throat from behind and she was pulled away from the wall. She brought the gun up, but she couldn't get a clear shot before the gun was slapped away from her. As she hit the ground, she saw someone else grabbing Stanton and disarming her as well. The man was tall and elderly, but he moved with the grace of a much younger man. He had a thick beard and his white hair was brushed away from his forehead. Kenzie knew she had seen him before, but couldn't place where.

She freed the water gun from her belt and fired blindly over her shoulder. The thing holding her wailed and its grip lessened. She grabbed her weapon and got to her feet. The creature holding Stanton looked up just as Kenzie put a bullet through its head.

Stanton kicked the corpse away and said, "Was that—"

"I have no idea," Kenzie said.

Stanton knelt and looked at the face and said, "Bernard Wright."

"The Angel Maker's first victim?"

Stanton said, "Zoe and Gillian."

Kenzie ran toward the front of the house while Stanton ran across the backyard to where Briggs had been standing before she disappeared.

Riley stepped into the hallway. Framed photos hung on the wall, the glass either cracked or too dusty to see who was immortalized within. More symbols were painted on these walls, and Riley saw a foreign language written in dried blood on the floor under her feet. A part of her yearned for Priest to be there, to explain what the designs meant, but for all she knew it was a trap to ensnare angels. It was probably best she wasn't there.

When she reached the end of the hallway, she found herself in a sunroom. The windows were all blacked out, and the hardwood floor was painted with pools of spilled blood.

The room was empty and had no other exit, so she turned to continue her search.

The demon's hand hit her flat in the chest, the force behind the blow hard enough to throw her back into the room.

Kenzie saw movement between the two cars on the loading dock, the grunts of a fight coming to its conclusion. A dark shape rose, the victor getting back to their feet, and Kenzie rounded the front bumper of the car and charged the silhouette. She brought her gun up as the figure turned, and she squeezed the trigger three times in quick succession.

Gillian yelped and knocked the water gun to one side. She blinked the water from her eyes and said, "What the hell are you doing?"

"I thought—" She looked down at the body of a man lying on the concrete behind the cars. His face was blistered and scarred from being hit with holy water.

"Sidney Lee," Gillian said. "I could have sworn he was dead when I autopsied him." She wiped the holy water off her brow. "Thanks for not using your real weapon."

Kenzie said, "I... forgot what hand I was holding it in."

Gillian smiled. "Maybe someone is watching out for me."

"Someone better be."

Stanton could barely make out more than vague shapes in the darkness. Someone was pressed against the side of the house, struggling with a taller, more muscular creature. Stanton managed to see a wide blue strap against white material and remembered Briggs was wearing a white T-shirt under her bulletproof vest. She grabbed the attacking creature from behind, wrapping her arm around its neck and wrenching it back away from Briggs.

As soon as she was free, Briggs pressed the barrel of her water pistol into the creature's mouth and pulled the trigger. The man recoiled and hissed, struggling to escape and run. Stanton pressed her gun against the creature's temple and pulled the trigger. It fell between them.

"Are you okay?"

"Fine. That was James Graham, the cabbie rapist."

Stanton said, "Kenzie and I were just attacked by Bernie Wright and I think the other one was Mitchell Reese."

"Bishop's victims."

"Looks like."

"Zombies?"

Stanton said, "Probably something to do with souls. If these people are as bad as Riley thought, then they probably went to Hell. After that, the demons could use them however they pleased."

Briggs scoffed and shook her head. "That means if any of us go down, we could be used as weapons against the others."

"You think we're all bound for Hell? We're fighting demons."

Briggs shrugged. "All I know is that I don't see myself qualifying for harps and halos. Where's Kenzie?"

Another round of gunfire came from across the street.

Riley grabbed for her water pistol and found a puddle of water on the bottom of her vest. She looked down and saw the impact of her tumble had opened the plastic stopper on the toy. The holy water and spilled over her hip. "Just fucking wonderful," she muttered, scrambling backward to the wall as the demon approached.

"I don't believe we've been properly introduced. My name is Aiperos, but you may call me Cain. I'm here to warn you."

Riley couldn't help but laugh. She felt the water from the useless toy wetting her fingers and palm as she hit the wall. "Warn me. That's nice of you."

"Yes, as much good as it will do you. I expected an angel to be with you. Zerachiel? Perhaps you discovered that she and I are quite good friends." He smiled. "But I still never expected you to come here without her. That would have merely been suicide. Coming with just a few mortals for support that's... that's... what was the movie where the cowboy rode a nuclear bomb to its destination?"

"Look, can we skip the movie recommendations and get this over with?"

Cain's smile faded. "Fine. You have no idea what is waiting for you upstairs. Terrence Charles Bishop was borderline psychotic when I entered his life. I merely gave him the push he needed to be truly great. For the first murder, he was still hesitant. The same for the first three or four. But once he got into the groove?" Cain laughed. "You foolishly believed that Allan McDade was an unfortunate eyewitness. That Terrence panicked because someone was in the wrong place at the wrong time.

"I was there when Terrence killed Sidney Lee, and then I watched as he waited by the stairs to the el station. I had no idea what he was doing until the first commuter arrived. We never discussed taking two victims at once. I discovered Terrence no longer needed me to okay his actions. He had become who he was meant to be. And it's all thanks to me. Well... me and Zerachiel, that is."

Riley used the wall to push herself up with her free hand, the other still pressing against her wet vest. She didn't take the bait he was dangling about Priest. "And what, exactly, was he meant to be?"

"A killer," Cain said. "He is the one you should fear. Not me. Although if you wish, I could make it painless for you. End it right here, right now."

"You're a saint."

"Bite your tongue." He stepped forward and said, "But it is a kindness I'm offering you. He will take pleasure in taking your life slowly, with as much anguish as possible."

Riley said, "Well, I would consider taking you up on that, but there's just one thing. I spent all last night on the internet. Researching. It would be a shame for all that information to go to waste." She brought her wet hand away from her vest and pressed it against the demon's face. He howled in pain and Riley said, "Myn tagazie p›arguceay. Coa ci'it myn ema."

Cain pulled away from her, but he didn't get far. The light in the room seemed to be drawn toward him, darkening the house even further until it exploded from him in a burst of energy that knocked Riley back to the ground. Cain's body was wracked by seizure, his arms and legs twitching as he threw his head back in agony. Burns scored his face in the shape of Riley's hand. With a final wave of energy, the light returned to the room and his body crumpled to the floor in a lifeless heap.

"Who needs an angel?" Riley muttered. She shook the droplets from her hand as she stepped past the body and went to find the stairs.

Gordon Dixon was holding Kenzie back, his face twisted in a grimace of hate and anger, while Russell Stone assaulted Gillian. Briggs slammed into Stone from the side, knocking him to the ground and freeing Gillian's hands. Gillian retrieved her water pistol and fired it into Dixon's face. He fell back, and Gillian switched the water pistol to her other hand as Kenzie took cover. She shot him twice and turned the weapon on Stone.

Briggs already had him taken care of, pushing herself off the pavement and letting his body fall to the side.

"Are you okay?" Gillian said.

"Yeah. He's dead again, which just sounds so peculiar." Briggs looked her over. "Are you?"

Gillian's face was red and swollen, and her eye looked ready to swell.

"Yeah. They caught us both off-guard."

Stanton was helping Kenzie to her feet when the shockwave hit. It knocked all four women to the ground, and Briggs was the first one back on her feet. "What the hell was that?"

"Riley," Gillian said.

The sky was now bright enough that they could see the house, its white paint peeling to reveal the gray boards underneath. It was the kind of ramshackle house that didn't register; something your eye would typically just pass over without notice. Briggs said, "How many have we got? The victims, I mean?"

"There were seven total," Gillian said. "Bernie Wright..."

"Got him."

Briggs counted them off on her hand. "Russell Stone, Reese, Graham... Sidney Lee, Allan McDade and Gordon Dixon. We've seen everyone but McDade, I think."

"The accidental victim," Stanton said. "Maybe the demons didn't have a hold on him."

"Maybe," Briggs said. "Keep your eyes out regardless. We don't want anyone surprising us when we get inside. Dr. Hunt..."

Gillian shook her head. "Don't even think of telling me to stay behind. I'm coming."

"I was going to say you could come with us this time, if you want."
Gillian smiled.

They started across the street. When they reached the house, Kenzie was the first onto the porch. She reached for the door, but Stanton shouted, "Wait!"

It was a moment too late. Kenzie grabbed the doorknob and was immediately thrown backward. She barreled into Gillian, both of them tumbling off the steps and onto the front lawn. Gillian recovered and knelt next to Kenzie, slapping her cheek lightly. Briggs tried to find the trap, but she couldn't see anything. "Stanton? Why did you call out?"

"There's no entrance here," Stanton said. "I... it's hard to explain. I'm seeing a barrier. It's blocked off."

"Riley got in," Gillian said. She was cradling an unconscious Kenzie in her lap, checking her vitals.

"Riley's the one they wanted," Briggs said. She holstered her weapon and said, "Dr. Hunt, stay with Kenzie. Chelsea, come with me. We're going to find a way into this place if we have to blow through a wall."

Riley moved slowly up the stairs with her gun ready, her finger tense on the trigger guard. The second floor had five doors along a single corridor, all of them closed. She tried the knob on the first one, finding it unlocked. It opened into a narrow sewing room and she nearly wasted a bullet on the mannequin standing in the middle of the room. The small window at the back of the space revealed it was dawn. She hoped her theory about Bishop being exhausted after a night of killing was accurate as she moved on to the next room.

Two empty bedrooms followed, filled with detritus from the teenagers and homeless who had made this home before Bishop and Cain arrived. The fourth door was a bathroom with such an odor that Riley doubted anyone could choose it as a hiding place without fainting. The final door, then, which led to the room in the turret. She tightened her grip on the Desert Eagle and pushed the door open with her free hand.

"Terrence Bishop?"

"That's not my name."

Riley moved to the wall so that she could see into the room. The Angel Maker sat on the window seat, his arms on his knees with the hands dangling between them. He was unarmed. His dress shirt was covered with dry blood; evidence left over from his murder of Gordon Dixon. He didn't look up as Riley moved cautiously into the room.

"What should I call you then? Just Mr. Bishop?"

"I'm the Angel Maker. That's the name I was given. The name you chose for me."

"I didn't pick it," Riley said. "You can thank Gail Finney for that. Put your hands on top of your head."

"But then I couldn't reach my knife."

Riley said, "That's kind of the point."

"I think I pass."

"If you take out your knife, I will have to shoot you. I don't want to do that, Mr. Bishop."

Bishop laughed. "Yes, you do. It would be an ending. The only ending. Because if you lead me out of here in handcuffs, then take me to trial, I'll plead insanity. I'll shout about demons and angels and Armageddon, and they'll put me in a nice little asylum. And eventually, I'll get out. Eventually, I will kill again. Or maybe I'll just kill inside the asylum. That would be fun. All my victims conveniently caged."

"Your friend is dead. Cain. Aiperos. I sent him back to Hell."

"And my other friend? Zerachiel? The one who tried to force me to kill only who she wanted dead? Have you shut that bitch up yet?" He looked up at her and smiled. "You freed me, Detective Parra. From the list of victims I had to follow. From the damned wings I had to paint every single time. I will be a much, much better killer now. Thanks to you."

"Mr. Bishop, one last time. Put your hands—"

He lunged forward, and Riley fired. He twisted so that the bullet missed him and broke the window. He lashed out with his right hand and Riley saw the light reflect off the curved blade of his knife. She fell back and the blade sliced across the POLICE on the front of her vest with a metal-on-metal scrape. He twisted his wrist on the follow-through and slammed it down, the sharp edge slicing through Riley's sleeve just below the elbow. She cried out as her muscles twitched and she dropped the gun.

Bishop kicked it away and pressed his weight against her, running her across the room. Riley shoved him away and brought her uninjured left arm up. She twisted her upper body, bent her arm and slammed her elbow into Bishop's jaw. She lifted her foot and wrapped it around his leg, knocking him down to his knees. She pulled away from him and dashed for her gun, dropping to one knee as she scooped it up off the floor.

Bishop grabbed her by the hair and yanked her head back, exposing her throat. She saw the flash of the blade as it came down.

Riley let her entire body sag, and Bishop shifted his weight without thinking. When he was balanced on the balls of his feet, she threw herself backward and knocked them both down. His knife scraped her throat, slicing her jaw, but she didn't even notice the pain until she pulled away from him. She grabbed her gun and spun around to face him. "I have every right to shoot you."

Bishop got to his feet and glared at her.

"Hands on your head. Now, goddamn it." Blood dripped down her chin in a steady stream and, when she spoke, the muscles felt strangely tight. She prayed he hadn't severed anything vital.

Bishop lunged at her, swinging the knife in a wide arc. Riley fired three times.

He slammed into her, eyes wide as if he hadn't considered she would actually do it. Riley took his weight without falling and turned to dump his body to the floor. Endorphins flooded her brain, adrenaline was making her shaky and she looked at Bishop's empty right hand. That didn't make sense.

She looked down at herself and saw the handle of the knife protruding from the arm of her vest. "Oh. Shit."

The knife was buried in her up to the hilt, blood pooling around it and streaming down the side of her blouse. She suddenly realized why her chest felt so tight, why it was so hard to draw breath. She gasped and brought one hand up, trembling as she considered whether it would be worse to pull it out.

"Oh, oh, shit," Riley said. She dropped to one knee.

Stanton hesitated. She stopped and looked back the way they had come and then at the window they were next to. "It just disappeared."

"What do you mean?"

"Everything, the… protection, the barrier. It's just a house now."

Briggs said, "Let's hope that's a good sign." Briggs tentatively approached the window, leading with her gun. When nothing stopped her, she tossed her water pistol inside and said, "Gonna have to trust you here. Give me a boost."

Stanton helped Briggs through the window and said, "I have to… I'm sorry. I know you need me, but… Mackenzie…"

"Go to her. I'll help Riley."

Stanton nodded her gratitude before she turned and ran back to the front of the house. Briggs picked up her water pistol, noticing it was nearly empty, and headed for the stairs. She saw the dead body in the doorway of another room and stopped at the base of the stairs. "Detective Parra?"

"Present."

The weakness of Riley's voice was alarming. Briggs hurried up the stairs, still wary of a trap. When she reached the open door to the turret, she saw Terrence Charles Bishop's legs lying in a pool of blood. She breathed a sigh of relief as she pushed the door open and stepped inside. "Riley?"

"Here."

Briggs looked down and felt her heart clench. Riley's entire left side was covered with blood, and the pool she sat in was growing by the second. Riley was deathly pale, but she lifted her eyes and managed a weak smile. "Got him."

Briggs dropped down and looked at the wound. "Jesus Christ."

Riley said, "Oh-oh. Guess it's bad." She pressed her lips into a thin line and rubbed them back and forth. "I'm thirsty."

Briggs picked up her water gun and said, "Take this." She uncapped the bottom and let the water spill onto Riley's tongue. Riley swallowed it and rested the back of her head against the wall.

"Mm. Thanks."

Briggs turned at the sound of running feet. Stanton appeared at the door and said, "Kenzie's awake. We—"

"Get Dr. Hunt. *Now.*"

Stanton didn't hesitate; she turned on her heel and disappeared. Briggs turned back to Riley and touched her cheek.

"Is she..." Riley swallowed hard. There was blood on her lip. "Tell her..." She frowned and then shook her head. "Oh, she knows. She already knows."

"She's on her way, Riley. She'll take care of you."

Riley smiled. "She always does."

"Just hold on a little longer." She grabbed Riley's hand and squeezed.

Riley grimaced and reached for the knife with her free hand. "Take it out. Take it out."

"No. It'll make the bleeding worse..."

"Doesn't matter anymore. Don't let me die with it in me. Please."

Briggs still hesitated. If there was even a chance Gillian could do something, she didn't want to ruin their chances by making a drastic decision. But one look at the blood pooled beneath Riley and the smear of it on the wall told her that it would require a miracle. Divine intervention wasn't out of the question where Riley was concerned, but there was a time to fold your hand and bow out. She could see Riley was there.

Briggs untucked her shirt, using the tail to preserve any prints left on the knife as she gripped the handle. Riley cried out as she pulled, and Briggs grimaced until the blade finally came out. She immediately pressed her hand against the wound to try to staunch the bleeding. Blood immediately coated her hand like a glove, streaming down her arm and staining the sleeve of her blouse. "God, where the fuck are they? Hold on, Riley."

"Get Gillian."

"She's coming, Riley."

"You have to get Gillian. I want..." She raised her eyes to the door and said, "Hey, Jill."

Briggs turned, expecting to see the others. But the doorway was empty. "She's coming, Riley, just give..."

Riley's eyes were focused on the door, unblinking. Her lips were slack. Briggs pulled her hand away from the wound and found herself barely able to stop the cry that came from her throat. She reached up with her clean hand and closed Riley's eyes.

"I'm sorry, Detective Parra. Riley. I'm so sorry."

Gillian nearly tripped on the stairs as she made the turn down the hall. Briggs appeared in the doorway, her right hand red with blood. Gillian didn't even slow down. "Move."

"Gillian, stop," Briggs said. Her voice was raw.

Gillian slammed into Briggs, but the lieutenant wouldn't be moved. "Stop. Gillian. You don't want to go in there."

"Riley needs me," Gillian said.

Briggs whispered, "No. She doesn't."

Gillian stepped back and punched Briggs in the face. Briggs was so thrown by the blow that she released Gillian and was easily brushed aside. Kenzie and Stanton arrived at the top of the stairs, Kenzie pale and clinging to the banister as Stanton helped her stand. Briggs put her back to the wall and slid down, resting her elbows on her knees. She pushed her hands into her hair, smearing Riley's blood on her forehead, eyes closed as Gillian began to wail.

Kenzie looked at Briggs. "No."

Stanton turned to Kenzie and hugged her, holding on tight as Gillian's voice echoed off the walls of the house.

As the sun rose, the angels who had lined the edges of the buildings in No Man's Land silently took wing. People on the street heard the departure, but they counted it down as nothing more than a particularly large kit of pigeons looking for somewhere else to roost.

The demons who had laid witness to the final confrontation also slipped away, joining with the shadows and fading from the material world to celebrate in darker caverns.

Priest went to the window and pressed her hands against the glass. She closed her eyes as she felt the grief wash over her, bowing her head and sobbing. She was a guardian angel; she could tell when her charge was no longer living.

Marchosias greeted the day with wine and a feast fit for a king. His minions ate better than they had in decades, and he reigned over it all with an evil smile.

The rest of the city woke without a champion.

The coroner's van parked on the lawn, its back end open to the front door. Five police cruisers blocked the side streets and held the reporters at bay as the bodies were wheeled from the house. Stanton and Kenzie supported Gillian as they left the building, her shoulders weighted down, her feet barely moving across the pavement.

When they got to the car, Kenzie placed Gillian in the backseat. Briggs looked toward the media. "I should probably go make a statement to the press."

"Gail Finney is out there," Gillian said. Her voice was broken from the screams that had prompted three neighbors in the dead zone of No Man's Land to call the police. The officers who responded thought it was some kind of record. "Don't... tell them about Riley. Not yet. I can't stand to think about her gloating."

Briggs said, "I won't." She touched Gillian's face and said, "Will you be okay?"

"No."

Briggs looked at Kenzie, who nodded. Gillian wouldn't be left alone. "All right," Briggs said. "I'll be at the hospital to check on you as soon as I can."

"No," Gillian said. "I... have to get to the morgue. I want the autopsy."

"Well... you're the chief medical examiner on the Angel Maker case. I'm sure no one would—"

"I want Riley's."

"Out of the question."

"We know who ki— killed her. He's dead. There won't be a trial. I need to do this."

Briggs said, "I'll see if I can okay your presence in a supervisory position. But that's the best I can do."

Gillian nodded. Her face was streaked with tears, her hands trembling against Stanton's. They all turned to watch the blue ME van pull off the lawn, slowly going down over the curb before it made the turn toward the morgue. Gillian closed her eyes and fresh tears rolled down her cheeks.

Stanton nodded for Briggs to go. "We'll take care of her."

"Okay. Gillian. I cannot express how sorry I am..."

"You were with her," Gillian said. "You held her hand. Thank you."

Briggs felt her own eyes starting to burn and had to look away. "Her last thought was of you. I think she knew she was going, but... she wanted to say goodbye to you."

Gillian smiled and nodded. Briggs impulsively leaned down and kissed the top of Gillian's head before she turned and walked away.

"...can now confirm that Terrence Charles Bishop, the serial killer, known as the Angel Maker has been killed after a confrontation with the police. That's all we're—"

"Lieutenant Briggs, Gail Finney. Can you confirm that the detective involved with the murder was in fact Detective Riley Parra?"

"Detective Parra was involved, but that's all we're—"

"Is it true that Detective Parra was killed?"

"Where did you get that information?"

"So it is true?"

"Detective Parra was badly injured during the fight, which necessitated her use of deadly force. We'll know more in a few hours and we'll have an update for you when the dust has settled. Now if you don't mind, Ms. Finney, that is all the information we're prepared to share at this point. Once we have more information, you'll be the first to know I'm sure. Thank you."

Gillian showered until her skin was bright pink, and then changed into a pair of crisp blue scrubs. The locker room felt different. There was nothing changed, but that somehow felt wrong. She felt the lights should have been out, or the room should be utterly silent. She shut the locker door and pressed her head against the metal. She felt like there was a reservoir behind her eyes, waiting to break. She forced it back, wiped at her eyes which were somehow still wet, and began the too-short walk to the morgue.

Riley was lying on a table in the middle of the room. Still dressed, hair brushed back out of her face. Gillian crossed the room with leaden feet and methodically undressed her. She catalogued the wounds.

Riley shrugged out of her blouse and bent down to untie her shoes. Gillian reached over and ran her fingers up Riley's spine, up to her shoulders, slinking across the mattress until she was kneeling behind Riley. When Riley sat up and reached back for her, Gillian kissed her neck. Riley twisted her head and they kissed as Gillian unhooked her bra and let it slide down her arms.

When Gillian finished with the preliminary findings, she put aside the report and walked back to the bathroom next to her office. She shut the door and dropped to her knees in front of the toilet right before she started to throw up. The pain cut through her, through her midsection and right down to her spine. The tears started again and she couldn't bring herself to stop them.

Finally, she got back to her feet. She stumbled to the sink and splashed cold water on her face. The sound of water on the porcelain of the sink sounded impossibly loud to her ears. She ran her wet fingers through her hair and looked at her reflection in the mirror. Maybe they had both died. She certainly looked the part. She blinked away a new round of tears and forced herself to leave the bathroom.

Caitlin Priest was standing next to Riley's table, and Gillian stopped in her tracks. "She wouldn't want you here," she said in a cold, neutral voice.

"I know."

"Then get the fuck out." Her voice was more resigned than angry.

Priest winced and said, "I just... there's just one thing I have to do."

Gillian held her hands out in surrender and crossed the room. "What? Do you have to steal her tattoo for the next champion? Do you have to do some damn ritual to pass it on? Part of your damned war? Well do it. And then I never want to see you again."

Priest put her hand on Riley's chest and said, "I don't know what this will do. Only one person has done it before, and he was more powerful than I am."

"Just get it over with."

Priest closed her eyes and her hand began to glow against Riley's chest. Gillian opened her mouth to ask what was happening when all the air was sucked from the room. She gasped helplessly, sure she would suffocate before the air returned with a colossal sonic explosion. The energy from it knocked Gillian off her feet. Secondary tremors rattled every metallic surface in the room like in an earthquake, and the tiles in the ceiling began to dance in their frames. The lights flickered once, then twice, and then stayed out before coming back on with an impossible brightness.

It felt like the entire room was being shaken, like a bad-tempered child who captured a mouse in a shoebox and then decided to see what happened if he kicked it down the stairs. There was a sound like a gunshot, and Gillian looked up in time to see Priest being thrown across the room as if she weighed no more than a feather. Priest hit the wall and fell in a heap.

The cacophony ended, and Gillian shakily got to her feet. "Priest? Jesus, what the fuck..." She stumbled across the floor toward the woman lying crumpled next to the door.

Riley sat up.

Gillian recoiled at the sight. Memories of the demon that animated the corpses in the morgue filled her mind, but Riley looked... the same. She blinked at Gillian and frowned as she looked down at herself. The terrible wound in her side was gone, healed without even a scar, and the various minor cuts - on her throat, on her cheek, and her right arm - were also missing. She held the sheet to her breasts as she looked down at herself, her skin erupting in gooseflesh.

"Riley," Gillian said. It wasn't a question or a confirmation, but something closer to a prayer. She moved down the side of the table and lightly touched Riley's cheek. "Riley?"

"God is a madman," Riley said. Her voice was rough as if it hadn't been used in years. "He told me so himself." She closed her eyes and pressed her forehead to Gillian's. "I feel like I died."

"You did," Gillian said. She couldn't comprehend what she was seeing, the warm flesh under her fingers. "Priest... oh, God." She reluctantly pulled away from Riley and ran to where Priest was lying. Riley slid off the table, wrapping the sheet around her like a toga as she followed Gillian to where Priest had fallen.

"What happened?" Riley said.

"She saved your life. Although... that's not entirely accurate."

Priest opened her eyes and focused on Riley. She laughed quietly and then closed her eyes again. "It worked."

"I guess so," Riley said.

Gillian put her hand on Priest's back to help her sit up. She ran her hand over Priest's jacket and hesitated. Something was wrong. "Riley."

"I didn't know angels could do that," Riley said.

"They really, really can't," Priest said.

"Riley," Gillian said more insistently. Riley looked at her and saw shock in her eyes. "Priest. Where are your wings?"

"Gone."

Riley frowned. "What do you mean 'gone'?"

"My divinity. Used it all up." She swallowed. "I used it all. Zerachiel is dead."

"But you're still here."

"Technically." Priest sagged against Gillian's arm, on the verge of passing out again. The last thing she said before fading from consciousness was, "I'm mortal."

Gillian looked up and met Riley's eyes over Priest's body. She could see that Riley was still reeling from everything that had happened to her, so dealing with Priest would have to wait. She pulled Priest onto her lap, then reached out and curled her hand around the back of Riley's head. Riley pressed her forehead to Gillian's, kneeling on the floor in silence next to her partner and her lover.

About the Author

Geonn Cannon is from Oklahoma. He writes the things he would like to read and reads things he wishes he had written. In his spare time he writes the occasional review for the online publication *Geek Speak Magazine*.

www.ingramcontent.com/pod-product-compliance
Lightning Source LLC
Chambersburg PA
CBHW070053120726
47909CB00002B/381